# The Holy Fool

## By Jason Liegois

Copyright© 2019 Jason Liegois

To all of the journalists past, present, and future, who work to let us know what's going on in our world, no matter what the cost.

ISBN: 978-1-62249-453-8

Published by
Biblio Publishing
BiblioPublishing.com
Columbus, Ohio

## Table of Contents

Chapter 1 .................................................... 1

Chapter 2 .................................................. 11

Chapter 3 ................................................. 23

Chapter 4 ................................................. 37

Chapter 5 ................................................. 57

Chapter 6 ................................................. 91

Chapter 7 ................................................ 121

Chapter 8 ............................................... 143

Chapter 9 ............................................... 147

Chapter 10 ............................................. 157

Chapter 11 ............................................. 175

Chapter 12 ............................................. 187

Chapter 13 ............................................. 195

Chapter 14 ............................................ 205

Chapter 15 ............................................. 213

Chapter 16 ............................................ 223

Chapter 17 ............................................ 233

Chapter 18 ............................................ 239

Chapter 19 ............................................ 265

Chapter 20 ............................................ 279

Chapter 21 ............................................ 283

## Author's Note

I've set this story, for the most part, in Chicago during late August and early September of 2008. In the process of writing that story, I have tried to keep the setting and events of those times as close to reality as practicable. Any discrepancies between the real events and features of those times and what you read here is either the result of an author's oversight or a sacrifice to the needs of fiction.

# Acknowledgements

First, to any I forget to name here, thank you.

Thanks to the Midwest Writing Center, located just across the Mississippi River in Rock Island, Ill., for their support and programming in recent years. Many of the revisions to this book were a result of workshopping opportunities the center provided.

Also, thanks to the Muscatine, Iowa writers' group Writers On The Avenue for their support and critiques. Special thanks go to members Misty Urban and Pat Bieber for their insight and advice on this project and ones currently in progress.

Special thanks go to my former educational colleague and fellow Eastern Iowa writer Bert Miller for his assistance in getting this book published.

Thanks to Biblio Publishing of Columbus, Ohio for making me a published novelist for the first time. I truly appreciate the opportunity.

Finally, I want to thank my family for their love and support of my passion. Thanks to my parents, Bill and Suzanne Liegois, for giving me my love for the written word and encouraging me to follow a career path that would keep me writing throughout my life. Thanks to my kids, Jacob and Madeline, who have been so encouraging to me on my new adventure in life as they are on the cusp of beginning their bright futures.

Finally, thanks so much for my wife, Laura, who has loved me for more than 20 years no matter whether I wrote or not, but always supported my type-type-typing away whenever I got an interesting idea. She is absolutely the best and the center of my world.

# Chapter 1

## Aug. 31, 2008, Chicago, Ill.

As Sonny Turner walked up to his apartment building, his attention was on anything but his home. That wasn't a surprise, given that there was no one there waiting for him at home and he was positive that someone was following him.

Once he got within a block of his building, that feeling eased somewhat. The figure on foot that had followed him from the El station had disappeared a block back, and the vehicle that had passed him three separate times had finally headed westbound when he arrived at his block. He suspected they already had someone watching his apartment. With the row of three-decker apartment houses lining both sides of the street in his Wicker Park neighborhood, it would be easy to use a nearby apartment as a surveillance point.

It was quiet as Sonny approached the front stone steps of his building, only to see someone sitting down and blocking his path – just barely. The man there was well in his fifties, nearly six feet tall but with a bare bones physique. He was balding, with what was left of his hair a grey dusting across his shaved skull, and had what Sonny considered to be the saddest eyes he'd ever seen in a man – dark, sunken into the hollows of his eye sockets. Never the sharpest dressed man around; he awaited Sonny in a more casual than usual Bears navy starter jacket and faded jeans.

Sonny was an inch or two taller than his unexpected guest - a beer-barrel tank, with a thick chest, soft but solid contours, and short legs and arms. Slightly shaggy but not long brown hair and a full beard and squared face framed the dark eyes that glinted as he stared down at the man. "Damn, Gus, what are you doing out here near midnight?"

Arthur "Gus" Pulaski shot up, swiveling as he examined the street. "Need to talk, kid," his boss spit out. "Invite me in?"

"I got your message three days ago; thanks for calling me. You and Ed were about the only ones I heard from."

"Not about your mom – something else."

"C'mon." He gestured for Gus to follow him into the building. Deciding to forgo the freight elevator in back, he led Gus up the staircase to the right of the front door up to the third floor. Once they were there, Sonny made his way toward the door marked 4C. He examined the doorway and found a wooden wedge there, lodged in the crack between the door and doorjamb halfway up. He unlocked the doorway and, making sure his body screened Gus's view, he pocketed the wedge and opened the door. "Get in."

Gus followed Sonny in. Sonny's place had only one bathroom and bedroom behind single doors. One wood table with two chairs occupied the kitchen nook at the far end of the apartment. The living area had three bare white drywalls and a brick wall facing the outside of the building. There was no other furniture, except for the roll-top desk and chair and the dresser and bed in his bedroom.

"Christ, aren't you going to decorate this place sometime? How long have you been here, eight years?"

"10 years. I'll decorate when I'm dead and have the time. Have a seat." Sonny pointed to the kitchen table. "You want something to drink?"

"Some beer, if you have any – I didn't drive here." Gus wandered toward Sonny's desk. "How was the funeral?"

"It worked out OK." Sonny turned his back on his houseguest while he swiped a Samuel Adams and a Coke from the fridge.

Gus' eye noticed a familiar photo framed on Sonny's desk. It was a picture of a younger Sonny, without the beard, sandwiched between two older men in shirts and ties. Someone took it during a late night in a Rush Street bar. The man on Sonny's left looked like a retired con man, silver-haired with a strong, jutting chin and with clothes just the right level of rumpled to look elegant. The man on the right just looked rumpled, heavier, with grey eyes that seemed to be scanning the room even as the picture was taken. <u>Jack, Sonny,</u>

and Ed On the Town a small note said on the frame of the small photo.

Gus sat down at the table as he stared at the photo. Sonny set down the drinks, then tossed something in front of Gus. "I appreciated the flowers and check you sent."

Gus opened it. It was a visitation notice, filled with pictures from the past century. *Gail Turner, 1950-2008*, it read.

"So, what are you doing out here? Aren't you supposed to be putting out the Monday edition?"

"Decided to take a day off from the *Journal* for once. I've got enough days for it."

"Yeah, that makes total sense," Sonny laughed. "But, Wicker Park's not quite your scene, Gus. It's rough out here, don't you know that?"

"Hell, kid, it's not Cabrini-Green."

"Cabrini-Green's just about torn down. Anyway, since you never show up around here, what the hell is your malfunction tonight?"

Gus leaned back in his chair, taking a long pull off his drink as Sonny sat down in front of him. "Something's going down and I need your help to figure out what it is."

"Hmm." Sonny had a drink of his beer, and then stared right at Gus.

"I was up in the Penthouse late Friday, turning in some paperwork for HR, when I decided to use the executive restroom up there. It's supposed to be for just the senior execs, but hell if I care. I'm in one of the far stalls when I hear a guy come in, start washing his hands, and then as he's drying them, his cell phone rings and he answers it. It was John Michael."

That caused Sonny to look up. It was the name everyone used for John Michael Edson, the CEO of Edson Media, the *Chicago Journal*'s owner for the past two years. "You could hear him?"

"He was talking low, but yeah. I stood on the throne and kept quiet as I could."

"Well, that was your workout for the day," said Sonny, taking a long drink from his beer. "Who called him?"

"The name I don't know, but from the conversation I heard, it was some guy from UUF Bank."

"Ah, our favorite hometown bank slash Wall Street wannabe."

"I wasn't able to catch it all, but I heard him specifically say, 'I need the valuation report for the *Journal* done by tomorrow, understand?' My gut says that he's looking to sell."

"Sell? He just bought the paper two years ago. You get that idea just from that?"

"From that, from the spending cuts, and from the next round of staff cuts that's apparently starting this week. Anyway, this is your new project."

"What?"

"Despite that column of yours, you're still a good investigative reporter." Gus drained the rest of his Coke and got up to start circling around the table. "I want you to start looking into this. I need to find out about what John Michael's plans are."

"What? Excuse me, brother," Sonny laughed, "But when did you start acting all renegade? You're not even sure you want me to go ahead with this whole other thing…"

"Look, kid, drop it." Gus spun around and pointing at him. "I'm willing to talk about that, but this is more important. This isn't just a story – it's our jobs, and the jobs of our co-workers."

Sonny sighed. "You really think there's something to this?"

"Three weeks from now, the paper's going to celebrate its 140th anniversary. I want to at least know if it's going to have a 141st. This has been my life for the past 35 years."

"You said it yourself; these newspapers close all the time. You told me about the Chicago *Sentinel* closing in the 60's. What are we going to do?"

"This paper, the guys who wrote for it, helped make you into what you are." Gus pointed at the picture on Sonny's desk. "Can you help?"

Sonny stared at his beer for a moment, took another drink, looked over at the photo on the desk, then back at Gus. "Coming back here, I just realized you and Ed might be the

# The Holy Fool

only people I have left. Isn't that just fucked? OK, I'll start tomorrow. But, we're going to talk about the other project."

"We will, but this is the bigger priority, even over your column."

"Well, hell, I'll have to start subcontracting that out to the Indian grad students again." He got up and shook Gus's hand. "I'll see you in the newsroom tomorrow?"

"Of course." Gus patted Sonny on the shoulder with his other hand. "Talk to me by midday at least and let me know where you're at."

"OK."

"Take care, kid."

As Gus walked out of the building, he wondered if he should have told him about the new kid coming to work tomorrow. He decided it was for the best that he didn't; he felt there was only so much Sonny could absorb.

After Gus left, Sonny sat down at his desk. The silence filled up the entire room, lit by just a single fluorescent bulb above his stove. It was right then that the isolation hit him. 50,000 followers on Twitter and he felt alone, and that thought and his laugh kept him company for a few seconds.

The only other light in the room was two LEDs on his landline, one flashing, located on his desk. He picked up the cordless receiver and punched a button next to the flashing LED.

After a beep, he heard a young woman's voice, dark and scratchy. "Sonny, still with us?" the message began. "It's Joey. Listen, I haven't heard from you in a while. Just... I was worried, OK? I was hoping everything's all right with you. I saw you run out Monday and not say anything to anyone. Call me? Bye."

He replaced the receiver, smiling. "She called. She called," he heard himself say aloud. He was scared when he burst into tears right after he said that, his fingers covering the LED light. "What the hell?" he muttered to himself. He was glad he had the blinds drawn, because he didn't want whoever was watching him to see this.

*\*\*\**

The kid Gus had thought of that evening started to stir in his bed the next morning just as the sun crept through the blinds of his apartment window.

Colton felt around for a familiar presence in the bed next to him but didn't find her. As he began to sit up in the bed, he heard a knock at the bedroom door. "Baby, you up?" a whispering female voice breathed from behind the door.

"Yeah, that you?"

With her foot, Kyra swung the door open and bounded in. Small-boned, somewhere just over five feet, with long black hair and wide blue eyes that reminded Colton of the anime characters he loved, she was already dressed for the day in a purple sweater, leggings, and leather boots. "I thought I'd be super nice and get breakfast all set before you headed out to work." She dropped a McDonald's bag by his lap and a McDonald's coffee cup in his hand.

"Wow, thank you." Colton took the briefest of sips and set the cup down. As she sat down on the bed, he leaned in for a kiss, which she accepted. "You're looking beautiful today. I don't suppose you wanted to take a moment and hang out before heading in…"

"Ooooo," she said, shaking her head in mock frustration, "I'm already dressed for school today." She was studying public policy at the University of Chicago, where he'd graduated that spring. She kissed him back on the lips. "You're so cute, of course, it's a temptation, but I've got to maintain that 4.0."

Kyra wasn't joking when she said she thought he was cute. He was six-three, short brown hair, a heart-shaped face topped with hazel eyes and a wide grin he popped out whenever he was happy or nervous. Many people mistook him for a basketball player or a distance runner, but he used a series of boards to shape his lean figure. There were the small boards in the summer for the streets of Chicago, slightly longer boards for the slopes, then an even longer board for the annual getaway to Hawaii.

"If you want to do something like that, we'll have to get to bed earlier and wake up earlier."

# The Holy Fool

"I'm game. You eating with me today, at least?"

"Two egg McMuffin meals for the two of us. Also, I thought this might be required reading." She took a newspaper with *Chicago Journal* written across it and dropped it on his lap.

"Good idea. If I'm going to work for this thing, I'd better know what we printed today."

"So, have you found out what they'll have you start doing?" Kyra said, as Colton got ready after breakfast.

"Not getting anyone's coffee, I hope." Colton finished tying his tie. He kept his outfit basic – black shirt and tie, khakis, and brown-suede shoes. "They wanted me to report to the city editor, Gus Pulaski, when I got in today, but that could mean anything."

"One thing I do know," Kyra said, sliding in behind him as he looked in the dresser mirror, "is that I hope this is what you want to do."

"Yeah, it is, definitely." Colton finished tying his tie and pulling her arms around him. "I want to work with my dad; I should know something about how it works. Letting people know about the world around them - to me, it always seemed worthwhile, and isn't it natural to do what your parents did?"

"If you're happy, I'm happy, then."

He tossed a brown bomber jacket on his shoulders to finish off the outfit. "OK, off to the station, then." They shared one more kiss.

\*\*\*

With a coffee mug in one hand and a plate with a bagel and banana in the other, Sonny went back to his desk. He noticed that he was getting an alert on an e-mail message. He clicked on the tab:

7:30 a.m. Chicago time.

With that, Sonny began to open another tab on the browser. A notice saying ENCRYPTION COMPLETE popped up as Sonny opened the chat program. Waiting for him was this:

\<hewoman98\> Ready to talk?
He sighed, then typed in:
\<SonnyT76\>Ready.
\<hewoman98\> Finally got back?
\<SonnyT76\>Yes
\<hewoman98\> sorry about mom again
\<SonnyT76\>Appreciated.
\<hewoman98\> You received the new package?
\<hewoman98\> 3/?
\<SonnyT76\>yes
\<SonnyT76\>in my possession, and saved to different places
\<SonnyT76\>3/? ????
\<hewoman98\> thought I would stop at 4 batches, but now decided I'd keep going and see how much I'd put out
\<SonnyT76\>Can't advise you on that one way or another.
\<hewoman98\> if you get them, you'll use them?
\<SonnyT76\>yes
\<hewoman98\> good boy.
\<SonnyT76\>Still trying to figure out who you might be. I know military, probably the Poly house. A lady for sure.
\<hewoman98\> More like the B word. You won't know until they finally catch me.
\<SonnyT76\>Prison sounds like fun to you?
\<hewoman98\> \>\>\>Implying there's things that aren't scarier than prison
\>\>\> Implying I haven't already been through it.
\<SonnyT76\>You've been to the Sandbox, then.
\<hewoman98\> Keep guessing. So, when am I going to see some scoops in print?
\<SonnyT76\>When I get through the material and make sure I won't get anyone killed if I dump it
\<hewoman98\> What's taking so long?
\<SonnyT76\>The number of documents you've dropped already? It might take me years if I go through it myself.
\<hewoman98\> I understand about troops, but don't worry about the rest of them. They're not worth it.
\<SonnyT76\>Terrorists? Civilians? American politicians?
\<hewoman98\> All of the above.

\<hewoman98\> 4/?
\<SonnyT76\>regular place
\<hewoman98\> regular time.
\<hewoman98\> This one's a doozy. FS cables...
\<SonnyT76\>These are just lying around?
\<hewoman98\> honey, you'd be surprised about how much of that "top secret" stuff just lies around.
\<hewoman98\> Signing off

    Sonny logged off, closed the laptop, and started staring at the photo again as if to ask the men in it a question.

## Chapter 2

It was less than an hour after Sonny had left his apartment, making sure to tuck the tiny wooden wedge into his doorway just below knee-height before leaving for work and the headquarters of the *Chicago Journal*.

As he later approached within two blocks of Lake Shore Drive, he noticed two men through his aviator sunglasses. He'd noticed them last night and long before then but made no effort to confront or even acknowledge them.

The first one was always on foot. His wardrobe vacillated between business casual and court deposition. He was in his forties, trim, with his grey hair trimmed military short. The Gentleman, as Sonny had nicknamed him in his mind, never had trouble keeping up with him on foot.

The other guy was in a grey Dodge coupe. He was in his forties too, but not as well preserved – rounder, balding but black hair, and a Ditka-shaped mustache. He'd seen the guy driving everything from a minivan to a gypsy cab, and he was the guy that usually tailed Sonny to just outside his apartment. He usually wore Bears or Cubs sports gear, although he had worn a Blackhawks jersey last Sunday. Sonny could not resist naming him The Superfan.

He was surprised that their presence no longer fazed him. It did make planning his daily schedule more challenging.

***

Colton got off at the Clark El stop. He knew that the *Chicago Journal*'s headquarters was right nearby. He needed to go down to La Salle, then head north until he was right at the river.

As Colton turned the corner of La Salle, however, he knew that despite only having been there a few times, he would be able to get there without Google Maps. The home of the

Jason Liegois

*Chicago Journal* loomed in front of him, overlooking the Chicago River.

The official name of the building was Journal Tower, but everyone in Chicago other than *Journal* executives called it The Keep. It was a monument in concrete, a massive rectangle that could have been Al Capone's idea of a castle fortification. Art Deco detail lined its walls, reaching for the sky, especially the four corners of the main building that were modern reflections of medieval turrets. A slightly smaller rectangle with smaller turrets, housing the company's executive offices, topped off the block. The Keep was never one of the tallest structures in Chicago, but it succeeded in being the most intimidating.

***

By the time Colton was beginning to come around the corner, Sonny was already inside the main lobby of the building and headed straight for the main elevators. As Sonny punched the button to bring down one of the eight elevators serving the building around its central core, he pulled out his Blackberry and noticed a text from Gus: *Stop over*.

Sonny got off at the $12^{th}$ floor, home of the newsroom. Each department of the paper, such as advertising, circulation, and pagination, had its own dedicated floor. The executives claimed the seven top floors of the building – the smaller top rectangle of the Keep - known by all as The Penthouse.

Except for a few load-bearing columns, the floor plan of the newsroom was wide open. Clusters of desks were gathered in different sections of the floor, separated only by fuzzy blue fabric and metal cubicle walls that reached their residents' heads while seated. Each section had signs hanging from the ceilings over the clusters indicating which section was which. Along the outer edges of the floor, there were individual offices, conference rooms, an employee lounge, and restrooms.

In the middle of the room were the Metro and City desks. Sonny made his way toward the City Desk, where Gus worked

# The Holy Fool

alone at the cubbyhole he reserved for himself, even though he had his own office on the fringe of the 12th floor.

"Gus, we're running through what I have on the I-project with you." Sonny said, using his own code for the data packets the mysterious woman had been sending him.

"Yeah," Gus said, "But I'm going to need another favor from you."

Sonny recognized the presence of a trip wire in that statement but went forward anyway. "On top of your little side project? ...OK, what do you need?"

"I need you to help babysit a new person who's coming on staff today. I'm going to have him do some City Desk duties, but I thought he could help you out, too. Here's his resume."

Sonny scanned the paper and a large sigh ran from his lungs. "Bloody hell."

"Sonny..."

"Wait, we're letting some... *kid* play reporter in our newsroom after all the people we cut? After all the people we're *going* to cut?"

"We're hiring new people every day," Gus said, hands up in what looked like a plea, though he seemed to be defending the paper more out of habit.

"Cutting news staff, then either adding more executives or inexperienced *garbage* that can't replace someone who's been on the job 20 years. Tell me this isn't some bullshit right here." There was silence, which was Sonny's answer. "Is he totally useless?"

"Graduated with honors at U. Chicago, MBA. The writing samples he submitted looked pretty good, actually."

With a sigh, he declared, "OK, I'll see what I can get him working on."

"Always know I can count on you, Sonny."

"I'm doing this for you, but you'd better believe you owe me." Sonny walked backward toward his own office. "And I'm collecting soon, I don't have time to mess around, and you don't either." It wasn't until he turned to walk through his door that he saw the girl sitting at the nearest desk to his office, in the area reserved for the Arts and Entertainment Desk, staring at him with a half-smile on her face.

Jason Liegois

She was the type of woman that earned a second look, not necessarily because she was hot but because of her uniqueness. Her eyes might have seemed a little too sleepy, her mouth a touch too wide, her nose a little too prominent, and her hips not as skinny as the current fashion gods would prefer. However, she had her own sense of fashion – a blend of pastels teamed with funky gold and silver jewelry around her neck and covering her wrists.

Then, he remembered. He remembered what he had decided to do on the way into work this morning. He was nervous, but he wasn't scared anymore. He was more scared about what would happen if he never tried it.

"Hi, Joey." Sonny waved to her as he walked toward her. A nameplate on her desk proclaimed it belonged to JOSEPHINE HALVORSEN.

"Hi, stranger, welcome back."

"Yeah."

She paused for a moment. "Where were you last week? I tried to call..."

"Thanks for that, by the way... Well, my mom died."

She sagged a little in her chair at that. "Oh, I'm sorry, Sonny," she said, her voice a whisper.

He smiled and nodded. "It's OK. I appreciated your call. How have you been, Joey?"

"You know, same stuff," Joey replied, reassured with Sonny's positive mood.

"Yeah. So, anything crazy been going on around here since I was out?"

She leaned toward him as he did the same, her voice parodying the gossips of the newsroom. "Well, I could tell you a few things, but we'd have to save it for drinks after work. Too hot for the office."

Sonny laughed at that for a moment, but then it tapered off as he began to look around to see if anyone else was looking at them. "How often do you think you've dropped that line on me?"

Joey blinked for a moment as she realized Sonny was going off script. "How many times? In the time I've been working here, maybe six or seven? And you've done it to me once or twice, as well."

"Yeah, fair enough." Eventually, Sonny sighed and looked straight at her. "What if I finally take you up on that?"

That brought her up short. "Oh, ah, OK... what was that?"

"I said... I felt... wait." He felt like he was about to trip over his words. He paused for a few seconds of silence, and then continued. "Sorry, I've trying to see if I can be an alpha male in real life, not just on the job."

"Alpha male, OK." She tried hard not to cackle, but kept her hazel eyes locked on his, not trying to avoid him. It settled him down without him realizing it. "What does that make you now, an Beta male?"

"Heh, maybe more Omega male."

"Ha-ha, all right, sorry," Joey waved him off but sneaking peeks at whether other people were looking on. "Go ahead."

"So, Joey, I'd really like to meet you after work for dinner. Since we always have good conversations at the office, I'd like to have one outside of it. That's it, that's all the poetry I have."

"OK." Her voice had shrunk but stayed clear. "You didn't have other plans?"

"Funny enough, usually every Monday I get suckered by Ed in having dinner with him at his place near Hyde Park. Kind of his way of keeping in the loop. I'll reschedule for tomorrow."

"Oh, yeah, Ed Mazur, right? I've seen his pictures all over this place."

"He's semi-retired, sticks to his house nowadays. He was one of the guys that showed me the ropes around here..."

"...him and Jack DeFoe, I remember you said that," she finished for him.

"Yeah. Listen, I hope you don't mind, but I'd prefer to meet there, wherever we go, rather than leave here together. Would that be a problem?"

Joey glanced at him, amused. "I didn't know you were that discreet, given some other people I heard you've dated around here."

"It's a good thing the ones I did date moved on," Sonny laughed. "That's part of it, but that's not the main reason." He lowered his voice. "I'll explain it to you. But, could we talk about it at dinner?"

That got her attention, her expression a mix of nervousness and curiosity. She sat still in her chair, her eyes focused down on her desk, before turning to look at him. "Sounds cloak and dagger," she whispered to him.

"Harry Carey's work for you? We could meet there, then go to Navy Pier, take a boat ride for a while and chill out."

"So, why now?"

"I really wanted to ever since we got into that conversation a few months back about media bias, Laurie Anderson's music, Werner Herzog's films, and God knows what else, but I was too chicken until now."

She leaned back in her desk chair. He could tell Joey was trying to act cool and collected, but he could sense the wheels turning behind her eyes.

"Quick question." She made a big show of getting out her reading glasses and giving him the once-over. "You're not too old for me, right? I'm too young to be dating grandpa material."

"Naw, I'm..."

"Thirty-two, that's right," she said at the last minute. Sonny had to shake his head. "Just five years older."

"Twenty-seven, then? Good, I hate jailbait."

She laughed at that. "OK, that was worth a meal. Why so nervous around me? You're always so take-charge when you talk with people on the phone."

"Well, I never have to worry about hurting those guys' feelings."

"Ok. Well, meet you there."

With a wave, Sonny made his way into his office. Josephine waited until he was inside before shaking her head and grinning in disbelief. "The fuck?" she whispered to herself.

*\*\**

Five minutes after that conversation, Colton walked into the newsroom. He saw Gus perched on top of a workstation in the City Desk den. He'd already had his shirt sleeves rolled up as he loomed over a reporter typing up a story.

As Colton got closer, he heard him say, "OK, does that mean if the city gets the money, they'll be able to make it work? Is that what they said, or are we just assuming that?"

The reporter, a skinny pale kid that looked not too much older than Colton, looked up, started to say something, and then finally shrugged his shoulders in submission.

"So, what's going to happen?" The kid pulled out his cell phone and started dialing. "Exactly."

Gus turned to face Colton. "Colton, right?" He reached out and shook his hand. "Gus Pulaski, city editor. Early today."

"I wanted to make sure I was on time."

"Fair enough. I'm going to let Kerry here get this taken care of. Let's head on over here and talk," he said, nodding his head toward his office.

"OK."

All the individual offices had cubicle-fabric walls with glazed glass doors. Gus's office was cozy rather than cramped. His narrow vertical window faced out toward Lake Michigan. A second desk and a sofa on the other side took up much of the rest of the space.

Gus indicated Colton should sit down on the sofa. "So, I've looked at some of the writing samples you submitted." Gus scanned several sheets of paper. "They looked pretty good."

"Thank you."

Gus gave him a look-over. He'd been waiting for the kid to act like he owned the place, but it hadn't happened so far. "OK, I'm going to see if I can be straight with you, and I'm expecting you to do the same."

"Yes." Colton nodded.

Gus sighed, laid the papers down on his desk, and leaned toward Colton over his folded arms. "Why do you want to go and play reporter?"

Colton hesitated for a moment. "I want to get to know everything this company does, and that includes newsgathering. I did a summer internship at the outdoor advertising division, so this isn't any different."

After a few quiet moments, Gus finally nodded. "OK."

"That's it?"

"Oh, definitely; you're in." Gus laughed. "With the cuts we've just had, we can use any extra hands."

"Fine by me. I don't want to just hang around."

"This is not going to be one of those 'take time and show you the ropes' situation. It's going to be more of a 'throw you into the middle of the Arctic and see if you can fish' situation, *capish*?"

"Ah, yeah." Colton nodded, even though he didn't know that last word. "Am I going to be working at the City Desk or somewhere else?"

"Partly. For now, I'll have you working mornings at the desk, checking the police blotter or other things. During the afternoons, I was thinking it might be useful to have you work with one of our columnists. Basically, helping with some legwork, things like that."

"OK. Who do you want me to work with, Carlton, or one of the sports columnists?" Sean Carlton was the paper's top political columnist, one of the few remaining Buckleyite moderate conservatives remaining in the wild.

"No, I'm going to pair you with someone else. We'll go over and meet him."

\*\*\*

"Turner? No, I never really heard of him," Colton said as he followed Gus across the newsroom.

"He started working on the city desk eight years ago, then conned me and Jack DeFoe into doing a column, not that we weren't overflowing with columnists at the time," Gus said.

"*The* Jack DeFoe?"

Gus nodded. "He was still editor-in-chief back then. Anyway, he starts off writing like the next Royko or Mazur, but he built on that, started writing about 'online lifestyles,' how people spent their time on the Web, how the Web connected to people in real life. He mixes politics into it. Recently, he's been doing a lot of media criticism, how he thinks journalism should work."

## The Holy Fool

"So, he messed up?" Colton was unsure if he was being stuck with someone on the editor's blacklist.

Gus laughed. "The Penthouse doesn't know what to think of him, but they leave him alone. He's been driving a lot of unique visitors to the Web site and all our Web and phone survey data says he's the only guy in our paper anyone under 40 bothers to read that doesn't talk about sports. As long as he's not committing felonies... OK, here he is."

They stopped at another door and Gus knocked. "Come in," Sonny growled from behind the door.

Sonny's office was half the size of Gus's cubbyhole. He hunched over a laptop on one end of an L-shaped desk while file folders and papers covered the other end facing the door. Two stuffed chairs faced the desk, and an old steel desk was tucked next to the filing cabinets covering the left-hand wall.

Sonny Turner got up, then froze, hands on hips, as he saw who was accompanying Gus into his office. "Sonny," Gus began, "this is..."

"Colton, right? Go ahead and have a seat." As Colton looked down to find his seat, Sonny mouthed the words "I hate you" to Gus as he took the other seat.

"Mr. Pulaski – ah, Gus – he suggested that you might need some assistance with your column," Colton said.

Sonny sat down as Gus took a seat beside Colton. "So, will you work at the City Desk then, too?"

"City Desk mornings, then some work with you during the afternoons for now," Gus specified.

"So, Colton here has the option of doing the job of two people and having no life or doing the job of two people half-assed and having a life. Just like nearly everyone else here." Sonny grinned at that.

"I'll be the first type of person rather than the last one. I can always have a life later," Colton said without hesitation.

That earned a laugh and a shrug from Sonny. "OK, Gus said you were game, at least... Gus, where do you want the kid to set up shop?"

"Well, there might be room for him out there, but I was thinking you could just install him in the spare desk in here," as he waved his hand at the steel antique. "He'll be in here a lot, anyway."

To Gus's surprise, Sonny nodded. "Sure, we can squeeze him in. Do you think we can get him a phone line and a chair that's not made out of rotten wood?"

"I'll talk to Maintenance and have them get on it. Sonny, when did you want to talk about that other thing?"

"I was thinking four, maybe."

"Sounds good; we'll do it in my office."

"OK. Listen, I know you want the kid to tag along with you – can I talk to him for a few minutes before he heads back out?"

"Sure." As soon as Gus walked out and closed the door, Sonny turned to Colton. "OK, so, you're in the Army now."

"Yep."

Turner got up and started to pace behind his desk as much as the limited space allowed. "What do you know about reporting?"

Colton leaned back in the overstuffed, fraying chair, deep in thought. "Well, my professors always said I did a great job with my research papers. But as far as what you guys do every day, I admit I don't know that much."

"Good. That's the first step of reporting – figuring out what you don't know about your subject."

"What are you working on right now? I'd be willing to help any way I could..."

"A lot of the stuff I'm currently working on, I need to keep close to the vest," Sonny interrupted. "Before I even consider..." He stopped pacing and started to stare at one of the walls of his office. "You see those pictures?"

Colton looked at the pictures. There were some old-time shots mixed in with recent ones. "Yeah?"

"Task #1, is that I want you to figure out the identities of the first eight people at the top of the wall. By the end of the day."

Colton looked at the photos. There was a hard-eyed man with hair neatly parted down the middle, an older man who resembled nothing less than a good-natured garden gnome, and someone who appeared to be a retired diamond thief, all on the left side of the wall. The other half had a white-haired woman in Victorian dress, a balding man with sunglasses and a cigarette holder, a similar-looking man, except in cartoon format with a spider tattoo on his head and glasses with one red and one green lens, and a rumpled fireplug of a man who smiled mostly with his eyes. "How do I do that?"

"Well, I'll leave that up to you. However, you have to tell me their names at 4:30 – no notes. Second, take a look at this."

Sonny pushed a paper across his desk and into Colton's line of sight. Colton looked down and saw this on the paper:

- 30 –

"I need you to explain to me the importance of that symbol."

"And that needs to be taken care of by 4:30 today."

"Exactly."

"Anything else you need by the end of today?"

"No, not really." He moved from behind the desk to shake Colton's hand. "Good luck with Gus today – he shouldn't run you too ragged."

"Thanks. I'll see you at one."

As Colton walked out and closed the door, Sonny muttered to himself, "Goddamn, save us from all the noobs."

Jason Liegois

# Chapter 3.

Colton walked back to Sonny's office at 1 p.m. "Come in," he heard before he could knock. "Welcome back – you get a chance to eat?"

"Yeah, someone sent out for some deli," Colton said. Looking around, he noticed that someone had brought in a new armless office chair and a phone extension for his desk.

"Sorry there's not a desktop yet, but there's plug-ins for it later."

"I've got the laptop Gus gave me – I could use it in here."

"Cool with me. Any luck on what I asked you to look up?"

"Not yet. I was going to keep looking for that now, unless you had something you needed me to do…"

"Naw, keep up with that." Sonny reached behind his desk and slung his leather satchel over his shoulder. "There is one other thing."

"Yes?" Colton draped his bomber jacket over the chair and sat down.

"I'm going to be out for a while. I've set up the phones in here so that my extension will ring out to your phone. Catch any messages for me. You know how to send them through to the voice mail?"

"I think so – Gus gave me this manual…"

Sonny tossed a long, narrow reporter's notebook onto Colton's desk. "Write it down before sending them over just to stay safe. Also, anyone asks, I'm not around here and I can't be reached, understand?"

"Got it."

"Hang loose." Sonny swooped out the door.

***

Sonny took the service elevator on the west side of the building to the Penthouse. Usually administration didn't let

Jason Liegois

regular staff up there without appointments, but he had a duplicate security key card that let him not only run the elevator, but gain access to certain rooms.

The elevator opened at the lowest floor on the Penthouse. No one was around as Sonny peaked out and saw an ornate oak doorway whose nameplate proclaimed:

## **JACK DEFOE**
## **Editor/Publisher Emeritus**

With one more look outside to see if the halls were clear, Sonny tiptoed out and fed the keycard through the door lock, saw a satisfying green light, and opened it.

"Was wondering when you'd get here," said the tall, rubber-limbed man behind the massive desk.

"Woot, would you get your feet off the desk? You know, for Jack's sake, at least?" Sonny whispered at him.

"Sure thing." He eased his feet down to the floor. "How about there?"

"Be my guest." Sonny gestured to one of the red leather couches nestled in front of the desk.

With a cackle, Jeff "Woot" MacKenzie got out of the high-backed red leather chair behind the desk and, with an exaggerated bow, offered Sonny a seat. As Sonny sat, Woot walked around and flopped onto one of the couches, limbs laying in all directions.

Sonny thought of him as a hipster Lincoln-meets-Einstein, long, rubbery, with a hawk nose, and frizzed sandy hair that shot out in all directions and down to his shoulders. He almost invariably dressed in vintage or joke T-shirts, jeans, and some version of Chuck Taylor sneakers.

Woot - the Internet handle came from his favorite expression of excitement – was a tech consultant for the *Journal*, but he was the closest thing that Sonny had to a friend left in the building except for Gus and Joey. Woot ran a small computer security firm, and Edson Media had subcontracted its network security to him. Sonny had used Woot as a source of information for his column, and as a liaison to other tech sources. Over time, they had bonded over their mutual fascination for online and pop culture, as well as politics, although a lot of their communication happened either online or away from the newsroom. The more he thought about it, the more Sonny realized it was a good thing that the level of their friendship was not common knowledge given what he had asked of him and what he was about to ask.

"So, you understand what's going on?" Sonny began.

"Oh, yeah. Apparently, Gus thinks Edson is looking to sell the paper right from under everyone and he wants you to find out if it's true."

"Like that. I'm going to need your help."

"What do you have in mind?"

"Everything. Email dumps, network and hard drive searches, phone hacks… everything, basically."

Woot stretched out on the couch, lost in thought and staring up at the ceiling. "Tricky."

"Can you get it done?"

Woot grinned again. "It's possible."

"Well, glad to know. I don't want to get you in trouble, but it's for the paper, you understand?"

"That's OK. But I really want to do it due to my urge to get back to some black hat activities after being a good boy for so long."

"Messed up," Sonny laughed. Woot had a past – some criminal mischief and computer trespassing charges before even setting foot in high school. He was usually vague about it, but Sonny got the impression that Woot was the hacker version of Sinatra – not a hardcore criminal, but someone who liked hanging out with the Outfit boys.

Woot flexed his long fingers together behind his head as he lay back on the couch. "I can direct penetrate them, but it's going to take some time, especially to escape detection in the process. That asshole Wyatt, the new security head, I think he's getting more paranoid every day…"

"We'll need to get inside their shorts pretty soon."

Woot looked back at Sonny. "How soon?"

"Two months, max, likely less, maybe a fortnight? I want to give you deniability on this, but we're going to have to move."

Woot sighed as he started at the ceiling, and then sat back up. "What the fuck is a fortnight?"

"Two weeks."

"Oh, great, I always wondered about that ever since I started watching Wimbledon."

"So, is there any way to speed up the process?"

"I'll think about it. I'm going to put some hardware in here tonight to help intercept their communications, but we'll have to keep out of here after that to avoid detection. Then I'll find a safe spot in the basement to tap into the network directly through the fiber-optic cables. Meantime, this might be helpful." Woot reached into his jeans pocket and pulled out a flash drive, black and the size of a stick of gum. "Some juju for you."

Sonny turned it around in his hand. There was a clown head sticker on one side. "What the hell is this?"

"Zombie Clown. I cooked up a little proprietary infiltration software. All you have to do is insert the drive, open its files, and click on the clown icon. It downloads a Trojan Horse program. They won't know it's even working. Hang onto it just in case you get near any important-looking computers."

Sonny started at Woot. "This will work?"

Woot stared right back, radiating confidence through his smile. "I've got this."

With a nod, Sonny pocketed the drive. "OK."

Woot looked around the room, and then turned his attention to the picture facing them from the opposite wall. "He really hung that here?"

It was a full-color oil painting of Jack in his prime, silver-haired, and confident, beaming with good cheer as he casually sat on top of the desk Sonny was behind now. "Naw, they put that up after he died. Jack'd never go for that."

"Hey, speaking of sneaking around, did Casey get through all of that other stuff? You know, what you had me set up the encryption for?"

## The Holy Fool

"Let's find out." He fired up his cell phone and selected another digit. After two rings, someone picked up. *"Chicago Journal* D.C. bureau, Barnes," a smooth voice with what sounded like a Midwest flatness said.

"Casey, it's Sonny."

"All right, Sonny!" Casey responded, his accent getting broader by the minute. "See you on Skype

Within two minutes, Casey's image flashed onto Sonny's laptop as they and Woot pulled on headphones. He was younger than Sonny and Woot, mid-twenties, slim and elegant, light-coffee colored complexion, and kept his dark kinky hair short. When he was working, he preferred collared knit shirts, sweater vests, and tailored slacks. Sonny called him "Kanye's twin." "OK, what do you need?"

"You already know that. What have you got?" Sonny said.

"Just a minute." Casey was typing away at the keyboard. "OK, I decided to pull out about 30 documents from the last batch we got. I started letting people in the know look at some of them."

"Who?" Woot broke in.

"Strictly family. One cousin in the Navy, a second cousin in the State Department, and my aunt with the Congressional Black Caucus staff."

"What's the verdict?" Sonny said.

Casey shook his head. "Everyone's saying either these documents are real or someone's done a master job at faking them. What are we doing with this?"

"Something," Sonny said. "I've already started putting together two stories based on info you've already seen. Woot, I'm going to need you to help me and Casey look through this deeper – you've got document recognition software, right, the stuff the law firms use?"

"Sure," Woot said.

"What do you want?" Casey asked.

"Basically, flagging anything that might be above top secret, revealing personnel, people under cover, stuff like that." Sonny said.

"OK, I'll get you guys the hook-up," Woot said.

Jason Liegois

*\*\*\**

At 4 p.m., long after Sonny and Woot had vacated Jack's office after Woot wired it, Gus ushered Sonny into his own office and closed the door. "This sort of thing, this... I-Project, I don't want spreading throughout the newsroom unless we're ready to spread it," Gus said, showing Sonny to a seat.

"What's the story with this meeting?" Sonny said.

"The Executive wants to meet with you tomorrow afternoon, to go over it."

"What do you mean by executive? You mean Connors?" Sonny said, referring to the editor in chief. "I haven't run into him more than twice in two years."

"Not just him. Cathy Boone's going to be there," Gus said, referring to the *Journal*'s publisher. "There's also a good chance Johnny Boy's going to be there," using his own pet name for the Edson CEO.

Sonny looked up at that. "What's the big deal?"

"Are you kidding me? You're talking about leaking classified government documents, many of them having to do with active war zones. Governments, *U.S.* governments, have tried to shut down papers for less than that. You remember your history class?"

"Not my history class. You know they never get around to the 'Nam and the Pentagon Papers in high school."

Gus groaned in response.

"What, they expect me to reveal the source? You know I'm not doing that. I'm tired of this..."

"No, they won't." Gus waved at him to calm him down. "They'll want you to go over what he or she's been giving you."

"Well, there's that mercenary stuff I mentioned before..."

"You mean Foxwood Solutions?"

"Yeah, that... and other stuff. Here's an example." Sonny reached over and handed Gus a printout.

"What is this?" Gus said, looking it over.

"This is an official after-action report on some war games in the Gulf back in '02 that the Navy and Marines ran. The Navy was running a carrier battle group and the Marines were simulating Iranian military. So, the Marine general decides he's not going to go toe to toe with the carrier group like a good Third World general should. Instead of putting out his front-line ships, he sent out a mess of smaller boats, ships, and even civilian aircraft. They were swarming around, and the poor Aegis radar operators couldn't tell who was what. You should see the communications from the Navy admiral where he all but demands the Marines fight like proper white men."

"So, what, the carrier group finally goes after them?"

"Naw, the admiral finally gets pissed off and starts to withdraw his ships, and right then, all of those little ships and planes go in for the attack. And the problem is, all those suckers have missiles, and most of them are anti-ship missiles." He paused for a second. "The carrier group lost two-thirds of its ships, including both carriers."

"What?"

"Oh, yeah, that was clever. What AA weapons they had that could conceivably stop anti-ship missiles in ballistic flight got overwhelmed by the number of targets."

"Can't believe it's that easy."

"Go into a bar sometime in Portsmouth, find some old Royal Navy guys, and ask them whether Exocets were a joke to them in the Falklands. Maybe you should go to Tel Aviv and ask some guys in the Israeli Navy why they don't run big ships any more ever since the Arabs knocked out their pride and joy cruiser back in '67. The Navy is sticking with the old way of fighting and it'll bite us in the ass."

"OK, then. You'll have some other examples to show them on Wednesday?"

"Sure." After he collected the file from Gus, he shook his head. "Or should I ask them whether we're going to have a newspaper to work for two months from now?"

Gus groaned at that and put his hand to his face. "Sonny, dammit, you're not going to do that. Anyway, Arturo wants to talk to you. He wants to see if he can help out."

"You mean, you want me to talk to him." Gus shrugged in response. "Thought his specialty was cop shop, not investigative."

"The guy used to *be* a cop, Sonny – he's an investigator. Check in with him tomorrow."

Sonny shrugged. "OK... When exactly will the execs need us there?"

"Noon."

"All right, then."

***

Colton was looking through a file folder and standing sentry over Sonny's desk when he returned to his office.

"So?" Sonny said as he came in.

Colton took a deep breath, then continued. "OK. The identities of the people you asked me to find. We have Jack DeFoe and Ed Mazur from the *Journal*..."

"I wanted to give you a couple of easy ones."

"Ah, Studs Terkel, a Pulitzer winner, used to write and do radio here in Chicago. This guy, H.L. Mencken, used to write for the *Baltimore Sun* back in the early 1900's. The bald guy there is Hunter S. Thompson, who used to write for *Rolling Stone* back in the 70's, and the cartoon guy is Spider Jerusalem, a fictional reporter for a comic called *Transmetropolitan*. A lot of people think Spider was kind of a take-off on Thompson, like Duke in *Doonesbury*."

"You read *Doonesbury*?"

"I read it in *Slate* online."

Sonny laughed. "Figures."

"The lady was probably the toughest for me to find. Her name was Mary Jones, and she was a labor organizer at the turn of the 20$^{th}$ century. She was better known as Mother Jones."

"Correct. So, where'd you source your stuff?"

"A mix of everything – Google searches, Wikipedia, a couple of the older guys on the city desk, this new site TinEye that does image-based searches."

"OK, not bad, but you always need to confirm those Wikipedia sources," Sonny took a moment to pull out one of his narrower, spiral reporter's notebook out of his desk and begin writing some things down on a page. "The next couple of days, I'll probably need you to get some research done, follow-up with some people for me for the column, and some other stuff. But this I want you to work on outside of the office."

Sonny ripped out the page he had been writing in and handed it to Colton.

"What's this?" Colton said.

"It's a list of movies – there's three of them on there. Rent them and look through them. I bet you can get through these by the time you get into work tomorrow, right?"

"OK. I haven't heard of any of these films..."

"Doesn't matter. Just pay attention – I'll have some questions for you tomorrow and I'll expect some answers with thought in them, right?"

"Right, *The Falcon and the Snowman*?"

"Just watch them, OK? So, you heading out? You can probably get going soon."

"Really? Great, I wanted to get back home before seven if I can manage it."

"What for? ...oh, you got someone waiting for you at home? I get it."

"Kyra," Colton fished a photo of her from his wallet to show to Sonny. "We've been together for about two years."

"Cool chick, good for you," Sonny handed back the picture. "Yeah, sure, just check around and see whether Gus needs something, and if he doesn't, you're home free."

"Thanks."

\*\*\*

Colton walked past Gus as he made his way around the City Desk. "You need anything else, Gus, before I get going for the night?"

Gus, who was proofreading one of next morning's stories, looked up for a moment. "No, I think we're set, Sonny didn't hassle you too much, did he?"

"No, no, he was fine. I got everything he wanted done, not a problem."

"OK, good. I want you to shadow Dana Parker when she goes on the morning cop run, give you a chance to see how that works. We'll try more beats over time."

Jason Liegois

"Sure, not a problem. I'll be there."

"Night."

"Night." Colton made his way across the newsroom and to the reception area where he got onto the west side elevators. However, instead of pushing the button for the ground floor, he waited until the doors closed before pushing the button to the fifteenth floor three floors up.

At the end of the hallway outside the elevator, there was a desk and a security guard overseeing the entryway into the elevator area. When he came up to the standing guard, Colton fished around in the inside pocket of his jacket, found the Journal ID tag, and showed it to him. The guard let him pass through to the executive areas.

Within a few seconds, he walked to the executive reception area. A single receptionist, not much older than Colton, awaited him behind an all-white desk. Big black metal letters spelling out Edson Media were on display behind her. "Yes, can I help you?"

"Hi, I'm here to meet with John Michael Edson."

"Very well, do you have an appointment?"

"Ah, no, but he was expecting me today."

Her brows knitted at that remark. "All right. Can you tell me your name, please?"

"Yeah, it's Colton...," he began, halted, then continued in a lower volume voice, "Colton Edson."

Her eyes flew wide after hearing the name. "Oh, sorry – I just started working here last year..."

"Don't worry about it. Just started work today, myself."

"Really? Well, congratulations."

"Thanks."

"If you just want to go up the hall there and to the left, I'll let Mrs. Kennedy know you are coming."

"Thanks. Have a good day." Colton waved goodbye to the girl and started down the hallway.

The doorways were fewer and the offices larger on the 21st floor, the highest of sanctuaries for the top Edson media executives. When Edson Media took over two years ago, they had decided to move their main offices into the Penthouse from their old headquarters, an aging and nondescript

# The Holy Fool

broadcasting center in the Near North area of Chicago. The size of the Keep meant that even after the move, there were still empty offices in the Penthouse.

Colton made it to the end of the hall, where the glass-walled main executive conference room sat, overlooking Lake Michigan and the lakefront. A T-hallway intersection led to the left and right, so Colton turned left and walked down that hall. A simple brass plaque at the end of the hall at eye level proclaimed JOHN MICHAEL EDSON, CEO.

Mary Kennedy waited at the desk just before the double doors. Slim, fortyish, conservatively dressed with hair going prematurely grey, she had been John Michael's administrative assistant for a dozen years and knew Colton very well. "It's OK; you can go right in. He's expecting you."

"Thanks." He opened one of the oak double doors leading into the office. John Michael sat behind an oaken frigate of a desk, tucked into the northeastern corner of the room and angle so he could stare out at Lake Michigan.

John Michael was handsome but in a bland manner, as if a beginning artist had drawn his idea of an older male model. He looked thick but not heavy; his hair was full and a mix of dust and ash color, and grey eyes that seemed indistinct. He preferred Italian suits exclusively when he was at work, even though he grew up on the Gold Coast and had never been to Italy.

As he turned around and his eyes focused on Colton, a smile spread across his face. "Kiddo?" He got up from his seat. "It's great to see you."

"Good to see you too. I'm not bothering you, am I?"

"Nah, I told you to come up here today, didn't I?" Edson strode over to the younger man. Somewhat to Colton's surprise, he found himself enveloped in a hug. "Glad you're here, Son."

"Thanks, Dad."

"Well, come on, then, sit." Edson pointed to an overstuffed leather couch and two similarly upholstered chairs flanking it in front of his desk. "Tell me about today."

"Not much to tell." Colton took the offered seat. "I got started right away down there, met Gus Pulaski – he got me squared away, met some of the guys on the City Desk, took a tour of the newsroom."

"Good to hear. So, you'll be working for Pul... Gus down at the City Desk, right?"

"He also wanted me to work for one of the columnists down there, Sonny Turner."

That got Edson's attention as he sat up straight behind his desk. "Really? Did Turner request that?"

"No, actually I think it was Gus's idea."

"Hm." Edson's brows knitted together and he leaned forward, balancing his chin on his hands. "That's a surprise, but I'll trust Gus's judgement on that."

Colton laughed at that. "You, trusting anyone? You said that was never the key to success."

"Well, what I said was trusting anyone when money changes hands was a sucker's bet. I trust Gus with teaching new reporters how to do their jobs."

His dad picked up a special digital picture frame that showed a rotating series of family pictures. One of the pictures was Colton and his parents posing at his college graduation; others featured him and his brother at family get-togethers or vacations. He stared at the frame for a few moments.

"I'm sorry – I have to admit that I've been down a bit since you graduated," Edson finally said, setting the frame down. "And it's not your fault at all. It's just that I expected your brother to be graduating first. It just reminded me what's going wrong with Mikey. And that's not fair to you at all."

"No, I understand. Have you heard from him? The last time he texted me was a couple of weeks ago."

"He's back at Northwestern again, on academic probation. I'm glad he's back in school, but he's still hanging out with that old crowd of his. Well, you don't need to hear about that. How was working for Turner?"

"Sonny? He seems like a real interesting guy – I might learn a lot from him."

"I've tried to read some of his columns, but it's not my taste. Our younger readers seem to like him, though, and anything attracting younger readers we've got to stick with."

"Anyway, let me see you out." Edson got back up out of his chair and made his way toward the door. "That girl of yours…"

"Kyra?"

"Is she graduating soon?"

"After next semester, actually."

"It would really be great if the three of us went out to lunch sometime."

"Ah, sure. We could do that."

"Maybe next week?"

"Sure. Mom come along?"

"Not sure. She's been busy with so much volunteer work that she's giving my schedule a run for its money." He patted his son on the shoulder. "I'm proud of you coming here."

Jason Liegois

# Chapter 4

Sonny slouched out of the Keep, his courier's bag over one shoulder. When he went outside of the building, he saw The Gentleman waiting for him, about a block away, buying a copy of the *Journal*. The Superfan was on the other side of the street, looking out of the back of his gypsy cab.

Sonny saw a bodega on the next corner. As the two men followed him, he walked up and darted into the shop's entrance.

The owner of the place was in the front, the register area enclosed in a Plexiglas booth. He was a Hispanic male, bulky, with a 50's style pompadour, and was watching America C.F. play Chivas on a television in the booth.

"Eduardo, *que pasa*?" Sonny said.

"Not too much," the man replied. "How about you?"

"OK. You still have that exit out the back?"

"Yeah, it's unlocked. What do you need?"

Sonny grabbed a copy of the *Journal* and an energy drink. "First, these. Then, if I could go out there, that would be great."

"Not a problem, Sonny."

"And, can you forget I was here after I go?"

"Sure, Sonny." Eduardo got up from his seat and shrugged. "What if the cops start asking around?"

"You can tell *them* you saw me," Sonny said as he walked to the back, "but I don't think that they'll be asking."

After threading through the storage area, he came upon the metal fire exit. He eased the door open, peeking out first to the right and then around to the left. There was no sign of the Superfan and his car, but Sonny knew that he could be there soon.

Sonny saw the alleyway running parallel to the doorway 20 yards to the right. He dashed toward it, the surrounding buildings hovering well over him but providing no cover on their own.

He managed to get into the alley at the exact second the Superfan began rounding the corner to the alleyway behind the bodega. Sonny saw a Dumpster near the intersection of alleys, off to the left, and ducked behind it. From behind there, he saw the Superfan drive to the back of the bodega and come to a stop directly behind the back door. He immediately called someone on his cell.

Making as little noise as possible, Sonny crab-walked down the alley to the city streets, yanked a black knit cap from his coat's inside pocket and pulled it over his head. Satisfied, he followed the flow of pedestrians headed first to Wacker Drive, then across one of the Chicago River bridges.

During the next half hour, he ducked into the Merchandise Mart across the river, toured several floors, entered a restroom stall, changed into a Blackhawks hoodie and khaki shorts, jumped onto the El's Mart stop, and rode the Loop until stopping at a station three blocks away from the restaurant. The Gentleman or The Superfan were nowhere to be seen.

\*\*\*

Joey was at a table at Harry Carey's, feeling alone even though diners packed the room. As she checked the phone for the fifth time, arms snaked around her neck and she heard, "Hello, stranger."

She jumped in her seat, letting out an *Eep!* before turning around to see Sonny coming around to face her. "Sorry it took so long." He sat down.

"Geez!" Joey clutched her chest.

"Yeah, it took a while to make sure I wasn't being followed. You order yet?"

Joey shook her head as her breathing returned to normal. "Someone was really following you?"

"Two people like before. I got rid of them at some bodega right next to the Keep."

# The Holy Fool

"OK, Mr. Flint," she said, leaning back in her chair and shaking her head, "so am I going to hear this story about why people are following you around Chicago?"

"Yeah, but I want to relax first." He picked up a menu. "What do you think you'll get to drink before we start? By the way, clever 60's spy cultural reference there." He stared at her for a moment. "You're looking nice today."

"I changed before leaving work too. You like it?"

He took her in. She had settled on a flowered skirt reaching halfway down her shins, a thin knitted blue sweater, and Doc Marten combat boots alongside her regular platoon of bracelets and wristbands. A single gold necklace sported a jade Buddha, and she had settled on a simple ponytail that managed to gather in her black hair that got more wavy the longer it was.

"You do look cute and... you. I feel underdressed."

"No, you look fine."

\*\*\*

"So, what prompted all of this?" Joey asked as she dug into her chicken fettuccine alfredo.

"What?"

"You know, finally deciding to meet me outside of work."

"I'm starting to recover from a life-long bout of workaholism," Sonny joked, taking an initial stab at his prime rib. "You know, one thing I never asked you before? I always wondered how your parents stuck you with Josephine for a name."

"My family's Norwegian, and it was one of those names that they're always giving girls in our family. They thought I was going to be a boy, so they had Joseph lined up. When I came around, they just added a few letters and they were set."

"No kidding?"

"I was fourth of five kids."

"Wow, that would have been cool. Maybe a little crowded, but... It would have been nice to have siblings, but Mom never remarried after the divorce."

"So, you don't have anyone else?"

Sonny shook his head. "Dad drank himself to death 10 years ago; he never really got over my mom. Mom and I were close, but I was busy with work and she was busy being a principal. I'm glad I was with her when she passed."

"Again, I'm so sorry."

"Thanks. Just to change the subject a bit, you're totally done with the Art Institute then? Graduated and everything?"

"Yeah, I finished up in May."

"Right, I remember. It's weird, you still being at the *Journal* now that you graduated."

"Well, I started with an English degree because I thought I was going to be some kind of novelist, but writing the Great American novel never worked for me. I fell more into art. I'd always been playing with art as a kid, and when I met some Art Institute students, I thought it might be the creative outlet I always wanted. But, the *Journal* job sort of fell into my lap. Maybe it was because I worked cheap."

"I remember seeing those sketches you had with you a few months back – they looked real nice."

"Not just those – some paintings, sculptures, photos, some installation pieces. I've actually sold some, but no big dollars yet."

"You'd ever think about going to New York, try and make it there?"

She sighed. "I don't really see any point to moving to New York or somewhere else; the art scene is as strong here as any place, and it's fairly cheap to live here.

"Your family lives here in Chicago?"

"Highland Park," she said, as if she was trying to pass along a state secret.

"Highland? John Hughes' turf? Oh, wow, this is a trip!" Sonny laughed and shook his head all at once.

"OK, OK, enough… I forgot where you live…"

"Wicker Park." Sonny grimaced. "It used to be somewhat sketchy when I first moved out there, but the yuppies are there in earnest now. They doing that in Pilsen yet?"

"No, it's divided between the Latinos and the art folks, but not that many yuppies."

# The Holy Fool

"I'd like to see your place." It got quiet at the table. She stared down into her lap for a few moments. "Was that the wrong thing to say?" Sonny finally ventured.

Sonny was relieved to see her look up at him with the smallest of smiles. "No, it wasn't wrong; I was just processing it."

"You hear that often?"

She nodded. "There was the first boyfriend in high school, the one who basically drugged me to sleep with him. I even knew about it beforehand, and I never said 'no,' so I guess you couldn't call it a sex crime."

"It's definitely bullshit."

She eased her left hand over the table and covered his right hand with it. "It's OK; you don't need to look the guy up. We broke up before graduation – I told him life was too short."

She felt the tension back out of his hand and arm. "What happened to him?"

"David? He went to UCLA and flunked out a year later. Last I heard he was waiting tables in LA and trying to get some acting work."

"You never mentioned any of this to me before."

"I never went on a date with you." There was a deep sigh before she continued. "There was Ricky in college, somewhere around my second year. That went well for a while until he slapped me one night after I'd beat him at bar trivia night out with him and his friends. I was impressed that I never considered staying after that." Her face clouded over after that remark. "There were a couple of other guys too, but nothing like that happened with them. I've been by myself for at least three years."

"Three years? That's been about as long as it's been for me, too."

"Hum. OK, that's officially a coincidence." Joey stopped to take a couple of bites of her dish before it stopped steaming. "So, tell me," she said when she was done, "what broke you and the last girl up?"

"I guess it was the same thing that happened with all of the girls I've dated," he finally said. "I guess I just got too obsessed with my work to pay attention to them over the long term."

Joey looked off into the distance, deep in thought. "Can you tell me why you finally decided to ask me out to dinner?"

He paused, then: "When my mom died... Last night, I was more alone than I ever felt until I heard your message. I suddenly realized I needed a life, and you were someone I'd always wanted to get together with and see what might happen. There's a couple of other reasons, but that's the main one. Why'd you agree?"

Joey folded her hands in her lap and sat up straight as if she was about to address a tea party. "I always felt you treated me as a person, not just another girl. That's unusual for guys I meet. I'm glad you finally asked me."

"So, you want me to tell you why I think I'm being followed?" Sonny dropped his voice, which could be heard throughout the newsroom easily, to at least half-power.

"Yeah?"

"It probably has to do with a story I've been getting the editors to try and run."

"What's it about?"

Sonny hunched over to try to stop himself from laughing. "Nothing much, but everybody's worried the federal government's going to bust us on an espionage rap if we publish what I've got."

"What?" Sonny was impressed that she was still trying to whisper to him and managing to do it. "What happened, did you hack into the Pentagon's computers and steal all of their top-secret files?"

"Nooooo, of course not, that would be crazy. I just got the files from the person who did steal them."

"Who gave you them?" she finally asked.

"The files? Haven't a clue. Well, I have a clue or two. I ran into... *her* in an IRC room."

"OK, wait, IRC?" Both had forgotten their half-eaten dishes at this point.

"Internet Relay Chat. An old chat room. I've been cruising the hacker ones to get some column ideas. About six months ago, I was chatting with some people in this room which specializes in deep Web surfing..."

"Deep Web?"

"The parts of the Internet the normal search engines don't pick up. It's a digital mix of the Wild West, the Walled City of Kowloon, and Amsterdam. Anyway, I'd been on there for a few hours, chatting with some people about Tor usage when this woman, entity, whatever, named hewoman98 starts chatting with me, asks me to go into private chat. She says she knew who I was through my handle – I'd listed it in a column somewhere – and that she has some top-secret files for me, stuff on the war in Iraq and Afghanistan."

"You believed her?"

"Not at first, but then she passed along a few gigabytes of documents."

"Gigabytes? It must have been a ton of documents."

"Not all of them were word or pdf files. Some of it was even gun camera footage of firefights, civilians getting whacked in Iraq. A lot of that first batch was of this one company, Foxwood Solutions, which operates around Baghdad. People that would have been called mercenaries a decade or three back; now, they're contractors. With the stuff I saw, a lot of those people need to be doing time somewhere. Maybe they could open up Abu Ghraib again for the fuckers."

"What *do* you know about her?"

"Nothing solid, but I have a few hunches, from a couple of things she said. First, she's working somewhere she has access to these files. Probably the Pentagon because she knows the building well, from the way she talks about it. She's very intelligent, has a sophisticated vocabulary. With the Top-Secret access and that, I'd guess she's a junior or mid-level officer, or at least a high-ranking NCO.

"She's never worried about getting caught or anything like that – no fear," Sonny continued. "You ask me, something out in the Sandbox put the zap on her head. So, what do you think?"

Joey blinked for a few seconds, totally in shock, her food orphaned on the plate. "Excuse me?"

"As a fellow journalist, what do you think I should do?"

Joey was quiet again for a moment. "It's our job to let people know what their government is doing, right? Even if they'd prefer people not to know for whatever reason."

Sonny stared down at their plates. "And you say you're not a real journalist. We might as well finish this off."

"I'm ahead of you on that," Joey dug in to her noodles.

\*\*\*

Sonny had chosen a boat at the Navy Pier that would take them on a leisurely trip along the western edge of Lake Michigan as the passengers could gawk at the sight of Chicago from the lake. After they boarded, Sonny found a table on top of the boat's observation deck and escorted Joey there, where they both sat down.

"OK, how about this?" Sonny said as the boat got underway. "How about we trade more stories? Go on, you go first."

Joey hesitated for a moment. "I forgot to tell you about this art show I'll be in Saturday. There's a gallery in Pilsen, The Bitter End, that's showing my work starting that evening. I've been in shows before, but this is the first one where I'm actually the featured artist."

"What are you going to show that day?"

"A mix of paintings, photos, and models. I had to do it when I was building my portfolio at the Art Institute. In fact, some of this work I did when I was still there."

"You'll be fine. Do you have everything ready to go?"

"Yeah, all set. Most of it's at my apartment; I've been experimenting with the set-up."

"You've got enough room at your apartment to do that?"

"Just barely. Either the landlord or the tenant before me managed to divide up the living room of my apartment into two spaces, so my artwork's taken up the front space."

"Cool."

"Well, now let's hear from you, unless you have something else going on other than this version of *All the President's Men*?" she said as she stared at the Gold Coast's lights dancing across the water toward the boat.

# The Holy Fool

"Funny enough, Gus told me he wants to find out whether or not the newspaper's getting sold."

Joey's jaw dropped at that. "You're serious?"

"He's dead serious."

"You think it might happen?"

"It happens all the time in the newspaper business. Whether it's happening now or not, I don't know. I just started looking into it today."

"If it happens, are any of us going to be able to keep our jobs?"

"Probably not."

"Oh, jeez." She covered her eyes with her hands and slumping down. "Uhhh, I don't need this right now..."

"Thought you weren't sure about journalism."

"Not necessarily. I need this job right now. I'd like to keep my apartment..."

"It'll be fine."

"What if it's not?" She stared back at him. Sonny was surprised to see the hint of starter tears around her eyes.

"I can somewhat guarantee no one's getting fired this week. If something happens for real, I'll warn you, even get you some help if you need it for a while."

"You going to do that for everyone at the paper?"

"Warn them, yes. Help them... I have a pretty small lifeboat, but you get the first seat. Look, don't worry about this tonight."

She seemed to relax after that, the tension draining from her shoulders. "OK." She looked out at the skyline. "It really is a beautiful night. Thanks for inviting me out here." She looked up at Sonny. "I'd like to have you come with me back to Pilsen. There's a corner store nearby my apartment, and we can get some rum because I'm out. After that, I want to take you up to my apartment and show you my paintings. That sound like a plan?" She covered her mouth to stop a giggle from forming. "Do I sound like one of those pervs from the 60's movies or something?"

"I'm down for it, perv or not."

\*\*\*

They walked out of the bodega, arms over each one's shoulders, as Sonny carried a bottle of rum in his other hand. There was a large mural showing a procession of Aztec princes promenading across the wall. "You run into the natives a lot?"

"All the time. A couple even bought my stuff."

"That's nice. Sometimes I see 'Hands off Pilsen' graffiti in Spanish around here; I was wondering if that was aimed at people like you."

"Not really; they get along with us. It's the… developers that they get nervous about. They don't want this place to get all uptown like Lincoln Park and Old Town has been."

"Don't worry; they've got their eyes on Wicker Park." He laughed.

"Well, it's nice out here now."

"I can understand why."

They made it to her building and walked past a set of hastily installed mailboxes up a wide flight of stairs. Joey caught her foot on the first step up and managed to land on her butt in the middle of the staircase. "Shit, I was trying not to wake anyone up by not taking the elevator."

"How many margaritas did you have tonight?" Sonny offered his hand to help her up.

"Apparently not enough," she said as she took it.

Sonny and Joey walked up to the top floor. It was a long hallway until they reached Joey's apartment on the back side. There were two deadbolts that she had to unlock before opening the door. "I wanted to make sure no one got in without my say-so."

"Smart."

Joey opened the door. The room behind the door had a pair of traffic horses nailed to double sheets of plywood that held various art supplies, tubes of paint, glue, duct tape, and unfinished projects strewn across it. Otherwise, it was barren of furniture except for a stool next to the table. Paintings, etchings, and other oddities lined the walls wherever there was space.

"Jesus, this is cool."

## The Holy Fool

"Not much, but it works." Joey circled around the room. "I had to buy track lighting for this room before I got a decent fridge."

"Good to know what your priorities are."

Sonny looked at one corner of the room. What he saw were several paintings that seemed to be pictures of Roman citizens wandering through American cities, hitting the clubs, and attending football and hockey games.

"I keep hearing everyone comparing America now to how Rome was, so I started to wonder how they would have reacted living in our world," she said.

Sonny looked back at the table. A city model covered at least half of the table. The city wrapped around the bend of a river of blue plastic. It was a mish-mash of ruined, classical buildings with naked columns, no roofs, and open spaces tucked in between ultra-modern skyscrapers. A few of the remains of old buildings served as facades for buildings with advanced, futuristic architecture.

"Jesus, how long did it take you to build this?"

"Six months, maybe? It's a mix of paper-mache, wood, and some plastic odd and ends, even a few Legos. See what it is?"

At what appeared to be the juncture of several streets in the city at the base of a hill, he saw the top of a battered but intact white dome on top of a classical building. After a minute of staring at the building, he finally whistled, saying, "Is this DC? Is this the Capitol?"

"My vision of it 500 years from now." Joey brushed her hand over the ruined Capitol. "Two years ago, I got to travel out to Rome as part of a class. There were all of these old ruins from the ancient Roman days just sitting there, all those old columns and piles of marble bricks right in the middle of those modern buildings and roads. I wondered how that might look in DC, where the old buildings were set aside and the city had moved on."

"You read my column when I talked about America being the new Rome, didn't you?"

"Dip." Joey snuck behind him and smacked him between the shoulder blades. "I thought of it first. I have to admit it was wild to see that online, though, how you were thinking about the same thing I was without even us talking about it."

"I didn't tell you about that column?"

"You *barely* ever talk to me about what you write except when I ask you about it," Joey shot back. "Most of the times, you ask me about Adult Swim on Cartoon Network."

"You love those shows, though."

"Don't change the subject. I think maybe I got interested in you by reading what you wrote, what you believed in, that New Democracy stuff. Is that weird?"

"Weird's good."

"Do you want to see the rest of the place?"

"Sure."

It was a combined kitchen/dining/living space. The kitchen area was compact and immediately to Sonny's left. It was basic: tile flooring, Formica countertops, with a fridge, gas oven, and microwave tucked under a cabinet and a bar area dividing the kitchen from the rest of the room. There was a four-person table immediately behind the bar, and then there was space right next to the outside windows where two overstuffed couches and two equally overstuffed leather seats surrounded a battered coffee table. Abstract and modernistic paintings of her creation covered all the brick walls in the room.

"That's not as expensive as it looks – all of the furniture I got from swap meets and the landfill," Joey laughed as they walked in. "I even refurbished and recovered the couches myself."

"Handy woman." Sonny found a bar stool next to the bar and parked himself there. He set the rum bottle down and deposited his bag with his laptop at his feet.

"Thanks for the compliment."

"No, I'm serious. I like the paintings, too."

He noticed Joey walking into the kitchen area – it was more like *sauntering*, like she was trying to make her hips sway but she was out of practice.

She opened one of the cabinets and fished out two square highball glasses. Joey slid over to Sonny and sat both down. She pointed toward the right-hand wall and the two black

# The Holy Fool

doors there. "Bathroom's behind the right door and the bedroom's behind the left." She then took the bottle, cracked the seal, and poured. "Listen, *I've* got to go to the bathroom for a second. Are you going to be OK?"

"Sure, no. I'll be fine."

Joey made her way around to Sonny's side of the bar. She took both sides of his face in her hands and placed a solemn kiss on his lips. "And what was that for?" he asked.

"It's not that big of deal, is it? The world didn't end?"

Sonny shook his head. "Naw."

"I'll be right back."

"I'll be right here waiting," he called out as Joey slipped through the farther of the two doors.

Slowly sipping his drink, he looked at a series of paintings of female figures along the left-hand side of the living room. Each one ran half the height of the wall and featured nearly life-size pictures of women, some who were nude and wrapped up in sheets, laying on a couch.

"These up here are nice," Sonny called out. "Who posed for these?"

"Actually, they're self-portraits."

Sonny took a closer look. He saw primary colors, several square feet of pale skin tone, and dark shadows pitting the eyes of the women. The darkest of the lot was to the left and featured a ravaged, lined Joey slumped on the couch, trying to cover her head with a sheet. The paintings got progressively lighter as they went down the wall until the final one was a brightened, contented Joey relaxing in her nightgown, or sheet, as she sipped a cup of tea.

"The first one I did six years ago. Would you believe the newest one I finished up last Monday night?"

"No, not really."

"I was going to turn on some music; do you mind?"

"Ah, naw, go ahead."

Sonny heard a familiar twangy, vibrating guitar chord, a rat-a-tat drum fill, and then a ghostly voice:

*Dreams and wishes, like shooting stars...*

Sonny's head popped up as he heard the song. "You a fan of Big Star too?"

"Well, I remember you writing that one column about it, so I downloaded two of their albums. Now I'm a fan."

Sonny laughed. "It feels awkward sometimes, you knowing so much about me and me knowing just a few things about you."

"What do those paintings tell you about me?"

"At first you seem real sad. But later on, it's like you're more peaceful. Someone who actually likes herself."

"Perceptive." Sonny thought he heard the brush of footsteps behind him. "Can you turn around for a minute?" Her voice was right behind Sonny.

He pivoted to face her. Joey stood there, wearing a white silk robe that extended just above her knees. All her jewelry was gone. She kept flexing her strong feet with long toes and nails covered in black polish up and down. She rubbed her hands together as her eyes darted from him to around the room.

Sonny stared downward as she stopped directly in front of him. "God, you've got cute feet," he finally said.

She immediately started giggling and crossing her arms in front of her. "OK, that was *not* what I was expecting."

"There's a lot of guys who appreciate cute feet."

"Ahhh, OK..." She waved at him as she began to get her breath back.

"So far the other interesting areas are covered up."

She cackled at that again and took a step forward so she stood right underneath Sonny's face. "Really?"

"Absolutely."

She started to lean toward him. As she did so, she reached for her glass and managed to empty the liquid contents in a single gulp. "So, what areas?"

"Honestly? Ever since you started moving it around here, I've got a big interest in your butt."

"Really?"

"Exactly."

She set her glass down on the counter and leaned in a little closer. Before she could come cheek to cheek with Sonny, he halted her with her hands around each of her biceps. Joey noticed her hands were shivering. "It's OK."

# The Holy Fool

"Why come here now, after all this time?"

Sonny's sigh was so deep it appeared to vibrate him. "I'm alone," he said at last. "I'm tired of being alone, and I'm tired of pretending that we couldn't be something because I'm afraid it wouldn't work out or we don't have time. I don't want to ask myself what could have been 10 years from now. My mother did that one too many times and she wound up alone."

Joey nodded. As she leaned into him and kissed him on the lips, this time he let her get next to him. "I'd like you... to... come into my bedroom. Could you do that? I don't want to be alone anymore, either."

Sonny leaned over her and kissed her on the forehead. He took her left hand into his right. "Lead the way."

She led him through the doorway. The bedroom was plain compared to the rest of the apartment; white drywall covered all parts of the room. A king-sized bed with a wooden waterbed frame dominated the center of the room, and there were two white-painted dressers on the opposite side of the room.

*Thank you, friends*
*Wouldn't be here if it wasn't for you...*

They approached the bed. Joey then started to crawl onto it on all fours and stopped, looking around and fidgeting as if she wasn't sure what to do next. Sonny let go of her hand and brushed his hand up the back of her thigh. He lifted the back of her robe up to her waist, freezing her in her pose. She had a curvy pair of buttocks, whiter than the rest of her, but with firm muscles and soft skin. His hand drifted back down across her ass. "God, you're beautiful. You're just... so beautiful."

"Shut up." It was a whisper. She turned around and started to reach for his clothes. She lifted his sweatshirt over his head. As he removed his T-shirt, Joey ran her fingers through the thick forest of dark hair across his chest and up to his beard. "Oh, what a cute teddy bear you are." Joey laughed softly, then started to unbuckle his belt.

"I'm not going to look as good as you naked."

"You're fine... ah," Joey stopped. Her hand had dived into the front of Sonny's boxer briefs and found him down there, fully aroused. It felt like it was of average length, but above average width. "OK, fuck it." With a quick motion, she shoved his briefs down his legs and around his ankles. For his part, he had managed to untie the belt of her robe and expose her from the front. Her breasts were modest, A-cup mounds, with darker than pink nipples standing up as Sonny began to touch them.

He looked down further and saw a wide V of dark curls, the same color and wavy texture as her other hair. Sonny reached down to touch her there. "You feel soft down there… it's nice." He noticed that her armpits also sported smaller tufts of hair deep in the middle of her pits.

"I'm on the Pill."

"Ah… OK… Where do you want to start?"

As she let her robe finally fall off her shoulders and land in a pool on top of the bed, Joey pulled the covers back. She rolled across the bed until she lay belly down on top. "Come here." She reached out her hand to him.

Sonny crawled onto the bed. He took her hand as he laid down on his belly next to her. With Joey's help, he pulled some of the sheets over them, then laid there without a sound for some time.

Joey finally turned her body sideways to face Sonny. "OK?"

Sonny turned toward her. "Yeah." He drew her into his embrace, pulling her mostly on top of him as he gave her a deep, probing kiss that melted what remained of her shyness. She took his left hand, guided it to her breast, guided his other hand to her butt, then crept her hand between his legs and slowly took hold of him.

"How do you want to do this?"

She kissed him in response. "What do you want?"

"I'm for whatever leaves you happy at the end."

"OK." Another kiss, this one drifting away from his lips and nestling into his neck. "What's going to make me happy is you doing with me anything that you want. It doesn't matter – It's been too long."

"God, I just want to eat you up."

Sonny barely got out those words before he threw himself on her. As he pinned her wrists above her head and onto the

# The Holy Fool

headboard, she felt him nuzzling and sucking on first one, then her other breast. His tongue drew a line between them and led back up to her neck as he sucked there for a moment, too. His kisses fell on random areas – her biceps, her breasts again, the tip of her nose, her earlobes (those made her feel warm and fuzzy), and even once on her left underarm (that pulled a yelp and a cackle from her).

Sonny finally let go of her wrists as it became obvious that she would not move them from where he had put them. As he continued to slightly knead her breasts, Joey saw Sonny move his head further up along her thighs; she realized his plan, and then slowly raised her legs and tucked them over his shoulders.

She reached down and pulled him up to face her. "Come here, I want you in me."

He moved up, took her hips in his hands, and rearranged them on the bed with a few tugs. Then he leaned forward and slid into her with barely any effort.

They moved together, Sonny going back to pinning her wrists above her head while he felt Joey ease her legs up around his waist, her feet moving between linking together and caressing his lower back like a second pair of hands.

Sonny felt himself building to a climax a lot faster than he expected and was trying to hold out until he looked down at Joey. She was staring right back at him, her mouth open in disbelief, a thin trickle of sweat moving across her forehead, and a pink blush that covered her face and had spread down to her neck and upper chest. "Harder," she said, the words croaking out of her throat, "do it harder."

Sonny met her gaze "Yeah?"

"I want you to."

By then the desire had built up so much he surrendered the last shred of his control as he plowed his hips into hers. He buried his face into her neck as she clenched her legs around him. As Joey cried out, Sonny finally felt himself come.

He took a final, deep breath as he lay on top of her, and he felt her hyperventilate through the connection the two bodies still had. Sonny raised his head and they found themselves staring at each other.

*Caught a glance in your eyes*
*And fell through the skies...*
"That was... I don't even know what to say," Joey said.
"OK, is that bad or good?" Sonny cradled her head in the crook of his arm.
"It was nice at first, and then it became something more than just that. I... don't want to overthink it, because I don't want to wreck it..."
Sonny nodded. "Yeah."
"This is not this a one-time situation, right?"
"No, it's not. It's not."
"OK." She held out her arms to him. "Could you come here?"
"Sure." Joey tucked her head into the crook of his right arm, snuggling up with Sonny.

***

The sun crept across Joey's face as she lay flat on her stomach in bed, a sheet gathered around her waist. She felt a finger trace the lines on the sole of her foot and finally raised her head, praying she hadn't drooled during the night.
Sonny stood by the bed, smiling. He dressed in his old clothes, and his hair looked more than a little rumpled. He held two mugs of coffee and leaned down to hand her one. "A nude lady in bed – this is a nice surprise."
"Thanks." She took the cup.
"I remembered you preferred it black."
"Good memory."
"I wasn't sure what you might want for breakfast, so I figured I'd wait until you got up to ask."
"Oh, thanks. Um, there's some bacon in the fridge and eggs; I could go for that."
"Sure." Sonny paused to sip from his own mug. "Any preference on the eggs?"
"Scrambled is fine, and I prefer my bacon not crisp."
"A girl after my own heart." He leaned over and kissed her, cradling her head with his free arm.
"Sonny?"
"Yes?"

"I figured we might want to go to work separately. It's not that I'm embarrassed, but I didn't want to make a big deal about it at work." She shook her head.

"I understand. Plus, with these guys I've had tailing me right now, I don't want to get you involved with that."

"But, I was wondering if you wanted to hang out tonight after work, maybe." She didn't quite meet Sonny's eyes.

"I'd like that. As long as I didn't get in your way – I might have to duck some tails…"

"No, that's OK. I've got to finish up some touch-up work on some of those installations in the other room, so you could do your thing for an hour or so and I'll do mine."

"OK." He kissed her on the forehead, then sat up. "Breakfast coming up."

As Sonny went into the kitchen, Joey propped herself up sitting in her bed and had another sip of her coffee. She shook her head, laughed softly to herself, and whispered, "Did that just happen?"

## Chapter 5

Sonny got in early to the office that morning, with both of his tails watching him enter the Keep, their MO's unchanged from the previous days, even in the same location outside the building. That told him one of two things; either they thought yesterday had been a fluke, or they knew they'd been made, and were staying in open sight to keep his attention. Sonny made a note to watch for other frequent faces.

As he walked into the newsroom, he noticed Joey staring at him from her desk with a smile as he arrived. She'd gotten there early. She'd had a smile for everyone in the newsroom, but Sonny noticed something she did with her eyes, sort of a half-peeking stare from the corner of her eyes, that was different.

"And how are you, Joey?" Sonny whispered.

"Quite well, Mr. Turner," she said, her voice lilting in a parody of an Oxbridge accent. "And you?"

"Can't complain, though I've been busy." Sonny said.

She gave a single nod, then raised her voice. "Must be rough having to write just three columns a week."

Sonny played along, realizing it was a little bit of a troll to him and misdirection to everyone else. "It wouldn't be so bad if the Wednesday, Friday, and Sunday columns were all I did. With all the blog entries I wind up posting for the paper's web site, tweets, and everything else, I bet I'm writing more than those five-days-a-week columnists from the old days."

"Well, I look forward to hearing more in-depth insight about the hard-professional life of a newspaper columnist. Hope you have a good day."

"You too."

\*\*\*

Jason Liegois

After speaking with Joey, Sonny made his way into his office and was surprised to find Colton there. "Aren't you supposed to be with Gus now?" Sonny asked.

"Yeah, I was just headed over there in a moment," Colton said. "You said we'd talk about those movies you wanted me to watch."

"Oh, yeah, that. Let's see, what were those movies I gave you?"

"Ah, <u>Princes of the City</u>, <u>Tinker, Tailor, Soldier, Spy</u>, that was a TV movie, I think, right? Also, <u>The Falcon and the Snowman</u>."

"So, what did they have in common?"

"Well, they were all spy films, except for <u>Princes</u>, that was a cop show, but it was sort of a spy deal because one of the cops was an informant."

"Exactly. Why do you think I wanted you to see them?"

Colton thought for a long moment as he settled into one of the comfortable chairs and Sonny settled behind his desk. "I have a feeling I probably do, but I'm not sure."

"OK, let's walk you through it. What's the main purpose of the news business?"

"We gather news."

"Easy answer. What's another word for news?"

Colton was silent for a few seconds, his chin cupped in one hand. "Information?"

"Good answer. Who else gathers information?"

"Intelligence people," Colton answered immediately.

"OK, you have an idea where I'm going with this. Where are the spies getting their info?"

"Some documents, sometimes electronics and bugging devices. Much of the time, they're getting it from people."

"All right, concentrate on the people. How do spies treat them?"

Colton stretched as he sat up in his chair. He picked his way through what he said next. "They treated them OK. I mean, they're not trying to betray them, but they're not palling around with them, either. They'd always listen to them, but, they wouldn't always trust them."

"Why not?"

# The Holy Fool

Colton shrugged. "They wouldn't always tell the truth about things. Sometimes they didn't want to give up friends, or whatever. Many times, they had their own reasons for giving info. The spies and the cops had to pick out what was good out of the BS."

Sonny leaned back in his chair and smiled. "OK. 'Featured interviews?' Bullshit. These are our sources, our hookups, our snitches, our rats, and we have to treat them as such. There are certain people in this business, and even, regretfully, certain people associated with this newspaper..." He stopped, looked at the walls and up at the ceiling as if he was searching for bugs. "...our distinguished executive editor, our Washington Bureau chief, and that fossilized columnist Sean Carlton – who believe that to be an effective journalist, you have to befriend your sources. The powerful and the wealthy get a sympathetic ear and a friendly publicist, and the journalist gets a gusher of quotes and information. If the guy's lucky enough, maybe they start to feel like *they're* the new mover and shaker, the guy who gets $30K per speech and gets to advise presidents, senators, and CEOs."

"Don't you want as much information as possible?"

"Ah, yes. The problem is, in trying to playact that you're like them, they forget that we're in the business of getting all the truth, not just info these people want to give us. You lose sight of your real goal, to sort the gold truth out of all of the ore and muck."

"And if someone is trying to roll me? Their information's no good?"

"Not always. Sometimes they give you truth because it suits their purpose. But you also have to realize what their game is. That's why you never rely on one source, and you never can have enough sources."

***

It was the start of another 10 a.m. news meeting at the Journal. Gus looked at the empty seats, then at those seats that were filled. "Are we going to get started?" Gus said in as neutral of a tone as he could manage.

Richard Connors had been editor ever since the Edson takeover nearly two years ago, hired from some community

Jason Liegois

newspaper chain in North Carolina. Gus's opinion of him ran to bland and unthreatening. There was the dark hair that never seemed out of place, the blocky chin that some newsroom jokers dubbed "Leno Jr.," and the Armani suits he always wore either at work or at any social gatherings. From what Gus observed, Connors seemed to talk more about running a great paper than running one.

Gus caught the eye of Carlo Massino. The burly, bushy-haired Massino, who saw nothing wrong with wearing ties with short-sleeved shirts, had been managing editor of the Journal for six months. He'd learned his job included providing excuses for his immediate boss.

"I talked with Richard early today," Massino said in a matter-of-fact tone. "He said he had a breakfast with the chamber of commerce early today, then the whole day was gonna be filled with editorial board and executive meetings." He paused as he started to unwrap a sausage and biscuit sandwich in front of him and take a quick bite. "That's what I heard from him, anyway."

It took every effort for Gus not to make some type of wisecrack. Carlo was OK. The Philly native had known the newspaper business from the ground up, unlike most Edson executives who knew the radio business at best and the outdoor advertising business at worst. He also had a habit of staying out of the way of his underlings' work, especially when it seemed to be running smoothly.

"OK," Gus said, turning back to Carlo, "Can we have a new rule here? Nothing big, but... since you're usually here and Richard isn't, can we say that these meetings start when you get here, not when Richard does?"

Carlo nodded. "Sure, sounds reasonable. OK, let's talk about next edition. What about Lifestyles?

Damien Coster, the editor of the Lifestyles section and most of the arts and entertainment news in the paper, leaned forward. At 25, he was the youngest of the department editors. He stood out among the journalists in the room with his black biker jacket, skintight Levis over a narrow frame, and Smashing Pumpkins concert T-shirt. The black hair over his eyes and skin that hadn't seen the sun in months made him

# The Holy Fool

look like an urban vampire in training, but few questioned his knowledge of the arts and entertainment scene in Chicago. He'd promoted his first house party at the age of 16, and by 19, he was publishing his own fanzine of Chicago's underground music scene called <u>Dead Bluesmen</u>. Damien had improved the local arts coverage considerably during his time with the <u>Journal</u>.

"Well, Lollapalooza is over with, but there's still a few festivals going on this month, like the Latin Music Festival in two weeks and Jazzfest at the end of the month, so we'll begin previews and features on all of those as they come," he said. "The summer movie season keeps going; <u>Dark Knight</u> and <u>WALL-E</u> are doing OK, but I think the next few won't be worth D1, so forget them. As for today's wood on D1, we'll do an update on the progress on the Art Institute's modern wing."

"They still think they'll finish it up by next year?" Carlo said.

"It seems like they're on track," Damien said. "Nothing A1 worthy, but that's what I've got."

"OK, Bill, what do you have?" Carlo said, turning to a bald, muscular man with a thin goatee in a Cubs jersey.

"Olympics are still going along – I've got a package on Phelps' endorsement package now that he's broken the medals record," said Bill Goldstein. He'd been one of the most opinionated and feared sports columnists in Chicago. Bill was always willing to rip one of the home teams whenever they failed to achieve for 15 years, and then he abruptly applied for the position of sports editor. "Every guy has a certain level of negativity in their lives, and I've already reached my limit," was his only explanation.

"Do you think that could stand somewhere on A1 if we wanted it?" Carlo said. He always was jittery throughout the day until he had his front page for the day set.

"Take it if you want; I wasn't going to put it on C1 anyway." Bill was infamous for ignoring national sports news in favor of local teams. Bill was proud of the fact that the <u>Journal</u> dominated coverage of the local high school sports more than any other media outlet, even the TV stations. "We'll have Cubs and White Sox updates on the front, and we're still filling up the fall prep season previews inside the section. Bears preview we'll save for the weekend."

"OK. What about B?" Carlos said.

The B section of the Journal was split between City, Metro, and Business news, as well as any overflow from the A section. The responsibilities for the section were thus split between Gus, Metro Editor David Palmer, and Business Editor Bernard Newton. Newton, an elegant forty-something golf hobbyist and fan of gold jewelry who habitually dressed like the commercial real estate agent he'd once been rather than a reporter, went first.

"No changes from yesterday's meeting," Newton said. "No significant progress with the Chicago Spire. If Gus has something, more power to him."

Gus nodded. "There is something. We've got a feature on this teacher in Lincoln Park that's getting her home foreclosed. Her and her two kids might be out on the street by the end of the week. It would be a nice A1 anchor. We've got photos, the whole package."

"Tell me why this is something that's A1 worthy, especially with the Republican convention going on," Carlo said.

"There's more problems with this bubble in real estate prices, and I don't care that all of these Realtors and market analysts are saying it's going to turn around," Gus said. "The bottom's falling out of the real estate market this past year, especially on residential properties. Most of the problems have been out on the West Coast, the Southwest, and the East Coast, but it's started to affect us. We need to get on top of it."

Damien turned to face Gus. "Blacks and Hispanics have been dealing with that here for years."

"You bring up a good point," Gus said. "The problems are starting with lower-class homeowners who got suckered into bad mortgage deals or deals they couldn't pay off. But because of all the foreclosures and other problems, it's starting to affect all homeowners. We want people to know what they can do, how they can avoid getting into trouble or at least make it manageable. The reporter, Harry Read, he's done a good job."

"Read's one of your new boys, right?" Carlo said. Gus nodded his head. "What's this caption I see here – 'The Way

# The Holy Fool

We Live Now.' Is this some sort of series? How long is it running?" Connors was always stressing the need for good series to submit for media awards, such as the mighty Pulitzers.

"More of an ongoing series," Gus said. "It'll be touching on new aspects of the economy as we get into trouble."

"You're acting like we're in a depression," Newton said. "There's still a lot of good economic indicators out there."

"A lot of these things are stuff that doesn't show up on the typical economic report. Like the fact, we keep hearing from storage facility owners that they're having to host twice as many auctions to give away lockers from people who can't pay rent anymore, or that those people find people living in those lockers sometimes. Harry's working on that for the weekend," Gus added.

Carlo cupped his chin in his hand, nodded twice, and then turned to two other men further down the table. "OK. What about national and foreign news?"

National/Foreign Editor Andrew Odom had most seniority there; he had arrived in the <u>Journal</u> newsroom just six months before Gus. He was gaunt and white-haired, and clamped an unlit, long Costa Rican cigar in his teeth in defiance of about a half-dozen state and company wellness rules. He'd been in a permanent sulk ever since he'd been passed over for the head editor's job two years ago. "We've got analysis on what the Musharraf resignation means for both Pakistan and our army's operations there and in Afghanistan," he said in a voice that sounded like rustling leaves. "Also, there's the ongoing reporting on the South Ossetia conflict, and an Iraq wrap-up."

"Can't believe we don't have a correspondent out in Iraq right now," Gus said.

"Guaranteeing security for those correspondents is getting more and more expensive," Odom said. "We can either have safe reporters or kidnap victims – there isn't a viable third option right now."

"Noted," Carlo said. "What's the schedule update for the Republican Convention in St. Paul?"

Jason Liegois

"They'll adopt the party platform today," said the second man at the end, columnist Sean Carlton. He was 50, athletic, tanned, with perfectly positioned hair shifting between sandy brown and grey. Reporters and columnists rarely made it to the editorial meetings. Carlton was one of the few exceptions because of his high profile in Washington, the level of his official connections, and because due to the most recent staff cuts, Carlton was the de facto political editor for the paper. "Tomorrow, they'll expect to endorse McCain, Palin speaks Thursday, then McCain accepts on Friday," he said, adjusting his bright red Hugo Boss tie.

"Still can't believe they named her the VP candidate," Carlo said to Carlton.

"It's a puzzle to me," Carlton responded. "I know for sure he wanted Lieberman, but the party elders nixed it. He didn't want Romney or Pawltney, so he got someone to make the right wingers and the ladies excited."

"I hate to say it, but what luck are you having with the story about her daughter?"

"The rumor about the secret baby is nothing. It's looking like a regular teen pregnancy. Of course, it's the Republicans with all of the sex scandals."

"Get it pinned down," Carlo said. He turned back to Gus. "OK, we'll go with your foreclosure story today unless we have other breaking news, but we'll have to bump the convention stuff up on the top of A1 the rest of the week short of Al Qaeda flying into the Sears. We'll have the Pakistan and Iraq stuff on A3 and fit the Phelps stuff below the fold. You still want to use that tag line?"

"Yeah," Gus said.

Carlo nodded. "OK, 'The Way We Live Now' it is. Anything else to add?" After several moments of silence, he continued, "OK, see you at the 5 p.m., then. Gus, can you stay for a second?"

"Sure." Gus got up to sit closer to Carlo as the rest of the editors and staff filed out of the conference room. "Yeah, what did you need?"

"You going to be in that meeting with Richard and the others about Turner's story?" Carlo said.

# The Holy Fool

"Yeah. If we need something, we'll let you know."

"I know I just got here, but I'm here to help. I know it's tough, with all of the uncertainty about our future."

Gus hesitated for a moment, then gestured with a finger to get Carlo to lean in closer. "You know, Sonny and I have been heading up an informal effort to look into that, as well."

Carlos snorted a lungful of air into himself at hearing this. "I'm hearing this now?"

"It just started up yesterday. I didn't even say anything to Sonny until Sunday night."

"Let's say I want to know something about it now."

"How much do you want to know?"

A smile started to spread across Carlo's face. "How about just enough to keep my deniability intact?"

***

As Gus' meeting with his City Desk wrapped up, he said, "Colton, can I talk with you for a second?" Colton was rearranging some papers where he was sitting.

Colton looked up. "Absolutely, Gus, sure."

As soon as the rest of the city desk reporters cleared out to their respective assignments, Gus leaned over to Colton. "Kid, you finished up putting together those stories on the quarterly reports for Boeing?"

"Yeah, I should be finished with them soon - I just have to give it the once-over and I can shoot it over to your inbox in maybe... 10 minutes or so?"

"OK, fine, that's great. Go ahead and do that quick because I need you to get on something for me as soon as you can."

"Sure, Gus, what do you need?"

Gus cranes his neck around as he checked to see if anyone could possibly overhear the conversation. Satisfied, he beckoned Colton to sit next to him in one of the cubbyholes of the City Desk.

"OK, keep this quiet, but I want you to start looking into USA Unlimited Financial."

"What, an earnings report?"

"There's something up with that company. I keep hearing from people I know in the trading business that some hedge funds are taking a closer look at Double-UF's financials. You know any lower-level people over there?"

"Yeah, I do," Colton said immediately, not pausing to think whether he did.

"I figured you might. I want you to shake a couple of trees, see what falls."

"Anything in particular I should be asking about?"

"The big question is their real estate portfolio. Most of it is in Chicago, and that hasn't fallen as badly as some of the regions around the US. But, I'm wondering whether the local market is about to start going down the tubes, or if Double-UF's involved with real estate out West or South that's in big trouble."

"I'll get on it right away."

"Let me know tomorrow where you're at. I feel like something is going to shake out very soon and I don't want to get scooped on it. Later." He dismissed Colton by getting up and striding over to his own office.

Colton sat there silently for a moment, the tapping of his finger on the desk the only indicator he was alive. Then, he picked up the phone at his desk and dialed a familiar number.
"Hello?" Kyra answered.

"Hon, how are you doing?"

"Oh, same old thing, classes going well, I'll head into work after the lunch hour for the afternoon. I won't be back home in time for dinner, I think... Sorry."

"No, that's OK. They're keeping me busy. I'll see you later tonight. Anyway, I had another reason to call you."

"Sure, what is it?"

"I was trying to get in contact with some people at UUF, somebody that might be able to talk with me about a story I'm working on. Do we know anybody there at the home office here in town?"

"Don't they have a PR office or something?"

"Of course, Kyra, but they'll just send a press release or something."

"Wait, I remember someone... there was that one kid on your floor, the MBA candidate, Bill... Drake, Bill Drake, wasn't

# The Holy Fool

it? He had gotten an interview with them to work in their real estate department before he graduated."

"No, yeah, I remember him. I'll check if he's at the Chicago office. Take care, hon. Love you."

"Love you."

Colton immediately hung up and started to flip through the nearby Chicago Yellow Pages for the main UUF number. He spotted it after a short search and immediately punched the number into the desk phone. "USA Unlimited Financial, can I help you?" a secretary answered before the second ring.

"Yes, I was trying to contact Bill Drake, with your real estate department?"

"One moment, please." There was a couple of minutes of jazz while Colton was on hold. In the middle of a trumpet solo, a young but tired voice came on the line. "Bill Drake."

"Hey, Bill, how are things? It's Colton, Colton Edson."

"Colton Edson from the top floor? Damn, how are you doing?"

"It's been crazy since graduation, but I wanted to check in."

"Yeah, I'm hoping for a transfer to the New York office sometime soon – it just feels like the same old faces and scene here in Chicago."

"Yeah, I know what you mean, I'm still around here."

"Surprised that you are, considering that you always talked about New York or overseas."

"Well, I get to head out to Switzerland every winter for skiing, so it's not like I'm totally deprived. Besides, I've got a paid internship here, so it's working out OK."

"Oh, a paid internship? Where with?"

"The *Chicago Journal*. My dad, obviously," Colton replied.

"The *Journal*? Cool. What are you doing for them now?"

"Well, I'm in the newsroom, actually."

"Really? Wow." Colton could hear him swallow over the phone. "Oh... oh, OK. I have to ask, is this an, 'official' call?"

"Something like that. My boss over here, Gus Pulaski, he wanted me to see if I can talk to some people here."

"Yeah, I'm probably going to have to cut this short, then." He could feel Bill's nerves vibrate over the telephone line.

Jason Liegois

"The management here is really getting picky about who can speak to media or anyone else without attorneys present and all that garbage. Listen, let me get your contact information and I promise to send it along to our communications director."

"Yeah, yeah, sure, I totally understand." He gave Billy his office number at the *Journal*.

"Do you have a cell phone? I can have them call you there if you're out," Colton immediately volunteered that number, too. "OK. We'll have to get together sometime when you're free. Good to hear from you."

"OK, take care."

Colton hung up the phone and spent the next few seconds wondering what Billy's reaction might have meant until he noticed his cell phone was buzzing. He picked it up off his desk and saw a text alert. Colton clicked on the message icon, and read:

Can't talk over phone. Can you meet later outside of Adler P? Maybe 6. Bill.

Colton's Blackberry had a full keyboard, so he was able to respond right away.

OK, I'm in. I will see you there. Colton.

Within a minute, Colton saw this pop up:

See you there.

Colton shook his head. His father had warned him that reporting wasn't like how it was shown in the movies, but this was looking a little like a movie scene to him.

***

Gus arrived at the main elevators to the Penthouse to find Sonny waiting for him there. "Nice for you to be on time," Gus said.

"Well, they might call me all sorts of names before this is done, but I don't want tardy to be one of them," Sonny said. "I even dressed up for the occasion."

Gus stared at Sonny. He had on a blue denim shirt, no tie, khakis, a dark brown sport coat, and hiking boots.

"For you, 'no jeans' is business dress."

"Exactly."

# The Holy Fool

Shortly after they exited the elevator, they walked down the narrow hallway toward the eastern side of the building to the two massive glass doors leading to the executive conference room. Gus reached out and opened one of the doors, and they heard, "Hello, hello, come on in."

Sonny identified the voice as Edson's, which he confirmed as he came into the room and saw him gesturing them to come closer. "Great, you're early. How about you come over here and we can get started?"

Edson stood at the head of the massive wood boardroom table that dominated the room, along with the view of Lake Michigan through the floor-length windows. Sonny and Gus sat down on the left-hand side of the table; Gus sat down right next to Richard Connors, the editor, who mumbled apologies for not being at the meeting earlier. Gus nodded and said nothing more.

Right across from the trio of newsroom men was the lone woman at the meeting, Cathy Boone. Edson installed her as publisher when the company had taken over two years previously. All Sonny knew about her was that she was in her 40's, had started out as one of Edson's top protégés back when he first started buying up radio and TV stations, and had an affinity for grey pantsuits. The fact that she let her curly blond mane fly behind her seemed to be the only casual thing about her. She was seated next to Perry Reeves, one of the lead attorneys for the company. He was 30, nearly bald, preferred to wear a fancy diving wristwatch, but was otherwise uninteresting as a person.

"Well, Gus, Sonny, thanks for coming up here to talk with us – I know you are keeping busy, so I appreciate you making the time," Edson said. "You do know everyone here, correct?"

Sonny nodded. "Yes, I think I've been introduced to everyone here at the table at some point, Mr. Edson."

"OK, great. Quick question, Sonny – you've been writing for us for about… eight years, now? Somewhere along those lines?"

Sonny nodded. "Yeah, it's been about eight years full-time."

Jason Liegois

"He actually started to submit articles to us back when he started with the Medill School at Northwestern, and that was 10 years ago, correct?" Gus said.

"Yeah."

"Wow, 10 years," Edson said. "All of that experience, and I don't think you're barely 30, are you, Sonny?"

"Thirty-two," Sonny clarified, keeping patient.

"Yes," Edson said, "despite your age, I'd still have to consider you one of the veteran members of the staff. Our focus groups and Internet data keep telling us that people are reading your stories and columns more than nearly any other reporter or editor on staff. We appreciate your work."

Sonny was taken aback. "Thanks."

"So, keeping that in mind," Edson said, "when Gus approached Richard with the story that you've been working on, and then brought it to the attention of Cathy and myself, it's something we took very seriously."

Sonny waited for a moment, waited to hear if there was a "But…" at the end of that statement. When one did not come, he said, "Again, thank you."

Edson nodded. "Now, I know that you've briefed Gus extensively on the project, and he's given Richard a good overview of it, but I was wondering if you'd take a few moments to go over it here with all of us, especially myself and Cathy. Do you think you can do that for us?"

"Certainly," said Sonny. It took him about five minutes to cover the basics.

"Thanks for keeping that easy to follow along," Richard said. "Since we have you here, I thought I'd ask John or Cathy if they had any follow-up questions."

Gus turned and looked Richard up and down for a brief minute, enough to convey *NOW you decided to take charge?* to anyone paying attention. Sonny was the only one who might have, and he was focused on John Michael.

"I had a couple, if that's OK, John Michael," Cathy said after a moment of silence.

"Go ahead – you might be able to cover my question," Edson said.

## The Holy Fool

Cathy turned to face Sonny as the lawyer next to her continued to fill a large legal pad with notes. "As I understand it, you basically have two stories that you want to run, is that correct?"

"Two stories?" Sonny said.

"Yes," Cathy said briefly pausing to look at Reeves' note pad, "the... piece about the "Haji-hunters" in Kandahar Province in Afghanistan, and their superiors, and the incident just outside the Baghdad Green Zone with the Iraq civilians and the employees of Foxwood Solutions. Am I right about that?"

"Ah," Sonny said, nodding his head. "OK, I see what you are saying. Actually, the answer to that would be yes and no."

"Pardon me?" Cathy replied.

"I'll explain. I have the two stories that you mentioned 'ready to go.' What I mean by that is that they're in draft form, I have contacted second sources for those stories, went to other sources to confirm the authenticity of the materials I've received, and reviewed all of those primary and supplementary materials."

"Have you officially contacted the White House or Pentagon as part of that second-sourcing you mentioned?" Edson said.

"Not as yet... John Michael," Sonny said, not sure if his main boss was serious about the informality. "We usually save that until just before publication."

"So, when you say you have two stories that are ready to go, you mean that there are others that might be generated from the material that you have?" Cathy continued.

"Yes, that's exactly right. I've received a massive number of documents and materials already, and there's a good chance more are coming. It's going to take a while to sort through that and see what can be made of it."

"Just to give us an idea, how many stories are we talking about? And, how long would it take you to get all of those stories ready?" Edson said.

Sonny leaned back in his chair for a moment and scratched at his beard. He realized it was getting time to trim it. "As far as number goes, it would come down to how much I could confirm and how different documents might help tell those stories. But, if I'm being asked to estimate, I'd be comfortable saying it could easily be dozens."

There was silence at the table for a moment, except Reeves' scratching pen. "Ah, Mr. Turner, did you say dozens, or dozen, just a couple of moments ago?"

"Dozens," Sonny replied.

"So... at least 20-30 stories, perhaps?" Reeves asked. "All of them of a 'feature' length?"

Sonny thought for a second, then: "Yeah, I'd be OK with that number."

"What about the amount of time it would take to get all these stories ready, then?" Edson said.

"That could vary a bit, too," Sonny said. "I'm assuming that we'd run the first two stories right away, and release the others as we got them ready?"

"Let's assume that for now, OK?"

"It might also depend on how many people might be able to help me out, and whether I'd concentrate mainly on that or I'd have to keep up with my regular column and blog schedule."

"Assume that you will keep up with your regular schedule, and you'd be relying on just whoever has been able to help you out at this point – how long?" Edson said.

Sonny shrugged. "I'd say it could very easily be several months, bare minimum. Over one or two years would not be a surprise to me, though."

The rest of the group other than Gus stared at him silently for a moment.

"Well, it would be a big task," Edson said. "Now, I had a quick question. What's the status of these files right now? I'm discussing their physical location and your possession of them."

"So far, I've made dozens of copies of those files," Sonny said. "None of these are located here at the paper or its servers, in case you were worried."

"Well, it's good to know," Edson said.

"Is there any chance of you telling us where these copies are located at?" Cathy asked suddenly.

# The Holy Fool

"Ah... I'm not really sure, under the circumstances, that you would want to have that information," Sonny replied. "Gus doesn't know where they are, for example, although I have shown him some files."

"We don't have to get into that now." Edson hunched his shoulders slightly and leaned closer toward where Sonny sat. If he couldn't hear what he said next, Sonny would have sworn that his boss was trying to imitate Brando in *The Godfather*. "Sonny, I have to say we appreciate the effort you've put into this story. However, we need to talk about some of the concerns Cathy, Richard, and I have regarding this. We haven't made a decision about whether this story can run, but I wanted to see what you might have to say about these concerns before that."

Sonny nodded. "OK."

Edson gestured toward both Cathy and Richard to prompt them. "Our first concern, obviously, is the sourcing of the stories," Richard said. "Relying so much on one source we don't know is one thing, but since you don't even know the exact identity of the source, how much can you rely on him or her?"

"Right now, I'm working to address these concerns, by both contacting other sources, quietly, and checking the authenticity of the documents. We're coming close to being done with the first part; the second part we've got pretty much done."

"As far as the authenticity of the documents, how have you been doing that?" Cathy asked.

"Casey Barnes in the D.C. bureau's spearheading that. All of his sources have been confirming that these documents are legitimate."

"Barnes, yes," Richard said. "I was a little surprised you hadn't talked with any of the more senior staff in either the bureau or the national desk back home. I'd have thought one of them would have had better sources or resources."

"With all due respect, Richard, I'd have to disagree," Sonny said.

"I have to admit the kid can write," Gus said.

"More important, he's a good investigator," Sonny continued. "He knows how to chase down stories. And the sources he has in D.C., I'd put up against anyone."

"That's strange – one of the few things I remember hearing about Barnes from Candace out in D.C. is that he doesn't seem to try to make contacts with senior political officials or their staffs," Richard said.

"That's because he doesn't need to hang out at congressional cocktail parties or K Street get-togethers to get whatever information they want to leak," Sonny replied. "Casey was born in D.C.; he's got relatives and friends working throughout the Beltway, from generals to janitors. If there's anything to find in Washington, I trust Casey to get it for me."

After a quiet moment, Sonny could see Edson nodding. "Well, obviously we're not keeping him on staff for show," Edson said. "I think what Richard was saying is that we shouldn't feel like we should just rely on him, that you could turn to others in the Washington bureau or other places if you need to."

Sonny shrugged. "OK."

"The second thing we have to take under consideration is national security concerns," Cathy said. "Obviously, we can't be releasing any information that might possibly cause any harm to American troops."

"I've been checking through these documents myself, and I'm not seeing anything from what I would release that would be dangerous to people."

"We understand that," Cathy said, "but we still feel that it's necessary that this project have some oversight in that regard. We'd feel a lot better if some of the national and political reporters we have, some people with more experience regarding classified material, would have a chance to look as some of this first, before it got published."

"You're not asking me to let you know about sources?"

"No, we are not asking you to do that," Cathy said.

Sonny sat for a few moments. Then he replied, "Could Gus put together a list of people we could find acceptable to do this?"

# The Holy Fool

Cathy, Richard, and John Michael, stared at each other for a moment, and then turned their attention back onto Sonny. "That might be a possibility that we can work with."

"OK," Gus said, "glad to hear it."

"Good," Richard said. "I'm sure that no one here wants to do anything to harm American soldiers or American interests."

"That's *not* my intent," Sonny said, lurching forward. "I'm not publishing anything that could harm troops in the field. As for 'American interests'... well, there's a lot of definitions for that, isn't there?"

"Sonny, just a second," Gus said, laying a hand on Sonny's arm.

"I'm not sure that's exactly what we mean," John Michael said. Sonny noticed only the tiniest of lines developing on his forehead as a sign that he might be mad. "I think the only thing we are saying is that there are a lot of things we need to consider before we give the go-ahead on this story, and we have to consider whether this is a right fit for the paper we have and want to keep."

Sonny leaned back in his chair. The air hissed out of his nostrils as he did everything to suppress what he was thinking right at that moment. "I understand."

"We'll let Gus know the situation by tomorrow. For now, just keep up with your regular work and let Gus know if your source contacts you."

"Understood," Sonny said.

John Michael stood up from his chair, the signal for the other administrators to do the same and that the meeting was over. "Sonny, Gus, I appreciate your time today and your work on this project."

Both Sonny and Gus nodded silently and prepared to leave the conference room. As Sonny stood up and adjusted his coat and stared out the windows toward Lake Michigan, he turned to John Michael. "John, can I ask you one more question?" Sonny said.

"Of course, Sonny – what is it?"

"I have to ask – if we decide we're not interested in writing about something this important, what the government does in our name, what's the point of us?"

With that, Sonny shrugged and made for the door with Gus behind him before John Michael could react.

"Christ, kid, are you looking to get fired?" Gus whispered as they made their way down the hallway.

"Right now, I'm seriously beginning to wonder. I love this place, but the longer I've worked here, the more that's been draining away."

"You think you can drag yourself out of your moping to get my column to me by Friday?"

"Nowadays, I can knock one of those out before Thursday's done. Don't worry, Boss," Sonny said as they entered the elevator and the doors slid shut.

*\*\*\**

After the meeting, Sonny returned to the newsroom and made a beeline for his office. He found Arturo Torres waiting for him there, leaning against his door.

Torres stood 5'9", with a close-cropped hairstyle he inherited from his years undercover among gangbangers and wore his sport coat and khaki ensemble uneasily. He looked more First Nations than Mexican – TT used to say it was the Mayan in him. The stare that Torres had developed from his years of intimidating informants had never went away, however, and it gave Sonny a pause as he walked past Torres and into his office. "C'mon in if you want to talk," Sonny said as he slouched into his office and toward his desk.

There was a hitch in Torres' walk that made him pull to the left slightly as he followed Sonny into his office. "How have you been feeling, TT?" Sonny asked as he eased into his chair and gestured for TT to take a seat.

"Actually, pretty good," TT said, sitting down. "The Department docs signed off on me being 100% disabled, but I've been moving around a lot better since I've been in physical therapy. Personally, I think I could get back on the streets, but after 20 years? It's more trouble than it's worth."

# The Holy Fool

"I thought you dug all of that undercover cop shit."

"Maybe, but that narcotics crap, that got old quick, putting brown and black kids into jail for 20 years on crack charges when white kids dealing powder coke would get half that, at best."

Sonny nodded. "OK, Gus said you wanted to talk to me about something."

TT lurched forward in his chair. "I want in. Whatever you're doing, whatever you're scheming, I want in on it."

"Want in with what?" Sonny spread his arms.

"With what you're doing. Look, this place has been good to me. Ever since I was shot, I was wondering what the hell I was going to do with the other 30, 40 years of my life, you know? Shit, most cops I know started to go crazy a couple of years after they retired. This place, it gave me something to do, it made me feel like I'm actually doing something that serves the public. If this place needs help, I want in."

Sonny let out a deep breath, then looked into TT's eyes. "OK, we could use your help. I don't have an idea of what the plan is, but I'll find out. Then I'll come for you. Until then, stay frosty."

TT got up and offered his hand. "OK."

"Welcome to the cluster fuck."

\*\*\*

By 6 p.m., Colton was on the sidewalk next to East Solitary Drive, the wind from Lake Michigan whipping across the causeway as he headed toward the dome of the Adler Planetarium. Although the temperature wasn't oppressive, he had hiked from the Roosevelt El station, and was working up a sweat.

As he got to the Adler, Colton looked for his appointment. He didn't see him by the entrance, so on a hunch, he decided to peer down at the walkway that wrapped around the planetarium facing the lake.

Bill Drake was there, leaning up against a lamppost, trying to hide in the open. The blue pinstripe suit Bill had on looked good on him, but he seemed to have lost a couple of pounds since last year. He'd remembered Bill being burned bronze from Spring Break in Cancun; now he seemed chalk-pale as the wind whipped his blond hair out of place.

Colton almost waved at him but checked himself at the last minute. It was only when Colton approached him that Bill tore his eyes away from the lake and turned to him. "Colt, thanks for not making me wait around here forever." He offered his hand.

"No problem," Colton said as he took it.

Bill looked right and left, scanning the crowds. "Anyone follow you here?"

"Jeez, no. I haven't even told my editors I was meeting with you."

Bill gestured Colton to follow him closer to the edge of the lake. He continued in a lower voice, "Listen, whatever happens, you *cannot* give anyone my name. I've got enough to deal with just with what's going on now."

"Sure. I'm not trying to get anyone into trouble; I just wanted to see what you know about real estate financing at UUF. With everything that's been going on this year, people are wondering how it's doing."

"That's what you're worried about? Hell, it's a lot worse than that." Bill gestured for Colton to lean in closer to him. "Last week, they let a third of the trading floor go, just marched in security to escort them out of the building. The word I kept hearing from everyone was minor losses, but that's not how all of the traders are acting. They keep waiting to get the call."

"Wait, what? What do traders have to do with real estate?"

"It's the bonds, not stocks. For years, the traders have been building these new financial packages and bonds to alleviate the debt and risk. It's turned into some real Frankenstein shit. I'm not even sure if the senior executives understand how all of it works. I barely understand it myself."

"And these guys are cool with that?"

"Who the hell cares as long as the money and bonuses are flowing in? Nobody gives a fuck as long as the card still works at the ATM, you know?"

# The Holy Fool

"Jesus." Colton let out a whistle. "I remember my dad buying me my first share of stock from those guys. They've been around longer than the Merchandise Mart."

Bill checked behind him again before continuing. "OK, what else do you want?"

Colton nodded, somewhat unsure of how to proceed. "This is what I'm thinking. I need to understand a little more about how these new bonds and items work. I'm an MBA, but *I'm* getting confused just listening to this."

"Look, I was willing to talk because you were cool back in college and I feel bad about getting people to buy these bonds when they're going to tank. But this is off the record."

"Hold on, off the record means I can't use it? I've got to be able to use the information, at least."

Bill sighed. "OK, but I'm serious, there's got to be a way that my name doesn't make it into the paper."

"I can do that."

He nodded. "I'm assuming you need the information soon."

"Yeah."

Bill handed Colton one of his business cards. "On the back there, that number's my personal cell phone. Text me tomorrow. Got it?"

"Got it."

Bill shook his hand. "Later." He was already 10 yards away before Colton stammered out a "goodbye."

Colton remembered one of the nights he'd spent out with Bill back in college, when they and some of their friends had bopped around some Rush Street bars the night after a Bulls game. That night the most important detail was what chick they were going to attach themselves to that night. Now they were discussing the fate of a billion-dollar-plus company. *How much changes in a couple of years*, Colton thought.

∗∗∗

Joey was working on a story involving a arts festival when she felt a tap on the shoulder. She turned around to see Sonny, who whispered, "I've got an idea about tonight."

"What?"

"I usually go visit Ed over at his place and eat dinner there with his family once a week. I had to cancel Monday because… but anyway, why don't you come with? They'll be happy to meet you."

"Are you sure? I didn't want to impose on them."

"Are you kidding? Ed's daughter has been begging me for years to bring some girl over. This will make her day for sure, much less Ed's. They always have decent food, too."

Joey started to say something, stopped, then finally nodded. "All right. I'll go with you. How about we meet up after work at Bobby's, have a drink, then head on down to his house?"

"Works for me. I'll have to brief him in on *Journal* stuff after we get there. You can hang out with us while that's going on."

"He still wants to hear about what's going on at the paper?"

"It's still his home. Plus, the old man's contacts, his brain – he might be able to help out with things coming up."

"All right, then, off to the South Side for dinner it is."

***

Getting to Ed's place that evening involved more than a little bit of drama. First, he met up with Joey at Bobby's, a popular bar in the Loop, after his usual evasive maneuvers. Then there was the dip into the basement of the building, leaving out of one of the service entrances, and then running over to the nearest El station before the Well-Dressed Man and the Superfan picked up his trail. Before they got on, Sonny's head was on a pivot, trying to determine which bystanders might be the next stalkers.

"You see anything?" Joey whispered to Sonny as they waited for the train to get going.

"I'd feel better if I did," Sonny replied. "If I did, I'd know if we were being followed."

After walking out of the 59th Street Metra station, Sonny led Joey north to South Harper Avenue, one of the side streets tucked in around the leafy, relaxed environs of Hyde Park and the University of Chicago.

Eventually, they stopped at a green, three-story house with steel siding somewhere in design between a brownstone and a bungalow, tucked into one of the small lots facing east. Sonny led her up the steps before knocking on the door. "Here we go."

A scrawny but coiled woman, someone who should have belonged in a pioneer photo from the West but dressed in a Cubs jersey and sweatpants, opened the door. "Sonny, great to see you," Melissa Mazur Eichoff exclaimed as she got the main and screen doors open. Even though Sonny thought of the home as Ed's place, his daughter and son-in-law had bought the place a decade ago and Ed had moved in later. "And who is this with you? It's about time you brought a guest."

"I didn't want to impose – this is Joey Halverson, she works over at the *Journal*."

"Well, of course – who else are you going to meet, working the hours you do?" she continued as Sonny found it difficult to stand still. "Joey, a pleasure to meet you. I'm Melissa, Ed's daughter."

"Thank you," Joey said. "I feel bad about just showing up here..."

"Absolutely not! Don't even think about it," Melissa said, taking Joey by the shoulders and maneuvering her in for a quick hug. "We've been pestering him to bring someone over with him for years. Sonny, you know we cook way too much food here. Well, come in and meet everyone. Ed's been asking about you for the last 20 minutes. 'Where's Sonny?'"

"Where's Troy?" Sonny said, referring to her husband.

"In the kitchen, of course. He's in Top Chef mode now, don't disturb the master," Melissa continued, giggling. "Joey, hon, you don't mind roast beef, do you? He's trying some new type of spice recipe..."

"That would be lovely, thanks," Joey said to Melissa.

"When have I ever turned down beef, Melissa?" Sonny replied.

Another woman wandered into the room. Melissa was pushing fifty; the other woman was maybe a decade younger, with a full, hourglass figure, but she shared the same squared-off face, green eyes, and dark hair. She wore a tan version of a D.C. power suit, but she'd had already ditched her high heels.

"Oh, I don't know if you two have ever met," Melissa said to Sonny, putting her arm around the other woman, and bringing her into the living room. "This is my sister, Mary. Mary, this is one of Dad's old reporter friends, Sonny Turner. Well, *he's* not old, but still…"

"Hello," Mary said, in a voice quiet but clear if you paid attention. "Dad's talked about you a lot."

"And this is Sonny's… friend, Joey."

"Hello," the two women said to each other.

"And he's talked about you as well," Sonny said to Mary, shaking her hand. "It's nice to see you other than some pictures. I know you were living in Texas, right?"

"Yes, north Dallas, actually."

"Great! Are you visiting?"

"Well, actually, she's staying with us for a little bit…" Melissa began.

"It's OK, Mel," Mary said. "I'm in the process of getting divorced. Melissa offered to have me and my son stay here for a while and get resituated. I just started work over at Boeing this week – I'm a structural engineer, I used to work over down at Rockwell Collins down in Dallas."

"Wow. Well, sorry for the divorce, but congratulations on the job," Sonny finally said.

"Thanks, although I think the divorce was overdue."

"Sonny, if you and Joey want to check in with Ed, go ahead; I think Troy's going to be a few minutes getting everything ready," Melissa said.

"OK. Nice to meet you, Mary," Sonny said.

"You too."

Most of the bedrooms and bathrooms in the house occupied the top two floors. The only exception to that was the section that Troy had turned into Ed's suite near the back of the house, near the kitchen and dining area. Troy had set up a bedroom/home office there, with a bathroom that had handrails and a zero-entry shower with seating in it.

# The Holy Fool

As Sonny and Joey made their way to Ed's room, Joey whispered to Sonny, "It's like you're the prodigal son around here."

"Well, he and Clara never had a son of their own. When I came to the paper, no family here in Chicago, Ed just sort of adopted me, in a way."

They walked into the room. The bed was nothing special, a queen-size contraption with a built-in bookcase as a headboard facing the window to the backyard. Photographs of family and old colleagues covered every inch of oak-paneled walls that didn't have bookcases or file cabinets in front of them. A couch sat in front of Ed's oak desk, which lined up directly in front of the window facing away from it.

Ed was behind the desk, seated in his wheelchair and dressed up in a dark brown sport coat and slacks with a khaki button-down shirt. He always insisted on getting properly dressed for work during the weekdays, just as he did for the fifty years before that.

As Sonny looked at Ed, he remembered the picture that ran alongside Ed's column, unchanging for decades. There was never a reason to change it. Ed's hair was white now rather than iron grey and his nose a shade more prominent on his face than it had been, but everything else had stayed the same – hair parted just so on the right, steel-framed rectangular glasses, and the paisley suspenders and matching bow tie he would have worn if he was heading out to see people.

There was a pale, skinny, sad-eyed kid in his mid-teens, with jet-black hair over his eyes, in a black Misfits T-shirt and jeans standing next to him and looking over Ed's computer.

Ed looked up. "Sonny Boy! Wondering when you'd show up. And you've brought a lady friend at last..."

"Yeah, yeah, Ed. Josephine Halvorsen - she works over at the paper, on the Arts and Entertainment Desk, but she's also an artist. She just graduated from the Art Institute."

"Oh, it's a pleasure to have you here," Ed said. Joey saw him grasp something at his sides. He wheeled out from behind his desk, seated in a composite wheelchair, and presented himself in front of Joey with surprising speed. "My apologies

– MS can be something of a pain in the ass." With one motion, he bowed in his seat as he took Joey's right hand and kissed it. "A pleasure to meet you."

"Thank you."

"Of course, you turn on the charm now, you goat," Sonny cackled.

Ed nodded, then gestured over to the kid. "I don't believe you've met this grandkid. Jack, this is an old colleague of mine from the paper, Sonny Turner – well, *he's* not old, but I've known him for years."

The name stopped Sonny for a moment, but then he walked up to the kid. "Nice to meet you, Jack," Sonny said, stepping forward to shake his hand. "I just met your mom coming in."

Jack looked up for the first time and tried to meet Sonny's eyes through his forest of hair. "OK, cool," the kid said, then did a double-take. "Wait, you're Sonny Turner? The online columnist?"

"Among other things."

"Yeah, I read your column. I don't usually go to the paper, but a lot of tech bloggers link to your stuff. Wow, Pap didn't say he knew you."

Sonny cocked his thumb toward Ed as he said, "Your grandfather taught me a lot of things about being a reporter back when I got started."

"Well, Jack's inherited more than a little of his mother's technical skills, so he's helping me sort out some of these computer things that I've had to deal with," Ed said.

"Most of it's regular stuff, but he said he wanted to start sending and receiving encrypted communications," Jack said. "I guess you guys need to keep some things quiet, especially interviewing sources, right?"

"Yeah," Ed said. "Hey, kid, can you head out for a minute? We have to talk some shop about some old stories."

"Yeah, no problem. Uh, Mr.... Sonny, I was wondering if I could ask you later about that one piece you did about the... ahhh, furries in Chicago."

Sonny laughed at that. "Does your mom know what furries are?"

## The Holy Fool

The kid shook his head. "Naw, no way."

"OK, we'll *try* to keep it that way, right?"

"Sure. See you in a bit." With that, Jack waved and walked out of the room.

"Jack's a good kid, really," Ed said. "He dresses like one of those, what, mopers?"

"Emos."

"Yeah, anyway, he's moping around about his dad not being around – he was a decent father but a shit husband – but he's got a decent head on his shoulders. He's doing OK with school here, but it bores him – spends maybe 15 minutes a night on homework and gets A's on everything. He's into computers, maybe he might be able to help Woot out and stay out of trouble."

"Relatively speaking."

Ed nodded. "We can trust him to keep quiet, anyway. He doesn't take to too many adults, but I guess I'm an exception, his 'Crazy Pap,' you know."

Ed turned to Joey. "Now, hon, you're with the paper, so stick around. Sonny, how much does she know about your... I-Project."

"Most of it."

Ed shrugged, but Sonny could tell he was making a big show of it. "Well, welcome to the foxhole." He settled back into his chair. "Anyway, speaking of the other thing... get me updated. What the hell is going on with our paper, Sonny?"

"Shoot, Ed, I emailed everything that I have to you so far." Sonny and Joey sat down on the couch in front of Ed.

"Aw, geez," Ed laughed, "What do you call it, too long; didn't read? Make it simple for the old guy."

Sonny leaned back, closed his eyes, and then nodded. "From what I know and Gus has heard, apparently there's panic talk in The Penthouse."

"It just seems strange. The company is Edson's baby. From everything I've heard, he wouldn't willingly give up part of his media empire without a very good reason."

"Exactly," Sonny said. "There has to be more to it than what we're seeing."

"Well, somebody's got to know something. Anyway, keep me in the loop – I might be able to help out."

"You're not worried about getting in trouble, Pops?" Sonny said.

"What are they going to do – cut my column? I'm already syndicated. Speaking of worries, though…"

Sonny leaned forward. "Yeah, the I-thing." He brought his voice down several decibels. "You've had a chance to look at some of the material. What do you think?"

"Ah, kid." Ed settled back in his chair. "What do I think? Other than the fact that you might be looking at an espionage rap if you print them? My opinion, everyone suspects that things are messed up, but all of this confirms it. And these guys, these 'private contractors,' in my day they called themselves mercenaries."

"Exactly what I said. You serious about the espionage? I'm not the one who dug these files out of the Pentagon or wherever."

"They busted Daniel Ellsberg for this, back in '71 with the Pentagon Papers, put him on trial and everything."

"Didn't they find him not guilty, though?" Joey responded.

"Ah, so you read up on it?" Ed nodded to her. "It's because the same idiots who did Watergate got caught trying to dig up dirt on him. They ruined the case for the prosecution. You might not get so lucky, Sonny."

"I can see Rove running an operation like that on me," Sonny said, laughing. "He's probably got icons of G. Gordon and Nixon right next to his Reagan pictures he has in the West Wing. But Ellsberg was the leaker, I'm not. They didn't put Punch Sulzburger or Katherine Graham in jail."

"To be honest, I think things are worse in some ways than back then," Ed said. "They didn't have this Patriot Act, for one. Another thing – you're just a reporter. I can't see Kathy Boone or John Michael sticking up for you."

Sonny was quiet for a moment. "I just can't let this go. What else am I supposed to do?" He pointed at Ed. "So, why aren't you worried for yourself?"

"Ah," Ed waved his hands around, "it doesn't matter as far as I'm concerned. I've lived a long time – longer than I ever thought I'd live, as much as I smoked and drank back in my younger days."

"What about Jack?" Sonny said.

"Ellsberg's kids helped him copy the Pentagon Papers, and they never got busted," Ed said. "Besides, he's a juvie. It'll be OK."

They both looked at each other and laughed at that, Ed so hard that he found himself dabbing at his eyes as he finally got control of himself. "All right, I'll keep looking through this. I still have some guys I know in Washington, some old contacts, I might fly these by them."

Ed inhaled deeply through his nostrils, then grabbed the wheels of his chair as he turned to Joey. "Well, I've been rude not paying attention to you. Interested in seeing some old photos?"

***

Jack had returned to the group as Ed was paging through a massive photo album balanced on his lap. "I was talking to Pops about how we could scan in these pics," Jack said. "I figure I could do it in a weekend or whatever." Jack extracted one photo of Jack DeFoe, standing over two reporters hunched over typewriters as they banged out stories on deadline, a hand on both their shoulders. "Was it true that Mom named me after this guy?"

"Oh, yes, yes it was." Ed took a closer look at the picture. "He knew your mother very well."

"The way you talk about him, it's almost like you guys were brothers." Jack pulled up a folding chair and sat beside Ed as he faced Sonny and Joey on the couch.

"Well, we were family. Not brothers, but... Jeez, let me do the math. Kid," he said, pointing to Sonny, "What's it called when two cousins have kids, what are the kids to each other?"

"Second cousins," Sonny said, "then their kids are third cousins, and so on."

"So, the relation between the first cousin and his cousin's kids would be..."

"I think first cousin, once removed?"

"Yeah, so, me and Jack were... second cousins once removed. You'd actually be his third cousin, once removed," he concluded, pointing at Jack.

"You never told me," Jack said.

"Ed doesn't like to brag about the connection he has with journalistic royalty," Sonny said.

"Who was that?" Joey said.

"That would be Jack and Ed's common ancestor, the man responsible for the *Journal*, Michael Bauer," Sonny said.

"Wait, he founded the paper?" Jack said.

Ed sighed, then finally nodded his head. "Yeah. Big Mike. He always wanted the employees to call him Col. Bauer after his service in the Civil War, but everyone called him Big Mike when he wasn't around. Ran the paper 40-plus years, from just before the Chicago Fire to just before the start of World War I.

"Jack D's great-grandfather was Jacob, Big Mike's oldest kid," Ed continued. "His mom, the Colonel's first wife, Hanna, died in the Fire, but Jack managed to save both the boy and several other young people from a burning building the night the flames reached his home and the paper's offices. My grandmother, Mary, was the younger daughter of Big Mike and his second wife, Anna. Anna was one of those kids Mike rescued, 12 around the time of the fire. He took her in because all of her family died and gave her a housekeeping job. It wasn't too long before they were playing a real game of house, if you know what I mean. They got married four years later."

"What, she got married when she was 16?" Jack said.

"Back in those days, most of the time, a guy wanted a kid, he'd just marry her with the parent's permission. Big Mike became her legal guardian, so you see how that made it pretty convenient."

"Geez," Jack said, quite horrified.

"Big Mike always planned on passing the paper over to Big Jake," Ed continued. "Big Jake ran the *Journal* for 35 years. The girls, though... Mike loved them, I guess, but they weren't boys. My grandmother, she wound up marrying a Polack bar owner and having his kids. My grandfather, dad and uncles only had so many bars around, and I was the fifth of seven kids, so I decided to go into the other family business after I finished school."

"Crazy." Jack shook his head.

"Well, we can't be rude to our guests, my boy. Sonny's heard this story so many times, he's probably tired of it. I'll fill you in on the rest later. Tell you what – you want to check out that scanner of yours, see how well it will get those pictures digitized?"

"OK, shouldn't be a problem," Jack said, getting up. "I bet I can get a dozen pages scanned before dinner." With that, the young Jack left the room.

He turned to Sonny. "Sonny, she's promising, by the way."

"That's a shock to you?" Joey said.

"A little... girls he hung around before, I think he had lowered expectations of them. I don't sense that with you."

"Well, I hope I don't disappoint you. I can converse about anything from horror films to the influence of Hollywood on refugees in America."

"Excellent. Since you're an artist, I'm assuming you do a good job painting houses?" Ed murmured.

"Well, my roller technique is a little bit off, but I've gotten plenty of compliments on how I can match color schemes."

"Oh, this *is* a keeper, then," Ed said. "Well, we should check in with the kitchen. I don't know about you, but the roast beef tonight might be interesting."

"Maybe." Sonny got up. "Here, I'll wheel you in."

Jason Liegois

## Chapter 6

Colton heard the buzzing of his cell phone even with his head under the pillows at six in the morning on Wednesday. Moving the pillows off his head and easing Kyra's arm off his chest, he managed to hit the call button before his phone rang a fourth time.

"Colton Edson," he whispered.

"Colt, great, you're there. Have a pencil or pen? You're going to need them before I hang up," Bill Drake whispered in turn.

"Yeah, one moment." He eased out of bed, walked over to his desk in the bedroom, and fetched a pair of pens and a yellow legal pad. "OK, what do you want?"

"It's what *you* want. I've got two names for you – Zach Davidson and Ty Polanski. They're on our risk assessment department. If anyone can give you an outside chance at letting you know if something's wrong, they can do it." Bill then proceeded to give him phone numbers and private e-mails for both men.

"Listen, thanks for all of this…"

"Enough. Look, lose my number for a little while. The heat is turning up in this office and I'm trying to find a new job. Talk to you later."

As he finished up taking down the names and numbers without waking Kyra, he thought, *Glad to know what I'll be doing today.*

*\*\**

Sonny was on guard as he walked into work that day. He wanted to know the decision on the I-project.

The newsroom looked vacant except for a few people checking on the morning wires and making sure there were no last-minute additions to the Web site or other items. For the people whose primary responsibilities were to assemble the paper and put it out, late morning was the start of their day and they wouldn't wind up until the evening's edition went to press at 9 p.m. on the dot, night after night.

As he came in, Joey was there at her desk. For the first time in a while, she didn't try to meet his eyes as he came up to her. He realized she was working hard at playing it cool like he suggested.

After quickly examining the scene and making sure no one was paying attention, he leaned in and whispered, "Are we still on for tonight?"

She looked up slowly at him from where she had been marking dates in her calendar. "Sure," she said with the tiniest smile she could manage with a mouth as wide as hers. "Good luck with today."

"Bribes and extortion might work better, but I'll take what I can get. See you."

"See you," Joey said as Sonny began to walk away.

Sonny figured that he would park himself in his office and spend the next couple of hours planning what to do over the next week, when he saw Gus by himself sitting on top of the City Desk. He waved at Sonny to come over. "We've got a meeting," Gus said simply. "Come with me."

"Where at?"

"Newsroom conference room, right now." Gus got up and gestured with a crooked finger for Sonny to join him, which he did. "The editors wanted to talk."

"About what?"

"What do you think?"

"Fuck."

"There you go." They got to Conference Room A, a row of frosted window walls facing out to the newsroom. "After you," Gus said, yanking open the glass door and gesturing to Sonny to go first, which he did.

Sonny had expected a crowd to be waiting for them, but there was only a single figure seated at the table – Carlo Massino. He sighed as the two walked in, which gave off an immediate warning vibe to Sonny.

# The Holy Fool

"Hi, guys, go ahead and have a seat," Carlo said as they approached him.

Gus and Sonny took the closest two seats next to him on Carlo's right. "Where's John Michael? Richard?" Gus asked.

Carlo shook his head. "They couldn't make it, and Cathy couldn't either –meetings all day," he said.

"So, you get to be the designated suit for today, huh?" Sonny said.

"Heh." Carlo leaned forward to face the other two men. "The senior management discussed the situation with your Iraq/Afghanistan stories. It got decided that you sit on the stories until we can get more information."

Sonny started shaking his head. "Wait, what? 'It got decided?' What the hell is that, 'It got decided?' Who actually decided it?"

"The editorial board," Carlo said. "Mainly John Michael, of course, but the board went along with him."

"Oh, good to know. I hate passive verbs." Sonny looked over at Carlo sitting, silent, across from him. "OK, that was a real obscure joke, I admit it."

"A grammar reference." Carlo said.

"Yeah."

"Grammar nerds," Carlo said, then shook his head.

"Wait, did John or Cathy or anyone say exactly what kind of evidence they were looking for?"

There was silence for a moment as Carlo examined the wood rings in the conference table rather than meet Sonny's gaze. "I have to be honest with you, they really weren't specific. They definitely didn't say 'you can't look into this anymore,' but they kept saying they needed more information."

"So, not kill the story, but keep it on the shelf," Sonny said, nodding. "Got it."

"Sonny..." Gus started.

"Garbage, that's what this is. Those guys have let single-source pieces run from the Washington desk all the time, pieces from congressmen designed solely to make themselves look good, and they're saying I don't have enough proof, with all the government documentation I've gotten? It's because they think it'll be bad for business, is what it really is. They'd rather focus on the political horse race going on right now or the Olympics rather than questioning whether we really screwed up getting into a war. There's a double standard here. And I'm *not* having those Washington guys learn about my sources; they'll either rat them out to their buddies to look good or brag about them to someone else – maybe both."

"I'm sorry, but that's the only option," Gus said.

"I'm telling you the story is there."

"I'm telling you it's not enough," Gus shot back. "You either have to get more evidence on those stories, be able to corroborate the evidence from either your own end or from someone else's sources, or both."

Sonny leaned back in his chair and drummed his fingers on the table for a few moments that were otherwise silent. Finally, he looked at first Gus then Carlo. "Is there anything else?"

"No, that's it," Gus said. "Like we said, there's nothing keeping you from working on these stories in your spare time, but we're going to need more."

"OK, then. Thanks." Without a glance back at his superiors, he pushed away from the table and walked out the door.

After the door closed, Carlo said, "Well, he seemed to take it well. You think he's going to pout about it?"

"Replace *pout* with *plot* and I think he will," Gus replied. "He's not done by any means."

"But you're OK with holding the story, right? I want to make sure you are on board with this."

"Yeah. Something this big, what it says about what's going on over there – I want to make sure we get this right. He's not going to give it to someone else."

"You mean the Lord's Men, then?" Carlos said.

"Exactly." It was the most recent nickname for the *Chicago Star*, the *Journal*'s main competitor. The name came from its English owner, Andrew Charlton, Earl of Melchester, and the head of WorldWide Media. Ever since Lord Melchester had bought up the competing tabloid, the paper had gone from a local joke to a persistent thorn in the side of the *Journal*.

"He hates the Lord's politics. I think we're safe there," Gus continued.

"Good to know."

***

Sonny started into the polished steel of the elevator walls as he wrestled with an unfamiliar tie, attempting to fashion it into a half-Windsor. The elevator doors eased open to The Penthouse as he made some last-minute adjustments to his tie and sport coat.

With the lightest of footsteps, hunched down to make himself as small-looking as possible, he took five giant strides out of the elevator and to the safety of the hallway. She never looked up.

Sonny continued to stride down the hallway, took the turn at the conference room, and headed in. He saw Mary behind her desk, typing but with a clear view of him as he walked down the hall. The door to John Michael's office was open just a crack, and there were some voices coming from behind the doors. As he got in front of Mary's desk, she looked up and said, "Hello, can I help you?"

Sonny switched on his improvisational genes. "Yes, I was wondering if Colton was in the office here. I just needed to talk with him to figure out if he took care of something for me."

"Well, I'm not sure about that..." Mary said.

"Sonny? Is that you? Come on in, it's OK," they heard John Michael say from behind the door.

Both Sonny and Mary exchanged shocked looks. "Go right in," Mary finished, waving him toward the door.

Sonny saw father and son on opposite chairs, appearing as if they had just been chatting. "Yes, what is it?" John Michael said.

"Pardon me, John Michael, but I just had two things for you – actually, one for Colton, here, and another for you."

John Michael's expression was the height of blandness. "Go ahead."

"Colton, that research for Friday's column; is that all set to go? I wanted to take care of that before leaving tonight."

"Oh, yeah, I got that taken care of," Colton said. "E-mailed that to you a half hour ago."

"Really? I appreciate it. The next question I had was for you... John Michael." He paused. Begging was just as unfamiliar to him as humility, and he didn't want to be obvious about it. "I didn't want to take up a lot of your time, but I wondered if you had two minutes."

"Hm," John Michael grunted. "Actually, I do. Can you wait here for a moment? Colton and I were going to get together for dinner after work tonight and I wanted to talk to him about where he would like to go."

"No, that's fine. Do you want me to wait outside in the hall...?"

"Actually, here is fine," John Michael said. "We'll be in my lounge over in the other room. I never showed you that part of the office, right?"

"No, I never did," Colton said.

"Great," Edson said to Sonny. "Come on, Colton, you'll like this." With a sweep of his arm, he led Colton through a small oak doorway leading to the room located directly to the west of the office.

As he stared out the window, Sonny noticed out of the corner of his eye that Edson had left his laptop on. The desk was otherwise empty except for the portable mouse.

There was a kaleidoscope screensaver on the laptop. With a shake of the mouse, Sonny got the screen to refresh. The screen was empty except for the desktop icons, but he noticed that Edson had minimized an Excel document. Glancing to make sure the door to the lounge stayed shut, he clicked on the icon.

When the first page of the spreadsheet came up, there were two things Sonny noticed immediately – the name of the *Journal* on one of the documents, and the color red. Both captivated his attention. There were comments about loans, banks, and plenty of numbers in red and located in parentheses.

## The Holy Fool

A real *deadline* reporter was a guys or girl willing to outhustle everyone else to be the first to get the story. Sonny hadn't been that type of reporter for some time. However, some of those instincts never went away.

Sonny found himself fishing in his shirt pocket for a small black plastic item, using a switch to slide its USB port out.

Sonny searched the sides of the machine until he found a USB outlet. He slid the flash drive in and accessed the computer's file manager. After just a few keystrokes and mouse manipulations, he'd copied the spreadsheet onto his drive, as well as a half-dozen other documents he'd found in the same file folder. He then clicked onto the flash drive and found the Zombie Clown head file icon. He clicked onto it, acknowledged it as an executable file, and hit RUN. Finally, a message window popped up, reading I'M READY. Sonny clicked OK, saw the window disappear, and ejected the flash drive from the computer.

After the flash drive went into his pocket, he made sure everything on the computer was in its previous position, even making sure to move the mouse and computer cursor onscreen exactly when it had been and activating the screen saver. He got back from behind the desk and into one of the white sofa chairs in front of the desk, trying not to look guilty.

Within five seconds after Sonny sat in the chair, Edson and his son came through the door. "Have a good weekend, Sonny," John Michael said to the departing Colton.

"You too."

After Colton had left the room, he leaned over to Sonny and said, "I'm taking him and that girl of his out to Charlie Trotter's tonight. I haven't had a chance to meet her, but I've heard she is quite the babe." He laughed at that, a small joke in confidence. "Have you had the pleasure of meeting her?"

"No – I have seen pictures, though. She seems nice."

"Yeah, that's what I hope." Edson leaned in closer. "I get the feeling I know why you're here. It's about the Iraq business, right?"

"Yes, sir. I understand your concerns about these stories. But I honestly believe that these pieces are solid and that we need to publish them."

"I see."

Sonny slid a plain white envelope with EDSON scrawled across it out of his jacket pocket and across John Michael's desk.

"What's this?" John Michael asked.

"This is a signed letter of resignation from me. If we publish these stories and they find a single wrong thing, a single inaccuracy, then feel free to date and initial that. You can put the whole thing on me."

Edson stared at it for a few moments. "Well." He leaned over and pushed it back towards Sonny across the desk. "I appreciate your sincerity. But, there are some other factors I have to keep in mind."

"OK." Sonny pocketed the envelope.

"As much as you would be willing to take the fall for a bad story, you should know readers would blame us anyway regardless of what you said. Many of them still support what is going on in Iraq. Right now, we need all of the readers we can get, especially with the Lord's Men breathing down our necks. If we're going to do this, I want to make absolutely, 100 percent sure that what we're going to print is totally correct."

As he heard this, Sonny kept a tight grip on his knees to avoid forming any fists. Inside he was screaming that they'd win more subscribers by being honest. Instead, he just said, "OK."

"Now, I want you to be totally clear that this is not dead by any means of the imagination," Edson continued. "By all means, I want you to continue your work on it. Understand?"

"I understand."

"Also, and let me be honest with you, I think it would give you a better chance of getting this thing to run sooner if you started to widen the group of people helping you. I'm sure Sean, Andrew Odom, or Candace Mooney could help if you open up to them, show them some of what you have."

"Understood."

Edson stood up. "Listen, thanks very much for taking the time to come in and talk to me about this. I appreciated your thoughts and opinion."

Sonny knew a dismissal when he heard it. "Of course. Thanks for taking the time to talk."

"Don't be shy in giving me updates on the story, by the way."

"OK. Have a good weekend."

"You too," Edson said as he made his way around his desk and back to his laptop.

As he took six steps to get out of the room, Sonny kept expecting to hear a "WAIT A MINUTE" from his boss. However, the only thing he heard was the tack-tack of the laptop keys.

He managed to get to the elevators without acting in any way unusual. However, the minute the doors closed behind him, Sonny extracted his iPhone.

There were two rings before he heard a beep on the other end. "It's Woot. What you need?"

"Need to meet – crash priority. Downstairs?"

"Yeah. OK, I'll shake loose in five."

"OK." Sonny hung up.

\*\*\*

Much of the Keep's basement was deserted except for storage areas, utility spaces and empty rooms. If two people came across each other wandering through the half-lit, white-walled hallways, it would be considered a traffic jam. Sonny was alone as he stopped at an anonymous doorway that led to one of those empty rooms but required the special keycard that he and Woot had.

As Sonny walked in, he heard, "What do you have?" Woot sat in front of a table lined up with desktop hard drives and monitors. He was wearing a white Pokemon T-shirt showing one Pokemon electrocuting another one.

"It's about that Trojan Horse program you gave me."

"Yeah?"

"Yeah, well, I managed to use it."

"Wait, what?" That almost brought Woot out of his slouch in his rolling chair.

"I got access to Edson's laptop and used the flash drive to download it on there. Also managed to snag a couple of files."

"Just like that?"

"Just like that."

"Fuck me. So, are you sure that the program installed?"

"The progress bar page counted down just like you said it would."

Woot propped his feet up on table. "OK, were there any cameras or surveillance in the office?"

Sonny thought for a moment, then shook his head. "No cameras in the office, just outside. I'm not sure if his computer was being monitored."

"I'll have to check that later. Second question; who knows about this?"

"Just us. Nobody else."

Woot nodded. "OK, good. Let's keep it that way for now. Killer. What now?"

"I'll look over the docs I got. Once you get the data dump, we'll look over everything."

"Sounds good. OK, don't you have that computer at home, the desktop one?"

"Yeah, yeah, I do, plus the laptop."

Woot nodded in return, then made a point to reach out and crack his knuckles before continuing. "OK. DO NOT, under any circumstances, look at that thing here or on any computers the Journal owns. You take it home and go over the whole thing."

"Fine."

"You also take that flash drive and copy all of the files you can find on it and stash that in as many places as you can think of, hard drives or online dead drops. I don't want to lose this just because it's in one place. Understand?"

"Absolutely."

"OK."

"Where are we with the e-snoop setup on the whole system?" Sonny said just as Woot got to the door.

"I'm getting everything lined up for the weekend. From here I can plug into the entire network and nobody will notice it."

# The Holy Fool

"OK. Pretty soon we're going to have to make this more than just me, you, and Gus. Big-ass man decisions need to be made soon."

Woot was quiet for a moment and turned back around to face Sonny. "So, you think they're looking at the sale for sure?"

"We'll see."

Woot sighed. "Outside the Keep. It's the only way we have a chance of not having people notice a good chunk of the newsroom is MIA."

"OK, I'll let you figure out a place."

"I'll put it on the to-do list."

\*\*\*

When Sonny made it back to the newsroom, he was surprised to find Gus waiting next to his office door. "You have a minute?" Gus said.

"Sure, come on in."

Gus snuck through the doorway as Sonny walked inside and quickly closed it behind him. "Hey, I wanted to check with you, making sure things were OK."

Sonny choked back a laugh or two as he tossed his cell phone on top of his desk. "Sure, Boss, things are great! Why wouldn't they be?"

"C'mon, don't blow me off."

Sonny gestured that Gus should have a seat. After Gus complied, Sonny did the same, then continued, "Honestly, what do you expect me to say? That I'm OK with this?"

"Sonny, I know you." Gus reached over and knocked on his desk. "You'll be able to keep this source on the hook, find more sources, and convince John Michael and the rest of them to go ahead with it."

Sonny shook his head. "You know, there's two really sick things about this situation. First, there's the fact that you believe what you're saying. I'd really like to know how you managed to keep your faith in journalism this long, Gus, because *I'm* having trouble with it. Secondly, I'm stunned to realize... just how much I don't give a shit about this stuff. The guys upstairs, what they want, I'm just over it. There's got to be a better way to do journalism than this, because this isn't working."

"Bullshit; I don't see that in your writing. Maybe you need to take a breather, maybe a normal schedule, a normal life, a steady girl."

Sonny laughed. "Really? What have you heard?"

"Should I be hearing something?"

"No, *Dad*," Sonny said.

Gus shrugged, his palms out. "OK."

Sonny paused for a second, then: "I probably need to let you know I technically went over your head a few minutes ago. I talked to John Michael about the stories."

He was expecting to have the volume rise in the room, but the only thing that did rise was Gus' eyebrows. "Really? Did it work?"

"Hah, not even a chance."

"All right, then."

"Hey, I got the column into you an hour ago. Anything you need me to change?"

Gus shook his head. "Nah. It's fine. Surprised you asked."

"Glad to hear my words sound so safe." Sonny sighed, then shook his head. "No, screw it, I'm trying to pick a fight. I'm done with feeling sorry for myself."

"Sounds like a plan. See you, kid."

As Gus walked out the door and closed it behind him, he tapped a few keys on his laptop and opened his custom e-mail account. A notice popped up on his screen: IN CHAT NOW NEED TO MEET WHEN YOU RECEIVE THIS.

It took Sonny about five minutes to get his computer encrypted and proxies set up before he went into the IRC chatroom. Within a few seconds of him entering, he saw:
&lt;hewoman98&gt; made it I see
Sonny sighed, then replied:
&lt;SonnyT76&gt; yes
&lt;hewoman98&gt; what's the word from your bosses?
&lt;SonnyT76&gt; not good they want me to sit on it.
&lt;hewoman98&gt; why?
&lt;SonnyT76&gt;not enough evidence, not enough time, all bullshit.

# The Holy Fool

\<hewoman98\>shit on my dick
\<hewoman98\>you said this was going through
\<SonnyT76\>It's still happening.
\<SonnyT76\>I'm still talking with editors, even the owner.
\<hewoman98\>no chance
\<hewoman98\>beginning to wonder whether this is worth it.
\<SonnyT76\>yes it is
\<SonnyT76\>don't say that
\<SonnyT76\>I will continue to fight however long it will take. People will read about this.
\<hewoman98\>You promise this will happen?
\<hewoman98\>Where I work, your word has to mean something. Does your word mean something to YOU?
\<SonnyT76\>Yes, I promise.
\<hewoman98\>What if you can't make your editors come around?
\<SonnyT76\>Plan B, I guess.
\<hewoman98\>There's a Plan B?
\<SonnyT76\>There will be.
\<hewoman98\>There better be
\<SonnyT76\>OK, Boss.
\<hewoman98\>Beginning to wonder if my supervisors are starting to suspect something.
\<SonnyT76\>How much of a worry?
\<hewoman98\>I should stay worried if I'm smart.
\<SonnyT76\>Speaking of making preparations, what about that list of other potential sources?
\<hewoman98\>I'm working on it.
\<SonnyT76\>When might you send it?
\<hewoman98\>Very soon.
\<hewoman98\>trying to limit the list to people I'm aware of OL, but have some connection to IRL job. I know that if this gets found out, a lot of people I know are going to get questioned about what they knew and when did they know it.
\<SonnyT76\>Watch yourself.
\<hewoman98\>aw, you worry about me
\<SonnyT76\>of course.
\<hewoman98\>so you can get the scoop of this century?
\<SonnyT76\>OK, yeah, but I worry about you, too.

\<hewoman98\>Aw, that's sweet.
\<SonnyT76\>When will I get that list?
\<hewoman98\>It's coming soon
\<hewoman98\> you'll get 4/? this evening.
\<SonnyT76\>Regular location?
\<hewoman98\>Same drop
\<hewoman98\>I'm expecting you to finally print something soon.
\<SonnyT76\>I will
\<hewoman98\>OK.
\<hewoman98\>got to go
\<SonnyT76\>OK
\<SonnyT76\>bye
\<hewoman98\>bye.

***

Gus made his way toward his spot in the City Desk cluster when he saw Carlo standing on the edge of the room, off to the left of the cluster. With a single finger, he gestured that Gus should change his itinerary, which Gus did, heading over to him.

As Gus got next to him, Carlo waved for him to get closer, leaning their heads in for a two-man football huddle. "I just got the word from upstairs," Carlo whispered. "They're going ahead with the new cuts now."

"The stop-gap cuts? I thought they were reconsidering that."

Carlo shook his head. "They figured they needed to get it started now."

"On a Wednesday, too. Who's out?"

"Several out of classified, two people in the New York office, a lot in printing. I'll fill you in on the newsroom situation upstairs." Gus swiveled his head around, scanning the floor. "HR already called all of them that's going upstairs. They'll have everything taken care of in 30 minutes."

"Amazing." Gus spat out the word. "What do they need me for, if I'm not going?"

# The Holy Fool

"They're going to want to talk with us about the press release, keep it low key."

\*\*\*

Sonny had "Wig Wham Bam" by The Sweet pumping through his iPod and keeping everyone else away as he opened the door to his office to find Colton there at the spare desk, typing away. "What's up, kid?" he said, leaning on the door jam and unplugging his earbuds.

"My one source on the UUF story got me contact information for some people in their risk department," he replied. "I'm trying to get in touch with them."

"Did the guy give you personal contacts for these guys?"

"Actually, yeah."

"Good. Don't even think about contacting these guys at work. You'll need to meet them in person, preferably out of the Loop, away from where these guys hang out after work. Keep Gus updated, too."

"I get it; will do. I'm also going over some of the questions I'll have for them. You mind looking over them, see if I need to add something?"

"Sure kid. No problem."

"I'm just worried about doing this right." Colton turned to face Sonny. "I just realized, these guys handle some banking for Edson Media. What happens if their investments go under? Couldn't that hurt us?"

*The kid's fast,* Sonny realized. "Maybe, but I wouldn't worry too much. As good as your dad is with numbers, I'm sure he'd be aware of any problems."

"Well, what if the bank's hiding something from them about those investments?"

"Say what?"

"Them keeping the money from us, obviously. Plus, if your clients don't know how bad something is, they can't start a run on the bank unless it's too late."

"Yeah, interesting," he said, trying not to show his surprise. *Spent all this time thinking about how Edson's lying to us, didn't even think that maybe the bank's lying to everyone. Could it be true? Could they both be true?*

From his peripheral vision, Sonny noticed that Joey had headed off to the newsroom lounge a few dozen yards from the front reception area. "Kid, I'll be right back. I'll look at those questions when I get back."

"Sure," Colton said to Sonny's departing form as he strode over to the other side of the newsroom floor.

The "newsroom employees break room" was more like typical elementary school teachers' lounge rather than the break room for a major metropolitan daily newspaper. A single row of tables placed end to end dominated the long room that would have barely fit a football team around it. Scuffed Formica tile covered the floor. On the side by the door, there was a row of cabinets and counters with dishes and supplies, two microwaves, two large coffee pots, and two 70's-era pale green refrigerators completed the ensemble.

As depressing as the place looked, few people spent any time there. Most of them would dart in to grab a cup of coffee or grab the lunches they'd stored in the refrigerators and take them back to their desks to eat or avoid it altogether and keep their own small cube refrigerators by their desks.

Joey looked up at him as he approached and she finished filling her cup. "Hi, Sonny," she said, keeping her voice neutral but friendly, "How did it work ou…"

With a final look behind him to make sure no one was coming through the door and that they were alone, Sonny strode right up next to Joey, cradled her face in his hands, and leaned in and kissed her. The kiss was in depth, with a slight bit of tongue movement at the end. When he broke off, she gasped, "Well, that escalated quickly."

"I missed you." He kissed her again, drawing her in for a hug and his tongue probed a bit further in depth.

"How'd it go with them?"

"Not what I wanted; I'll tell you later."

"OK. What do you want to do for dinner?"

"You into Chinese?"

"Sure."

# The Holy Fool

"I'll bring over Chinese. Don't worry about it. Anything you like?"

"Surprise me."

"I thought I already did," he responded, and that prompted a big smile from Joey. "Hey, thought I'd bring over a movie I just bought and I haven't even had a chance to see it."

"What did you get?"

"<u>Southland Tales</u>. It's by the guy who directed <u>Donnie Darko</u>. I remember you loved that movie, yeah?"

"Yeah, that was a mind freak, I remember. Jake Gyllenhall was so cute in that – no offense."

"It's OK, I dig his sister." They both had a laugh at that.

"You inviting me to watch it?" she said in a softer tone.

"Sure, I can bring it by tonight," Sonny replied with a whisper.

"Okay. Am I going to have to worry about molestation in the workplace, now?"

"No worries." He took a quick look behind him as he backed away from her. "See you later."

"Bye."

Sonny backed out through the door, still looking behind him and at Joey. He tried to think about whether he'd ever pulled anything like that back when he was in high school in Des Moines, but he couldn't think of anything other than holding hands with some girl in front of some teachers. *Trying to relive some of my youth, maybe,* he thought.

He made his way back into the middle of the newsroom and deliberately forced himself not to watch her leave the break room. Instead, he saw TT standing around a bank of police scanners taking up cubicle space between the City and Metro desks.

"Anything of interest?" Sonny said, walking over to him.

"Nothing that belongs on A1, but I'm taking some notes for Dana or whoever she's going to have make the cops and responders run," TT said.

"You want to talk with me?"

"Yeah, I'm done here. Take a walk?"

"OK." He unslung his cane and put away his notebook. "Lead the way."

"Come on." Sonny led TT to the men's restroom on the classified ad floor a couple of levels below them. It was usually reliably empty around that time of the day, which Sonny confirmed by checking the four stalls in that room.

Sonny started to pace in a semi-circle around TT, stopping every few moments to face him. "You told Gus you were down for anything, right?"

TT chuckled at that, resting his cane upon his shoulders. "Yeah, I did."

"We are doxing John Michael big time."

"Doxing?"

"Basically, opening up someone's life like a tin can."

"Wait, you saying you...?"

"I want to know what he does, what he says, who he meets from now until further notice. If you can open up his head and tell me his hopes and dreams, I want to know about that, too."

TT leaned forward on his cane and finally nodded. "Yeah, it's done. When does this start?"

"Right the hell now."

"You know where he is now?"

"Brother, you're the detective." Sonny replied. "We may have to cover things for you, but I can make it right with Gus."

TT laughed at that, then leaned over to shake his hand. "Well, I'm not going to hang around here if I've got work."

Sonny shook his hand. "Fair enough. Let me know what I can do to help you out."

"When do you want to update you on what's going on?"

"Contact me tomorrow at least, and then at least every other day. We're going to need information fast."

"OK, later." With that, they were off.

***

Sonny found Gus looking over Harry Read's shoulder as he was putting together one of his features, something on squatters in the west suburbs. "Christ, Harry, quit using 'they were found' all over your copy, will you? Just say 'The authorities found them.' It sounds better, more direct, got it?"

## The Holy Fool

"Also helps that it's less words," Harry said, nodding.

"Finally, the boy gets it. Ah, Sonny, what's the word today?"

"Got a second? Needed to get a coffee break."

"OK, with me, then?" Gus replied. "Christ, I've got McCain named as the nominee tonight, Andy Odom's got what's left of the national/foreign desk and most of the DC bureau divided between Denver and St. Paul, with maybe your guy Casey and maybe one or two others left in the capitol. Bush could invade Syria tomorrow, we might not find out about it until next week."

\*\*\*

As Sonny and Gus went to the elevator, they found a surprising figure coming out of one of them that made both men stop in place.

"Hey, Mr. Pulaski, Sonny, good to see both of you," said Wyatt Walker as he walked up to them. The security chief for Edson was somewhere between Sonny and Gus's age, a shade under six feet tall with a marathoner's build, pale eyes, and short hair so blond to almost be white. He preferred a sport coat, khakis, and hiking boots to three-piece suits – Sonny decided it was probably because if he ran into any physical action on the job, he wanted to be comfortable doing it.

"Hi, Wyatt."

Wyatt nodded. "John Michael wanted me to pass something along to you. It turns out he's getting picky about security. He wants everyone to be wearing their badges – can you pass that along to the newsroom employees?"

"Sure, no problem," Gus said.

"Also, he's getting picky about having people in parts of the building without prior authorization, especially the Penthouse. Technically, I'm not supposed to let anyone there anymore without executive clearance unless they have prior permission."

"Understood, understood, Wyatt. We're not going there today, but next time anyone needs to go up dere, we'll clear it with you first, prawmise," Gus said, his North Side accent

109

getting broader as he continued, trying to sound unsophisticated.

"OK. Sorry to bother you," Wyatt said, waving them through to the elevators.

"No problem," Gus said.

After going down in the elevator, with Gus right behind him, Sonny strolled to the basement room, used his key card, and opened the door to see Woot behind the long table, working on his laptop.

"Hello, bro. Gus, surprised to see you," Woot said.

"I thought I should check up on you delinquents," Gus said.

"Hope this place is safe," Sonny said, recounting the run-in with Wyatt.

"No worries, but he's asked me about network security in addition to the physical security of Edson Media," Woot said.

"You think he knows you're with us?" Sonny said.

"I'm sure he suspects it, but he doesn't have any proof; at least, he doesn't have any proof that he's confronted me with. He also doesn't have any cybersecurity background, and neither do any of the goons he has working for them."

"OK, keep an eye out on him. First, the surveillance on John Michael," Sonny said. "TT's handling the physical part of the investigation, although I'll probably help with that, too."

"It's going to be difficult to put a physical tap on the phone," Woot said. "However, the Wi-Fi networks around here are public, and John Michael links up to them when he's using his cell phone."

"OK, make sure if you find out anything about his movements on that, pass those along to TT."

"Will do."

"Is that all you'll be watching, though?" Gus said.

"We've got access to his laptop," Sonny said, which earned a surprised gaze from Gus.

Woot said, "I'm hoping with the access, I can get into other people's stuff, too. Not sure who exactly we need to have..."

"Cathy Boone for sure," Sonny cut in. "Then that CFO, the accounting guy, who is he, Henry Walsh..."

"Hector Walsh," Gus finished for him.

"Right. Then the main attorney, Perry Reeves. Oh, getting Mary Kennedy's access would be a good investment, too – she basically runs John Michael's whole life from that office," Sonny said, pointing to one of the 3x5 cards on the board which showed the organizational structure of the paper.

"Consider it done," Woot said, typing a note to himself. "Anything else?"

"Not right now," Sonny said. "Next thing is finding out what the buyers for the Journal or Edson Media are making as offers."

"You're acting like you already know who John Michael wants to buy the paper," Gus said.

"Well, I do. It's obvious who it is, isn't it? It's Lord Melchester and his merry men."

Gus looked up. "Just like that?"

"Exactly. Who else has a financial incentive to buy it? So, Woot's going to continue the electronic portion of our surveillance, TT's handling John Michael detail, and I'm looking into the Lord's Men, among other things."

Sonny paused for a moment, lifted his hand, and snapped his fingers a couple of times. "I just realized something, something that Colton just mentioned this morning. If things are going bad with UUF, maybe John Michael and the rest of the executives here don't realize it."

"What?" Gus said.

"Think about it. John Michael and the rest of the clients find out something's wrong with the bank, their first instinct is going to be to pull all of their money out of their investment accounts."

"That's a hell of a lack of customer service," Woot said.

"I think these guys skipped those lectures at university," Sonny said.

"More than just us are going to have to meet, though," Gus said.

"OK," Sonny said.

\*\*\*

Soon afterward, Sonny was reviewing the questions Colton had written down for his interviews. "So, are these OK?" Colton asked.

"Right now, I'm liking them," Sonny said. "Looks like you're avoiding true-false answers, always a plus."

"OK, anything else?"

"Two things in particular." Sonny settled into a seat next to Colton. "Obviously you're planning to meet with these guys today, if you can."

"Yeah." Colton nodded as enthusiastically as he could to show he was up for anything.

"I know you're willing to put the work in, but we have to be really careful. What you said about this possibly having repercussions with the paper makes sense. We need to careful, understand?"

"Absolutely."

"I might have said this before, but you talk to *nobody* about this until our work is done. The only people you discuss this with are Gus and me, and that even goes for your dad, understood?"

"OK." Colton was looking a bit unsure, but his response was immediate.

"Who were you going to get in contact with first?"

"I was going to try this guy, Zach Davison…"

"The guy in their risk department?"

"Yeah, one of them."

"OK, we'll work this one together. Say, ask if he's into Mexican. I've got a good meeting spot in Pilsen – it's close enough that he can get back to work right away."

*\*\*\**

Colton gazed around the restaurant he sat in with Sonny and commented, "I'm honestly not sure Zach's going to be comfortable being here."

"He can just fucking chill and enjoy the atmosphere, yeah? Besides, he wanted to make sure none of his buddies saw him talking to us. And, this will calm things down exponentially,"

# The Holy Fool

Sonny said, nodding at the waitress approaching with a large pitcher of margarita and glasses.

"Didn't know we could drink while working."

"Desperate times call for desperate measures. *Gracias, senora.* Also, a benefit of working on the road. Ah, here he is."

Sonny spotted him right away. Zach Davidson walked into La Ranchera Primera scared. He looked like he was wondering whether he was overdressed for a Mexican joint with his grey pinstripe suit and ostrich-skinned shoes. He looked behind him as if he was expecting someone to be tailing him. Zach also scanned the predominantly Hispanic crowd as if they were a different species. He finally spotted Sonny and Colton in the booth. Sonny gave him a low wave to come on over.

The guy was about Colton's age, below average height, fit but pale with short black hair and dark, unfocused eyes. He hesitated, then walked over to the booth and sat next to Sonny and across from Colton, shaking Colton's hand. "Hey, you're Colton, right? I'm Zach; we talked on the phone. So, you used to be roommates with Bill back at U. Chicago?"

"We were on the same dorm floor," Colton said. He pointed over to Sonny. "This is Sonny Turner, my boss. He wanted to hang out with us."

"Pleasure," Sonny said.

"Wait, I think I know your name," Zach said. "You're the columnist, right?"

"I do that."

"Some of my bosses called you a socialist."

"Shoot, Marx would be disappointed to see how easy it is to qualify as a socialist nowadays," Sonny said. "You look goddamn nervous this early in the day. Pour yourself some 'Rita and relax a bit."

"Usually it's only the older guys nowadays who get drunk at lunchtime, but today I'll make it an exception," Zach said, reaching for one of the glasses.

"I've only been at the bank for 18 months now," Zach continued. "When I got there, I was hoping for a spot in the real estate section or the trading floor. But they didn't have anything on the trading floor – they'd just cut a couple dozen people – so they stuck me in risk assessment. I had an in; my uncle used to work with Gil Lott before he retired."

"Lott, you mean the bank president?" Colton said.

"Yeah, exactly. Lott was still a mid-level exec when my uncle, Frank, worked with him. But Uncle Frank always said Gil was going to be on top someday."

"Let me ask you a question, just for us, not really for the story," Sonny said as Colton examined him. "What was your Uncle Frank's feelings about Gil getting the job?"

"Honestly?" Zach said, taking a deep sip of his margarita before continuing. "Frank always liked Gil – he was OK to joke around with, he could relax, be one of the guys…" His voice tapered off.

"But?" Sonny said.

"He was someone who was willing to try the newest thing, getting involved with the latest market where he thought he could make money. You've got to remember, UUF opened for business back in 1890 as Marshall Central Bank. For years, it was a 1-2-3 bank - loan one customer money at two percent and get onto the golf course by three in the afternoon, right? It was like that even 20 years ago, but the higher up Gil got in the organization, and the more his boys were part of the bank, the more freewheeling it got."

"What do *you* think about it?"

"With all these new securities they're dealing in, these new bonds… a lot of this stuff I think the old guys don't have a clue about how it works. But that's not the scary part," Zach continued, finishing his margarita and pouring another the second he finished the first. "I'm not sure the new guys in charge really know how they work, either. And they seem to be keeping it secret from the rank and file employees, the risk-management staff, and our clients."

"So, do you know how many of these securities and bonds might be in danger?" Colton asked.

"No, not for sure."

"Let me figure out what your biggest concern is," Sonny said. "Basically, you're worried that Daddy had a bad several nights at the sports book. Now, on top of that, you haven't seen him around for a day. So, now you're thinking he's raided

## The Holy Fool

the college fund, driven off to Vegas, and looking to go double or nothing to see if he can win everything back. Is it something like that?"

Zack thought for a moment, then nodded and took another drink. "Yeah, that kind of captures it."

"You don't know what's wrong with the place, but can you find out what's wrong, can't you?" Sonny asked.

"Maybe. That depends. What's in it for me?"

Sonny nodded at that, then looked around and tapped Colton on the shoulder. "Now, this part you need to pay attention to," he said to Colton. "Most reporters, they'd get nervous when a source asks them that question. For me, I came to realize that I have to give them an honest explanation, to help build that trust. Are you ready to hear that now?" he finished, facing Zach.

"Sure."

"OK. We want a story. But you, you want to look out for yourself, right?"

"Exactly."

"Let's use another metaphor. Right now, you're on the <u>Titanic</u> and you think there's an iceberg in the fog off the bow, but you're not sure. So, you want to find out as bad as us. Best case scenario, you find out there's no iceberg; your worries are over. Next best scenario, you find out there is an iceberg, and we get the word out soon enough that the captain can get the ship turned away from it."

"What about worst-case scenario?" Zach said.

"Worst case… you see what's coming and get the first seat in the lifeboats," Colton said before Sonny could utter a word.

Sonny looked across the table at Colton, chuckled quietly, and then nodded. *Well played.* "Exactly. It may be unpleasant, but it's better than your balls freezing in the Atlantic."

"But why do I need to give *you* guys the information, too?"

"Another good question," Sonny replied. "Basically, we can put pressure on these guys. Pressure to act nice they wouldn't have if no one was watching or talking about them."

"You're not going to jerk off all over the couch while watching S&M porn if you know someone's looking through the windows, right, bro?" Colton said. "Nobody likes to be bad news." Sonny chuckled at that.

Zach appeared to deflate at their words. After a few moments, he nodded. "OK, what might you be interested in?"

"I think we should probably review what you already know about these bonds, and cover what information we're interested in," Colton said. "That sounds like the best strategy."

"I agree," Sonny said. He got up out of the booth. "To be honest, I have to get going right now – I've got some other people I need to meet before the day gets done. I'm sure Colton'll be able to sort things from here."

"Sure, no problem." Colton got out his notebook.

Sonny stared at the margarita glasses and pitcher on the table. "You drive to get here?" he said, pointing to Zach.

"No."

"Good deal. Might as well finish that up," pointing to the margarita pitcher. "You guys might need a lot more of this stuff before everything is done." With that, he scooped up his nearly full glass and downed it in several gulps. "Later."

As Sonny walked out of the restaurant, he noticed that the Gentleman and the Superfan were waiting for him as he exited the building. *Zach was so worried about someone tailing him, but the only ones doing any tailing don't even give a fuck about him,* he thought.

It took two train stops and a dodge onto Lower Wacker Drive over the next hour to lose them.

***

Sonny walked up to Joey's building, while managing to hold a plastic bag full of Chinese takeout boxes in one hand and a six-pack of Chinese beer. Lacking a free hand, he managed to push the doorbell with his head. He heard the ring and waited for a few moments. Finally, a chorus of locks shifting in the door let him know she was there.

"Ah, the deliveryman's finally here," Joey said, laughing. Her hair was loose around her shoulders "You were looking for popcorn and a movie, right?" Joey said as she opened the door. She had a massive metal bowl of popcorn in her left hand.

"Exactly."

"Like the outfit? You didn't have a chance to see it today." It was a floor-length, tiger-stripe dress, with just some straps up front and around her neck keeping her top up.

"Actually, I do."

"I think I remembered something about this film - I think they played it at Cannes two years ago. It just came out now?"

"Earlier this year," Sonny said. "They released it in theaters last year, but it didn't do too much there."

"The movie sucked?"

"Probably because it was too weird."

"What's it about?" she asked as they made their way into her bedroom.

"Wow, where to start... OK, it's a sci-fi fantasy set in an alternative universe America. America's at war with the entire Middle East, the government's watching everyone..."

"What's the sci-fi part?" Joey cracked.

"The part where a German company hired by the government comes up with a new energy source that basically rips apart the space time continuum in the process?"

Joey set the popcorn down at the foot of the bed, kicked off her black sandals, and lay down on the bed. "OK, that's sci-fi. There's some Coke in the fridge. Could you get me one?"

"I'll get two, then," Sonny said, then ducked into the kitchen.

"Who's in it?" Joey asked as Sonny returned with the Cokes.

"Let's see, The Rock, Stiffler, Justin Timberlake, Buffy the Vampire Slayer, and half the former cast of Saturday Night Live."

Joes burst out laughing. "Well, shit, I'm there, then," he said. "What are you waiting for? Let's start this thing up."

After taking off his shoes and coat, he joined her on the bed, laying down and facing forward. As he took his first bites of popcorn and Chinese and cracked open the Coke, they began to watch what unfolded.

Jason Liegois

They saw a third of Texas get nuked and America at war with the entire Mideast as a result. They saw an organization called USIDENT that saw everything and monitored everything – basically, Sonny's worst nightmare. He saw comedians turn into Marxist revolutionaries. He saw Buffy get most of the good lines; the ones he laughed at included "Scientists are saying the future is going to be far more futuristic than they originally predicted" and "We're a bisexual nation living in denial. All because of a bunch of nerds. A bunch of nerds who got off a boat in the 15th century and decided that sex was something to be ashamed of. All the Pilgrims did was ruin the American Indian orgy of freedom."

"My personal opinion," Joey said, laughing.

"You serious?" Sonny said, grinning in disbelief. "You've actually tried that?"

"There were a couple of times that I fooled around with some girls," she said. "Nothing really serious, we were just friends. In one case, she wanted it to be more than that, and that caused some drama. It was… different."

Sonny nodded at that. "OK."

"That's it, OK?" Joey said, surprised.

"What's the difference between that and ex-boyfriends?"

She settled back down on the bed. "True."

They continued to watch the movie. They saw time and space fold in on itself and The Rock actually acted and they wondered if the two were related. As he watched Justin Timberlake lip-synch The Killers with a chorus line of naughty nurses, Sonny said, "This almost feels like what's inside my head right now, all the craziness."

"Same here."

"The bad way that things could turn out, you know." The smile grew across Sonny's face. "The weird thing is, I see myself trying to change things, alter history, you know? Maybe it's arrogant, but I think I can do something about this."

"What do you want to do?

"You know, important journalism stuff. I'm talking Woodstein and Pentagon Papers level shit. I'm just not sure I'll be able to do it at the Journal."

## The Holy Fool

"What do you mean? You don't think Gus will back you when it comes down to it?"

"It's not his fault, not really. What do you expect when the fucking paper has to make 30, 40 percent profit margins to make stockholders happy? For once I don't want to have to worry about that, but I don't know how I can avoid it."

"There's a lot of organizations that are nonprofit that do journalism, like NPR, the *Guardian*, other groups."

"I'm not sure John Michael, Gus, or anyone else at the Journal would be in favor of that."

"Who says you work for them?"

"I'm working for them now."

"That can change."

"How's that? Didn't know *Mother Jones* or *The Guardian* was hiring."

"Everyone's building their own web site. Why not you?"

"What, I do my own thing? Like I know how to do that."

"I could help you. I used to work for different nonprofit organizations, and I wound up doing a lot of things with them, learning how they worked, even helping design their websites. It could happen – something like that would be a place I'd want to work for."

"Really? I don't know if I could be convinced of that..."

She untied the straps at the back of her neck as she leaned down for a probing kiss. "Maybe I'd be able to..."

***

"OK, I have to admit this is nice," Sonny said.

They were covered with just a sheet as the closing credits of the film ran across the screen of her TV. "Yeah. It's nice to relax," Joey said.

He turned to her. "Joey, something went on today?"

"Well, not so much with *my* work... I'll try to explain. You have any more popcorn?"

"Yeah, you want some?"

"Sure, I'll come get it." With that, she leaned over his lap to reach for the bowl at the nightstand on his side of the bed, baring her rear right in front of Sonny. Sonny found himself leaning down and nibbling on her right cheek just at the junction between her butt and the back of her thigh.

"Shit, Sonny, you're going to make me drop everything," she laughed as she squirmed for a moment in his lap.

He sat up straight and popped in a kernel. "Sorry, that was too much temptation."

"God." She shook her head in mock exasperation, as she straightened up and sat next to him. "So, anyway..."

"Anyway."

"I'm going to be having that exhibition this Saturday, remember?"

"Yeah, I remember. You need me to paint something?"

That earned him a shove from a giggling Joey. "NO, dork. I was wondering if you could write something."

"OK, I'm listening."

"For these exhibitions, there's these artist statements. I've got one written out for myself, and you can look that over if you want, but I was wondering if you'd write commentary for my exhibits."

"Me? I know a little about art, but I don't know a lot of technical terms."

"No, that's the point, Sonny. I remember that column you did about Washington being the new Rome, the decline, and the themes you talked about, those were incredible words. Something like that would be a better commentary on what those pieces mean than something I could spit out."

Sonny set his empty beer bottle on his plate and patted her head. "Sure. Was this some trick to get me to help do your homework?"

She leaned over and kissed his forehead. "Maybe."

"Well, I'm OK with that."

# Chapter 7

It was 7 a.m. Thursday as Gus made his rounds as usual, stopping by each of the reporters' desks. He was surprised to see Colton, right on his heels, hearing toward Gus right as Sonny was.

As he approached Gus, Sonny said, "Gus, hey…"

"Gus, can I talk with you really quick? It's urgent," Colton interrupted, tucking into Sonny's immediate right side so he and Gus were face to face.

"Excuse me?" Sonny said.

"Gus, I think you really need to see some of this stuff I had…" Colton began. It's about the UUF assignment you put me on. I've got something here."

Gus looked up and down at Colton. "OK. Sonny, I need to talk with the kid for a few minutes. I promise as soon as we wrap up, I'll be in your office."

Sonny furrowed his eyebrows and stared down Colton, but otherwise he kept his opinion to himself. "OK, not a problem," he said. "I'll be ready when you get there."

"Great. Colton, we'd better get to my office." Gus turned on his heels and marched in that direction with Colton in tow.

Gus waved Colton into his office and gestured for him to sit down. "OK, what's so important you needed to hunt me down?"

"I've got my laptop here," Colton said, pointing to his backpack. "Where do you want me to set this up?"

"Just do it on my desk. I'll pull up a chair behind you and look on. So, what does it look like?"

"You want my technical opinion? Weird." Colton opened the laptop.

"OK, I guess I need to see it, then."

\*\*\*

As the spreadsheets started to open across Colton's screen, Gus loomed over his shoulder. "OK, tell me what's going on here."

"OK, this has to do with the bonds that they're creating out of the home mortgages they are financing. Actually, 'mortgages' seem to be a little bit simple, considering how they work."

"So, tell me what the hell we've got to worry about."

"They've blended various forms of home mortgages and business mortgages together and started selling them as securities. This has been going on for a while, at least – maybe 10 years ago in the case of UUF. They've been very lucrative for the bank and its clients.

"Of course, not all of these securities have mortgages that are at the same level of risk." he continued. "Some are very solid; some are to more risky first-time buyers, no money down deals, that sort of things."

"So, the idea behind that is, with the variety of risk, you're able to make buying these things not as risky." Gus was surprised he was following along.

"Exactly. But what I'm hearing around and seeing here, is that there's a lot more risk than almost anyone realizes. See these numbers here?" Colton pointed at the screen.

Gus gazed at where Colton pointed for a few moments. "Those numbers?"

"Yeah."

"Are those potential losses?"

"As long as the financing levels stay within these historic norms, everything works out fine. But as you see... here... and here, the market has already gone beyond those historic norms at least twice, and have the potential to do it again in the next couple of weeks.

"Here's another thing." He reached around Gus's arm to gain control of the mouse and move to another window. "This is an e-mail from Hector Walsh here and Melvin Berg at USA Unlimited."

"OK, I know Walsh – well, not really..."

"The CFO."

# The Holy Fool

Gus nodded. "In the two years he's been here, I haven't met him. Anyway, who's this Berg guy?"

"Melvin Berg," Colton said. "My contact told me all about him. Apparently, the senior VP of corporate accounts – basically the main hand-holder for their big-ticket clients. They've been in communication with each other for the past few months."

"About what?"

"Apparently, Edson is buying up USA UF bonds – some they originated, some that they originally purchased through Lehman Brothers in New York."

"OK, MBA grad, what happens if those numbers you talked about before keep traveling outside of those 'historic norms,' as you call them?"

"There's definitely potential losses, but it's tough from these numbers..."

"Guess."

"OK, say they keep having a couple of off days every week, like they are now. If that continues for a couple of weeks... God," Colton said, the last word exhaled.

"What?"

"Losses here could be as much as 70 percent of the bank's entire estimated assets. That's just if things stay the same. If it gets nastier, I don't even want to think about that. Oh, God."

"What, you worried about your friend?"

"No... well, a little, but it's not that. This was the bank that Dad used to help finance the purchase of the *Journal*. He was getting in on these mortgage securities years ago."

There was silence for a moment. "Go on."

"He used some of them as collateral for the *Journal* purchase. If something goes wrong with them, is it going to affect us?"

Colton only heard a sharp intake of breath from behind him. Finally, Gus said, "That's a very good question that we need to look into." Gus gestured for Colton to lean down toward him. "OK, you need to write up everything that you know, put a story together on this *now*. When you're done, I want to see it   don't share it or show it with anyone else, understand? That includes your dad."

"Got it."

"This is your only priority."

"I've still have those two quarterly report stories to do and some research for Sonny today, probably…"

Gus shook his head and waved him off. "You can get the quarterly earnings stories done in a half hour, tops. And I'll talk to Sonny and tell him to not bug you."

"OK."

"We need to find out what's going on – for the sake of the bank's customers and clients, as well as our own sakes. But we're going to have to proceed carefully with this. I'll have to talk with some people myself."

"Who, the business desk?"

"Not sure I'd trust Bernie over there – he's always been a little too close with upper management. Maybe Andrew Odom might be able to help. Too bad we don't have a New York bureau anymore, because it would be good to have someone who's covering The Street in person."

"I thought we had a New York bureau?"

"*Had* is the appropriate word. That closed yesterday, all but a couple correspondents scattered to the four winds."

Colton shook his head. "I'm sorry."

"What your old man does is not your fault. What you *can* do is to get this story together, understand?"

"When do you want it?"

"You can get me a first draft before you leave tonight, then we'll revise it over the next few days."

"Few days?"

"We have to be really careful with this piece, understood?"

"Understood."

Gus nodded. "OK, get going."

\*\*\*

Two minutes later, Gus walked into Sonny's office. "OK, tell me you have better news than the kid did."

"Wait, what did Colton talk to you about?"

"I'll tell you in a minute. First, let's get into what you have."

# The Holy Fool

"OK, come around here so you can see." As Gus made his way around the desk, Sonny took a long, deep breath before starting. "All right. What we have here, in both the spreadsheets and some of the memos I found, is basically a financial overview of the paper since Edson bought out the *Journal*."

"Um... how did you came across files from our CEO's computer?"

"Honestly, Gus, it'd be better..."

"...if I didn't know. OK, moving on... The good news, how about that? I don't want to get immediately depressed."

Sonny nodded. "OK, the pre-buyout numbers, then. Just a second." He started sorting out documents on the computer desktop.

"OK. So, the financials on the *Journal* looked... OK. Not crazy good, but not a disaster, either. From what I could tell, the newspaper was losing about 100K per month."

Gus laughed at that. "That's nothing. The *New York News* was losing a million dollars a month 20 years ago. That should be survivable."

"Well, you're right when you factor in the TV and other advertising revenue. But, you've got to remember that this is a company that's used to getting 40, 50 percent profit margins yearly."

Sonny shook his head as he continued. "All of those Bauer bozos owning the paper forever, they started thinking of the place as a piggybank rather than a business. And it finally fell to shit."

"Whining for the good old days isn't going to bring them back, kid," Gus growled.

"How about better days? How about a Silver Age rather than a Golden Age if our only other alternative is a Lead Age? I'd be OK with that. How about a profession that's not obsessed with making fucking profit margins over actual reporting?"

"And you have the magic solution to that? Go on, get on with it."

Sonny had been around long enough to know that comment was just Gus telling him to get to work.

"OK, so, the reasons for the losses... Subscriptions are down 45 percent from their peak in '75, classified revenue's been killed by Craigslist et al, print ads are down by 20 percent in the past 10 years. The online advertising revenue's grown threefold in the same time, but it hasn't been enough to make up for the shortfalls."

"And that leaves us..."

"Like I said, not that good, but tolerable. Basically, when Jack died, the family had the option of... how many people would be part of the family now?"

"Depends. I figure if you're counting those with voting stock, there were about... I don't know, maybe a dozen to 20 people at that time?"

"Well, they had the option of modernizing some equipment, streamlining some services, and better exploiting the Web, more than what they were doing at the time. They would have had low profit margins, but things would have been sustainable, for sure. Or, they could look for another buyer for the *Journal* and the affiliated properties."

"And guess which one they decided to go for?" Sonny continued. "Ha. Of course. Once owning the paper actually started to look like work, you know what route they'd take. Jack was the last one of them with any guts – the rest had it bred out of them."

"That's when Edson came around looking into buying JournalCorp," Gus said. "It was weird. He was a real estate guy; His main thing was flipping properties in the Midwest, building those up. No communications background except for some of those radio stations he bought into."

"Anyway," Sonny interjected, trying to get back onto some sort of schedule, "He only had a little bit of cash to help make the deal work. About 80 percent of the financing he got from transferring title of about $400 million in securities bonds to the *Journal*."

"So, that leads us to now."

"Basically, these securities are bonds backed by long-term real estate debt. But these securities are a little different from normal. They mix a wide variety of different types of loans

## The Holy Fool

into these securities, to diversify the securities. The idea is to reduce risk."

"OK, what's this number here? The one that's smaller than the estimated total debt? Is that our revenue for the year?"

"No, that's an all-asset number. Basically, that represents the total market value and assets of Edson Communications. The debt would be at least... 80 percent of that."

"That's also assuming optimal conditions," Sonny continued. "If they get into a fire sale situation where they must dump all of it, those losses would likely be greater, maybe a billion over total asset value."

Gus's eyes were frozen in position, straight ahead, as he settled into the chair and continued to stare at the computer screen. "So, this debt Michael used as collateral to buy the company, it's going bad."

"Correct."

"Total assets for the company are being dwarfed by this debt. If they collapse – they're not going to have enough cash to cover those drops. You remember Colton bugging me just now?"

"What got him all gung-ho to report today?"

"Basically this." Gus took a few minutes to fill Sonny in.

"Urrgh, are you kidding me? The entire economy's about to collapse and take down the paper with it? This is bonkers," Sonny concluded. "So, what happens next?"

"I'm having him continue to work on the story. He may not be doing as much for you..."

"Understood."

"I'm starting to wonder – you think the kid is a plant? You think maybe Edson wants him here to check up on us?"

"What, you think he's a spy?"

"I'm beginning to wonder."

Sonny shook his head. "It's too obvious a play. We're going to be careful what we say and do around him anyway. It wouldn't make sense."

"Sonny, I hate to break this to you, but most of the people in charge of this place, me included, aren't as smart as you think we are."

"So modest. No, he'd try and get someone else. Otherwise, he'd contend himself with whatever Wyatt could dig up."

"*He'll* be a problem."

"I'm beginning to wonder if I can flip Colton. He might have enough latent rage or daddy issues that we might be able to get him to our side of things. You never know."

"Be careful."

"Always."

"So, what's the answer to my question – what are you going to do with Colton's information?" Gus said.

"It's his story, isn't it?

"I'll want him to keep working on it. This will factor into whether the *Journal* stays open or not."

"Our guys are going to have to talk."

"I'll leave you to it. I've got a staff meeting now," Gus said as he eased from behind Sonny and his desk and prepared to leave.

"Aye, aye, Cap." Sonny saluted his editor's departing form.

Two minutes later, Sonny dashed into his office, but what he saw inside caused him to decelerate from speed walking to solid standing within a second.

Wyatt Walker stood behind his desk, gazing off to the side at Sonny's collection of pictures. An unknown man in a dark grey pinstripe suit occupied one of the chairs in front of the desk.

As Sonny stopped, Wyatt turned to face him. "Hey, Sonny; sorry to drop in like this." He smiled and leaned back, hands clasped behind his head. "Like the pictures here. Say, do you have a few minutes to talk?"

Sonny's gaze focused on Wyatt. "I'll talk as soon as you get out from behind my desk."

Wyatt looked Sonny up from head to toe, assessing everything, his grin slowly fading into a neutral expression. Sonny got the feeling he was trying to see how much of a threat he might be in a fight.

There was a tightness in Sonny's throat as he considered the possibilities. Sonny was more solidly built than Wyatt, but the slightly older man would be in better physical condition than him and knew more of fighting. In an open environment and space, Wyatt would mop the floor with him, but in these cramped quarters, the odds might be more even…

Wyatt snapped him out of his speculations with a quick "Sure, Sonny," and darted from behind the desk to sit in an open chair. "Sit down. I wanted to introduce you to someone I met back in Iraq, in the First Gulf War… this is FBI Special Agent Clark Heiden."

Heiden was Wyatt's age, his hair reduced to a thin sheen of grey stubble that partially covered his scalp, and pale grey eyes that tracked Sonny as he got back to his seat. The image came to Sonny's mind, unbidden, of Heiden in the robe of a Franciscan monk torturing heretics in 16th-century Spain for the Vatican. Maybe he had in a previous life.

"I'm glad to get a chance to meet with you, Mr. Turner," Heiden said. "I've read your past work."

Sonny leaned back in his chair and tried to get the eye of Spider Jerusalem on the wall for inspiration before turning his attention to the Fed. Spider would have pulled a gun or grenade at this point, but Sonny wanted to be a little subtler. "So, what are you doing here?"

"Well, in talking with John Michael, he discussed some of the work you and some of the other reporters have been doing on Operation Iraqi Freedom," Wyatt said. "Agent Heiden was on a stopover at O'Hare and we got talking. He's been helping with an investigation into possible unauthorized leaks at the Defense Department. He was wondering if you could help out." Wyatt said "help out" like he was trying to recruit Sonny for his church 18-inch softball league.

Heiden jumped in. "We were wondering if you've been in contact with certain people, either in the Defense Department, with the Pentagon staff, any private Defense Department contractors…"

"White boy, are you even fucking serious?" Sonny said in a low, even tone to Heiden.

That made Heiden sit up in his chair. "I… excuse me?"

"I'm saying, are you fucking serious with that question? You even expect me to answer it? I'm really hoping you're not that stupid."

Heiden shrugged and Sonny realized he thought it was a longshot, too. "I was a little surprised when Mr. Walker invited me down, but he said he was sure you'd be willing to help out, so..."

...*even if it's a stupid idea, even stupid ideas paid off sometimes*, Sonny thought. He got up and leaned over his desk, staring right at Heiden. "Do you or any other law enforcement agency have an arrest warrant for me right now?" he said.

Heiden fidgeted in his seat, like he didn't want to give the answer. "No."

"Do you have a search warrant for this office or any other place in this building?" Sonny said.

"...No..."

"OK. I'm sorry you wasted... wait, I could care less. Agent, I'm done talking with you. I'll ask you to find your way out." Sonny waved toward the door.

Heiden got up without argument. "Very well. Have a good day. Wyatt, good to see you again," he added, nodding to his former comrade. He turned and exited the room with almost no sound, leaving the door open.

After Heiden left, Wyatt turned back to Sonny. "Look, Sonny..."

"You might want to close my door right now," Sonny said, his voice still low but losing an effort to stay in control. "You probably are not going to want all them to hear what I have to say."

"Sonny..."

"Am I stuttering at all? Think about it."

The last sentence appeared to take that last bit of bluff out of Wyatt. He closed the door and took Agent Haiden's now vacant seat.

Before Wyatt said anything, Sonny plunged ahead. "I have no idea whether you know what, exactly, a journalism organization is supposed to do, or if you just don't care. And right now, I could actually care less."

"Sonny... there's a lot of guys that are shopping around top-secret intelligence all over the place, for whatever reason, usually to embarrass their bosses or make some sort of statement. Reporting is one thing, but revealing top-secret information is something else."

"Who put you up to this? Richard? Cathy? John Michael?" Wyatt stayed silent.

"Let me try and explain this at a fifth-grade level, like they teach us to do back in J-school, right?" Sonny continued, not adding *so you could comprehend it, dumbass*. "Journalists don't write what other people want them to write. They write what the truth is. Almost anybody who wants us to write "the truth," they really want us to lie our asses off for them. We're not supposed to protect the powerful, we have to make them nervous. People in government want to classify everything they do, their fuckups most of all."

"And *you're* the one to judge that, not the people Americans elected to lead them?" Wyatt shot back.

"If you want to go back to work for the government, OK," Sonny pointed at Wyatt. "But I don't, and you're not welcome back in here."

"I beg your pardon?" Wyatt drew himself up to his full height.

"You're not fucking deaf, *mano*. I don't see you in this office, my office, ever again, unless you're escorting me off the premises or escorting cops in here with a warrant. And maybe you should think about whether this is the right business for you to be working for."

There was a long, uncomfortable moment as Wyatt stood still that Sonny thought he might have to force Wyatt to leave, and he didn't want to think about what was going to happen. Finally, Wyatt said, the words sounding like a snarl, "You should probably think about whether this is the right business for yourself." With that, he exited the room and shut the door with a bang.

Sonny leaned back in his chair, closed his eyes, and counted to what he believed was a whole minute in his head. When he was finished, he leaped out of his chair and headed straight out of his office and toward the City/Metro desk, now combined under Gus's leadership due to the cuts.

Gus was standing over Harry Read at his desk and was talking to him, possibly about another story, but Sonny could not care less. "Gus, need to talk."

"In a minute, Sonny. I'm working out this thing with Harry," Gus said, calm and undisturbed. He immediately turned back to Harry.

Sonny closed his eyes and fought every instinct in him to yell. His response came out in the same manner as Gus, instead: "I have to ask you a question, and how you answer it is going to tell me whether I can trust you again or not."

That got Gus to get back up and face Sonny. Excitability about work was a Sonny trait, but he rarely did ultimatums. "Go ahead." Gus remained calm.

"Did you have anything to do with, or have any knowledge of, Wyatt Walker bringing a Fed in to my office and asking if I knew any classified leakers?"

Gus's skin turned a darker shade of grey, and he even grabbed a corner of one of the nearby cubicles. There was a long, shuddering sigh as he seemed to flash between horror and disbelief. "What...? Are you serious?"

Relief flooded through Sonny as he realized he had nothing to do with it. "Yes. This actually happened. It went down two minutes ago in my room. What the hell is Wyatt doing?"

"Harry, just a second, OK?" Gus recovered himself enough to gesture to Sonny to come to a spare desk away from the rest of the City/Metro cubicle farm and sit down next to him. "How did this happen? Could he know about the I-Project?"

"Does he know? Maybe not. Could he know? Hell, yes."

"How did he find out about it?"

"I've been encrypting. So, someone said something."

"What? You think I..."

Sonny shook his head. "I'm thinking someone a little higher up than us."

"Higher up... Edson."

"Or Cathy or Richard, yes. More likely Edson. Wyatt always seems to be report directly to Edson, as his right-hand man."

"So, this was Edson's idea?"

"Or maybe he just wondered out loud whether someone would get rid of a bothersome priest."

Gus rubbed his eyes and shaking his head for a moment. "Look, as much as I think we need to wait on the story, I don't like the idea of giving this up to anyone. What did you say to the Fed?"

"Nothing except to fuck off."

"You... shit, are you serious?"

"Not in so many words. I did ask him if he was fucking serious at one point."

"Goddamn Wyatt, still thinks he's some government agent or something."

"Or something. OK, I've got stuff to do. Later."

"Talk soon."

\*\*\*

The *Journal* reporters who had to use cars either to get to work or to move around during the workday invariably parked at a lot two blocks south of the Keep. There were about 12 levels of rectangular block parking for workers at the *Journal* as well as some neighboring businesses. To avoid Superfan, The Gentleman, and who knows who else, Sonny took the trouble of hitching a ride in one of the delivery vans leaving the paper that morning, then slid out of a side door after hitting a few intersections.

TT was waiting at one corner of the garage in the most anonymous late model grey Lexus possible. The motor was running as Sonny, wearing big sunglasses and a navy Bears hat, eased himself into the front passenger seat. The minute Sonny belted himself in, TT shifted into park and glided out.

"You know where Carlton's is, right?" Sonny said.

"Not that I ever ate there, but... yeah, I know it," TT said.

"OK, if we know it, let's go to it."

As they motored out of the parking lot, TT nodded in the direction of a black camera bag on the floor next to Sonny. "You know how to use one of those, right?"

"Seriously?" As TT drove on, Sonny unlatched the straps holding the bag closed. He pulled out a solid black Canon full-sized digital camera with a heavy zoom lens. "All charged up?"

"And with an empty memory card, too. We should be good to go."

As Sonny continued to check the camera and they pulled up to a stoplight, TT turned to face Sonny. "OK, these are the rules for the car, OK? I am in charge of this operation, not you, to ensure its safety. Understood?"

Sonny finished his inspection and turned to TT. "I bow down to your kick-ass skills in the dark arts of information gathering."

"OK. If someone must tail this guy on foot, up close, that's going to be me and me only. John Michael isn't familiar with me. You have any idea where he's going to park when he gets there?"

"They've got valet parking right next to it."

"Any security?"

"Yeah, plus cameras."

"Shit." TT groaned. "OK, here goes."

They saw the Carlton down the street. Even in the early morning, cars lined the few precious street-side parking spots.

"Here's how we play this. We're going past this place and down a block. I'll get out there. You take over driving and continue to drive around for a while, no more than two blocks away."

"Got it," Sonny said.

"I've got a laser mike and recorder with me – it's smaller and not as good as the bigger models, but I should be able to hear something. Once he gets going, you pick me up."

"OK, got it."

"I want to get a bug onto his car, but we'll have to wait for that."

As TT tumbled from the front seat and ran-limped to the sidewalk, Sonny ducked out of the passenger's seat, circled around the front of the vehicle, and eased the still-running car down the road.

It took Sonny 10 minutes to find a parking spot two blocks away from the restaurant. After he fed the meter and got back into the car, he found his cell phone playing the tune "Fortunate Son," by Credence Clearwater Revival. "Colton, how are things?"

"Hey, Sonny. Just wanted to update you on the UUF story."

"Sure, go ahead." Sonny belted in.

"Last night I got in contact with Ty Polanski, the other guy with UUF's risk management team. Sort of helpful, mostly confirmed what Zach talked to us about last Wednesday."

"OK. Just remember, whatever him and the rest bring to us, only you, Gus and I see it."

"I know, I know. See you."

"Bye."

Sonny tucked his phone into his coat pocket but heard "Dream Police" ring from the phone. "Yeah, TT?"

"Pick me up on the south end of the building. Looks like John Michael's on the move."

Sonny made it there in less than two minutes. "Where are they headed?" he asked as TT slid into the passenger's seat.

"You see the car, right?"

"Yeah, the black Toyota limo, right?"

"Right. Go, go, go!"

As Sonny eased into traffic and followed the limo three cars behind, he turned his attention back to TT. "You have any idea where he's off to?"

"He mentioned some place called Maximum Performance. You know what that is?"

"Private health club over on the Gold Coast. He's a member over there."

"Well, no wonder the man looks so good."

"Whatever."

"So, what's the parking situation over there?"

"There's a parking garage to the north side of the club building. They share it with a couple of other businesses. Most of their parking is on the top of the ramp. It's minimal security - I don't even think they have cameras."

"Solid. Once he parks and gets to working out, we'll be in business."

Jason Liegois

\*\*\*

It had been an hour since TT had parked the car as far away from the limo as possible but remain within sight of it. Sonny heard another ringtone. "TT?"

"Yeah, I'm in the restaurant. I see John Michael and... huh, it's just Cathy with him. It looks like they're both in workout clothes; John's carrying a racquetball bag with him."

"Do you think you should be talking right now?"

"No, my talking isn't going to mess up the laser mike – it's pointed at them, not me. My hidden camera's working as well."

"Good for you. You get the bug on the car?"

"No problems – right under the steering column. Sonny, I've got a question. Is all of this actually going to accomplish anything?"

"Honestly? We're probably fucked. But we've got to keep trying, right?"

"Yeah, doing nothing doesn't come natural to me."

\*\*\*

"So, be honest. You think John and Cathy are doing each other?"

It was the first question Sonny asked TT as they sat down in the Wrigleyville bar just a block from the home of the Cubs. Cubs memorabilia covered so much of the walls it was sometimes difficult to see the wood paneling.

TT stole one of Sonny's fries as he considered the question. "Maybe. The way they talked with each other, it was intimate. Whether they just flirting for fun or was there more to it, I couldn't say. The other thing I noticed is when they left the restaurant, it almost looked like they were going to the same locker room area. I couldn't tell for sure, because it would have been too risky to try and sneak back there."

"What about business talk?"

"That was interesting." TT stole another fry and dunking it in a ketchup bowl. "Cathy sounds like she has a good portion of Edson Media stock herself."

"Not a surprise. How's she feels about a possible sale?"

"Actually, she's very interested in it. She appears to believe John Michael should sell the entire company to a bidder or set of bidders. Melchester's interested in the papers, and maybe the Chicago radio and TV, but the rest he could take or leave. John Michael seems to think maybe they should just get rid of the papers and keep the rest."

"Good. We need *any* bit of information, cause information is leverage. When it comes to saving the paper, we are *not doing this thing* by the book. This is about survival, pure and simple, and it won't be like they taught me at Northwestern."

\*\*\*

"Fuck, how far north are we going, Wisconsin?" Sonny and TT had followed John Michael for a half-hour through midday Chicago traffic as his car wandered further and further north. "At least we're taking the lakefront route, I guess," Sonny continued.

TT laughed at that, then suddenly leaned forward over the wheel. "Look, he's turning. Where is he headed...?"

"Loyola Park? That's the only thing I can think of over in that area."

"Getting some rays?"

"Maybe catching Cathy in a bikini."

"Fuck that," TT replied, waving Sonny off.

\*\*\*

"Christ, he's not worried about getting sand all over his Guccis," Sonny said.

Sonny and TT had parked a dozen cars down from John Michael's car. TT had a pair of binoculars out and tracking him walking onto the beach while Sonny wrestled with the telephoto lens. "At least he ditched the tie," TT said.

"Funny. But what the hell's he doing here?"

"Mellowing out? Anyway... wait." TT leaned forward again in his seat. "I'm seeing something. You seeing something?"

"Yeah." Sonny watched as John Michael, his jacket thrown over his back and another hand shading his eyes, started to walk toward a woman in a gold bikini who was putting sunscreen on a girl in a pink Minnie Mouse swimsuit.

"OK, I've got John. You zero in on the lady. Shit, it's not Cathy, is it?"

Sonny zoomed in and focused on her. "Blond, but no. This one's younger, mid-twenties, maybe."

John smiled as he got closer to the woman. "Get ready to shoot when he gets there," TT said, his voice tight and soft.

"All set," Sonny said. "You don't think... ahh." His camera shutter erupted in a dozen clicks.

What Sonny shot was John stopping in front of the woman and baby's towel, laying down his jacket, and in a single motion picking up the child and enveloping her in a tight hug. After a few moments, he sat her back down by the woman, leaned over to her, and they kissed for several seconds before he sat down next to her.

"Whatever the living holy fuck," Sonny breathed. "You seeing this bullshit?"

"You shooting this bullshit?" TT responded. Sonny responded with more shutter clicks.

From the angle they were at, it appeared that John was watching the little girl build a sand castle. He appeared to be talking to her as he shed his shoes and socks.

"You ever seen this woman before?"

"Never. Does she look like someone who works at Edson?"

Sonny shook his head. "Nobody that I ever remember seeing. How are we handling this?"

"We stay on the girl. We can pick John Michael back up with the bug."

The trio hung out on the nearly deserted beach for another half hour. At the end of it, he gave the woman and the little girl kisses, got his shoes on, and headed toward his car. The woman put on a white cover-up, packed up her towel and swim bag, and carefully balanced the little girl on her hip as she walked off the beach.

"All right. John Michael's pulling out. He's not seeing us. Stay on the girls."

"Got them, getting close-ups. They're coming this way... No, they're stopping six cars away from us. They're getting in the Mercedes, see?"

"Which one?"

"The grey one, the four door."

"She see us?"

"No."

"*Bueno*. Make sure you get shots of the license plates."

The woman fired up the car and pulled out of her stall. After another series of clicks, Sonny spoke up, "Got it, Illinois plates," then rattled off the number. "What next?"

"We follow the mystery family."

\*\*\*

The mystery family led Sonny and TT to a historic old brownstone in the Lincoln Park district of Chicago, between the beach and the Loop. "This lady has to have access to some *cash*," Sonny commented after writing down her address when they passed in front of it. "Most of the condos around here average $2 million easy."

"So, the question is whether John's giving her all that cash, or if she's getting it from somewhere else..."

"Or both."

TT sighed, the creases of his face deepening in the growing shadows of the coming evening. "This is fucked up for more than one family."

"We don't know for sure what we're seeing. But yeah, this sucks." Sonny sank into his seat as TT circled the block.

"Now you're getting a conscience?"

"This shouldn't be easy, otherwise I'd know that I was really fucked up."

As they got back within sight of the house, they saw a woman in her fifties, dark-haired, elegant, and slim, hug the woman. As the older woman walked into the house with the toddler, the younger woman hopped into her car.

"Grandmother babysitting?" TT said.

"I've got shots of her, too," Sonny said. "Tailing the woman, again?"

"Yeah, but I have a feeling I know where she's going."

*\*\*\**

*The Drake Hotel,* Sonny said to himself. *Sure, why not?*

It was one of those Chicago institutions, an 88-year-old khaki stone icon from the days when they built specialty destination hotels and Super 8's were only an illusion. Sonny sat in a nearby Michigan Avenue parking garage. The mystery woman's car was 12 cars away from him; Sonny had followed the valet parker into the ramp while TT had trailed her as she walked into the hotel.

He'd been there for an hour in the garage when he saw a text from TT:

Get over here now; fifth floor elevators. Bring all your gear.

Within 10 minutes he was inside the hotel, avoiding eye contact with the front desk and making a direct line to the elevator. When the doors opened on the fifth floor, TT was standing there waiting for him. "What happened?"

TT was fiddling with his own camera. "Come here, look at this," TT said, gazing down both ends of the hallway to make sure no one was present.

There was a series of photos showing the woman entering one of the suites with a key card. "She didn't see you?" Sonny said.

"I know how to sneak, brother," TT replied.

There was a second series of photos showing John Michael walking down the same hallway, knocking on the same doorway, and seeing the door open and the mystery woman poking her head through the doorway. Smiling, she took John Michael by the hand and drew him into the room, closing the door. "Shoot," Sonny said.

"OK, go ahead and get your laptop out."

"Excuse me?"

"I want more than just me to have a copy of these pics."

"Got it." Sonny eased his laptop out and began to go to work, sitting down in the middle of the floor.

# The Holy Fool

As Sonny worked, TT said, "Once you get all this stuff, get home, and make sure to copy it over, understood?"

"You don't want me here to keep you company?"

"Nah, I've got this. I'm staying here to see when or if John Michael's heading home tonight. After that gets done, we'll start tracking down who the woman is and go from there."

"All right."

\*\*\*

Later that evening, Sonny took the stairs up to Joey's apartment. After she unlocked all four door locks, Joey swung the door open to greet him. "Hey."

"Hey yourself."

She was wearing a grey garage mechanic's coveralls, black Chuck Taylors, and had her head covered with a white bandanna. An assortment of paints and crafting glue covered her. Joey, who had worked up an obvious sweat in the near past, waved Sonny into her studio area, where she was putting the final touches on her Rome display and a couple of other works.

"So, your text seemed a little bit weird this afternoon," Joey said as she rearranged some of her supplies and began to get out some packing boxes to move the displays. "Can you tell me what's going on?"

Sonny hesitated for a moment, but blurted, "Not too much, just ruining one, two family's lives, maybe," as he plopped onto a stool. Before he knew it, he'd recounted the entire tale of the tail.

"God, what he's doing to his wife, Colton, even." Joey sat down on one of her work benches. "What are you going to do?"

"As desperate as we're getting, it's going to be leverage. I don't like saying this, but anything we can use to is something we have to consider using."

As she cleaned her hands off with a WD-40 covered rag, Joey thought for a moment. "Leverage on him? Why not go directly to his wife?"

"Diane? I've maybe seen her once around at company parties. Never talked with her myself. She seems like she's always going around somewhere else…"

"She keeps busy with a lot of charities around town, but her big thing is art. She's a big patron of a lot of the downtown galleries…"

"Yeah?"

She shook her head. "I don't talk much about my art at the office, except for you. I wonder if Diane might be interested in attending a show by one of her husband's employees? It might be a chance for you to run into her, give her the news."

"You sure about this?"

"Well, I'm not happy about her finding out about her husband, but that's John Michael's fault. She'll find out about it eventually; why not let it do some good?"

"Do you think she'll come?"

"I know one of the dealers she works with here in Chicago. Let me reach out to her and see what might happen. You mind hanging out here, helping me clean up?"

"When did I ever mind hanging out with you?"

## Chapter 8.

With his usual tails in tow, Sonny made it to work early Friday morning. Instead of the newsroom, he took an isolated staircase from the ground floor to the lowest subbasement of the Keep, down to his and Woot's secret war room.

Woot was seated in front of a desktop PC that joined two other desktops on two tables arranged in a T-shape. A single fluorescent track light illuminated the tables. Woot faced the doorway but did not look up as Sonny entered.

"Freeze, security," Sonny said so quietly it was an obvious goof, but Woot continued to work at his station. "Really, not even a single fuck given?"

"I saw you on the outside cameras."

Sonny took a seat behind another computer. He noticed another row of desktop hard drive cases lined up in a row on one of the tables, away from the others. "Where's their monitors?"

"That's the server farm," Woot said. "Once I get the air conditioning set for those tonight, I'll get it up and running."

That got a laugh from Sonny. "Hell, you *love* this. You really love this, don't you?"

Woot leaned back in his chair. "You've got an idea that I was a little nuts in my youth..."

"You're only 25, Woot."

"...It was kiddy-scripting at first, but not for long. I wound up getting interrogated by the FBI and got probation, but I thought it was a lot easier than dealing with the drama around my parents. I finally figured out that they'd never get back together, so that ended that.

"But there was some other thinking behind it, ideas about information flowing freely and powerful people shouldn't be keeping secrets. It's why I dug your writing, what you had to say. Doing all of this, it's like hacking, but righteous hacking, you know? I couldn't pass it up."

"I appreciate it. OK, where are we on the electronic monitoring?"

"I've gotten access to John Michael's phone via the wireless setup in his office. I'm in the process of getting Cathy and Richard's phones hacked too. I've got access to the security system already, but I'm ducking in and out to make sure Wyatt's boys don't catch on. Finally, I have one of the cleaning staff who's quitting next week to move down to New Mexico with her family to plant a listening device under John Michael's desk and the executive conference room."

"We'll be able to listen to all of that?"

"No problem; we're tied into the fiber optic connections down here."

Woot looked over at one of the monitors. "Ah, TT is here." On cue, TT came into the room after using his own card.

Sonny acknowledged him with a wave. "OK, where are we at?"

TT opened his laptop from his bag. There were a series of photos, the same ones TT took on Friday of the mystery woman, both in the bikini at the beach and headed into the hotel. At the end were four photos of the same woman, in a KWCN polo shirt and jeans, at a KWCN live broadcast from some music festival in Grant Park.

"Shit, we just hit the jackpot, didn't we?" Sonny said.

"Meet Jenni Hardin," TT said. "Twenty-eight years old, originally from the Lincoln Park area. Her father owns a real-estate agency, mom works part-time there, used to be a Realtor herself."

"So, what does Jenni do for our sister radio station, then?" Sonny asked.

"She's in charge of public relations and special promotions," TT said. "Started with an internship the year before she graduated from Illinois-Urbana."

"I bet," Sonny said. "Christ, this is just so clichéd when you think about it."

# The Holy Fool

"It tends to be that way," Woot said. "One of the things I've noticed is, he always seems to be thinking of work, even when he's having a good time."

Sonny turned himself to stare at Woot. "Pretty insightful for someone spending more time around machines than people."

"Oh, I communicate with people all the time; I just use machines to do it. That's the difference."

"Well, cheers, then," Sonny said. He turned back to TT. "I honestly hate to say this, but do we have any ID on her kid?"

TT nodded and tapped a couple of more buttons, and a document flashed onto the big screen. "Found a birth certificate for Caity Hardin, born 7/10/2007 at University of Illinois Hospital in Chicago. Jenni's listed as the mother, no father listed."

"That's going to be difficult to prove. Short of going over to Hardin's place and getting some saliva off the kid's juice cup, that is," Sonny said.

"I'm probably going to have more luck with the financials," TT said. "We'll have to find out how much he's been sending her."

"Who's going to do that?" Sonny said.

"Partly me, partly TT," Woot said. "He's going to check out the public records, leases, etc., while I keep trying to peek into his calls and e-mails."

"OK. I'm actually thinking about presenting all of this to John Michael's wife," Sonny said. "This might give her incentive to screw him over, which would be helpful since she's a part-owner, too."

"You know anything about her?" TT said.

"Did my own digging on that. Diana and John Michael met each other at Harvard University and married just after he got his MBA there."

"She got an MBA too? Or a MRS?" Woot said.

"MSW, actually," Sonny replied. "She's been active with many of the social action organizations in Chicago, on the boards of many of them, also very active with the arts. You think you guys can have all of that about Jenni and the kid ready by tomorrow?"

145

Woot and TT turned to stare at each other, then turned again to face Sonny and nodded. "We can do it," TT said to Sonny.

"OK. Now we've got to take this to the boys."

# Chapter 9.

Sonny was glad that there didn't seem to be that much traffic around the Denny's Friday night. It was part of one of the commercial strips through Oak Park, one of the older Chicago suburbs, charming enough that Frank Lloyd Wright built homes and raised a family he deserted there and where Hemmingway would grow up and want to leave as soon as possible.

As he pulled into the lot, Sonny hit a number on his cell phone. "Hey," he heard Joey say.

"Hey. I got your text a bit ago. You said that Diana Edson's coming to the show?"

"She called me. She's excited about seeing what I'm going to have up tomorrow. She might actually buy a canvas from me."

"Great."

"There's a 'but' in there. She said she's bringing Edson down with her. Can you believe that?"

"It'll work – we'll make it work."

"Diana sounds like a nice lady. She was going on about being supportive of staff and the *Journal* family and all of that."

"Right as her husband's planning to sell the place out from under our feet. Maybe he got talked into it because he wanted to meet a young *female* artist that works for him."

"Oh, you really think he's that shallow?"

"The guy's seeing two women on the side; why not keep his eye on others?"

"Oh, great." He could hear her exhale a deep sigh over the phone. "Actually, if I distract him, he's more likely not to notice you talking to his wife."

"You'd agree to do that?"

"You're not asking me to sleep with him, right?"

"No."

Jason Liegois

"Then it's not a problem. Not sure if it will work."
"Why?"
"From what you said, I'm probably not his type."
"He doesn't know what he's missing. Let's just make sure that everything's set up for tomorrow and the rest will take care of itself."
"The perils of art."

Sonny hung up. As he exited his car, he saw Woot sitting out in the lobby, stretched out on one of the benches, wearing a rust-colored T-shirt with an Atari 2600 controller on the front and the words OLD SCHOOL below. "Hey, bro," Woot said, waving as he got up, "I was waiting for you."

"Everyone else here?"
"Most all of the important guys. We ready to get this thing started?"
"Yeah."

After they entered, Woot led Sonny to a group of tables shoved together in an isolated corner of the Denny's. A dozen or so people, the heart of the growing conspiracy, were there.

Bill Goldstein was at the head of one of the tables. He represented the Newspaper Guild members at the paper, still a sizable force at the *Journal* despite the decline in union membership, especially among the newsroom staff.

A burly, balding man in a blue work shirt with OSCAR above the left pocket, sat next to them, nursing a coffee with the subtlest hint of black on his fingers. Oscar Johnson was the main print production supervisor, the head of the new print facility in the west suburbs, and another Guild member. Johnson had built his own little fiefdom up during the past 20 years and wanted to preserve it at all costs.

There were some other faces he knew there, including Damien Coster and Andrew Odom, the newly minted National/Foreign Affairs editor, a Polish bulldog, an ill-mannered, gruff grinder who wore cheap suits and was happily unmarried but who provided the best national coverage the *Journal* had in a generation with half of the staff. At the head of the table was a familiar face.

"Hey, Gus," Sonny said as he took a seat next to him and started to scan the menu.

"Hm," Gus grunted, finishing off a cup of coffee and immediately reaching over to the pot sitting on the table for a refill. "Well, after our little conversation earlier today, I figured that I should be around when we let everybody else know what's going on."

"Well, OK." Sonny said, his attention now turned to the menu.

After deciding who was eating what, Gus spoke up. "I don't want you to think that I'm trying to take charge here, or that I want to boss anyone around," he began. "Bill and the union have been working very hard on trying to get a handle on what's been going on with the paper. Sonny, TT, and... Woot..." – he stumbled a bit with having to use Jeff's preferred name – "have been doing the same thing, and I know there have been other individual efforts. The point I'm making, is we have to start coordinating our efforts and come up with a unified plan to deal with what's coming up."

"I had friends in the printer's unions in New York, guys who go back to the 60's," Oscar volunteered. "I remember their stories about how they never expected their papers could die until it was too late. I don't want that happening to the *Journal* – I'm not going to allow it if I and my brothers and sisters can do anything about. If anyone has a plan, we're all listening." He leaned back and crossed his arms over his chest.

Sonny now leaned forward. "Gus is right," he said. "We need a unified strategy. From everything that we know, there isn't too much time left."

"Like how much time?" Andrew asked.

Woot answered for him. "Three weeks, at best. It'll probably be shorter than that."

"*We've* got three weeks, says the contractor," Bill said.

"Listen, this guy cares about this paper and the people who work here, and we're probably going to need his skills to get it done, so you may want to chill out right now," Gus said, his voice low, even, and controlled, trying to prevent himself from screaming at Bill.

Bill leaned back, hands up in surrender. "OK, ok, my mistake," he said with a smile and the hint of a joke.

"Thank you, Daddy, for not arguing in front of the kids," Sonny replied.

"Sonny, you talked to me about how you had some additional information about management plans," Gus interrupted.

"Yeah." Sonny obliged, adding in the additional info from Colton.

"I've got a question," Oscar said when Sonny finished. "The kid… how much does he know about what's going on with us?"

"Other than what he's shared with us, nothing," Sonny replied. "Right now, I want to keep him in the dark, but he is a good source of information."

"Fuck, he's John Michael's boy," Andrew said, shaking his head. "How do we know he's not going to eventually go to his old man and break up this party?"

"First of all, all of us in this room are going to keep operational security, not gossip about this like the pack of bitchy reporters we usually are," Sonny said. "Second, he's working directly with Gus and myself. We can see what he does, who he talks to."

"OK, he might be safe for now," Oscar said. "What about later?"

"I'm getting a closer look into John Michael's personal life. There might be something in there that might let us make more use of Colton."

That earned Sonny a surprised expression from everyone except Woot at the table, but they collectively discovered their poker faces again. "Fine," Bill said.

"So, the *Journal*'s looking for a buyer so that they can get the cash to cover themselves," Sonny concluded. "They want to do it quickly and quietly, before their investments go in the toilet."

"OK," Bill said. "What we have to ask ourselves is what can be done about it?"

There was a long silence at the table as the men and women around it suddenly found their coffee and dinner fascinating rather than that question.

## The Holy Fool

Damien Coster raised his hand to get everyone's attention. "I might be a bit naïve here, but would a new owner necessarily be a bad thing right at this moment?"

Gus chuckled at that but nodded his head. "Yeah, I know kid," he said, "it sometimes seems like anyone could do the job better than John Michael's crew, as tone-deaf as they are."

"Ah, I'm the computer expert here, and not the business expert," Woot began, "but the problem is that whoever the new owner is, they're going to have to deal with all of the current debt load."

"Woot's right," Sonny said. "To prevent the paper from going belly-up immediately, a new owner'll slash operations to the bone and beyond. The *Journal* will be a ghost."

There was another silence around the table. Then, Oscar finally spoke up. "So, what are we talking about here? A strike? I know we have to do something that will get their attention, but I've got the feeling that they're not going to give a shit."

"True," Gus said.

"Yeah, I agree," Sonny replied. "The union's not going to get anything done that way. I've been thinking about... well, *plan* is stretching it a little, I'll admit. It's a ghost of an idea."

Bill tipped back his chair over and over as he listened. Finally, he said, "OK, Sonny. Please feel free to bless us with this ghost you have."

"There's a very small chance of having an out." Sonny paused for a moment to fill his coffee cup and have a drink. "I've noticed this about people with a lot of money. The thing that hurts them more than anything else is <u>separating</u> them from their money. But, do you know what's the one thing that makes them willing to get separated from money?"

"Something that crushes their enemies, drives them before them, and brings on the lamentation of their women?" Woot piped up out of nowhere. Everybody had to stare at him for a moment.

"Ahhhh... yeah," Sonny said. "However, I've noticed the only way rich people will accept losing their money is to avoid losing an even bigger amount of their money. And that's the key to making this work."

"What are you talking about, Sonny?" Gus said.

Until right then, Sonny wasn't exactly sure what the main plan was. Then he remembered something about what Ed had said to him on his first day on the job, about the *Journal* being a fighting paper. It spilled out of him in a few sentences.

\*\*\*

Everyone sat around the table, staring as what Sonny had just thrown onto it. Sonny was relieved when he saw Woot nodding, but not so much the ear-to-ear grin as if he could visualize the chaos he was about to help create.

"Christ, I'm not sure about this," Andrew said.

"If we do nothing, we'll be out of a job anyway," Sonny shot back.

Bill chuckled at that. "OK. Hoffa would admire your balls, kid. How does this start?"

Sonny nodded. "We'll look for any further information about the *Journal* and USA Unlimited's finances. Any background about how the *Journal* got into this situation, and what their pet bank's situation is, is going to help us out."

"We're also increasing surveillance on John Michael and certain senior executives," Woot said. "We need to know if there's any additional information about them and their personal finances that might explain why John Michael is looking for a new buyer."

"And, you two are coordinating all of that?" Bill said.

"Basically," Sonny said.

"Who else do you have working on this?" Damien said.

"A couple of other people; TT, like we said…"

"Glad you're listening to me for once," Gus said, cracking a smile for the first time that night.

"Yeah. Casey Barnes over in the DC bureau, for example. People we can trust."

"I love my job, love this paper, and I've done plenty over the years to make sure it kept going." Gus said, turning to face everyone around the table as he was speaking. "Now, it means working on our own to protect it. I'm not comfortable with it, but it's not something I can walk away from."

# The Holy Fool

"Well, daaaamn," Sonny said. "Looks like you decided you want to be the chairman, then."

"Chairman of what?"

"The committee, of course," Sonny said. "We'll call this The Committee to Preserve the Journal, CPJ for short."

As Gus shook his head in disbelief, Woot added, "Since we're going all 70's Parallax View/All the President's Men here, we decided we might as well go whole hog."

"I thought this was a Woodward and Bernstein-style operation," Gus said.

"Nah, acting like Nixon's a lot more fun."

Gus cackled. "OK."

"Great," Sonny continued. "So, you're chairman, Billy's vice-chair and head of the Union Subcommittee, Oscar's in charge of the Newspaper Operations Subcommittee, I'll head up the Intelligence Subcommittee, and Woot will chair the Technology Subcommittee. I'm sure we can make everyone here chairman of something or another."

"And yet, to make it work, we have to keep as many staffers in the dark as possible," Damien said.

"Yeah, one of several contradictions about this whole mess," Sonny said.

\*\*\*

The meeting finally broke up. Only Sonny and Gus remained at the table, coffee cups and piled dishes between them.

After a while, Gus stared into Sonny's eyes. "OK, I've got one last question."

"Shoot."

"Do you think we can make this bullshit you spewed out actually work?"

"If you have a better option, I'd agree to it in heartbeat."

"I don't. You didn't answer the question."

Sonny grew sober; he gazed out of the big picture window behind them before he turned his attention back to Gus. "It's going to be difficult, not impossible."

"I'll take that."

Jason Liegois

\*\*\*

As Sonny began to get ready for bed later that night, he looked around his room, with the simple mattress stuck into an old waterbed frame. He thought to himself; *This room is just so... white. Like no decoration around at all.* It was right then that he realized he missed staying with Joey.

He realized there was a buzzing from his cellphone next to his bed. As he picked it up, he saw an alert on the screen:

hewoman98 alert.

With that, he strode over to the small desk in his bedroom where his laptop sat. He had a very good idea what the conversation was going to be like, and he wasn't looking forward to it.

After booting up the computer, engaging his Tor program and the proxies, he accessed the IRC room that had prompted the alert. As the chat room screen came up, he saw this message:

\<hewoman98\>you there?
Sonny took a deep breath, then typed in:
\<SonnyT76\>Right here. What's up?
\<hewoman98\>Wondering what's going on. You got everything I sent, right?
\<SonnyT76\>Yes
\<SonnyT76\>everything's there
\<SonnyT76\>Haven't had too much time to go through everything, but I've started.
\<hewoman98\>Good to know
\<hewoman98\>but im wondering what the point iS?
\<SonnyT76\>Excuse me?
\<hewoman98\>You've been getting all of this inside information
\<hewoman98\>But you haven't done anything with it.
\<SonnyT76\>Not true, I've been putting together stories on it.
\<hewoman98\>that haven't gotten printed.
\<SonnyT76\>They will get printed.
\<hewoman98\>I keep hearing that but seeing nothing.

## The Holy Fool

\<hewoman98\>You want this to keep going on, or don't you care if the war stops or not?
\<SonnyT76\>I do care
\<SonnyT76\>I'm working on my editors to see if they'll change their mind
\<SonnyT76\>It would help if I had this list of people, other sources that you've been talking about.
\<hewoman98\>I want you to know, it's not like I know these people personally IRL, just OL exclusively.
\<hewoman98\>I can tell you really want this list, don't you?
Sonny found himself mopping his brow with his T-shirt before he could type his answer.
\<SonnyT76\>Absolutely.
\<hewoman98\>So, you have the press and I have the info. Seems like this is where I have to make a deal.
\<SonnyT76\>What are you talking about?
\<hewoman98\>I want the pieces we've discussed published, and I want them to be in the paper soon. I don't want this to be going out to people who aren't going to use it.
\<hewoman98\>That doesn't happen, I go, take my list with me, and start shopping this around to other news organizations. So, you lose me and my other potential sources.
\<SonnyT76\>Are you kidding? After what I've tried to do to help you out?
\<hewoman98\>Talk is just talk. I'm looking for action. Are you the person who will give me that action?
\<SonnyT76\>I will.
\<hewoman98\>Is that A promise? I've got a deadline in mind.
\<hewoman98\>You should know what that is
\<hewoman98\>A time by which you get things done.
\<SonnyT76\>OK
\<SonnyT76\>What deadline do you have in mind?
Sonny waited for two minutes before the answer popped up.
\<hewoman98\>I was thinking Patriots' Day. How about that? Both a reasonable amount of time and a symbolic date.
\<SonnyT76\>Patriot's Day?
\<hewoman98\>Sept 11
\<hewoman98\>that's what they've named it, anyway

&lt;hewoman98&gt;I keep wondering which stores will start offering Patriot Day sales
&lt;hewoman98&gt;My moneys on Wal-Mart
&lt;SonnyT76&gt;I can't guarantee I'd get it done by then.
&lt;hewoman98&gt;Too bad for you, then.
&lt;SonnyT76&gt;I'm asking for an additional week to get it done.
&lt;hewoman98&gt;I'll give you an xtra day, but that's it.
Sonny leaned back in his chair and cradled the back of his head with his hands for some time.
&lt;SonnyT76&gt;This would count if I published online or in print?
&lt;hewoman98&gt;yes
&lt;SonnyT76&gt;If it publishes at 11, 11:59 p.m. for next day's issue?
&lt;hewoman98&gt;Yes, if you provide proof.
&lt;SonnyT76&gt;Via dead drop?
&lt;hewoman98&gt;Yes. My reply will be to your dead drop and include what you requested.
&lt;SonnyT76&gt;OK
&lt;hewoman98&gt;Is that your promise, your deal?
&lt;SonnyT76&gt;Yes
&lt;hewoman98&gt;OK, then. I agree
&lt;SonnyT76&gt;Great.
&lt;hewoman98&gt;Remember, if it's 12:01 on Sat the 13, I'm gone for good.
&lt;SonnyT76&gt;Understood. You can trust me.
&lt;hewoman98&gt;Trust doesn't really come into this.
&lt;hewoman98&gt;Either you come thru
&lt;hewoman98&gt;Or you don't
&lt;SonnyT76&gt;Understood.
&lt;hewoman98&gt;Keep track of the calendar. Bye.
&lt;SonnyT76&gt;Bye.

Sonny logged off. *One week,* he thought, staring at the calendar on his computer.

## Chapter 10

Sonny had been to a couple of art shows before. As a kid, his mom had dragged him out to some exhibits at the museums in Des Moines when they lived. He'd had a girlfriend or two drag him out for a date to the art shows in Iowa City, then to the Art Institute in Chicago.

The Dark Arts gallery was a 1930's bank abandoned for many years before artists looking for cheap areas to work came around. The vault was a particularly auspicious display area. The artists who were too young, too weird, or both for the uptown art houses were featured here.

"Sonny, it's good to see you!" Carla Martinez waved him over to join her by one of Joey's displays. Carla was an Art Institute graduate who had met Sonny several years back during some long-forgotten story early in his *Journal* career. She was slim and dark, with black straight hair nearing her waist and wearing a flowing, khaki dress. Pilsen was her home neighborhood, and this was her gallery.

"Cheers," responded Sonny as he walked up to her. "Where's the crowd?"

"Most of them show up at least 10 minutes after the start of a show. It's almost like a rule with these things. Come on, look at how it turned out."

They approached Joey's main model of a burned-out DC. Carla had it displayed for optimum effect; the lighting above allowed the ruins of DC to cast ominous shadows across the scattering of modern buildings in the ruins.

"Everything looks great," Sonny said.

"I have to admit, I loved the commentary notes you wrote for this. She's lucky to have you around."

"Well, I was just trying to help out a friend." Sonny was trying to play it cool.

Both of Carla's eyebrows shot up at that statement, and it looked like she had to suppress a chuckle with a couple of coughs. "Uh, yeah, sure. Say, can I ask you something? Can I ask you about the quote you have here, by the end of the display?"

"Sure, lead the way." They walked to the other end of the room. "Speaking of Joey, where is *she*?"

"Oh, yes. Diana Edson said they're interested in picking up a few of the pieces here for her and her husband's personal collection. As part of it, she asked if Joey could paint something for her, a big display, so she's putting the last touches on it. It is a bit unusual, but it was a big honorarium that Diana gave to both the gallery and Joey, so she was happy to oblige. Here it is."

The long quote was on a plastic plaque next to the Capitol Hill area of the display. It read:

"'Most empires, dynasties, they go through three generational cycles. The first generation are the pioneers, the ones that build the foundation to what's coming. The second generation are the empire builders, the ones who reach the peak of power and dominance. The third generation… well, they sit on their asses, relax in the empires their parents and grandparents built them, and act entitled. Most times, that's the generation for whom everything falls apart. And by the fourth generation, it always does.

Think of America. America in 1750-1850 – that's the first generation. America in 1850-1950 – that's the second generation. Then, the third generation for America runs 1950-2050. I'm not sure I'll see the end, but I know you'll see the beginning of the end.'"

Sonny Turner, *Chicago Journal*, 2007

"Who did you quote in that column?"

Sonny finished reading it over again and turned to Carla. "My father. It was one of the things he told me in the last few weeks of his life, just before I moved to Chicago. It was weird – most of the time, he liked to keep things simple, not rock the boat. But by the end, I think the two of us identified with each other more than we could have imagined." He shook his head in disbelief.

"It's a shame, the two of you realizing that only at the end."

# The Holy Fool

"Well, at least we did – I was taking bets for a long time that we wouldn't speak before he died." He let out a short, barking laugh. "Typical him, getting stuff done at the last minute."

"Well, I'm glad you at least managed it." Carla's parents cut off contact with her right after high school after they discovered she liked girls more than boys. Since then, she communicated with her younger siblings via private e-mail and Skype.

Carla turned to see a snakelike procession of people winding their way through the front door and around the exhibits in a random pattern. "Well, it looks like the guests are finally here. If you'll excuse me." She glided over to the head of the snaking crowd, making sure there were champagne cocktails for all requiring them. She led the crowd on a path around all of Joey's exhibits, pointing out and explaining each one in turn.

Exactly two minutes after the scheduled start of the exhibition, Edson and his wife walked through the door. Edson had dressed down as much as he could manage in a public place, sporting a black knit short-sleeved shirt, brown sport coat, and khakis. Diana was wearing a red strapless velvet gown and matching heels, in a design that drifted between classic and contemporary.

For the first time, Sonny got an up-close look at Diana. He now had visual confirmation that his boss had a type when it came to women - medium-blond, barely wavy hair, whether it was natural or salon-generated, and blue eyes. Her body type was something of a hybrid of Cathy and Jenni – not as stringy as Cathy, yet not as curvy as Jenni; it was more of a swimmer's build than a model. Her features were nice and symmetrical, but not as sharp as Cathy's or as heart-shaped as Jenni's. Diana was a prototype; the other ladies were later-model variants. Sonny noted that even though they linked arms as they walked in, their eyes never met each other's.

He saw Carla make a beeline for the couple once they got around to Joey's installations. After a few words and some champagne cocktails, she led the two of them to another section of the bank-turned-gallery.

Jason Liegois

There were several rows of seats surrounding a large blank wall that faced what were the tellers' windows. It was wide and high, normally covered by a WPA-era mural of factory workers at their jobs. Carla had some classmates who specialized in art restoration give it a once-over, and the results had been excellent. Tonight, the view of it was mostly blocked by a canvas eight feet by 12 feet.

After that was a little more hurry up and wait as the reminder of the audience came in and sat down. Sonny stayed on the fringes of the crowd but moved closer to the couple. They sat in the center of the aisle, Diana off to the left and John Michael off to the right.

Carla brought three of the other artists out before the crowd to introduce them. They gave pocket bios of themselves – like Joey, the others were young – and answered a couple of questions about what they had chosen for display.

After they finished, Carla told the audience, "Regarding our featured artist, who I consider a friend, what always impressed me about her was her vision of what her art was about, the message she wanted to convey. Her craftsmanship, sense of design, her ability to take older images or ideas and use them in news and interesting ways – these were things that grabbed my attention. You'll hear more about her soon. Ladies and gentlemen, Josephine Halvorsen."

Joey came out from stage left to join Carla. She had on the same black Chuck Taylors she had on the other day, and he could still see some of the paint splatters on them from in back. However, the rest of her outfit consisted of a pair of light blue denim coveralls. From the back, it looked like she wasn't even wearing a shirt underneath all of it. Upon closer examination, he realized she was wearing a string bikini top that matched her skin tone almost perfectly.

She also had a lot less hair than before. Joey had cut it pixie-short, straight, and tight in the back and sides while varying between standing up and drooping on top. Her smile and nose were a lot more prominent without the hair hiding it. Sonny thought she was more beautiful than ever.

As she took the microphone from Carla, she took a quick look down at Carla's outfit and her own. "Sorry – I would have dressed up for this, but I was working," indicating the canvas behind her that two assistants were bringing into view and setting up on a large easel, "sooo..." That got a big chuckle from the audience.

After a quick review of the technical details about the collection and answering a couple of questions from the audience about what brought her into art, she saw John Michael raise his hand. "Hi, Mr. Edson. He's my boss at the *Journal*," Joey said in an aside to the rest of the audience. "What was your question?"

"I had a question about this model, *Vision of DC*," John Michael said. "Is this how you picture Washington being like this someday?"

"I could see how some people might see it that way, but I don't think that's the exact theme," Joey said, nodding. "My thought process was, there have been many empires throughout human civilization that have risen to power, reached their peaks, then collapsed and made way for something else.

"I'm not saying that's what's going to happen to America," Joey continued. "We have a chance to be something else. But it's definitely a warning for what could happen to us." Both John Michael and Diana nodded at that.

The custom canvas was an image of the Chicago cityscape on the shoreline of Lake Michigan looking south. It almost reminded Sonny of one of the Miami skyline murals he'd seen in *Scarface*, but Diana appeared to like it.

After the Q&A, Joey continued to talk with John Michael, who was doing a good job trying to think of technical questions to ask her while watching the muscles in Joey's back flex and play as she pointed to different parts of the canvas. As for Diana, she got up in her seat and made her way toward the restrooms.

Sonny made sure he stood between the entrances to the men's and women's restroom as Diana approached, not looking up at all. "Hello, Mrs. Edson," Sonny said as she arrived.

She finally looked up, wary for a moment, then her shoulders and neck relaxed just a little bit. "Mr. Turner, a surprise to see you here, although I guess you did help out your co-worker with this exhibit."

"I was wondering if we could talk for a moment."

"Perhaps some other time..."

"It has to do with your family. Specifically, your husband's... social activities."

That brought her to a stop within a couple of steps. She turned to him, standing calm, erect, her eyes appraising him with a cool stare. "Mr. Turner, how do you know that I'm not aware of them? And that I want something done about them?"

Sonny did not hesitate. "Are you just aware of them, or do you have proof of them?"

"You're saying that you do?"

"That's right."

She turned back to stare at her husband gazing at Joey working on her picture. "I don't know if you can tell this from here, Mr. Turner, but my husband's beginning to get a bit bored. After he leaves, I'll listen to what you have to say. Understood?"

"Understood."

She nodded. "Very well." With that, she strolled through the bathroom doorway.

Sonny had to hand it to her – either she was a real cool customer or a better actor than he'd ever seen at Steppenwolf.

***

As Diana had predicted, within 10 minutes, John Michael checked his watch from the front row of seats and then walked up to Joey. After a brief whisper in her ear, the two exchanged business cards. John Michael walked back to Diana, leaned over, and whispered in her ear for a moment. He kissed her cheek and took his leave.

Diana rose and walked toward where Sonny was leaning up against a wall. When she got to him, she said, "Perhaps this conversation needs to take place elsewhere."

"You pick the spot." Sonny gestured for her to lead the way.

They walked up to the second floor, with torn-out cubicles and offices serving as smaller display areas there. The center of the floor was open to the atrium below, so the two of them walked to a railing where they could overlook the activity below.

She nodded towards Joey. "She is talented, I will say that."

"Definitely is."

"She's an attractive girl – not my husband's type, but enough to trip his radar." She turned to face him. "You've been working with my son."

"That's right."

"He seems fascinated by you. Do you think he has talent as... a writer, a reporter, I guess?"

"He's got potential – knows what he doesn't know. That's a first step."

She nodded. "I'm glad, but I get the feeling what you want to tell me is not something you wanted to share with my son. Go ahead, then."

Sonny nodded and took a deep breath before continuing in his low but carrying voice. "I have evidence that your husband has been involved with at least two other women. I'm almost certain that he's conducting affairs with both women, and I'll have full proof of it soon.

"I have strong circumstantial evidence that one of these affairs has produced a child." Diana closed her eyes at that, but he continued. "I'm getting evidence of that, too. Once that happens, I'm willing to turn that information over to you."

There was silence for a moment, then Diana opened her eyes again and stared down into the atrium. "Just like that? Out of the goodness of your heart?"

Sonny walked up next to Diana and leaned on the railing as he stared down. "Well, I want to help you. I admit, I am looking to get something out of this deal. For the paper."

"What are you talking about?"

"We know John Michael wants to sell the *Journal*. I would like your help to try and stop that from happening." As he saw her eyes grow wider as she stared off into space, he continued, "What, Johnny didn't mention anything about that?"

She turned back to him. "No, no. He'd talked about maybe doing some reorganization of the company, but selling the paper... no."

Sonny saw her regaining her cool, her reserve, the more that she spoke. "I'm going to be honest with you, I'm wondering why that would necessarily be a bad idea, as least where I'm concerned. It would get us out of the newspaper business, which is dying. Besides, you'll still keep your job if the paper gets sold to someone else – is it going to WorldWide Media?" Sonny nodded, not speaking. "Lucky guess. So, tell me. Why should I care?"

"Wouldn't that put your son out of work?"

"I'm sure John Michael would find another spot for him in the company for him, not that I think it would do him any good."

"What?"

She leaned back against the railing and gazed upward. "As much as he doesn't talk about it in public, he's very much a believer in having his children join him in the family business. My oldest son, Michael, felt so much pressure to be his father that I think it's part of the reason he's an alcoholic and drug addict. The jury's out on how it's going to affect Colton." She let out a deep sigh.

Sonny joined her with his back to the rail. "I've never really been a fan of relying on family to keep things going."

"I'm still not seeing why your concerns should be my concerns."

"John Michael is representing the *Journal* as a strong investment, but it's likely to collapse within the next few weeks, maybe sooner. Part of that's due to mismanagement, but part of that, I believe, is that John Michael is siphoning some of that cash off for himself, hiding it from you and everyone else. I want to make sure that you and your kids aren't in the middle of a felony embezzlement and fraud case.

"I'm going to need your help to closely examine his financials," he continued. "You give me that access, you get all of the information about your husband and his flings."

"After you publish a story about it, of course," Diana said with a laugh.

"That story'll be coming out regardless. I'm trying to look after you and your kids…"

"What do you care about me and my kids?" Her voice rose a fraction. "I barely know you; you barely know me and my kids…"

"Twenty years ago, I *was* your kids." Sonny clenched his jaw. "My dad was a smart guy, smarter than a lot of people thought. But he shit all over every relationship with a woman he ever had, my mother included. He had to screw every woman he knew, and it wasn't until he was nearly dead that he realized he'd been an asshole.

"When my mom and dad broke up, it was a rough fight." Sonny turned and stared at Diana. "If you decide to leave him, or stay with him, I want to make it easier for you, in a way I couldn't for my mother. Also, I have a fear that the newspaper I've spent my entire career at might be dying and doing this is probably the only tiny chance I'm going to have to save that paper."

There was silence between the two for what seemed to be an eternity. As Sonny wondered if he needed to continue talking or wait, Diana reached into her purse and fished out a red and white pack of Marlborough cigarettes. She extracted one with her mouth and used a green Bic stashed in the pack to light up. After taking a deep drag, she said to herself, "That's something *I* need to change." Then, she stared at Sonny as if she noticed him for the first time. "I'm still listening."

"We're going to have to work fast on this."

"How fast?"

"Two weeks at best, probably less."

"All right. Come over to our house Sunday afternoon. John Michael will be gone then."

"You sure?"

"He'll be out of sight and out of mind," Diana said with conviction.

"I just want to make sure you're not found out. I was under surveillance earlier this week – I don't know by who."

"Surveillance? Who?"

"Not sure. Could be company guys; it could be Feds about a different unrelated matter."

"That being…"

"Due respect, Ms. Edson, I can't get into that."

"All right." Diana reached into her purse and took out a business card. "Here is my personal cell number. Sunday morning, after breakfast, you call me and let me know where you will be. I'll have one of my staff pick you up and bring you to the house."

"OK." Sonny nodded.

"Very well." Diana extended her hand as she took another drag on her cigarette. "I can't really say it's been a pleasure… but I think it's *necessary*."

"I understand, under the circumstances." Sonny gave her hand a single shake.

"Very well. I'll be returning to my skyline, then. See you Sunday." With that, she turned around and headed toward the stairs.

Sonny walked down and found Joey talking with Carla. "Hi, Sonny," Joey said, shaking his hand in front of everyone.

"So, what's all this?" Sonny said, gesturing toward her head.

"Decided a new look was in order," Joey said. "You like?"

"Actually, it's really nice."

She leaned over to him and whispered, "Did it work out?"

"It worked out. How about you?"

"Oh, I don't know," Joey said, looking away from him as she sat her tools down and dunked her hands in her pockets. "We started talking about how he was interested in art, fascinated that he had such an artist working for him, and a cute one at that, and why shouldn't we get together some weekend when we had time…"

"Liar," he said, laughing.

"Oh, he was a lot subtler in his word choice, but the intent was there, especially when we exchanged cards."

"OK, you can give me the details later. Are you going to be here a while longer?"

"Maybe another hour or two."

"OK. I'll meet you over at your place in a bit, after I stop at my place."

"Got it."

***

As Sonny walked up to his door, he looked at the door jamb of his apartment. Right at the bottom of the doorway, invisible to anyone who wasn't looking for it, was a tiny wooden wedge on the ground.

Sonny kneeled and tossed his hood off his head, then picked up the wedge and examined it as if to hope it would tell him something different than what he was thinking. After taking a deep breath, he pocketed the wedge and pulled two other items out of his hoody pockets: his keys and a large folding knife. With the greatest of care, he unfolded his knife, then inched his keys over to the lock.

He eased the door open and peeked in. He heard no one in either his kitchen, the bathroom just across from the closet next to the front door, or what there was of his living room. As he scanned his cubbyhole of a bathroom to make sure the intruder was not in there, he heard *tack tack tack tack click* from the open door of his bedroom.

Inside, Sonny breathed a small sigh of relief. Using the same care as the best of bomb-disposal efforts, he lifted his backpack off his left shoulder, and laid the backpack onto the floor. For good measure, he laid a jacket over it.

Sonny pulled out his iPhone and examined it for a minute, but then put it back in his pocket. A black camera bag sat on the top shelf in his closet, and Sonny opened it up and extracted a compact Sony camcorder. Leaving the bag on the floor of the closet, Sonny tiptoed toward the open door.

He peeped into the bedroom. There was a man about his size, wearing a black tracksuit with white stripes on the sides, sitting in his chair at a desk in his room, his back to the door. He was in front of Sonny's desktop computer mounted on the left of the desk, typing on it, and clicking the mouse.

He was thankful that his apartment had carpets. With the man still tapping away, not looking behind him, Sonny placed the camcorder on a shelf in an open closet and used some sweaters to keep it hidden from view but with enough exposed that the lens could still capture everything in the room.

Sonny approached him from behind, trying to find and lock in his memory every detail about what the man looked like. His beard appeared to extend down to his chest, but the hair on his head was almost a crew cut. Finally, Sonny walked up behind the man, and in a low but clear voice said, "What's up?"

For all the attention Sonny was paying to what the man looked like, he hadn't noticed him reaching into his tracksuit jacket for something. In one swift movement, he brought a collapsible baton out of the jacket, snapped it out to full extension with a flick of his wrist, and brought it down with a *thud* onto Sonny's wrist, the one holding the knife.

Sonny dropped the knife before he even felt the flash of pain. Within an instant, the man had pinned him against the wall, and he was attempting to use the baton against his throat to strangle him. Sonny was using both hands to keep it away, but the baton kept creeping upward.

The man leaned closer in to Sonny, smelling of cabbage and stewed meat, growling "fucking idiot" in an accent Sonny tried to recognize but couldn't. He was strong and Sonny knew he didn't have much time. As Tracksuit's head leaned in closer, Sonny reared back his own head and launched it forward.

The head butt crashed down on the precise location of the bridge of Tracksuit's nose. He jumped back a step and let the baton fall from his hand. As Tracksuit began to reach back into his jacket for something, Sonny raised his foot and stomped down on the top of the guy's left knee.

Tracksuit howled twice, once with the strike, then a second time when his knee hit the ground as he dropped to the floor. Sonny sent a right hook sailing at the guy's head and connected, sending him backward. Jumping on top of him, Sonny crashed his right fist into the guy's face repeatedly. He began to lose sensation in his knuckles by the fourth punch.

Tracksuit got his hand free from his jacket and came away with a Glock 17 in his hand, which he used to smash the right side of Sonny's face. Sonny fell off him and rolled to the side of his bed. Tracksuit hobbled to his feet, and began to extend his gun...

...which went flying across the room and under Sonny's desk when Sonny swung a baseball bat he'd had underneath his bed at Tracksuit's gun hand. With another howl of pain, he took a step back and wrung his hand out as Sonny stood between him and his desk, his bat cocked and ready to swing.

Tracksuit stared at him, all blocky features, dark eyes, pain, and rage. All Sonny said was, "Did you need your gun back?"

Sonny could tell Tracksuit thought about going for the gun, but only for a second. After that second, the guy turned on his heels and sprint-hobbled out of Sonny's bedroom.

"Hey, wait a minute!" Sonny ran out of the room after him, but Tracksuit already had gotten out the front door and down the hall.

Sonny turned back and headed into his bedroom. He thought about sitting down at his desk, but he found himself feeling tremors in his hands and shoulders and decided on the bed. He pulled out his cell phone, but he had difficulty dialing with his right hand, so he shifted it to his left. He dialed in a number and waited, lying on his back on the bed.

Someone picked up on the second ring. "Singer, Major Case," he said.

"Eric, it's..."

"Sonny Turner, yeah, yeah, I saw caller ID," Detective Eric Singer, Chicago PD, said. "*Long* time since I heard from you, man. How's TT been?" The two men had been partners in the Narcotics division some years back.

"He's OK. Hey, is there any way I can talk to you in person? Official capacity?"

"What's the matter, you need a story?"

"More like I need a cop. Somebody broke into my apartment tonight."

"What? Fuck me. The guy still there?"

"Ran off. I might have some footage of the guy, but I'm not sure how good it is. You got time to deal with this?"

"Yeah. Fuck me."

"Need the address?"

"Already got it. I'll see you in 30." He hung up.

\*\*\*

"OK, you have a description?" Singer said.

Singer was in his forties, lean, bullet head shaved, looking almost like an eagle with a powerful, blue-eyed stare. TT said he would trust Eric with his life without hesitation and had to at least on one occasion.

He'd brought his partner with him, Detective Marisa Kotas. She was Sonny's age, very fine-boned, auburn with high cheekbones and green eyes. TT had never worked with her, but there were rumors backed up by torn-out pictures from Vogue and Bazaar that she'd been a model in her teens before deciding on a law enforcement career. She looked like a strong wind could blow her over, but TT had said many of his former colleagues considered her one of the best young investigators on the force.

Both stood in front of Sonny, who had led them to his bedroom and sat down on the bed. "About my size, late thirties/early forties, brown hair and eyes, full beard down to his chest. He was wearing a black Adidas tracksuit with white trim."

"Did he say anything to you?" Kotas asked.

"Just cussing me out a couple of times. Nothing much."

"Any idea of an accent?" Singer said.

"Eastern Europe, maybe. Actually, more like Southeastern Europe."

"The Balkans, you mean?" Kotas said.

"Yeah, that's it."

"You said that he was trying to access the computer? Any idea of what he was trying to do with it?" Singer said.

"Maybe trying to see something I was working on, perhaps?"

"Any idea of what that could be?" Kotas said.

"I'm working on some stories having to do with… national security issues."

"Can you be more specific?" Kotas said.

"Nope," Sonny said.

From her screwed-up face, he could tell Kotas didn't like the answer. Cops never liked it whenever you held anything back from them, because they thought that little piece of information would be the key to solving the crime. Sometimes they were right, but not always. Journalists had a similar attitude towards their sources, so Sonny understood that.

"Anything else tampered with or searched in here?" said Singer, who had seemed more sympathetic to Sonny's need for privacy.

Sonny looked around the room. "I don't know for sure. Either the answer is no or he did a really careful search where he didn't tear anything up. Right now, I don't think so."

"Have you ever seen this guy before? Anything weird happen today?" Singer asked.

"No, I haven't seen *this* guy." Sonny recounted both being followed during the past few weeks and the visit from the FBI agent.

"You have no idea who the guys were that were following you?" Kotas asked after Sonny finished his story.

"I didn't know. I was wondering whether it was anybody from Chicago PD."

That seemed to shock Kotas. "Why would you think that?"

"You tell me."

Singer, the more experienced of the detectives, was less fazed by the claim. "I can ask around department headquarters to find out. We can also try and contact the Chicago FBI office, see if they know anything about this."

"OK."

"You think you can make it down to our office tomorrow, look at some photos?" Singer said.

Sonny nodded. "It might be the afternoon, but I should."

"We're going to look at that footage you shot with your camera too," Singer said.

"I figured. Sure."

Kotas looked at Sonny's face. "Do you need to get to a hospital?"

"Me? No, I'll be OK."

Kotas scanned the room. "It might be better if you stay somewhere else for a couple of days. Is there anywhere you can go?"

Sonny thought for a moment, then realized *of course*. "Yeah. Can you give me a few minutes to get a couple of things packed up?"

"Sure," Singer said. "We'll seal up the place. Do you need a ride?"

"No, I'll be OK with that."

\*\*\*

Joey was sitting in her living room at 2 a.m., watching the late news on MSNBC and still in the outfit she had been in at the show, although with the shoes flung in the corner. She'd been checking her cell phone for the past half hour after she'd gotten a text from Sonny saying *I'll be there soon*.

She was about to try and call when she heard a knock at her door. She marched to the front door. After confirming it was Sonny through the peephole, she undid all four locks and opened the door.

"Sonny? What the hell took so long..." She took a half-step backward at the sight of him. "God, are you OK?"

Sonny had his backpack and a duffle bag slung over each shoulder. Blood was running down from outside his right eye and off his right knuckles onto the backpack strap he held. "Someone busted into my place tonight," Sonny said at last. "Sorry I couldn't make it earlier."

Without a word but still worried, Joey took him by the left elbow and guided him into her apartment.

By the time he'd finished explaining everything, a half-hour had passed. Joey had been listening the whole time as she'd broken out her first aid kit. She'd gotten his hand wrapped in gauze and Neosporin, while using three butterfly enclosures near his eye to take care of that cut. "You honestly think the cops or the FBI's behind all this?" Joey said at the end.

"I don't even know." Sonny flexed his right hand. The knuckles there felt tight and swollen, but not fractured.

"If you're asking me, and I know you aren't..."

"Why not? You could probably figure this out as well as anyone."

There was a small shake of her head. "I was thinking this Walker is about as likely as anyone else to have organized this. If he was that willing to help out a friend or Edson, why not see if they could find any files or contacts you had?"

"That's probably my co-number one suspect along with the Feds," Sonny said, settling into the couch.

She sat down next to him, took off his cap, and began to run her fingers through his hair. "Are you worried he managed to get something?"

Sonny could barely shake his head to avoid it hurting. "Nah. That desktop computer, it's just a decoy. I wind up saving everything to flash drives and virtual dead drops. All I keep on the desktop are old Word, Excel, PowerPoint, and video files – nothing of importance."

"Very cautious."

"Cautious has let me keep my head." Sonny held up the little wooden wedge from his place. "This always goes into the door after I leave my place, so when this was on the floor, I knew something was up."

"What about now?"

"Shit's getting real fast." Sonny let her take his bandaged hand in hers. "This deal with the paper's going to happen real soon. Plus, I've got this deadline to deal with on my source – if nothing gets published by first thing next Saturday, I'm out a source."

"That's later. What about tonight?"

"I'm going to find a hotel for now. Might as well – my lease is up at the end of September, I was thinking about trying something else..."

"You're staying here. That's all there is to it." Joey nodded to herself as if it was already true.

"I can't haul you into all of this mess..."

"Are you fucking kidding me?" Joey's voice rose as she faced him. "We're a team. I know you would do the same thing for me, even if I was on the run from a biker gang or a former cult or the KKK."

She was still a foot shorter than him, but he found himself backing down from the ferocity coming from her like a summer wind. "OK, whatever you say."

"Hell, I got all of this cut off because I wanted to get your attention. You said back before we started dating you liked girls with short hair."

"I did say that, didn't I?"

She leaned over and kissed him. "And, you're staying inside for the weekend." She put up a hand to his face when he tried to respond. "It's not up for discussion. You shouldn't have to haul yourself all over the place. Get at least a little rest, because you'll need it soon enough."

"I've got to meet Diane later and then the police, but I'll stay home otherwise."

"I can live with that."

Sonny looked off at the television rather than meet her gaze at that moment. "I get the feeling things are going to change for me no matter what happens. I want you to be part of that."

"I admit, I first developed feelings for you from reading your writing. Why wouldn't I support you standing up for that?"

"OK. OK. Just realize at the end of this, I might be asking you to jump off a cliff with me."

"How much rope will we need?" Joey stared straight into his eyes.

Sonny stared right back. He reached over and unbuttoned one of the straps on her overalls and saw how the front leaned away from one of her boobs. "God, you have no idea how hot that looks." He leaned over and kissed her forehead. "My girl."

"My guy."

# Chapter 11.

Highland Park was exclusive even among Chicago suburbs. This section of the town had graduated from rinky-dink McMansions to the real deal, where homes went for multimillions of dollars. Sonny knew one of the nearby mansions had been Michael Jordan's main castle for years when he played for the Bulls, but he'd lost it to his former wife in the mother of all divorce cases. Sonny idly wondered if the Edson divorce might match the numbers in the Jordan case.

Sonny remembered the rumors about how John Michael was able to see his home from the Keep using a telescope in his office, and now realized that it might not be a rumor.

The house was imposing, around 50,000 square feet. It was a two-story structure, with two wings angling back and away from the main house, reaching out to Lake Michigan. It looked like John Michael had managed to salvage all the marble that had fallen off the old Standard Oil building and covered his house with it.

There was what appeared to be an eight-car garage off on the left-hand side of the property. The car Diana had sent for him drove past that onto the private drive leading to the house.

Sonny walked up the carved stone walkway to the door and rang the bell. A series of classical music chimes tinkled for several seconds. After about a minute, Sonny was pondering whether to ring the bell again, but Diana opened the door.

"Mr. Turner, hello." She was by herself, as promised. Diana was wearing a white sleeveless blouse with a generous cleavage, straight-legged jeans faded almost white but with no holes or fraying, and no shoes. Her fingernails and toenails were a fresh bright red. Then there was the gold – three thin necklaces, various rings and bracelets, bracelets on both ankles and what appeared to be a toe ring on the index toe of her right foot. "You're looking tired today, and a bit bruised, it seems."

"No worries, Ms. Edson…"

"Diana, please."

"Then I'm Sonny."

"Where did you get that name? I remember your real first name is Samuel," she said as she waved Sonny in.

"Just something my mother started calling me. It started before kindergarten and I guess just kept going."

"Ah."

The kitchen had all the extras. Twin stainless steel refrigerators, twin gas burner ranges, two tub-sized stainless-steel sinks with disposals, copper and non-stick pots and pans hanging around the room, oak cabinetry, granite countertops, and a kitchen island with the same cabinets and countertops and oak barstools surrounding it. Pages of documents covered the island, where Diana asked Sonny to sit down.

"Do you like the house?"

Sonny gazed around the kitchen and nearby formal dining area. "It's not my design taste, but it looks like somebody spent a lot of time building it."

"It's over the top," Diana said. "When I married him, I wanted a nice quiet, elegant home that I'd be proud of, not some castle that helps scream 'I'm the best.' Do you know that we own five different properties?"

"I knew you owned more than one house, but I didn't know how many."

"It's true. Five residences at a time when most people are trying to hold onto one home or apartment or trailer."

"I took a tour of some cities four months back. Went to LA, Vegas, Detroit, where some of the worst of it is, turned it into a whole series. Some people, especially those who haven't had it happen to them, like to think it's because those owners were lazy or got greedy. That did happen, but many more just got hit upside the head with job losses, medical bills, a decline in house values, or a whole combination of things." He turned to look at Diana, who had eased away from him without noticing it and appearing increasingly disturbed. "Tell me about your homes."

# The Holy Fool

Diana monitored Sonny for any signs of sarcasm, but she found none. "There's this one, of course. We've owned it for the past 10 years. There's a condo in New York on the Upper East Side where we stay when we're out on the East Coast. We've got a ranch out in Western Montana, a working ranch, 1,000 acres, I think, although he hires out the help and managers to take care of it. There's also a flat in the Chelsea section of London; that's our base of operations whenever we vacation in Europe. Finally, we have a beach house on the North Shore of Oahu we go to occasionally, to get away from things. It's small, quiet, intimate." She was silent for a moment, then said, "It probably seems strange, hearing about my worries. Most people think I probably don't have them."

"Oh, everyone's got problems. But when it comes to the rich, they can throw money at problems to make them go away."

"Does that always work, in your experience?"

"No, not always. But it works a lot better than it does when poor people try to do it."

That made her relax a little. "Point taken. Here, come take a look at this." Diana handed him two pages of documents.

"What are these?"

"This is the official report we received from our accountants regarding last year. It's the family balance sheet, so to speak."

Sonny was already skimming it as she spoke. "He made $40 million last year?"

"Less than half of that was salary. Most of it comes from investment income, most from Edson Media, of course."

"OK. Has he ever had any problems paying any bills?"

"No, never. Not even late payments."

"Ever noticed him spending compulsively on himself? What about gambling?" Sonny continued to check through the documents.

"Nothing like that. Even when he goes to Vegas, he's barely at the tables – he'll drop a thousand on baccarat just as a courtesy to the casinos, but nothing compulsive. Nothing he hasn't been able to pay for."

"So, he's doing well, the family's doing well. Anything in here about Edson Media itself? Its books?"

"No, nothing in the papers I have. There's the yearly stock reports, but you know how basic they can be."

"Yeah, I think you're right. He's got a home office here, right?"

\*\*\*

He did.

It was everything Sonny might have expected of his boss, a melody of dark oak, leather, and tapestries shaken and stirred together to create the man-cave for the upper crust. There was not a paperback in sight, nor did any of the books have paper dust jackets. Persian rugs in green, red, and gold covered the hardwood floors. Two dark brown leather sofas formed a U in the center of the room with John Michael's desk.

The pedestal desk was a heavy oak monolith on its side, with so much volume Sonny wondered if it was a decommissioned yacht whittled down to fit into the study. The only signs of advanced technology in the room were the multi-line phone and the desktop computer monitor and keyboard on top of the desk, which was otherwise barren.

As Sonny sat down in the high-backed leather chair behind the desk, Diana curled into a tranquil position on the couch closest to the window. He confirmed that the only lock appeared to be on the narrow center drawer. After turning on the PC hard drive stashed underneath the leg space, where it had more than enough room to sit, Sonny looked up at Diana and said, "You wouldn't happen to have the key to this, would you?"

"Sorry, I don't."

Sonny shrugged. "No problem." He reached into the interior pocket of his leather bomber jacket and took out two slim pieces of metal no longer than one of his fingers. He started to probe at the center lock with the tools.

Staring out the window, her expression bland, Diana said, "I suppose this must be old stuff for you, breaking into strange rooms to find information for your stories."

# The Holy Fool

"Actually, you let me in. However, this is the first time I've ever tried to pick someone's lock before."

"Do you think you'll be able to manage?"

"Well, I will say this," Sonny said as he carefully wiggled one of the metal picks in the lock and eased the drawer open, "I don't have much in the way of experience, but I have done my research."

"Bravo," she said with a quiet smile and a nod.

"Yeah..." Sonny turned his attention to the contents of the drawer. It took him about a minute of searching before he looked under a pen and pencil tray and found a Post-It note with what appeared to be an obvious password. "Crazy that he'd just leave this in here and not memorize this."

"He probably wasn't expecting someone to pick the lock on his desk."

"True." He typed in the password when the computer requested one. "We're in business." The password screen changed to the Windows boot up screen.

"Now what's the plan?"

"That's going to be pretty easy."

Sonny pulled out a black plastic item the size of a man's wallet. He used a short black cable that plugged one end into the wallet-shaped item and the other into one of the desktop's USB ports.

"What is that, then?"

"External hard drive. It's a little bit of a custom job designed by one of my friends. Rather than trying to search through all the files on here myself, I'm just going to copy everything over to this and have them look at it someplace else. The faster this process gets done, the less exposure there is for us. Plus, it adds some malware so we can track what else he does."

"Hoping to find where you think he's stashing all of his secret funds?"

"Likely. I'm downloading all of his e-mails, documents, pictures – I have to think it's going to give us a clue as to where he might be moving funds, either for the company or for himself he doesn't want anyone to know."

Diana stared out the window. "I think I might have an idea of who might be helping him."

"Yeah? What are you thinking?"

She turned to face him and stretch out on the couch. "Personally, I think if anyone might be helping him to hide money, it's Gil Lott."

"Gil Lott? The CEO of UUF Bank Gil Lott?"

"Of course. Didn't you know they went to Harvard together? Those two have been thick as thieves ever since they started hanging out in Cambridge bars their first year in Harvard Business School."

"Makes sense. It's like most crimes – usually it's the obvious suspects who committed the crime."

"The same with white-collar crime."

"Yep. I've been having Colton do some digging around UUF the past week or so. Maybe he can help us out." He looked at the computer monitor. "OK, maybe 15 minutes, and we'll be copied over."

"Can you come over here?"

He gawked at Diana. She was stretched out on the couch, her bare feet rubbing up against each other on the leather of the couch. She still gazed out the windows, but Sonny felt she was monitoring him in her peripheral vision.

He found just enough space on the end of the couch for himself. "On a related note, when were you planning on telling Colton your plans?"

"Honestly, I was waiting until the very end to break the news to him. I don't want him running to his dad."

"Running to his dad? That's your concern?" Diana cackled. "And I thought I was treating him too much like a child. No, I'll tell him. I can guarantee that he will keep his mouth shut around his father for a few more days until you and your colleagues pull whatever scheme you've got in mind. Deal?"

Sonny leaned back in the couch. "Guess it would be too much to expect that he doesn't try and punch me out when he finds out, isn't it?"

"I think that you should be able to take care of yourself, based on your battle scars. Let me ask you something else."

"OK." Sonny settled in.

Diana began to ease her way closer to Sonny on the couch, slow enough that he didn't notice it until she was halfway across. "Do you think it makes sense that John Michael is seeing other women? Is there a reason for it?"

"Well, the dating and partnership habits of men and women, I'm not an expert on that. I'm definitely not an expert on how women think." Sonny stretched his arms down one arm of the couch and across its back. "With some men, it doesn't matter who their wives or girlfriends are. They just have to have different women, the more the better. Whether their partner is attractive or not's got nothing to do with it. They just always have to have something new, or they can't stand it, even if they're married to a supermodel."

Diana's hand crept up to touch Sonny's wrist on the back of the couch. "Would you say that John Michael's like that?"

"He probably is." Sonny remained still. "Right now we think he's with more than one woman, so..."

"Was your father like that?"

"He was."

"It's interesting, trying to figure out people, especially in your line of work, isn't it? I can see the attraction." Her hand had crept up to his shoulder.

"It can be."

She eased her left leg over his, her foot brushing across his right thigh as she did so. "I have a question for you."

"Yes."

"You're not the type of man I'm typically attracted to, but... What would you do if I said I was going to kiss you right now?"

"I'd wait and see," Sonny responded. "Saying and doing are two different things."

"Very true." She slid over to Sonny's lap, took both sides of his face in her hands, and eased their lips together. As she used her legs to entwine his right leg, she moved her head into different positions, probing with her tongue into Sonny's mouth. He let her explore, just taking hold of her by the shoulders, but otherwise remaining still.

She finally eased away from him, but still half in his lap. "I'm thinking about going upstairs for a nap. What would you do if I asked you to come up there with me?"

Sonny was silent for a while, his gaze at Diana asking a question that Diana finally realized. "Are you coming up with me, then? We kissed; you have a problem with more?"

"I'll admit that I'm my father's son. However, I'm also my mother's son, too."

"You can't be that concerned with interfering in my marriage. According to you, there's not any marriage to interfere with."

Sonny nodded. "True. I'm not worried about you staying true to that relationship. But, I do want to stay true to the relationship *I'm* in."

"Wait… is it the artist? Of course it was; that seemed too convenient the other night. How would she compare to me?"

"She's the one for me."

She leaned back in the sofa next to him, her eyes now locked onto his. "So, what would happen if you weren't attached and I made that request?"

"For real? I'd probably take you up on it."

"Really?" her question both a joke and a challenge.

"Yeah. Some guy's going to be lucky when they meet you. I'd bet you won't be alone for long."

Diana closed her eyes for a moment. Wiping them, she then stretched, got up from the couch, and leaned over and kissed Sonny on the forehead. "You might have more of an idea of how to talk to women than you think," she said. "You said it would take you another few minutes to download everything?"

"Yeah. I'll check around the office too, to see if I missed anything. That won't do more than add another few minutes, then make sure I put everything back."

"Good. Well, since you seem to have everything in hand, I believe I will take that nap and let you get to your work. I'll make sure to call the car service to pick you up before I lay down. We'll talk tomorrow night?"

"Yes."

# The Holy Fool

"Excellent. Thank you. Don't worry about locking the doors when you leave. Take care." With that, she turned and padded out of the room.

Sonny wasn't quite sure what to think, since what had just happened was new to him. So, he got off the couch and continued to search John Michael's desk.

\*\*\*

Sonny knocked on the door of Joey's place, and she unlocked the door to greet him. "Hey."

"Hey, yourself," he replied, and stepped inside before exchanging kisses with her.

"I got some sausage pizza tonight – this place in Little Italy just delivered it over here."

Sonny could see the box on the kitchen countertop. "Great, no problem." He sat down at one of the stools in front of the counter.

"How'd the king's castle go today?"

"That went well, too. I ripped and copied his entire hard drive, got pictures of some documents of note, and Diana kissed me halfway through the whole process and invited me up to her room. I declined."

"What?" Joey whirled away from the pizza so fast that one of the slices nearly came off the plate she was holding.

"Diana kissed me halfway through me searching her husband's office and offered to meet me upstairs in her bedroom, and I turned her down."

Joey had got a hold of herself and her pizza and sat down on the stool next to him. "So, what made you say no?"

"Well, a bit of journalistic ethics, and you. I might have, but I hadn't said anything to you first."

"Hadn't said anything to me?"

"Cheating means you have something to hide. If I was even thinking about spending time with someone else, I'd talk to you about it, get your OK."

"And if I said no?" He was surprised that she didn't make it sound like an accusation, but more of a straight question.

"I wouldn't do it. But, maybe you wouldn't say no all of the time."

"And you believe that because..."

"I know how open minded you are about a lot of things."

"Ah." She reached over and squeezed his thigh. "What if I asked permission to do the same thing with some guy? Would you be OK with that?"

"I'd probably do the same thing – say no sometimes, but not all the time."

There was a long pause. "OK."

"Everybody's got urges, have things happen. But you're my partner. That goes beyond just physical affection. I want you to know you can rely on and trust me, and that I can do the same for you."

She leaned over and kissed his forehead, then took a second to wipe off the pizza sauce she'd left there. "Thanks for trusting me and being worthy of my trust."

"Of course."

"I was thinking," as she reached an arm around his waist as they sat together and ate, "that now might be the time to tell you John Michael called here and left a message asking me to go out with him."

He glanced at her. "A date-date?"

"Dinner at this hotel on the Gold Coast, Wednesday night. What's the plan?"

"Well, go ahead and call him back, say yes. You might find out some information that might be useful."

"You're OK with this?"

"Well, under the circumstances, I don't think it would be good to sleep with him, so just dinner." Sonny slid an arm around her shoulders and giving her a squeeze.

"OK, then." She picked up a Budweiser can and clicked it against the one he was drinking. "Here's to the modern Bonnie and Clyde."

"Or the reporter couple, I guess. Hopefully this isn't the craziest thing I ask you to do this week."

"Oh, hey, I have something for you."

"What is it?"

She reached over to a corner of the counter and picked up a sketch pad which she flipped open. "I drew something for you. Tell me what you think about it." Joey handed him the pad.

Sonny stared at the middle of the pad. There, by itself on the blank white page, was a drawing of a jester's head. The skin was white, and the head had black eyes with dark red irises that matched his lips. It wore a four-pointed jester's cap half-dark red and half-black, with silver bells, and a half black and half-dark red collar. Just a few lines here and there across the shield-shaped face brought out the trickster in the character.

"I like it."

"It's for you."

"Me? Well, thanks, but what am I going to use it for?"

"I thought it might make a nice new logo for our new project?"

"Project? What are you talking about...? Oh." He took another look at it. "OK."

"That story you told me, about the Holy Fool, remember? That's what you want to be, right?"

For a moment, as Joey stared at Sonny gazing at the picture in his hands, she could swear he was about to start crying, or have at least one tear escape the corners of his eye. Instead, without a word, he leaned over and kissed her. "Thank you for this."

"Are you OK?"

"Yeah, yeah. This makes it more real."

"Well, I guess I'd better help you get ready for that, shouldn't I?"

"From the looks of it, you have already. Thanks." She kissed him in response.

## Chapter 12

Sonny was realizing that trying to run an in-house newspaper rebellion and still do his job was a little difficult.

He was in his office at the *Journal* first thing Monday going over ideas for his midweek column. Back in the day, Ed had to write five columns a week. Sonny did three columns a week, a maximum of 5,000 words each, but often pushing the outer edges of that.

He'd finally settled on discussing a checklist for how to meet your online sweetheart for the first time and the mental health measures you'd need when you found out that person had lied to you when Colton walked through his open door. "Hey, Sonny."

Sonny's eyes darted up to Colton, looking for any sign of rage or suppressed rage. Finding none, he realized Diana hadn't sprung the news yet. "Hey, yourself. Gus keeping you busy?"

"There's been a couple of articles, a piece on a new law firm opening its doors. Today we're running something about the Chicago Spire."

"What are you hearing?" Sonny grinned because he had a feeling he knew the answer.

"People are starting to get worried," Colton explained as he sat down at his tiny desk in the office.

"If they're not, they'd better. Chicago used to be the place where they'd build bigger and better – now we're lucky to get new holes in the ground."

Colton did a double-take at that. "Wow, kind of dark this early in the morning, aren't we?"

"It's like I read in this fantasy book one time, Colton," he replied. "Trolls might have heads made of rocks, but even they know which way the wind blows. Right now, it's blowing weird. Things like UUF, for example. Speaking of that, how's that coming along?"

"Still going. I'm trying to contact some of the bank's local clients to see if they've had any complaints about them. Candace Mooney in the DC bureau is trying to get me in contact with her sources in the SEC."

"OK. We need to ask specifically about the securities Edson used to finance the *Journal* deal." Sonny reached over and grabbed a Post-It note from Colton's desk and began to write something. "I'm going to give you Ed Mazur's number. You know Ed, right?"

"Ah, Ed? Yeah, I know his work. I mean, I don't know him..."

"It's OK. He's expecting your call. Ed knows a couple of guys who recently retired from UUF. They might have a pretty good idea where bodies or bad loans are buried."

"OK. I'll give him a call in the afternoon."

"So, you've got this?"

"I've got it." Colton sank back into his chair from relief. "Thanks to you and Gus for trusting me with something like this."

"I know you'll pull it off." Sonny had to choke down the hypocrisy for that to sound convincing.

***

Before he left the office for the day, Sonny went looking for Gus in his office. "Come," Gus growled after Sonny knocked on his door.

"You have a second to talk?"

"Sure. What did you want to talk about?" Gus leaned back in his high-backed chair and took a sip from his coffee mug.

Sonny would have gotten down on his hands and knees to beg if he thought that would have gotten him anywhere with Gus. Instead, he simply sat down in the chair in front of Gus's desk and tried to keep his head bowed as he spoke. "I really didn't want to bother you with all of this, since this sale is going down, but I really need to talk with you about the I-Project."

# The Holy Fool

Gus's expression was neutral. "Go on."

Sonny nodded, then: "Last weekend I got an ultimatum from my main source. She contacted me and said that if we don't run something by this Friday, she's breaking off all contact with us. We need to run something."

"Are you kidding? Since when did we let sources dictate to us when stories run or not?"

"Normally, I'd agree, but this is not a normal situation." Sonny sat up straight. "All of Casey's sources have confirmed the documents are legitimate."

"My point is, we have to be very careful about it. We don't want to make waves like that. To be honest, I don't want to be wrestling around with this when we're having to deal with whether or not this place is getting closed down."

Feeling antsy, Sonny lurched out of his chair and walked over to the far wall to lean on it. "I understand." He rocked back and forth as he stood. "But, that means I don't get any more information from her. Her deadline's Sept. 12."

Gus began to reply but shook his head and sighed before continuing. "Sonny, look, right now it just sounds too dangerous. You can wait, right?"

Sonny closed his eyes and leaned back against the wall. As he digested Gus's words, it felt liked something clicked into place inside Sonny's head.

"You know, honestly, you're right," Sonny said to Gus, who tensed up in surprise at his words. "I can see how we don't have time to hassle with it right now."

"Really?" Gus eased back into his chair, relieved.

"Really. I'll take care of it." Standing up straight from the wall, he added, "Is there anything else?" Gus shook his head.

\*\*\*

Chicago dive bars can be depressing if gone to seed, and the dive bars that journalists hung around in could be especially so. Jerry's Place on the Near North Side was that type of place: barely any lighting that wasn't neon, ads for various booze companies plastered in random spots on the dark wood paneling, wood floors that looked like someone took a sledgehammer to them, miscellaneous items of Chicago sports memorabilia covering most other surfaces in the room. Above the bar was a row of pictures of deceased Chicago journalists; Jack's picture was up there somewhere. It was the kind of place that a woman wouldn't feel comfortable in unless she was a reporter, had an arrest record for assault, or preferably both.

Two facts made Jerry's Place the default bar of the *Chicago Star*. The beer and mixed drinks were almost too cheap to be believed, and it also happened to be just a half-block from the *Star*'s headquarters.

However, it was not rare to see random *Journal* members making the odd stop into Jerry's. So, Sonny went unnoticed as he wandered into the place and made a beeline for the most deserted part of the bar. The man Sonny had an interest in speaking with preferred to get drunk alone in one of the back booths.

He was rumpled, in his late 40's, grey, bulky, and worn, in a sport jacket whose elbow patches needed patches and shoes that had at least one hole in the soles. He sipped from one old fashioned in a plastic cup and was surrounded at the table by a half-dozen empty glasses and a black porkpie hat.

Sonny stopped in front of the man and looked around at the half-empty bar. "Jesus, Robin, you wanted to stay depressed, I can suggest some Cure albums for you. It's gotta be cheaper than this."

"I don't know about that; the whiskey specials around here are pretty reasonable," Robin Greene responded.

"You have space for me here?"

"You willing to buy the next round?"

"Sure, why not?"

"Well, then, get comfortable."

"Appreciate it."

"Haven't seen you around in a while. One of the boys told me about your mother – sorry to hear about her."

"Thanks, I appreciate it."

"You found some girl finally?"

Sonny cracked the briefest of smiles, then turned away. "Not confirming or denying."

# The Holy Fool

"Well, one of these days you need to bring her down, meet all of the boys. She'd enjoy herself."

"Enjoy getting eye-fucked? I'm not sure she'd be willing to brave this sausage parlor."

"Sonny." Robin put on an innocent face which immediately slid off. "who would do something like that?"

"You would in a minute, you goddamn grifter," Sonny laughed.

"You're my pal." Robin had just gotten out of his fourth marriage last year and had plenty of plans for women but no plans for another wife. As a waitress in a tight black tank top and painted-on jeans passed, he said, "Excuse me…"

"Yes, hon?"

"I need another one of these," Robin said, holding his glass up. "Sonny, you want a Sam Adams?"

"Wouldn't mind. A glass of ice water, too," Sonny said.

"OK."

"Thanks, hon."

"I always thought you Lord's Men always preferred to hang out together."

"You're the only guys who call us that, nobody else. We call each other the Stars, of course."

"You guys are so tight-lipped about what goes on over there we just wind up making up stories."

"Everyone thinks that we're like all of the other right-wing rags he has on three continents, but it's not… exactly like that. Sure, the editorial board is totally reactionary now, and the Guild is dead there, but they don't tell us what to report. He doesn't like getting scooped, that's for sure."

Sonny nodded. "Thank you," he said to the waitress who had arrived with their drinks. "I have to admit, he can be charming in person."

"You've hung out with him? I've seen him maybe twice since he bought the *Star*."

"I've had drinks with him at some charity party a year back. The guy actually tried to recruit me to the *Star*, did you hear about that?"

"Really?"

"He kept saying, 'You're the fresh new voice we need, you'd be a hell of an addition to the family.'" Sonny shook his head and took a drink of water. "I think he had the idea of making me into the *Star's* tamed liberal. Not that I necessarily consider myself a Democrat."

"Well, Democrats and liberals are two different things," Robin said before diving into his own drink.

"Anyway, I was wondering something. I was wondering if he was interested in recruiting me again..."

"Oh, boy, here we go..."

"And by recruiting me, I mean buying the paper I work for," Sonny finished.

Robin fumbled his drink for a moment but managed to not spill anything. "Really?"

"Exactly. You heard anything about that?"

Robin scratched his head and did everything possible to appear puzzled. "I always hear vague rumors – Melchester's one of those men who's always looking for a deal – but I hadn't heard anything about him making a play for the *Journal*."

"I think he is, even though he's keeping it quiet. You think you could find out more?"

"Ah, hah, Sonny, really," Robin said. "That'd be breaking a few confidences..."

"Oh, please, all of us are a bunch of bitchy whiners," Sonny interrupted. "Get us free booze and food we'll talk about how we know who killed Kennedy, who really started the Chicago Fire, and how many boys Anna Bauer fucked after she divorced old Col. Bauer. How could we do our fucking jobs otherwise? Maybe we don't print it, but we sure as hell talk about it."

Robin laughed at that as he drained the old fashioned and moved on to the new one. "I always told Jack whenever I saw him that you were one of the few young lads who truly understood journalism. But, why should I help out with this?"

"I know there's a deal going down; I'm just trying to find out whether this deal is permanently fucked."

"For who, the *Journal*?"

"Maybe. But, I'm also thinking about you guys."

"The Lord's willing to take a few losses. You know the *Star* lost $1.5 million a month last year? This coming year it might be $2 million per month."

"I'm talking bigger than that."

Robin stared at Sonny, then looked down and sighed. "That bad?"

"That bad."

"Looking for a front-page headline, my boy?"

"Honestly, I'm still trying to figure out what I'd do with the information if I get it."

Robin nodded. "OK, let me ask around. It might take a few days."

"A few days might be all we have."

"Melchester's that desperate to close a deal?"

"I think it's my guys who want to close the deal right away."

"OK, I'll see what I hear."

"Beautiful." Sonny took one last drink from his water and laid a twenty on the table before leaning over to shake Robin's hand. "Have the next round on me."

## Chapter 13

Sonny was in the newsroom's break room alone later that afternoon when Joey snuck in. "Hi," she said, "any dinner plans for the evening? I was thinking of picking up Chinese tonight."

"Sounds good to me..." Sonny began to say but was interrupted by the buzzing of his cell phone. "Sorry, it's Ed – I need to see what he needs."

"Hey, kid," Ed said on the other end, "looks like our poking around got an audience. You had dinner yet?"

"Sort of."

"I got word from some people – you need to get down to the Second Star tonight for dinner."

"What the hell, you taking me out?"

"The Man wants to speak to you. Tonight."

"Ah," Sonny said, realizing who he meant. "I need to call anyone else?"

"He's expecting you at six. You just show up. For Christ's sakes don't look like a bum as usual when you get there, OK?"

"*OK*. Take care, Ed."

"You too, kid."

Sonny disconnected, then looked at Joey. "What's up?" she said.

"I've got a work thing to go to tonight. Catch up later?"

"What, you have to meet with Richard or John Michael or someone?"

"Different Man," Sonny replied.

\*\*\*

The Second Star was one of the more popular dinner stops for Chicago's elite end powerful. It occupied the 40$^{th}$ floor of the Rainier Building, a Gold Coast high-rise overlooking Lake

Jason Liegois

Michigan, including condos, offices, and a five-star hotel. The Second Star was the high-end restaurant that served the hotel.

Sonny didn't have a tie that evening, but he wore dark khakis, brown leather shoes, and a dark brown sport coat over his denim shirt. By now the bandage on his hand and his face had been joined by a faint bruise around the cut near his right eye.

When he got to the lobby, an elegant black man, whose navy custom suit was well set off by a diamond-ringed Rolex and pinky onyx ring, approached him as soon as he entered. "Mr. Turner?" he said in a BBC-quality British accent.

"Yes?"

"Follow me, please." He ushered him into the dining area with a sweep of his arm.

The dining area was occupied but not filled with customers. Diners guarded their seats at glass tables and Bauhaus-derivative chairs, ready to be seen but not looking at anyone else. The only sounds that could be heard were the clink of stoneware, the footfalls of the wait staff across the bright bamboo-wood floors and the whispers between that same wait staff and the guests.

Black Bond led Sonny to a corner booth. As the two approached, however, Sonny slowed down as he recognized the single guest at the table - Andrew Charlton, Earl of Melchester, owner of WorldWide Media, parent company of the *Chicago Star*.

He was smaller than he appeared in pictures and television, but he seemed to fill the corner of the room with his presence. He sported a grey suit, Guccis, and a matching crème shirt and tie. He'd shaven his head bald ever since he lost the first millimeter of hairline around the age of 30, and it had stayed the same in the three decades since, more Professor X than Mussolini. Except for a single plain gold wedding band, there was no other jewelry. The handful of lines in the corners of his eyes and mouth were the only hint at his true age, except for the steel-rim glasses he used to gaze at a copy of the *Chicago Star* laid across his table, his glass of water and tea cup off to the side.

Lord Melchester waited until Sonny was next to the table before he looked up at him. "Samuel, glad you could make it to dinner. Thank you Randall; that will be all for now."

"M'lord." With that and a short nod to Melchester, Black Bond was off.

Sonny took a seat opposite of Melchester as a slim blonde waitress showed up. "Hello, sir, what would you like to drink to start off with?"

Sonny scanned what Melchester had before answering. "One coffee, black, and ice water."

The waitress nodded, not writing out a ticket. "I'll be right back."

Melchester scanned Sonny as he eased into his chair. "Taken up prizefighting recently, Samuel?" A brief chuckle, then suppressed. "No, I'm just having a go. Sorry to hear about the break in. Do the authorities have any leads?"

"Still up in the air at the moment. Unfortunately, I already promised I'd talk to my paper first. I'll talk to you guys after, though. Honestly, for a moment I thought one of your boys was behind it."

Melchester kept his face neutral. Only his "Indeed," hinted at his disturbance at Sonny's suggestion. "Is this a thought you're still... entertaining?"

"Nah, not your guys' style. Now, your boys might find out who hit my place and try and get an exclusive with him, but not that."

Melchester held up the *Star* as if he was reading something up close but he was hiding the tiniest of smiles. "We still might at that."

"No surprise. Thanks very much," he said to the waitress who brought him his drinks with full efficiency and silence. "Lord Melchester, I was curious as to why you wanted to have dinner with me."

"Why? Well, I thought my understanding was that you wanted to speak with WorldWide Media executives about a potential story. Since I'm CEO of the corporation, of course, I thought I might be of some assistance."

Melchester folded his paper and folded his arms as he turned his full attention to Sonny. "Samuel, you must be an excellent poker player, with how calm you are. But really? Chatting Robin up at the local bar, having old Edward ringing up his past drinking friends at my paper, you don't think I'd hear about that? I daresay one of the reasons the FBI had me under surveillance off and on since the Eighties is that they want to know how to do counterintelligence properly."

"I'm sure you could teach them a lot." There were persistent rumors that Melchester had worked for MI-6 for a time while traveling as a graduate student in continental Europe, and that he continued to pass them the odd tidbits of info.

"So. Why the subterfuge? I'm sure I could answer the questions you have. Whether you will approve of the answers is another matter entirely." Melchester leaned back in his chair and looked out the window.

"Maybe it would be best if we put our orders in first," Sonny noted, picking up the 10-page menu in front of him. "What would you recommend from the value menu?"

Melchester scowled at that. "The value menu? Good Lord, Samuel, your money's no good here tonight."

Sonny scanned the menu for a moment. "OK. In that case, I see fish and chips. What Michelin two-star has fish and chips?"

"A Michelin two-star that makes the best quality cod fish and chips around," Melchester said as if he was spilling a dirty secret to Sonny.

The waitress appeared for their order. "OK," Sonny said, "the fish and chips meal, plus a clam chowder bowl."

"Very well," the waitress said, still no ticket visible.

Melchester ordered a French duck entrée with some wine-based sauce, as well as a Bordeaux red. "None for me, thanks," Sonny said regarding the wine.

As the waitress left, Melchester turned to Sonny. "There, then. You had questions for me."

Sonny nodded and took a sip from his coffee before plunging in. "OK," he said, "do you currently have an interest in either buying the *Chicago Journal* or merging it with the *Star*?"

# The Holy Fool

Some sailboats below in Lake Michigan caught Melchester's eye. "Hm. I'm not quite sure those would be words I'd use." *Rephrase the question* was what he was really saying.

"Fair enough. Have you had discussions with Edson Media executives or representatives about the possibility of purchasing the *Journal* or other Edson Media properties? Or," he continued after a brief pause, "have your representatives had such discussions?"

"Ah." The lord shared a private Cheshire grin. "I have not had such meetings with executives or representatives, but *my* representatives have had such meetings with *their* representatives. There has been considerable... preliminary discussions, hypothetical proposals, and the like, but matters are starting to... solidify. If I may ask a question or two?"

Sonny took a second to react, as he was still trying to digest Melchester's admission. "What? Yeah, of course."

"Would I be objectionable as the owner of the *Journal*? Wait, strike that – I would not wish you to speculate on your co-workers' feelings. Let me ask how *you* would feel as my employee. You turned it down, as I remember."

Sonny laughed. "If I *was* to speculate, I think the opinions of my co-workers would range from calling you the Savior or calling you the Antichrist."

"Ah. So, typically what people have said of me for at least the past quarter century. Your opinion?"

"I guess that would depend on whether you'd be willing to let me write about what I wanted to write."

"A man of your abilities? I'd let you write a great deal, I'd wager."

"What about something that made the US not look so good? What about something that would make the UK not look good?"

Melchester offered the smallest of shrugs. "Well, I've always believed any articles that sell newspapers are good articles. Of course, I would have final say regarding the article and its... tone, its approach. Such a thing is just common sense, isn't it?"

"Maybe. Even if we have a different view?"

"Of course," he said. "Let me ask you another question. Who, in your opinion, would be a superior leader for the *Journal* – Mr. Edson or myself?"

Sonny whistled at that, linking his fingers behind his head. "Now, that's tricky."

"If we are to be candid, Edson has a native talent for business. He can not only smell a dollar from 100 paces but knows 100 different ways he could use that dollar.

"But he's not a newspaper man, is he?" Melchester continued. "I toured my first printing press 60 years ago, Samuel. I've worked at newspapers for 50 years, and I've founded or turned around two dozen different newspapers on three continents and led them to prosperity. Do you seriously think I would *not* be an improvement over this Chicago yuppie?"

Sonny waited for a second for the words to sink in before he gave his reply. "I can see your point of view. However, I guess my answer would depend on the effect your ownership would have on the *Journal*. You talked about all of those success stories over the years, but you've also shut down your fair share of papers, even whole chains, during that time."

"A good counterpoint. However, if the *Journal*'s really that bad off, what makes you think it wouldn't collapse without me buying it?"

"That's also a good point. But if that is true, and our paper's about to die... it's our dog. We need to shoot it, not have a stranger do it."

Melchester gazed at him for a long moment. "Indeed."

"OK, next question. Thanks," Sonny said as the waitress brought his chowder. He took an experimental dip into the chowder with his spoon and took a taste as it glided across his tongue. "Wow, that is seriously good."

"Wait until the cod comes out."

"I will. OK, next question. Is there a timeline for this deal to go down?"

"If I do answer, it couldn't be for publication."

"Not for publication? You mean never?"

"That's usually what not for publication is... but of course you know that."

"I could agree to an embargo now, but I think eventually I'd want to have the right to publish it."

Melchester brought a finger to cover his mouth and pondered the proposal. "When would you want the embargo to end?"

"Within 24 hours of final negotiations beginning."

"Hm. That might have the effect of torpedoing those negotiations, wouldn't it?"

"Possibly."

"Why would I wish for that?"

"Maybe you'd prefer it to be torpedoed."

"Lad, if I worried that one division of my business was losing money at a particular time, I wouldn't be able to do any business, would I?"

"I'm not talking about a little money loss. I'm talking a money bomb, a *Cleopatra* or *Heaven's Gate* bomb, the 1987 crash."

Melchester was silent for several moments after that. "If that information was to come to me before a deal was made... that would be doing me a favor – one I would have to return."

"I believe so."

After a beat, Melchester reached into the inside of his suit jacket and produced a crème-colored business card, which he handed over to Sonny. "Samuel, my direct mobile line is printed on the bottom of the back of the card. Before you run anything, I would like you to call that number. I think I can reliably say by that time, you will have confirmed the date of the meeting through other sources. Would I not be correct?"

Sonny nodded. "Correct."

Melchester reached over the table and extended his hand. "Then, I believe I have your word on the matter."

Sonny shook on it. "You do."

"Edson has proposed a face to face meeting between him, myself, and some of our senior executives to begin final negotiations."

"Where and when?"

"Mr. Edson was interested in meeting away from Chicago for those purposes, so he chose for us to travel to Las Vegas by private jet for a working vacation."

"Vegas seems to be a strange place to keep a low profile."

"The casino we'll be staying at, the Milan, has a... long working relationship with Mr. Edson. They pride themselves on service and discretion."

"I'm waiting for the when, though."

"We will be leaving first thing Friday morning."

"This Friday? That's... shit."

To Sonny's surprise, Melchester never even flinched at the obscenity. He thought that might be above English earls, but he guessed not. "Yes, the weekend before September 19, the anniversary of the *Journal*'s founding. The... 140th anniversary, I believe?"

"On the money."

Melchester indulged in a slight chuckle before continuing. "From what Edson's representatives have communicated to us, he is eager to have the *Journal*'s status resolved in time for the anniversary celebrations, to ensure that the event goes off without complications."

Sonny had a realization that made him shake his head. "Two deadlines for Friday, then," he whispered to himself.

"Come again?"

"An unrelated matter." Sonny focused on Melchester again. "So, you'll take my call Friday night?"

"I shall."

Sonny nodded, and the two shook hands. "OK, then."

They spent another half hour eating. Sonny had to admit it was better than any fish and chips he'd ever had, even though he had to put up with a stare from Melchester when he asked for some ketchup.

\*\*\*

"So, he confirmed the meeting for you, right?" Woot said on Sonny's cell phone. "Glad he did – I wasn't hearing anything on Edson's phone."

"He's been doing everything through intermediaries."

"Great, now I'm going to have to figure if I can hack his junior executives' cell phones."

"You can try, but don't make it a priority. Right now, we need access to Edson and Cathy's full files. Maybe his AA, Mary. The financials are the most important thing to nail down before this happens next weekend."

"Later." Woot signed off.

## Chapter 14

It was 6 a.m. the next Tuesday. The sun was shining but still out of sight and the streets unpeopled when Sonny made his way down to the Keep. Sonny would have glided through the main doors, but a flying Starbucks cup stopped him in his tracks, landing just a foot in front of him, blotting his sneakers and the bottom cuff of his right jean leg.

Colton stood in front of him, gasping for breath and mayhem, if not murder, in his eyes. With no tie, an untucked shirt, and smudges on the elbows of his sport coat, Colton appeared to Sonny if he'd slept in his clothes last night, but Sonny suspected he hadn't slept. "Motherfucker," Colton wheezed.

"Now kid," Sonny said, "I'm guilty of a lot of different things, but that's not one of them."

Colton shook his head and started to approach Sonny. "How long were you planning on just using me, not saying anything? God! Who do you think you are?"

"Calm down," Sonny said, but Colton continued to move forward, chest first, bumping Sonny back and threatening. "This is bullshit! What do you have against my family, my father…?"

Colton stopped when Sonny locked narrowed eyes with him, any sense of deference or peacekeeping done. "You will get yourself together and stop doing business in the street, or I will grab that head of yours and snap your fucking neck."

The words stopped Colton in his tracks, but the mayhem stare remained. "I *will* talk to you, but not here when anyone can hear us. You want to get it out, you come with me." Sonny held the main door open with one hand and waving Colton in with the other. "Let's get this over with."

With not a word, Colton followed Sonny inside.

✻✻✻

Sonny took Colton down to his basement headquarters. "Sit down." Sonny pointed to a chair around the last long table in the room.

"I'm standing right now, thanks." Colton began pacing in front of the table. Sonny shrugged and took a seat in a chair opposite of the one Colton had refused.

"If you're looking for some sort of apology from me, you'll be waiting a long time." Colton froze in his tracks and turned to face him, but Sonny held up a hand. "Let me finish. When you first showed up, we'd just heard about your old man considering selling the *Journal*. We honestly didn't know whether you were some sort of plant for your dad or not."

"That had nothing to do with it. It was *my* idea! I wanted to work with the newspaper, be a reporter. Dad didn't pressure me in taking the job; I hounded him."

"I know that now. So, we put you to work, see if we could get any use out of having the boss's son in the newsroom. Turned our you had some talent. The more I got to know you, the more I got to like you."

"Well, thanks for having faith in me, I *guess*. But tell me. Why should I keep quiet about this, like my mom and you want? What's the point? I mean, all you want to do is save your jobs."

"No." Sonny jumped up. "The point is, I think our jobs are lost no matter what. This is about him paying for what he's done. We're scheduled to celebrate the 140th anniversary of the founding of this newspaper next week, and because of your father's financial incompetency, greed, or both, we're more likely to be announcing the *Journal* closing its doors. That can't stand," he finished, slamming his palm on the desk in front of him. "It's about making them pay."

"Making them pay? What about reporting this to the cops, if it's illegal?"

"It likely is legal when you get down to it. The cops, the SEC, they won't do shit. I've seen how long it can take for justice, and I'm not interested in waiting. One thing I've come to realize recently, it's like what Eddie Murphy said in *Trading*

*Places*, the best way to get back at rich people is to make them poor. That's what's going down."

Colton laughed. "Shouldn't I be trying to oppose you because he's going to be broke if you do this?"

"I'm going to try something with you that probably nobody's ever tried with you before. I'm going to treat you like an adult. You ready?" Colton said nothing but nodded. "Right now, I don't even care whether you hate me or not. I don't care if you think trying to keep this paper open is stupid or that your dad did nothing wrong. Hell, I even think it's a fool's errand, but I owe my mentors to give it a shot.

"What I want from you is just two things. One is, do your job and get that story on UUF. Chicago and the rest of the country probably need to know for sure that the biggest investment bank in Chicago's about to go belly-up.

"Second, I need you to keep your mouth shut until the end of Friday," Sonny continued. "Not because of any affection for me, or Gus, or the paper. No, the reason you'll do this is to look out for your mom, to make sure she gets the money she needs to live comfortably. It all comes down to self-interest."

"You have a deal." Colton stuck out his hand. "Not for you, but for my mom and the people working here. For them, I'm willing to keep my mouth shut for now. You, though? I could care less if they let you go tomorrow."

Sonny accepted it. "A good day to be pragmatic. When do you think you'll get the UUF information?"

"Later tonight. You want me to bring it over to you?"

"Yeah, to me, personally, outside of the office. Christ, most of the stuff we've been doing the past week has been out of the office. You, Gus, and I are going to talk about it. You ready for this?"

"No," Colton said, getting up, "But I'm doing it anyway."

"My man."

\*\*\*

Gus was sorting through e-mails at his desk when Sonny showed up. "Can we talk?" Sonny asked.

"Might as well do it here." Gus waved at him to sit in a nearby chair. "Nobody's here just yet."

"Assuming that they haven't bugged your desk or whatever." Sonny sat down and immediately scanned the underside of Gus' cubicle.

"Not likely. You had anyone else follow you, kid?"

"If I'm being followed, they're either not doing it as closely as they were before or they're being a lot more subtle about it. I'm continuing to take precautions."

"I think that if someone's following you, it has to do with you and that Iraq project." Gus leaned back and scratched his head before continuing. "Either the Feds might be watching you and seeing whether you're contacting a source or Walker's doing it for them to get in good with his old buddies."

"Either one makes sense."

"Did you work everything out with your source? You managed to talk him or her down from that ultimatum? We just have to be careful with how we present this."

Sonny looked away for a moment, away from the city desk bullpen, and then turned back to Gus. "Yeah, I worked it out. It's fine."

"Glad to hear."

\*\*\*

It was the morning news meeting for the *Journal* when Richard Connors made an appearance, to the surprise of Carlo, Gus, and everyone else there. Hesitating to stand up and make his presence known, he got to his feet when he realized they were waiting for him to do something.

"Normally, I wouldn't come down and make a fuss," Richard said. "Carlo's been doing an excellent job running the daily meetings, but I was wondering if I could take a minute to make a couple of announcements?"

"Absolutely," Carlo said without hesitation. "The floor's yours."

"Thank you," Richard said. "First, I wanted to give everyone a heads-up that a good portion of senior management, including myself, Cathy, and John Michael, will

## The Holy Fool

be out of town this weekend beginning early Friday. It's actually going to be a working vacation – we'll be meeting with prospective business partners over the weekend."

"Where will you be at?" Carlo said.

"Las Vegas," Richard said. Then his face drooped for a moment as he realized who he was talking to. "Oh, I'm sorry, Carlo. Did you get the email invite Cathy sent?" Carlo shook his head. "Well, you're certainly invited if you are interested."

"Who else is going?" Gus said.

"Most everyone else we're going to need here to hold down the fort. Gus, I hope you're not put out staying here."

"Nah," Gus said, "Not really a gambler."

"Carlo, what about you?" Richard said.

"Can I get back to you on that?" Carlo said.

"Of course, of course." Richard had some 3x5 note cards when he spoke earlier, and now shuffled them before continuing. "During that time, we'll also be making some plans regarding the anniversary celebrations next week. Big anniversary, one hundred and... 20th, am I right, Gus?"

"140th."

"Ah, yes, 140th, big anniversary. It will be a big celebration in the main lobby downstairs, plenty of food, drink, and music for everyone." There were several affirmative grunts at that news. "Depending on how the working vacation goes, we might have some great news to share then regarding news partnerships and business arrangements that will take us well into this new century of ours."

"Any clue as to what those might be?" Carlo said.

"Sorry, can't get into details right now, before everything's finalized," Richard said. "Hope you understand. Anybody else with any questions? No? OK, I'll let Carlo go on with the meeting. Thank you, everyone." He gave his note cards a hesitant shuffle, turned, and eased out the door.

Carlo glanced at Gus, then turned to his notes and ran through one of the shortest daily meetings in memory. He did praise Casey Barnes for his work on Freddie Mac and Fannie Mae going into conservatorship – "Someone needs to get that kid a case of whiskey or something," he said. "The longer I'm here, it seems like he's the only one in the DC bureau breaking stories."

"He deserves it," Gus said.

After reviewing that and the rumors that Washington Mutual's CEO was on the way out due to losses at that investment bank, Carlo turned to Gus. "What's going on with UUF again? I thought Colton was working on something with that?"

"Yeaaah, he's working on something, but I'd need to brief you in private on this," Gus said.

"Hhm." Carlo reviewed his notes again. "In any rate, he won't have anything ready for tomorrow's paper, right?"

"True," Gus said.

"OK, we'll talk after the meeting." he said.

Carlo and Gus waited for everyone else to clear out. "OK," Carlo said when they were alone, "This getaway Richie Boy's talking about. Am I losing my mind, truly, or is that going to be where John Michael and the rest of our so-called brain trust are going to meet to see who they're selling the paper to?"

Gus heaved in his chair and sighed. "Yeah, that's the general idea."

"Fuck me," Carlo said. "So, what do you think? Should I get some sun in Vegas, or should I stay here and see what you and your kids do?"

"I guess it depends on how you feel about your job, Carlo."

Carlo folded his hands in front of his face and leaned on his elbows as he stared off into space for a few moments. "Might not matter either way. I stay here, John Michael and the rest of them will think I knew about this all along and can me. I go with them, I look like I didn't know anything about it and John Michael cans me for not knowing what's going on in my own newsroom."

"Yeah."

"Fuck me." He got up from his seat and started to walk laps around the conference room table. He stopped when he got to Gus. "Well, I guess I'm telling Richard that I'll be sticking around this weekend. Why waste money in Vegas when I'm going to need it until I get my first unemployment check?"

*\*\*\**

By mid-afternoon, Gus was reviewing the initial pages for the next day. Sonny walked out of his office and went past the now combined City/Metro desk. "All right," Sonny said, "I'm out the rest of the day. Call me when we have a location for tonight."

"I'll text everyone," Gus said, "It'll be faster that way."

"No problem," Sonny said, slinging his bag onto his shoulder.

"Where are you at with your columns?" Gus said.

"Wednesday and Friday's are in the can already," Sonny said. "For obvious reasons, I'm holding out on Sunday's to see what shakes out."

"OK. Don't forget the blog posts, though. I don't want static from up top that you're not producing."

## Chapter 15

Sonny was walking toward Jenni Hardin's apartment when his cell phone when off. Noticing the number, he hit respond right away. "Hey, hon."

"How are you?" Joey said.

"Great. Did he show up there?"

"And already put my drinks on his tab. Apparently he knows the executive chef here. We're going to try a seven-course chef's table special."

"Lucky you, I might have time for a burger tonight."

"He's in the restroom now. Any advice?"

"Well, try not to go home with him, but otherwise… if he wants to get together later, maybe set a date for next week or whatever. Let him at least think you're interested."

"OK."

Sonny was quiet for a moment as he stopped in the middle of the street. "Thanks for doing this. There's a little less stress knowing he's not coming out here any second. And anything he tells you will be useful, so keep your ears and head open."

"Well, I wanted to help you, right? See you tonight?"

"Of course. I'm going to be late, though."

"Sure. I'll wait up for you."

"OK."

Sonny went to a parked grey Toyota Camry where TT was keeping watch over the apartment. He knocked on the windshield, and TT rolled it down.

"Anyone there with her right now?" Sonny said.

"No, just her kid and her mom; that's it."

"Well, then. You ready to ruin someone's life?"

TT rolled up the window, opened his door, and eased out. "I was in the narcotics division for 10 years. This won't even make the top 100 list."

***

Jason Liegois

    Jenni Hardin, her mother Olivia, and her daughter Caity had just finished a dinner of Olive Garden takeout. Caity had made something of a mess with some cheese ravioli, but her mom had helped her clean her up and she was now tooling around with a kitchen playset stashed in one corner of the living room when they heard the bell ring.
    "Ugh." Jenni slid the last of the food containers into the refrigerator. "I'll get it."
    "You don't have to answer it," Olive said. "They can't expect people to answer the door at dinnertime."
    "It's OK, it'll just take a minute." She was still irritated, though; she was already set for bed, wearing a comfortable pink sweatshirt and grey yoga pants, no shoes. If some door to door salesman insisted on bothering her at dinner, they could deal with her being unfashionable…
    She opened the door to find Sonny and TT standing on her doorstep. "Ms. Hardin?" Sonny said.
    "Yes, who are you?" Jenni said. "Who are you with?" Then she took a closer look at the bigger man and recognized his face.
    "This is Arturo Torres," the bigger man said, "and I'm…"
    "Sonny Turner," she said. "I… I recognized you from the ads on the buses. I did a promotion for the radio station for your column once."
    "Yeah," Sonny said, "So, we have to talk with you about a story we're working on."
    "I don't know what I can help you with…"
    "It involves your relationship with our boss, and your child," Sonny said. "We're running a story about this, and it's going to happen whether you talk tonight or not."
    She started to ease the door closed, taking shelter behind it as she did. "No, I have no idea what you're talking about. If you could just go…"
    "Ma'am, you might think he's looking out for you, but he's not," TT said, his voice soft and even, reaching over and placing his hand on the upper part of the doorway. "Your boyfriend is a guy who seems to have a lot of money, but his company's in a lot of trouble and he might be hoarding money. Plus, he's seeing someone else."

She stared laser-hot holes into TT but stopped closing the door. "Ma'am, we want to help you. Could we just talk for a few moments, please?" TT said.

Without a word, she stepped away from the door and waved for the two men to enter.

\*\*\*

As the little girl played with first her kitchen set and then with some expensive American Girl doll setup, Jenni sat down on one of her plush leather couches and stared at the two reporters opposite from her, seated on a matching couch.

Olivia came in with two mugs of coffee and handed one each to the reporters. "I'm sorry," she said, "when you first came in, I thought you were the police, that something had happened to my husband or something like that."

"Arturo gets that a lot," Sonny said, taking his first sip.

She turned to face TT. "You're a police officer?"

"*Retired*," TT said. "I'm on my second career."

"You were with the Chicago PD?"

"Yes, ma'am."

With a satisfied nod, Olivia went to the kitchen, retrieved mugs for her and her daughter, and sat back down. "And I did recognize you from your pictures, Mr. Turner. I can't say I'm a fan of your column – a bit vulgar for my taste."

"Yes, ma'am," Sonny said.

"Very well." Sonny noticed that Jenni was easing back into her seat, not acting like she wanted to say anything at all. "Now that we have introductions out of the way," Olivia continued, "I'd like to ask you why you think we should even talk to you."

The two men glanced at each other and called a silent play. As TT took his first sip of coffee, Sonny plunged ahead. "This is a story that's of the highest importance to our newspaper, Mrs. Hardin."

"Well, I know newspapers print many different things now that used to be restricted to *The National Enquirer*, *Confidential*, and gossip at the hair salon," Olivia said.

Jason Liegois

"This story will impact more people than just your family, Mrs. Hardin."

A bemused grin crept across Olivia's face as she cradled her coffee cup in her hands. "I'd be interested to know how what you think my daughter has done with her boss, your boss, has any impact on anyone except for her."

On instinct, Sonny glanced around to see if anyone was watching or listening in. Then: "What I'm about to tell you right now, if it gets out or you let people know about it, it would mean the end of my job, the end of Arturo's job here, the end of the careers of basically everyone at the *Journal*, and maybe even your own daughter's career. I'm going to have to put a lot of trust into you."

The demeanor of the two women changed. Jenni sat up straight in her seat, fear starting to tighten her facial and shoulder muscles. Olivia did a better job of controlling her emotions, not moving, but a sense of alarm seemed to be creeping behind her eyes. "Could you explain yourself, please?" she said.

Sonny nodded. "You recall that two years back, John Michael and Edson Media purchased Journal Media from the Bauer family and the estate of their cousin, Jack DeFoe. The difficulty with that purchase is that he didn't have a lot of liquid cash flow. It was a leveraged buyout, using securities owned by Edson Media as collateral. Those securities are based off home mortgages, which have been very lucrative in recent years.

"There are several problems that are now facing Edson Media," Sonny continued. "We now believe that the paper has been losing more money than John Michael and senior executives have admitted to up to this point. Part of that might be unexplained losses, and part of that might be John Michael skimming some profits off the top. Also, we are about to obtain information confirming our suspicions that the securities that Edson has been using as collateral, that were initially purchased through UUF Bank, are about to lose a lot of their value due to, let's say, major market corrections. So, we have a newspaper owner desperate to sell a property he knows is a money pit, so much of one that the first thing a new owner would do is scrap the whole paper and sell off its assets."

After a moment of silence, Olivia said, "Even if all of that is true, what does that have to do with my daughter and granddaughter, other than Jenni possibly, maybe, might have to find another job?"

"Your major concern, I think, would be about whether John Michael continues to support your daughter and granddaughter financially, correct?"

"I and my husband can help our daughter just fine, thank you," Olivia said.

"Regardless, you want to make sure that your grandson gets what he is due from his father, right?" Sonny said. "If he's hiding money left and right and dumping part or all of his media empire, do you think he's going to be worried about a secret family?"

"We're going to be fine," Jenni said, causing everyone to turn and face her. "I see Johnny every other day, and he always takes time to be with Caity! And honestly, he's not going to hang around that woman for the rest of his life, now that his other kids are grown." After hearing her name, Caity turned from her toys and began wandering toward her mother.

Olivia unleased the deepest of sighs and sat her cup on the coffee table in front of them so that she could manage a double facepalm. "Jenni, please," she said.

"But Mom..." Jenni said, the pleading in her voice dropping 15 years off her age.

"But nothing." Olivia turned back to Sonny. "I grew up in a very strict household. My parents went to church activities twice a week with the local Catholic church, taught me to make the right choices in life. But, they also told me about keeping things private and not interfering with the business of others. And, as I've gotten older, I've realized being judgmental about people doesn't do any good. Would I like my daughter to get married and have a partner? Sure. Is it necessary? Not if he's not committed to her. If women can shoot insurgents in Iraq and win the Silver Star for it, they can be successful mothers on their own."

"You don't know he's not faithful, Mom," Jenni said. She picked up Caity, who had started hugging her leg, up and into her lap.

Olivia turned to TT. "How many other women do you know that he's been with?"

"We know for sure one is Cathy Boone – we've observed the two of them out together socially," TT said.

"Cathy Boone? You mean, the publisher?" Olivia said. TT nodded.

"What?" Jenni said. "But why? She's past 40." Then she saw her mother giving her the evil eye off to the side and decided to stay quiet for a while.

"He's out on a date right now with Joey Halverson, another *Journal* staff member," Sonny said.

"You know that for sure?" Olivia said.

"She volunteered to do it for me," Sonny said. "He approached her first, but she's playing along."

"You still haven't answered why doing this story is so important to you."

"To be honest, we're trying to do anything that's going to cause John Michael public and economic stress," Sonny said. "If he's worrying about his wife and you after his money, that's just one more roadblock to completing a financial deal for the paper."

"Do you think that will actually work?" Olivia said.

"Happens all the time. Tom Clancy had to stop his plans to buy the Minnesota Vikings a decade ago because he was getting divorced," Sonny said.

"Look, we admit that we've got our own motives for doing this, but we're also mad that he's doing this to your daughter," TT said. "Sonny's parents broke up because his dad couldn't stop fooling around on his mom. I've got two daughters, and I don't even know what I would do to any guy that did this to one of my girls. We want things to be better for you."

There was a long silence. "What really bothers me is that he's never come out and said that he's Caity's father," Olivia finally said as Jenni bounced the little girl up and down on her knee. "He's never denied it, but he's never admitted it. Jenni offered to get a DNA test done before she was born, but John

Michael has just kept putting her off. I'm not sure he even wants to think about it."

"We can get that taken care of," TT said.

"Taken care of?" Jenni said.

"Yes, we can do that." TT turned to Sonny. "Sonny, can you get the video on your iPhone fired up?"

As Sonny began to pull out his iPhone, TT reached into the tan briefcase he'd brought in with him and pulled out a plastic tube, a small manila envelope, packing tape, and a bite-sized Snickers bar. He laid them out on the couch next to him. "Ms. Hardin? Can you have Caity come over here to me?"

Jenni glanced over to her mother, who gave the faintest of nods. Jenni leaned down and whispered to the little blond girl in the long red cotton nightgown on her lap. After a moment, the girl hopped off Jenni's lap and started to walk toward TT. "You mind her having a Snickers?" TT said to Jenni.

"Tonight, I think we can make an exception," Olivia said.

Caity made it all the way over to TT when she stumbled for a moment and steadied herself by holding onto TT's knee. "Hi, honey," TT said, "can you do something for me? I'll give you a treat if you do."

Caity looked over at her mother. "It's OK, honey," Jenni said. With a wide smile, she turned to face the bronze man and nodded. "She's still a little shy with talking," Jenni told TT.

"It's OK," TT said. He unscrewed the top of the plastic tube. The top had a cotton swab attached to it. "Caity? Can you do something for me? Can you open your mouth wide? Like this?" He mimed opening his mouth wide, even extending his tongue just a touch. "Can you do that, honey?"

Caity nodded and imitated him, opening her mouth. "OK, Caity, just keep your mouth open just a moment. Just a second, OK?" In a swift but soft movement, he picked up the cotton swab, brought it to Caity's open mouth, and brushed the swab against the inner sides of her cheek.

By the time Caity realized what was happening, TT already had taken the swab out and placed it back into the specimen tube. "All done, honey. *Good* girl."

After sitting the tube down next to him, TT unwrapped the Snickers bar, gave it to a very puzzled little girl, and hugged her. "Very good girl. Go back to Mom, OK?"

Caity hugged his arm, almost but not quite dropping the bar in the process. With a satisfied grin, she turned around to walk back to Jenni. Caity had half the bar eaten by the time she made it back.

Without TT having to say anything, Sonny had kept the iPhone focused on the now sealed tube. He continued to film it as TT dropped it into the manila envelope, sealed it with the packing tape, and wrote down the time and date. TT also made sure to pull out his own phone and show it to Sonny, indicating the time and date.

"So, that's the idea?" Olivia said, intrigued. "Would that be allowed into a courtroom?"

"Probably not," TT said. "But at the least, it's enough to convince a judge to order his own DNA test."

"We'll match that sample with either a sample we can recover from John Michael or perhaps one of his family," Sonny said.

Jenni got up from the couch. "Oh, wait," she said, "I think I might have something you can use in the laundry or the bathroom. Just a second." She eased out of the room.

***

As Sonny and TT walked back to TT's car, Sonny said, "Thanks for saying what you did in there. You really managed to... mellow out the situation."

"No problem."

Sonny's phone began to buzz, so he stopped in the middle of the sidewalk to answer it. "Turner," he said.

"It's Gus," was the answer.

"Yeah?"

"We're meeting at The Briarwood," Gus said, mentioning an out of the way bar in Uptown, not a usual hangout of the *Journal* staff.

"We sure?"

"Yeah."

# The Holy Fool

"What time?"

"10:30, like before."

"Fine, we'll be there."

"We?"

"TT's with me. Does Woot know?"

"Hadn't had the chance to contact him. I'll do it right now."

"No, I'll call him myself; I need to check in with him anyway."

Gus grunted over the phone. "Fine."

"Later." He cut off the phone conversation. "Gus," he said, launching into a brief review of the conversation. "But still, thanks for helping with the girl," Sonny said, changing subjects. "How did you manage that?"

"Had practice with crime victims before. Besides, I remember when my girls were still that age. It just sort of comes back to you, even after all these years. You'll see how it works."

"What do you mean, I'll see how it works?"

"You'll see how it happens, when you get kids of your own," TT said as they got to his car. TT started to get in but stopped when Sonny was just standing there out on the sidewalk. "What?"

"When I get kids? That's a bit of an assumption, isn't it?"

"What, you never thought about having kids?" TT said, laughing.

"Honestly? I've never thought about it one way or the other."

"I'm thankful me and my first wife never had kids. We were close, but she had a miscarriage at least twice. Best thing that ever happened to us, though. Five years in, I realized she couldn't even handle life, much less being married to a cop. My girl Anita, now, she handled being a cop's wife and now a reporter's wife. It's the rare ladies you have to hang on to, right?"

Sonny shrugged. "Yeah."

## Chapter 16

The Briarwood wasn't the first place you'd expect Chicago newspaper journalists to hang out. It was more of a home for the new hipsters, old hippies, and in-between weirdoes that were making the Uptown neighborhood an intriguing place to be rather than the backwater it had been for the past 30 or 40 years. Now residential prices were climbing to a new upscale level. However, it hadn't affected the Briarwood.

Gus, Sonny, TT, and Woot met in one of the booths in the back. "The kid here yet?"

Woot craned his head high above the other members of the group, staring out into the crowd. They followed Woot's eyes to Colton Edson, slumming in Abercrombie and Fitch denim, speeding walked toward the ground without looking up at them the entire time.

As Colton sat down directly across from Sonny, Sonny asked, "You find something about UUF?"

There was a bitter laugh from Colton as he slapped down a reporter's notebook and file folder onto the table. "Yeah, I found something."

"What did you find out?" Gus said.

Colton stared out into the distance at nothing, keeping his hands at his sides. "I've been talking to these guys over at UUF, trying to get some solid information on their financial condition. One of them was a former classmate of mine. He's been the most reluctant to talk to me, passed me off to some guys in their risk management department, all that. But today, he told me everything."

"Do you think we can go with a more specific description?" Gus said.

"Yeah, UUF is terminally fucked." Colton slouched back in the booth.

"How so?"

Disgusted, shaking his head, Colton went on. "All of these complex mortgage and debt securities that UUF's been specializing in, that have been making the bank billions? They're beginning to run into trouble because the value of the mortgages and the likelihood they'll get paid back is falling through the floor. Most of those securities aren't worth a half or a third of the 'fair market value' these things supposedly are. And now, the bank is scrambling to see if they can pawn off the paper onto someone else before everyone figures out that fact."

"That even possible?" TT asked.

"As B... my friend explained it, the bank sees that they have two options. Either they try to dump it all at once, a fire sale, or they try and sneak it out the back door for the next two weeks and hope no one notices."

"What's the difference?" Gus said.

"Fire sale, it's more likely that they get rid of the paper in time before it's guaranteed to take down the bank. The bad news is, something that big is likely to ruin the securities market for the next decade, ruin their relationships with their clients, and is guaranteed to get the SEC snooping around their books. The second way, they keep a low profile, have a chance of continuing to do business with securities, and there's no panic. However, if they get caught with the paper and the prices begin to skydive, the company might not make it. It's like they're trying to decide whether to pull off a Band-Aid super-fast or super-slow."

"Which one have they decided on?" Sonny said.

"The slow way," Colton said.

"They've started the trades?" Sonny said.

"Yeah, and everyone, especially the traders, are trying to put a brave face on it, but most everyone else is scared to hell."

"And your friend?" Gus asked.

"He's trying to stay on until the end," Colton said through his fingers. "He's trying to pull off as many deals as possible, but he was in hysterics with me. The guy asked me if there was a way he could get on with the *Journal*, or something in Edson Media. He could barely hand me his resume; his hands were shaking so bad. I told him I'd look at it; what else was I going

# The Holy Fool

to do?" He uncovered his face and looked at the group. "He always was the cockiest bastard in the room, the guy who'd always come out on top, but now..."

"Welcome to the poor man's world, kid," Sonny said. "What I want to ask is, do you have enough there to put together a full story or not?"

"A story? Hah, yeah, sure, there's enough for a story here, why not? 'House of Cards,' something cinematic like that? When do you want me to write the final draft?"

"We need it ready for Friday night." Gus' voice was vacant.

Colton said nothing for a few moments, then dread and comprehension spread across his face as he sat up straight in his seat. "You want me to write about everything."

"Yes," Gus said.

"For Saturday's edition."

"Yes."

Colton let out a long breath. "Shit," he said. "I remember what Mom told me. That's going to torpedo their whole plan to sell the paper off. Once this gets out, it's going to be a feeding frenzy."

"That's the general idea," Sonny said.

"Christ, all of them are going to be out on the street by the end of Monday."

"It's either them or us," Sonny said. "You're not on board with this, consider your position, leave those files here, get up, and get the hell out of here. We'll take care of business, even if you're not."

There was a long moment of silence after Sonny finished talking. Colton sat stock still at his seat. "How about it, Colton?" Sonny said.

Colton stared at Sonny before answering. "I'm a reporter," he finally said. "This is what I do, right?"

"Exactly," Sonny said.

"OK," Colton said.

"OK," Sonny said.

"OK," Gus said, waving the two silent. "What else do we need to get settled before Friday?"

\*\*\*

Sonny walked out of the bar 20 minutes later, waving goodbye. The minute he hit the sidewalk, he took off at a fast pace around the block, out of sight from the bar.

He finally stopped three blocks away. As he stood there, a black stretch Cadillac pulled up and stopped in front of him.

A rear window rolled down, and Sonny could see Diane Edson in the back seat. "Need a ride?"

With a nod, Sonny stepped off the curb, opened the rear door, and eased into the car.

The back of the limo was empty, and the black-tinted window separating the driver's compartment from the rear was all the way up. As the Cadillac eased away from the curb, Diana said, "Not too hard to find me, I hope."

"No problems."

"So, what have you pulled out of my husband's computers and phones?" She eased back, reclining in the rear bench seats.

"A lot of things that you wouldn't really care about. Some things you would, like communications between him and his mistresses. The most interesting thing, however, is his bank records."

"What about those?"

"There were three special accounts at an entirely different bank than UUF that were kind of... off to the side, I guess. We aren't sure what is in them, but we get the feeling that if he's hiding any money, that's where it might be."

"Any reason for that?"

"Well, first, you don't know anything about those accounts, do you?"

"This is the first I've heard about them."

"That's interesting, because he has you as the owner of those accounts."

She took in a deep breath as she stared out the window. "Really?"

"Yes. That's also related to why we couldn't check and see what was in the accounts. They're set up so that the designees have to come in in person, with the passwords to the accounts, before they can deposit, withdraw, or even check the balance."

She turned back to face him, curious. "Who are the designees, then?"

"You, and John Michael. So, one of you has to walk into a bank with the password to do business."

"So, I have the description…"

"And I have the password," Sonny finished.

"Ah." She smiled at him. "It appears that you're making a business proposition."

"We get together Friday. I'll be there with the password, and you'll be there with yourself. Together, we'll get the money. Is it a deal?" He held out his hand.

Diana took it, then gave it the lightest of kisses before letting go. "Deal."

"How's Michael John doing, by the way? I heard that he was arrested the other weekend."

"It was a DUI, his second. It's a sad thing when you're praying that your son doesn't kill anyone when he goes out partying on the weekend."

It was quiet in the car for a moment. "I'm really sorry to hear that; is he out on bail?"

"Still in Cook County Jail. One of the few things John Michael and I agreed on lately. He because he doesn't want to be in our son's presence, and I because he needs time in jail to realize what he's doing to himself. If he were your son, how would you feel about it?"

"No offense, but I'm not really an expert at parental decisions."

"What would you do?"

Sonny stared at Diana as he opened them again and leaned towards her in his seat. "I'd try to get him out of jail as fast as possible, then into the best treatment center I could find for six months, maybe a year even, and then get him into a sober living house for a year minimum."

"You know a good place?"

Sonny shook his head. "One of my bosses, he's been sober for 20 years. I'll reach out to him."

She patted his arm. "Thank you. So, when should we meet again?"

"Friday 8 a.m. We'll go to the bank, get business taken care of."

"All right. Should we pick you up at the same place?"

Sonny shook his head and handed her a sheet of paper. "That address instead. I'm not positive if someone is still following me, but I don't want to give them an easy time of it."

"All right." She tucked the paper into her purse. "Should I drop you off at your apartment?"

"No. Just get me to Halstead and drop me off there. I need the walk, anyway."

"More operational security?"

"Yeah." Sonny leaned back into his seat.

"That sounds like a pretty exhausting way to go through the day."

"Believe it."

\*\*\*

It was pitch black by the time Sonny got back to Joey's building and started to walk up the stairs to her apartment. When he got to the door, he didn't bother knocking; the previous weekend, Joey had presented him with four keys on a ring that would open all the front locks she had on the door.

After noting there was no wedge in the doorway and opening all the locks, Sonny swung the door open. He noticed there was four white, lit candles along a work table to the right, in a straight line through Joey's studio to the door leading to the remainder of the apartment. "Hi, Sonny, that you?"

"Yep. Everything OK?" he said as he closed the door and fastened all of the locks behind him."

"It went OK. Come on in. I have something to show you."

Sonny walked through the door and into the living room. The lights were out, but thick white candles topped the kitchen counter, the coffee table in the living room, and the living room windowsill.

She was wearing one of her black silk robes that just dropped down to her mid-thigh. Her feet were propped up on the table, and he saw her smart phone on the table, alongside what appeared to be an airline boarding pass. Joey patted the section of the couch next to her. "Sit down."

Sonny did. As he turned to her, he noticed a small but clear round red mark on the right side of her neck. "Hi."

She looked nervous and unsure at first. "He was really sad to see me go."

"I imagine. I'm the same way with you."

She smiled, realized he wasn't mad. "Dinner was nice, but he was a little disappointed I wouldn't follow him to this really nice hotel on the Gold Coast. I told him we'd have to do it some other time. This was the consolation prize," pointing to her neck.

Sonny ran a hand over her head. "Are you OK?"

"No, it's fine. I'm not upset. I guess you can make it bigger if you want..."

"Girl," he said, using his best Barry White voice.

"...anyway, after the hickey, that's when he gave me the plane ticket; he wants me to travel out to Vegas and meet him out there Friday. I guess he's expecting me now."

"Vegas not your thing?" Sonny laughed.

"He's not you."

"Of course not. He's wealthier, probably has a better body than me, even though he's older..."

She leaned over and kissed him on the lips. After she broke off the kiss, she touched her finger to his lips to keep him from talking. "I know you're trying to be self-deprecating but stop. It's you, all right?"

Sonny eased her finger off his mouth. "OK..."

"I'd been talking with him for 20 minutes at dinner," she said, her eyes intense and staring straight into his. "You listen to him and there's *nothing there*. You, I'm always discovering new things. Anyway, I didn't want you to worry about..."

"Do I look worried? To paraphrase Ice-T, better to have one down girl than 10 freak hoes."

"Of course; I forgot how much of a b-boy you were." Joey smiled at her own joke. "So, am I your down girl, then?"

"Absolutely."

She eased up from the couch. "I wanted to show you something."

Joey undid her robe and let it slip off her shoulders as she stepped toward Sonny. She was wearing a black silk cropped camisole on top, and on the bottom, there was a thong that was a black triangle barely covering her crotch and two strings. She turned around. "You like it?"

"Yeah," Sonny's eyebrows raised at the sight as he leaned back and draped his arms across the couch. "It looks very nice."

"It was a present from him." She looked over her shoulder, balancing on one foot as she brushed the other one over his thigh and moved it closer to his crotch. "He said he wanted me to wear it when I went to see him in Vegas, but I thought why waste it?"

"Yeah."

As she continued to play her brand of footsie with him, she leaned over and pointed to the phone and envelope on the coffee table. "I managed to record most of our date on my phone. And when he went to the restroom, I went ahead and swabbed his glass like you asked."

"You're a better reporter than you think." Sonny held her by the hips in front of him as she straightened up.

"I'm still more of an artist at heart."

Sonny let out a deep breath, then turned her around to face him. "Something wrong?"

"No, no," he said, shaking his head. He brought his hands up to her shoulders and drew her down to a kneeling position between his legs as he still sat on the couch. "But, I have to ask you something. With my mom dead, you're the main person in my life now. I'm worried that what I'm about to ask might be too much to ask of you."

She brought her fingers to his lips to quiet him. "We love each other, right?"

Joey drew her fingers away after a moment, and he said right away, "Yes."

"People who love each other do things for each other." She looked down at her outfit and frowned as she gazed back at Sonny. "This isn't involving me getting on a plane and meeting John Michael in a hotel room, is it?"

Sonny laughed. "No, no, it's something else."

"OK, what?"

He continued to hold her shoulders as he came closer to her. "I want you to jump off a cliff with me."

"Ah, at last." A crooked smile crept onto Joey's face. She leaned over and kissed him on the neck right below his ear. "I'll make a deal. I'll fool around with you after you tell me what the view looks like from the cliff."

"OK."

\*\*\*

At midnight that evening, Sonny lay wide awake in bed, a fast-asleep Joey cuddled against his left side. He hadn't even tried sleep, thinking about what he had to do. He was about to jump off the cliff he'd told Joey about.

He used his cell to dial one of his contacts. "Hey" Casey Barnes replied, sounding as awake as Sonny was.

"I've got a question. If we had to reach out to reporters, who would it be in DC?"

"OK, why's that?"

"You know why." The finality in Sonny's voice stopped Casey for a moment. "Which ones you want to approach?" Casey finally replied.

"One domestic, one foreign, preferably English-language."

There was another pause. "Jackie Carcetti with the *New York Times* and Bobby Walcott from the *Guardian*. Both are good and they don't give up sources, which is good for both of us..."

"You've got nothing to worry about. Whatever happens next is on me."

"OK, Sonny."

"Get me their contact info and let them know I'm calling tomorrow. I'll do the rest."

## Chapter 17

After all the worrying about what was going to happen on Friday, Friday arrived.

By two minutes before noon, Sonny found himself standing on a random corner on the South Side, coffee in one hand and a copy of that day's *Journal* in the other. Joey had beat him out of the apartment by at least an hour, leaving a text saying *I'll check in soon*.

Exactly two minutes later, the black Buick mini-limo pulled up directly in front of him. Switching his paper to his coffee hand, he yanked the door open and ducked into the back of the car, which pulled away from the curb before he shut the door.

Diana was waiting in the back seat, in a navy suit with a pink, collared blouse, a fashion call-out to Hilary Clinton. "Looking nice today," Sonny said.

"As you are, too. A little bit formal for you today, isn't it?"

"Well, I thought I might as well look nice if I'm going to one of the main branches of National Bank of Bern."

"I see," Diana said. "I was wondering what you were wanting for the passwords..."

Before she could finish, Sonny tossed the newspaper onto her lap. Diana half-raised out of her seat, arms outstretched, trying to scoot the paper off. "What..."

"Open it up. You'll want to see this exclusive."

With a thumb and forefinger, Diana opened the paper. There, written on the back of one of Sonny's business cards, were three blue-ink written series of numbers.

She stared at Sonny. "I don't understand."

"I'm not interested in money, and I'm not holding this up just because I want to score."

She looked down at the card, chin in her hand, then stared back at Sonny. "What do you really want?"

"What I really want to be? Big Mike."

"Mike Bauer? Do go on, my curiosity's building now."

"Look, when you get down to it, Mike was a dick. Underage girls, double-deals with politicians, keeping the unions out of the *Journal*. But what he did, building something important, something longer lasting than him – that's what I want to do. But better."

"How would you do it better?" Diana reclined back in her seat.

"It'd be online – lean, mean, also nonprofit. For-profit journalism is dying – the chicken's still running around the barnyard but the head's cut off. I'm sick of basing what we publish on what some advertiser says or what the right people think, rather than information that people need to know to be informed about their world. All we'll do is pay the bills and have enough to take a vacation occasionally."

"That's your dream?"

Sonny stared ahead. "Yeah, it is. I don't know how it's going to happen, but I have to try. Even if I fuck it up."

"Well, I can understand... Ah, there it is. Pull over," Diana said to the driver.

Sonny followed Diana into the light blue glass tower of NationalBank Der Bern in the heart of the Loop. They entered a nearly vacant lobby, all white with minimalist steel and white chairs and furniture. They strolled over to the reception area, where a young blond man in a company blazer and tie asked "Can I help you?" in a Bavarian accent.

"Where is customer service?" Diana asked him in perfect German.

The kid was shocked for a moment, but recovered himself and replied, "Second floor, Madam."

As they headed to the elevators, Sonny remarked, "Versatile language skills."

"You speak anything other than English?"

Sonny shook his head. "Four years of high school Spanish didn't really stick with me, I guess."

"Too bad. Different languages might prove useful to you."

"Yeah."

\*\*\*

# The Holy Fool

After a couple of more stops on the second floor, Diana and Sonny found themselves in the private office of one of the account vice presidents for the bank. His silver hair matched his suit and tie, but he otherwise blended into the furniture.

"I'd like to access three accounts under my name here at the bank," said Diana.

"Of course," the man, whose nameplate said Breuer, replied. "May I have your name and the accounts, please?"

She complied, passing along her driver's license for good measure. "Very well. The account numbers match, and so does your identification. What would you like to do?" Breuer said.

"First, I'd like to check and see what the balance is on those accounts. Then, I would like to open some new accounts and transfer the funds from the existing accounts into the new accounts. Is that possible?"

"Of course," Breuer said. He looked over at Sonny. "And you are, sir?"

"My apologies," Diana said, "he's with me – one of my employees."

Breuer raised an eyebrow for a moment, but shook it off. "Ah, I see. Of course, ma'am. I'm assuming you'd like to see the balances now?"

"Thank you," Diana said.

After a few moments of typing on his laptop, Breuer looked up at the two of them. "Very well. The first of the accounts has a total of $25.2 million. The second account, $15.4 million. The third account, $10.4 million, for a total of $50 million."

Diana nodded like $50 million was $5,000 to her. "I'd like to take that money and divide that in half. The first half will go into an account under my name. I'll leave it to my employee, Mr. Turner, to explain how to divide up the remaining funds. Do we understand each other?"

"Of course. I will set up the first account. While we have you fill out the necessary paperwork, I can discuss with your associate how to divide up the remaining funds, yes?"

"That would be fine."

It took Sonny every trick he'd ever learned to appear neutral from the outside. Breuer had to notice that Sonny was

235

all but clawing the handles of the seat he was on after he finished the initial setup and produced some additional forms for Diana to sign. "Sir?" he said.

"Yes?" said Sonny.

"Mrs. Edson said you will explain where the remaining funds will be sent, true?"

Sonny looked up at him and relaxed his hands. "Yes," he said. "Are you ready?"

"Of course," Breuer said.

Sonny nodded. "Let me ask something first. I know this bank is based in Zurich. Where else do you have branches?"

"Ah, yes. In addition to the New York and Los Angeles offices, there are branches in London, Paris, Brussels, Geneva, and Tokyo."

"Very well." Sonny nodded. "I want them to go into different accounts, and I guess we'll set those up now. The first account, I would like to place $20 million in."

Breuer nodded as he typed. "We will handle paperwork on this and the others in a moment. Who will this account be accessible to?"

Sonny gave his name and also made it accessible to Ed and Joey.

"There's going to be a second account, accessible to the same people," Sonny continued. "That will be $2.5 million in that account."

A third account with $2 million would be accessible only to Woot. "This leaves, still, $500,000 left," Breuer said.

Sonny broke up the remaining cash into several smaller accounts, accessible to himself and Joey. By the time he was done, there was just $30,000 left.

"Can I get half of that amount in traveler's checks and the other half in cash?" Sonny said.

Breuer, appearing pained, said, "It's a bit unusual… we would have to have Mrs. Edson sign for those funds…"

"Of course, I'd be willing to do that," Diana said, handing back the remaining paperwork. "Where do I need to sign?"

"We will take care of that," Breuer said. "Would you prefer the cash in $100 bills?"

"If you want to throw in some twenties, that's fine, too," Sonny said.

***

An hour after they went into the bank, Diana and Sonny walked out, with Sonny toting the newfound cash and traveler's checks in his satchel without stuffing it to excess. "I have to say I'm not sure I really understand my motive for today," Diana said, "but it felt good to do it."

"I know the feeling," Sonny said.

"If there's one thing I've learned being married to John Michael, there is such a thing as having too much money. Besides, I believe most of your share is going toward a... nonprofit concern, am I correct?" Sonny said nothing but nodded. "Well, I wanted to indulge my charitable tendencies. As Jesus advised us 2,000 years ago, however, I'd prefer this gift not be publicized."

"Of course."

"I think that if you're right, in some ways I might have had a hand in building a media concern that will likely last longer than John Michael's tenure at the *Journal*. There's a little satisfaction in that." She smiled as her gaze found the Keep several blocks away. "Anyway, I'm surprised you didn't insist on returning it, or some of it, to the *Journal*."

Sonny shook his head as he readjusted his satchel. "Even if they got all the money, it wouldn't be enough to bail them out."

"Hm. Well, I'm also surprised you took so little for yourself." Diana got into the car. "Everyone needs a retirement fund, but you didn't take much."

"This isn't a retirement fund." He nodded at the bag.

"Then what is it?"

"Insurance. Insurance for what I have to do the next few days." Sonny reached over and offered him her hand. "Good luck to you and yours, including your boys. Enjoy Hawaii."

She hesitated, then shook his hand. "Thank you – for everything. Good luck to you, too." She then opened the car and closed the door as the limo pulled away from the curb.

Jason Liegois

Sonny took another look at his satchel. *I'll feel better about this when I get off the street and get into the Keep,* he thought.

## Chapter 18

It was about 4:30 p.m. when Sonny walked into the newsroom. It was packed with reporters and editors at their desks, putting together stories and pages or calling up sources before they left for the weekend.

Hugging his satchel closer to his body than he realized, he found Gus at the City/Metro Desk, reviewing what the reporters in that department were doing that day, when he looked up at Sonny approaching. "Hang on, guys," he told them, and met Sonny halfway.

"Day going OK?" Sonny asked.

"About as good as could be expected," Gus said. "You?"

Sonny hugged his satchel closer to him without really thinking about it. "It's been intriguing. Do we have confirmation that John Michael and his guys are on the ground in Vegas?"

"A couple of guys I've been in contact with at the casino, say they've checked in. They're expecting the Lord and his court to be wandering in within an hour or two. You said J… Woot had an idea of their schedule."

"Yeah. Dinner and a social hour at 6 p.m. our time, social hour after that, then the whole group's heading down to catch a Cher concert by seven. After that, I think it's going to be every person for themselves."

"Good for us."

"When are we going to send the word?"

"We're waiting another hour and a half."

"Six, not five?"

"We want to make sure that we push it as late as possible."

"What's the difference? The minute we let people know what's going on, someone could drop a dime on us."

"They have to be back here for anything to happen, but they're an entire time zone behind us," Gus said. "Assuming someone calls right when we make our move, assuming they get the message right away, assuming they can immediately leave the casino, rearrange flight plans, get to McCarren, board a flight, assuming that there's no delays, assuming they make it to O'Hare on time and catch a limo back to the office – even if we assume all of that is true, that's still five hours of travel, minimum. I don't want them to have the slightest chance of stopping us from getting the paper out."

"I also wanted to let you know, Woot's managed to set up a jammer for cell phones throughout the building. He's reprogrammed the phone system so that he can shut down long-distance calling from the landlines, too. He'll have everything cut off unless it's needed."

"Shit. Really?"

Sonny nodded. "He can turn them on and off when we need them to be, and control it from the conference room…"

"Yeah, I saw him bring that equipment in." Gus whistled in amazement. "But people could still walk out of the building to drop a dime on us, and I'm not interested in anything that even looks like kidnapping."

"It'll be five minutes for these guys to figure out what's going on, another five to decide, and another five, 10 minutes to figure out the communications devices in the building aren't working and try to make a jail break, and maybe another five to make a second call. That's… 20, 25 minutes extra time, isn't it?"

"That true."

Sonny looked around and made sure no one but they were there. "Listen, Gus, I have to tell you about something."

"Can it wait for tomorrow?" Gus' eyes narrowed as he scanned his copy sheets.

"Afraid it can't. I really need to talk to you about this tonight."

"What's going on? Can you let me know now?"

"Not in front of everyone."

Gus shrugged, not taking his eyes off the sheets. "Can we talk after we give the news to the staff?" Sonny sighed and nodded. "Good." Gus pointed toward Sonny's office. "TT's in there – said he's about to get Wyatt Walker out of the way for us."

"That'd be a trick. He's been my biggest worry about tonight, coming in here with armed guards or something."

"Anyway, TT said he's got it taken care of. Go in and look."

"All right." Sonny turned and headed to his office.

As Sonny walked in, he found TT behind his desk on TT's laptop. "Make yourself at home, bro. What's going on?"

"Most of the security guys in here should be fine, but we always said that Wyatt would be a problem. I think I've got a solution."

Sonny walked behind the desk to see an underground parking garage on the screen, with the camera focused on a silver Mercedes sedan parked near the top of the garage. "What's this?"

"Wyatt's car, in the garage. He's out at dinner, but he'll be headed back to the car for home in a moment. Woot managed to get a feed from the security cameras."

Sonny leaned over and got a closer look. "OK, so what's the big plan?"

"Nothing much, just me anonymously calling in a suspected bomb threat to some of my former colleagues, telling them there's a bomb in the trunk."

"How the hell is that going to work?"

"Because there's a bomb in the trunk."

Sonny whirled to face TT, horrified. "What the fuck, TT?"

"Well, he only keeps a shotgun and AR in his trunk, so I decided to use a couple of IED's. Without actual gunpower or C4, though, just enough of a trace for the dogs to get a hit."

"*Shit.* Isn't *that* traceable?"

"Got the items from some odds and ends in his home workshop."

"Oh, man." Sonny sank into his empty chair with his head in his hands.

"I'll be fine. Oh, look, here it goes."

TT pointed to a familiar figure wearing a blue suit and lighting up a long Costa Rican cigar with a butane lighter. It was Wyatt.

"And here's the target heading toward the car to pick up the briefcase he left there... getting closer... closer... wait for it, wait for it... and... *now*," TT said as Wyatt reached the driver's side of his car.

As TT said "now," five police officers in navy SWAT uniforms, helmets, and M4 carbines swarmed Wyatt, screaming "PO-lice! Freeze!" They wrestled him to the ground, sending his lighter and cigar flying. One officer handcuffed him in a single motion while a second officer searched him. Two others covered Wyatt with their M4s and the others scanned the surrounding area ensuring there were no other threats.

The second officer relieved Wyatt of his Beretta M9 and car keys. He handed the gun and keys to a third officer, who used the latter to open the trunk over Wyatt's howled protests. The minute that he glanced into the trunk, he began to back away and chatter into his shoulder-mounted radio, gesturing for the other officers to back away and drag Wyatt from the ground with them.

"OK, that's that. He's out of commission until at least midnight."

"Was that even legal?"

"Maybe not enough to get into court, if he has a good attorney, plus the fact that it's not a real bomb." TT logged off the camera. "Of course, that doesn't matter; we just want him gone for a few hours."

"True." Sonny got up from his seat. "I've got to check in with a few people. Can you clean up before you take off?"

"Sure."

"Later." He waved to TT and headed out.

As he walked out of his office, he got a text saying *Meet me in break room fifth floor*. He took one of the side stairways to head down to the break room on that floor, for the classified ad staff. It was deserted that time of the day, the classified deadline already passed and their numbers having been more affected than some others by job cuts. When Sonny got down to the room, only Joey was there, seated on a faded blue leather couch. She was taking a sip of something from a bottle in a paper bag and patted the seat next to her.

"How's it going? Getting started early? What is that?"

"Bacardi. It may not be appropriate for the situation, but given the circumstances, maybe it is."

"And you said you'd never be a proper journalist." Sonny removed the bottle from her hand, took a quick sip himself, capped it, and sat it between her knees in her dress as he leaned over and kissed her on the head. "I wondered for a moment if you were headed to Vegas."

"I just called him to say I was at the airport about to board."

"What do you mean?"

"Winona is, actually. She's from circulation - we kind of look like each other now, with my haircut. Anyway, she's wanted to head out to Vegas for a while, but never had enough time or money. So, I gave her my Vegas ticket and a couple of hundred bucks, and she said she'd fly out there tonight."

"Seriously?"

"She's into it." Joey took another sip as he put his arm around her. "She even borrowed some of my dresses. Depending on the lighting in the club, he might even mistake her for me for a while."

"What?"

"Here, have another drink."

He did, then turned to face her. "Come up with me?"

"Really?"

"There's no point in keeping quiet now."

"OK."

"Besides, Gus is calling everyone up to the newsroom for the big announcement anyway. We might as well have some more of this while we wait for that." He held up the bottle in the bag.

"You sure that's a good idea?" Joey smiled.

"I haven't given Gus the talk yet."

"What talk?" Sonny stared at her for a moment, then put her hand to her face. "Oh... that talk." She liberated the bottle from Sonny's grasp for another sip.

\*\*\*

A few minutes before six, Sonny wandered into the secondary conference room on the newsroom floor, where Woot was manning a desktop computer with three different monitors and six large drives lined up in a row underneath the table. "Hey, bro," Woot called out with a wave as Sonny came in, "driving a newspaper is something else, I'll tell you."

"Yeah, I'm sure," Sonny replied, sitting next to him. "Everything's set."

"Thanks to Jack."

"And you'll be able to handle things in back here on your own?"

"Shouldn't be a problem. I'll run things until 11 p.m., then Happy Jack takes the reins after that. It seems that I've motivated him to be quite the interested hacker." Woot laughed. "Corrupting the morals of a minor, wonder if they'll charge me with that."

"Don't think so. Why 11?"

"I get the feeling that John Michael's going to tear up my contract once he finds out what's going on. I've been thinking it's been time I head out of town for a while, wait for things to cool down."

"Headed out of town?"

Woot nodded. "Thought about traveling to Europe. Always wanted to go to England and catch a Premier League game. I've got to get to Amsterdam, too; get a chance to smoke some of that legal weed."

"So, off to O'Hare after the paper goes down?"

"*Hell* no. You know I hate flying in those stupid metal tubes where you don't even have room to breathe."

"OK, smart guy, you have any idea how you're going to cross the Atlantic?"

"Same way my ancestors did. I'm taking the Lake Shore Limited from Union Station all the way to NYC, and then I'm getting on a damn boat to London."

"Heh, didn't realize you could still go to London via cruise ship."

"It's a cargo ship. There's cabins available all the time if you know who to contact."

"Really?"

"Shit, all I have to do is stay out of their way and make conversation at dinner with the captain. Plus, they'll even let me log onto their Wi-Fi if I need to, although I may stay off that for a bit."

Sonny reached into his satchel and pulled out a long envelope and handed it over to Woot. "This is for you."

"OK, but... hey," Woot said, peeking into the envelope, and extracting a bank book. "What the hell is this?"

"Your severance package," Sonny said. "It's the least I can do, after getting you into trouble and everything." Woot glanced at him sideways like he was expecting a con job. "It's best not to know where it all came from. There's a branch of that bank in New York, so you may want to stop over there before getting on that boat."

Woot tucked it back into the envelope and tucked the envelope into his jean jacket covered with Guns N' Roses patches and artwork. "I appreciate the sentiment, I do. But I want you to know that I would have done it anyway. We're friends. I know you would have stuck your neck out for me if the situation was reversed."

"But really, you wanted to screw around with people like you did back in your misspent youth." Sonny cackled and doubled over.

There was just the smallest of shrugs from Woot, the subtlest of grins. "Yeah, maybe," he admitted. "You think you might need my services again, one of these days?"

"You might come in handy."

Woot reached into the backpack by his feet and pulled out a small flip-phone. "Here's a burner," Woot said. "I've got it programmed with some of the other burner phones in my possession. Wait a couple of months, because I want to get to know some of those Dutch girls. Save that one; here's another one you can use now."

Sonny accepted the phones, hesitated, then hugged Woot. After a moment, Woot was returning the hug. "Absolutely. I know not to get in between a guy and his weed."

"Better get out there." Woot broke off the hug and hunkered down in front of his terminal. "Looks like Gus is about to give the talk."

"Take care, Wootie."

"You too, *Sammie boy*." Woot's eyes were back on the screen, so he didn't see Sonny wave good-bye and lumber out of the room.

As Sonny walked out into the newsroom, he saw the clock's time of 5:55 p.m. He could hear Gus's voice over the PA system asking for all the employees to gather in the newsroom for a meeting.

It was a slow gathering. Most of the reporters with desks on the floor elected to sit at their seats while the ad reps, design staff, support personnel, and others had to find either seats or empty spots around the floor to stand. Eventually, the floor would fit in a couple hundred people.

They were greeted by Gus, standing on top of the City/Metro Desk, his head barely clearing the foam-tiled ceiling, a clipboard with notes in one hand and a metal pica ruler in the other. Sleeves rolled up, tie knot undone, sweat was already starting to form at his grey temples and shirt collar. "C'mon in everyone, come on in."

Almost by instinct, Sonny found himself gathering in front of the City/Metro Desk alongside some of Gus's current and former subordinates, forming what amounted to a palace guard in front of Gus. He saw Harry Read and TT among those lined up in front of the desk.

He looked out among the growing crowd. Another surprise was seeing Colton slouching as he leaned against one of the office walls. Carlo Massino was behind the City/Metro Desk and off to the right and in the background. Joey was threading through the crowd toward him. He could see more filing in from the main entryway in the back.

Gus had a mini karaoke machine left over from a holiday party a couple of years back, and he'd kept it for use as a PA system. He picked up the microphone to the machine and turned it on. "Everyone, everyone, try and get in as close as you can."

# The Holy Fool

Gus looked around and made sure that everyone was paying attention before he continued. "As of October, I'll have been at this paper for 35 years. There have been many ups and downs during that time, a lot of great stories and a lot of times when we've screwed things up. But right now, tonight, for the next few hours or so, is the most critical time for the *Chicago Journal*. During the next few hours, we're going to prove once and for all what type of paper we are."

The crowd murmured, their puzzlement obvious.

"For most of you, what I'm about to say shouldn't be a total surprise. Since Edson Media bought out the Journal Corporation, this paper has gone through three different staff reductions, the most recent of those last week. Those and other cuts have been to maintain those wonderful 30 to 50 percent profit margins we absolutely must have under any circumstances.

"Anyway, you're not here for that," Gus continued. "What we've gathered to tell you about is how dire the situation is with our paper, and how we plan to address it. I'm going to have Sonny Turner explain what we discovered, because he was responsible for how we found out about them.

"Once he's done, I'm going to discuss what I, Sonny, and some of the other staff at the *Journal* have decided is going to be our response. Finally, you'll have a decision to make about that. Understood?" There was general silence from the crowd, but Gus nodded anyway. "Sonny, you there? Can you come up?"

Sonny looked up at Gus. "That desk can support both of us?"

"There's more than one desk. It's OK."

Sonny nodded and began to head toward Gus, but Joey laid a hand on his shoulder. Her hand drifted down his arm and found his hand for a quick squeeze. "Good luck," she said.

Gus had used a small step stool to get on top of the table; Sonny used the same one to get up there. He sat his satchel down at his own feet, took the microphone from Gus, and took a deep breath.

"Like Gus said, thanks for listening," Sonny's voice rumbled from the karaoke machine. "All of the details will be online very soon, but I'll try and summarize it as best that I can."

He took a deep breath and plunged forward. "What it comes down to, is a lot of dishonesty from our owner and management. They have consistently lied about circulation numbers and advertising revenue. The purpose of this falsehood is to make the paper a more attractive location for advertising dollars and a better candidate for purchase.

"This and other things have resulted in some income for the paper that went underreported," Sonny continued. "Exactly how much and where those missing revenues went, whether to John Michael himself or someone else, we don't know for sure." *Maybe some of it's in the bag by your feet, asshole,* he thought to himself.

"Right now, John Michael and the executive board is negotiating with Lord Melchester and the Worldwide Media board to buy out at least the *Journal,* and perhaps some of Edson Media's other properties in the Chicago area. Edson is doing this because he believes the paper is within a year of collapse. He's hoping that this will give them enough time to survive this economic downturn, but later expand.

"However, Edson himself is being conned by the bank that handles financing for Edson Media, UUF. What UUF is hiding is that many of its own investments, which include the bonds that Edson used as collateral to finance the purchase of this paper, are falling in value. In many cases, they are nowhere near the value they've long claimed. Right now, traders with UUF are trying to very quietly dispose of these loans, very covertly, before everyone discovers how they've been overvalued. They have been trying to run a shell game on a lot of people. But they're about to run out of shells." With that, Sonny handed the mike back to Gus, picked up his satchel, and dismounted the desk.

"So, that's the deal," Gus said. "Like Sonny said, you can look up the details online.

"What this all means is that within two weeks, everyone will be losing their jobs and this place will close." That started the murmuring to increase to a low rumble and people jabbering with each other, processing the finality. "Edson and

# The Holy Fool

UUF both may think that they're going to get out of this without going broke, but they're not. So, this is how we're going to respond.

"First, we're going to run stories about everything Sonny talked about in tomorrow's paper. Carlo and I, as well as some of the other senior editors, are doing this without the permission of the publisher or management. We fully expect to be fired for our actions upon the return of the executive board to Chicago.

"These stories cover the misstatements Edson Media has made, the financial difficulties of the company and UUF, and the fact that this is about to all come crashing down on our heads," Gus said. "To be honest, this is going to speed up that process, and that's our intention."

"There's also a story in there about John Michael having at least two affairs, one with the publisher, another with an Edson employee who he has a child with," Sonny broke in from the floor, to the gasps of those near him. "Normally that wouldn't be a story, but since his relationships might have led him to hide money for different purposes, we thought it was relevant."

"Yes," Gus said. "Right now, our intent is that this kills the sale. We don't know if what we're going to do might save everyone's jobs or not. Probably not. But if this newspaper is closing, we want to make sure that it is our hands closing the door, not some middle manager. After 140 years, if this place is going to die, it deserves a wake from us."

With that, Sonny began to clap from the front, the sound ringing off the walls, sounding isolated until, with some hesitation, some of the other newspaper people began to join in. The applause lasted for a minute, with some, like Sonny, also adding to the noise by pounding nearby desks.

"So, you have a choice," Gus said. "You can stay here and support what we're trying to do. That would be great. Or, you could decide that you're not comfortable with what's going on here. That's fine. We'd ask you to take the rest of the night off, then. We are going to ask you to make your decision as soon as possible, because we have work to do."

Jason Liegois

"For those of you who are wondering if there's any way that you can stop what we're about to do, there isn't," Sonny said, his voice rumbling out into the crowd. "If you want management to know what's going on, that's your business."

Sonny was surprised to see Colton raise his hand and call out, "Gus, can I say something?"

"OK, kid; go ahead."

Colton turned to the crowd, unsure but plunging ahead. "I'm betting all of this news is pretty hard to take," Colton said, his higher, bouncing tenor not as deep as Sonny, but just as capable of reaching the farthest parts of the crowd. "It's hard for me, too, believe it or not. As for you, all of you could support this, or decide this entire exercise is bullshit, walk out the door, and find a saner profession." That earned him the first, quietest, isolated chuckles from the crowd. "Or, like me, you can choose not to take a side right now and just keep doing your jobs like you have been doing them. I know I came here to this newspaper to learn how to be a journalist. I'm going to keep coming here as long as I have my job."

Colton looked over his shoulder and tensed up as he caught the gaze of Gus examining him. In the end, Colton relaxed as Gus nodded approvingly. Gus turned back to the crowd as Colton took a step back away from the front.

"OK, does anyone have anything to say for the good of the group before we let you go to wherever you need to go?" Gus asked.

"I'd like to say something very quickly, if I could," a voice called out from the back of the room.

Gus got up on his toes to see who it was, then: "Yeah, sure, Ed, come on in."

The crowd parted just enough so that Ed could wheel his way into the center of the newsroom just in front of the city/metro desk, pushed by Jack. Another man stood with them; he was somewhere around his sixties, taller than but as big as Sonny, white-haired but tan, in a full grey business suit. Even from as far as Sonny was standing from the man, his eyes that were so blue they were nearly pale stood out. They reminded Sonny of a series of portrait paintings in the lobby,

# The Holy Fool

predating the current ownership. In a flash, Sonny realized the identity of the man next to Ed.

"Most of yous know me, so I'm not gonna get into introductions," Ed said. "This place was a big part of my life, and I guess it still is. I'm here to help out."

Gus nodded. "We appreciate all of the help we can get." He stared at the the man standing next to Ed and looked like he was unsure of what to say next.

Ed noticed his confusion. "Ah, yeah," Ed said. "We've got a guest here, although he's connected to this place. He can say something if he wants to." He gestured towards the man.

He stepped forward and looked around the room, appearing if he was trying to recall something. Then: "My name is Mark Bauer." Whatever murmuring there was in the crowd went silent. "And if you're wondering, yes, my father was Chris Bauer, and yes, he was publisher of this newspaper. Jack DeFoe was my second cousin. My great-great-grandfather, Big Mike, he founded this place. I never worked here a day in my life, myself. For years I've run a publishing company in New York that's worked out well, but I'm sort of semi-retired now." He was silent for several moments. All the eyes of the crowd, including Gus and Sonny, were on Bauer.

"When Ed talked to me earlier this week about coming out here tonight, I realized that it was exactly 35 years ago today that my older brother, Michael III, killed himself right here in this newsroom, in front of our father," Bauer said. "I'll admit my brother was a very disturbed individual. He always had a problem with depression, and alcohol and drugs. It also didn't help that my father just expected him to be the next publisher of this place whether he could or wanted to do the job or not."

He shook his head. "He should have just run like I did – it worked for me. And looking back, it was the right decision then.

"But talking with Ed reminded me about all of the good things this paper has done over the years. We told the story of this city's rebirth after the Fire. We've told the stories of our boys going off to war, and what it meant to the country. We started letting the world know about what the Chicago Outfit and the Daley Machine really was, at great risk to this paper and the people working for it. And, we stood alongside the New York Times and Washington Post in publishing the Pentagon Papers."

Mark looked around at all the staff before continuing. "Anyway, I thought one weekend out of my life to lend a hand wouldn't be a bad thing. That's all I have, Ed."

"Thanks very much, Mark," Gus said. He looked around the room. "Anyway. If you want to stay, stay, and if you want to go, go ahead. Carlo and I will have an editorial meeting in a few minutes. Let's hear it." Gus began clapping, and most of the crowd joined in for lack of any other better idea.

As Gus got off the table, Sonny, Bill, and some of the other committee members surrounded him to find out about the next steps. "TT, we've got some computer equipment over in Conference Room B right now – can you make sure nobody's trying to get in there without our permission?

"Bill already has a couple of his guys keeping an eye on things," TT said. "It'll be fine."

Eventually, the group was gathered in Conference Room A after shutting the door and settling into chairs around the long conference table. Carlo, Gus, and Mark were at one end. Sonny, TT, Harry Read, Ed, and Colton were at the other end, and Read, who was at one corner of the table, had pulled out his camera phone and began recording the whole proceedings. Bill Goldstein and Oscar Johnson, as well as some of Oscar's foremen, were around both sides of the middle.

"Our package covers the first three pages, and the left half of our Op-Ed pages," Gus said. "Sonny and myself collaborated on the main wood piece, detailing the proposed sale of the *Journal,* and summarizing the reasons why it won't work. TT, you had the piece detailing us fudging the circulation numbers?"

"It's ready to go," TT said.

Gus nodded. "Sonny has the piece on the financials, right?"

"I've gotten enough evidence that some of those dollars that should be in company accounts are missing," Sonny said, "but where that money went to has just led to dead ends. We might need more time on that."

# The Holy Fool

Gus waved him off. "Print what you have and follow-up the rest."

"Already done."

"Also, you and TT finished the piece on John Michael's... activities, right?"

"That's completed," Sonny and TT said together.

Gus laid a dummy copy of the front page on the table in front of him. "Sonny, do you think we can get a response from Melchester for the main piece? You said you had a line on him?"

"I do. That's set. I'll call him right after we get out of here."

"OK. Harry, you'll be doing the coverage of what's going on at the paper tonight, correct?" Gus said.

"Absolutely," Harry said.

"And Colton, I saw that you turned in the piece on UUF," Carlo said.

Colton, who had been staring at his smart phone for the past couple of minutes, looked up. "Yes?"

"Great work, very detailed," Carlo said, nodding. "You actually explained it so a fifth-grader could understand."

Colton looked surprised at the news. "Thank you."

"Is this the front-page workup?" Mark said, staring down at the page on the table. "Nice layout."

"Thanks," Gus replied. The main central picture of the front page was a stock photo of The Keep with a cartoon FOR SALE? sign stuck in the sidewalk next to it. In the main story, itself, there was a logo, which was the logo of the *Journal* cracking in two with the phrase LAST STAND OF THE *JOURNAL*? typewritten underneath. The same logo appeared in all the other related stories on the front page. Also, there was a long distance shot of John Michael and Cathy Boone exiting a health club together, holding hands; John Michael and Gill Lott at a rugby match at Harvard; mugshots of John Michael, Melchester, and Lott; and a picture of *Journal* delivery vans lining up outside of the press facilities on the South Side.

"Finally, two pieces on the Op Ed page. There's going to be an editorial from Carlo and me, going against the sale of the paper, and Ed has contributed a column, putting this whole issue in the historical context of what the paper has done for Chicago. Ed, nice work, by the way."

"Aw," Ed shrugged, "Maybe it was because I had a short deadline this time. Those always got my creative juices flowin'."

"Anyway, thanks again," Gus said. "One thing I didn't mention to everyone outside. All of this is going online in 30 minutes. The presses will run 10 minutes after that."

"Press time of 7?" Harry said.

Gus nodded as Joey entered the room without garnering attention from anyone but Sonny. "I want there to be as little chance as possible of anyone stopping us getting this paper out. I don't want the police charging in here and arresting us before we get things done."

He turned to Goldstein. "What's the word, Bill?"

"The prep coaches are going to get pissed missing the Saturday edition," Bill said. "Any chance at a late edition?"

"'Fraid not, Bill. We want to make sure the papers get out ASAP," Gus said.

"Agreed," Carlos said. Joey sat down in the back of the room, trying for invisibility from those around here. Sonny was trying to oblige her by not glancing in her direction.

Bill nodded as he stood up and stretched. "As far as the Keep goes, all of the entrances are barred and blockaded except for the south service entrance. That's locked from the outside, but people can still leave from there. I've got guys keeping an eye on all of the entrances and others directing those leaving to go through the south entrance. Most everyone except for what there is of the news and sports staff still working have jetted out."

"OK, keep that up, and make sure those that want to leave get to go out the south entrance," Gus said. "Oscar, how's the press plant looking?"

"We'll have everything ready to go and start printing immediately at 7, no problem," Oscar said. "We're going to shoot for everything to be printed and off for delivery in two and a half hours."

"We'd like you to be done in less than two hours," Gus said. "The faster this happens, the better."

Oscar's jaw fell for a moment, then he shook his head for a moment to clear it. "Well, I'm not 100 percent sure I can meet that, but we can try."

"You will do it; I know you can," Gus said, then got up and looked around at the room. "Anything else? All right, we'd better get finished up here if we're sending this out."

As everyone began to pack up and leave, Sonny approached Gus and Carlo. "Excuse me, I think that there might need to be one more story for the edition," he softly said.

"What are you talking about, Sonny?" Carlo said.

"One more piece, something I've been working on…"

Gus sensed what he was talking about. "No, that ship's sailed, kid – We already talked about it. You said you put it off for later, right?"

Sonny scanned the room. "Can we talk about this after these guys go?"

"No, no, no," Gus said. "We'll deal with it later, like I said. It's too much to deal with right now."

Sonny screwed up his face and reared back in frustration. "*Dammit*, Gus, are you really going to make me do this in front of everyone? **Really**?"

There was silence in the room as everyone stopped in their tracks and stared at Sonny and Gus staring each other down. Harry had his iPhone up and walking as far back in the room as he could to get the whole panorama of the room. "You're talking about the Iraq project?" Gus said.

"Yeah," Sonny said.

"What project?" Bauer said.

Gus realized that he, Sonny, Carlo, and Ed were the only ones in the room that had any idea of what he and Sonny were talking about. "Some mystery source has been feeding Sonny classified material on Iraq over the Internets," Gus said. "We decided that we needed to have everything more certain before moving forward."

"The information was solid, and so were the stories," Sonny said. "You just didn't want the additional heat while we were trying to save the *Journal,* and I was about to lose the source because she was worried that we were getting cold feet."

"You said you took care of it for later, right?" Gus repeated.

After a long pause, Sonny said, "I don't think I took care of it in the way that you'd preferred."

"What do you mean?" Gus finally said.

"I talked with some people, about the stories."

"What people?"

"*New York Times*. And the *Guardian* in London."

Gus started to ease back into his seat, hanging on to the corners of the table, as he threw the death stare down at Sonny. "When did you give the stories to them?"

"Two days ago. Both are running them in full online in four hours, last I heard. The *Guardian* put out a late teaser story in its late edition for tomorrow that ran five hours ago but didn't mention me as the main source. They'll do that with its Sunday edition. NYT's going with everything in four hours." Sonny's hands dropped to his sides as he looked at everyone staring at him.

Gus looked up at Sonny like he'd just shot one of his kids. "Sonny," he said, his voice croaking, "how the hell am I or anyone here supposed to trust you after this?"

Sonny shuddered just a bit as he took in a breath and reached into his jacket pocket. "Yeah," he said, extracting two long white envelopes from there. He tossed them onto the table, where they slid across the surface until they stopped right in front of Gus. "I'll save you the trouble."

Gus opened the envelope with his name on it and opened up the paper inside. He, Carlo, and Mark read:

9/12/2008

To Whom It May Concern:

I resign my position as Contributing Editor and Columnist for the *Chicago Journal* as of the above date.

Samuel Victor Turner

Gus looked back up at Sonny as he said, "The other copy is for John Michael when he gets back from Vegas."

Sonny scanned the room. A few, like Gus and Bill, looked at him with disgust and disbelief; most of the others, including Colton, were in shock.

Sonny turned to the left, fearful, to see Ed's reaction. As he faced his old mentor, Ed looked thoughtful, then gazed up as he shrugged. "Well, kid, when you have to go, you have to go," Ed said.

"Yeah," Sonny whispered. Ed leaned over and patted his arm as Sonny looked back at Gus and said, "What now?"

Gus's eyes regained focus at Sonny with the question. "You've still got to call Melchester and get comment from him," he said. "You don't get out of that. If you can't get him, leave a message. If he answers, don't fuck it up, got it?"

"Got it."

Gus turned to Colton. "You follow him. Once he's finished on the phone, you interview him and put together a piece on him leaving. Keep the story under seven inches, got it?"

Colton, still stunned, said, "Yes, got it."

Gus faced Sonny again. "Once the kid's finished talking with you, you grab what you can carry and get the hell out of my newsroom. Your stuff here, we'll ship it to your apartment."

"Just box it up," Sonny said. "Ed's kids will come by to pick it up later. I'm heading out of town for a while."

"How long?"

"A *while*. Hell, Gus, I've had guys burglarizing my apartment, FBI officials visiting me at work. I don't think staying's a good idea."

"You're a journalist, not a terrorist," Gus said. "You've got nothing to worry about."

"Really? When we're conducting covert operations against US citizens? What's the difference, Gus? I don't want to hang around to find out." He got up, grabbed his satchel, and started to head out the door.

"Can you tell me why, kid?" Gus said before Sonny could leave.

Sonny stopped in his tracks and shook his head. "I wasn't following your orders. I was following Jack's."

There was silence in the room for a few beats before Sonny continued. "It was the last time he was here in the newsroom before he went off to hospice. He told me the proudest thing he ever did was convince his Uncle Dan to go ahead with The Pentagon Papers back in '71, and that his biggest regret was not letting us look more into the WMD evidence before Iraq kicked off.

"He made me promise him that if I ever had a chance to make a difference like that, I had to take it because he wasn't going to have another one himself. I also told my mother about the stories before she died, and she told me they needed to get out too."

Sonny stopped slouching and stood up ramrod straight. "The stories are still in the system if you feel like running them. I'm sorry you and the others are pissed, but I'm not apologizing for what I did. Goodbye."

With that and a wave, Sonny stalked out the door, followed by Bauer. As Carlo said to everyone, "OK, show's over, guys. Let's get back to work," and the remainder of the group started to file out of the room, Joey walked up to Gus. "Excuse me? Excuse me?" she said to Gus.

Gus looked up at her, eyes narrowed. "What is it?" he barked, but then calmed down as he saw her. "Joey?"

"Look, I'm leaving this with you." She gave him another envelope.

Gus looked at it. "You're quitting? What…?" He looked back at Sonny's envelope, then hers, then her face. "Sonny… ohhh, man," Gus laughed, wiping his eyes, "now I get it."

"Yeah," she said. "This… it was kind of sudden."

"There seems to be a lot of that nowadays." Gus shook his head and tucked all the envelopes into his jacket. "Good luck trying to deal with *him*," waving toward the door.

"Well, thanks." Joey joined the crowd out the door.

Carlo looked over at Gus after she left. "You OK?" he asked Gus.

He shook his head. "I'm not relying on one guy to make this place go, not even Samuel Victor Motherfucking Turner."

"Well, it's good to know you're moving on, Gus," Carlo said, the irony thick around his statement.

# The Holy Fool

"What I'm worried about right now is Chicago PD charging through that newsroom shutting us down."

That stopped Carlo in his tracks. "OK, that might be a worry."

***

They shouldn't have worried.

Out of the hundreds of staff members who had been at the Keep earlier that evening, only four of them cared enough to try and inform upper management of the situation in Chicago. Literally or figuratively, those efforts fell on deaf ears.

One told her friend, one of the junior female administrative assistants on Edson's staff. She decided to keep it to herself rather than chase down John Michael, wherever he was. One of the biggest rumors in the Penthouse involved an unlucky female AA who had to drag John Michael out of a strip club to get to a dinner party for top advertisers on time. The girl was allegedly out of a job by the following week.

A second e-mail went out to someone in Edson's public relations department. The young man read it, then promptly ignored it. He was absolutely *done* with *Journal* drama and having to pretend that he cared about Renaissance-era media. He'd already given his two weeks' notice and would start his job with Governor Blagojevich's press office in time for the re-election run. *Finally, some stability*, the young man thought.

Publisher Cathy Boone had her phone set on silent, so she did not see the text someone had left for her. She was too busy in the front row of Cher's show, cheering and singing along with the ladies she'd befriended when she'd first come into the company 10 years ago and who had remained true even though she'd moved up the ranks faster than them. She vaguely wondered where John Michael was but dismissed it. It'd just be awkward if they were hanging around all the time at a company outing. Besides, he'd be cramping her style right about now.

The Johnnie Walker Blue had begun to kick in for John Michael right around the same time Gus was giving his speech to the troops. All his electronic devices, including his

Blackberry, were stowed away in his hotel room, where a voicemail message from Wyatt Walker was waiting for him.

He was feeling loose and casual at a dimly lit baccarat table while everyone else was headed into the concert arena to see Cher. He'd been there for a half hour, but he guessed from the pile of chips at his table that he'd lost somewhere in the low four figures.

He turned to his left and found a young girl hanging on his arm. She had on a little black dress and high heels, but her brunette hair was cut off sharp and short, like someone he knew... someone he'd wanted to hook up with here...

"Jo... wait, you're not Joey, are you?" he said to the girl.

"No, I'm not," she laughed, offering her hand to him. "I'm Winona, one of Joey's friends at work."

"Really?" John Michael examined her. She seemed more classically cute than Joey, more like the other Winona who had been in the movies years back that Colton had lusted after as a boy. "You had dinner yet?"

She shook her head. "Just landed in town. Happened to have my vacation the same night you were all out here, Isn't that weird?"

"Yeah, weird." John Michael shook his head back and forth in a mainly unsuccessful effort to clear it. "I was going to get a late dinner and go out to a club upstairs. Want to tag along?"

"You buying?" Winona said, a sparkle in her eyes considering a night on Vegas.

"Always. Shall we?"

Winona took John Michael's offered arm, and they left the baccarat table behind.

\*\*\*

Just moments after he left the conference room, Sonny headed to his office with Colton trailing behind. "Excuse me? Excuse me?" Sonny heard from behind.

With a harrumph, Sonny stopped in his tracks and turned around to see Bauer standing right behind him. "Colton..."

# The Holy Fool

"I'll be in your office," said Colton, who ducked in there immediately.

Sonny turned to face Bauer. "Evening Mr. Bauer. What can I do for you?"

"Mark," he said, offering his hand to shake, which Sonny accepted. "I just wanted to say I'm sorry the paper will be losing you. Jack and I didn't get to talk too much – the family reunions started to go out of style after my father's death – but he always spoke highly of you."

"I appreciate that."

"So, these stories that are running in the other papers, are they that important to you?"

"Well, one of them talks about civilian American contractors slaughtering some civilians in Iraq a year ago and getting away with it. The next one is how a report questioning the occupation strategy of US forces got buried by military officials. I thought they were a priority."

"Yeah, sounds like Pentagon Papers outtakes. You have any idea what you'll be doing now?"

"You mean, other than not working for the *Journal*? Maybe do something on my own."

Mark nodded, then reached into his wallet and pulled out a card. "When you have a moment later," he said, handing Sonny the card, "I'd appreciate it if you'd give me a call. I'd like to talk."

Sonny nodded, tucking the card into his coat pocket. "OK, I will."

They shook hands one last time, and Mark went back to the conference room. Sonny went to his office to make a call.

\*\*\*

"I've had the chance to review the material that you've sent, Samuel," Melchester said as his voice slid so easily into Sonny's ear canal over the speakerphone.

"What are your thoughts?"

"Officially: 'This information will be a factor in reevaluating the viability of this purchase.' Samuel, would you be so kind as to review for me the quote that you just wrote down, for accuracy's sake?" Sonny did. "Fine. Would you be willing to talk off the record, now?"

Sonny set aside his pad and paper. "Sure, no problem."

"It appears that I do, in fact, owe you a favor. And, a job with one of my holdings is still off your list? Or, perhaps not?"

"Still off. If I'm working for anyone, it's going to be myself."

There was a light, breezy chuckle on the other end. "You being a manager would be a sight."

"I'll get by."

"You might, at that. Perhaps you might have some other idea as to how I might repay you, then?"

"Can I think about it, call you back some time?"

There was silence, then: "You may. Please, call this number instead of my office. I will be waiting for your call."

"OK."

"Goodbye, Samuel."

Sonny hung up and faced Colton, who was seated facing him, pad and pen in hand, and a recorder lit up on the desk he'd been using since he'd gotten there. Joey stood by the doorway, lost in thought. "So, we'd been talking about whether this whole thing was worth having to resign," Colton said, all business. "What are your thoughts on this?"

Sonny nodded as he took a few pens and notebooks and tucked them into his satchel. "George Orwell said, 'Journalism is printing what someone else does not want printed; everything else is public relations.' Do I think we, as journalists, need to be writing stuff every day that's going to get people mad? Maybe not. But, if we're not *prepared* to do something like that, then why call ourselves journalists? Don't forget that, Colton."

"Right now, I'm not in the mood for words of wisdom." Colton finished writing.

"Yeah, I figured not."

Gus appeared in the doorway, metal pica ruler in hand. "You get that quote from Melchester?" Gus said.

"Right here," Sonny said, holding up the notepad.

"Kid, you done?" Gus asked Colton.

"Yeah," he said.

# The Holy Fool

"Good," Gus said. "Sonny, you give the quote to Colton." Sonny tore the quote from his pad, handed it to Colton, and stuffed the pad in his satchel. "Colton, you type that up and the resignation piece. We'll need them in 20 minutes, so you'll have to get going."

"All right," Colton said, getting up. "Sonny, Joey." He darted out of the room.

"So, what are you here for? Oh, yeah."

"Oh, yeah. I'm here to bang you two out of here. It's time."

Sonny looked behind Gus. "They're all out there ready to do that? Just for me?"

Gus shook his head. "Well, the both of you, but I'm making sure to bang out everyone when they go tonight."

"How about that? OK, I'll be out in one minute."

Gus nodded and walked out the door without a word. Sonny hefted a long red duffle bag onto his desk, unzipped it, and checked to make sure everything in it looked like it belonged there before zipping it back up and setting it next to his satchel. "You've got your stuff?"

"Sure," Joey said, indicating the black backpack and grey duffel bag at her feet. "What does he mean by 'banging out?'"

"Old newspaper tradition. It's what they did whenever someone left the paper. When they do it for everyone like Gus said, they usually do that the day a paper closes for good. I guess Gus is covering his bases in case the worst happens."

"Huh," Joey said. "Are you ready?"

"Just one second." He walked up to the wall of his office with a permanent marker in his hand. Finding just enough space on that wall not covered with pictures, Sonny wrote -30- on that section of the wall, then signed his name in smaller letters underneath. Capping his pen and letting it fall on his desk with a *thwack*, he said, "Time to go," as he slung the satchel and gym bag over his right shoulder.

Sonny and Joey walked out of his office together. Gus stood there, with a ruler in his hand. There were about a dozen other newsroom staffers out of the floor, also holding rulers or other implements. Ed was a little closer to the newsroom entrance, a ruler in his hand as well.

Gus gave him a single nod. "See ya." With that, he started tapping the ruler on a nearby table in a steady rhythm. The other staffers began imitating him in turn.

"Later." Sonny and Joey passed through the newsroom. There were scattered calls of "See ya" and "bye" throughout the room, although others were silent. Colton was not among the group; Sonny saw the back of him at one of the City/Metro desks, not looking up, keys tick-taking, an early deadline to meet. Woot was out of sight in Conference Room B, directing the electronic traffic.

Just before they left the room, Sonny and Joey crossed Ed's path. He was banging his ruler on one of the arms of his wheelchair. "Bless ya, Ed. I'll remember everything you taught me."

"Yeah, yeah, whatever. You two kids take care of each other, OK?"

Joey walked to Ed, leaned over, and kissed him on the forehead. "Thank you for everything, Ed. I'll miss you."

Ed smiled as he looked up at her. "A lady like you, what's not to miss?"

She hugged him, then returned to Sonny. They went to the nearest open elevator and stood in it and closed the door behind them. "You think everything is going to work out for them?" Joey said.

"Probably not in the long term. You know, I might sound like an asshole, but it's not my problem now. I did what I could, and what I said I would do."

She nodded. "So, what are you worried about now?"

"Keeping us safe."

## Chapter 19

It was 4 a.m. Saturday when John Michael realized he'd been had.

He woke up next to a still sleeping and very nude Winona in his room, and padded off to the bathroom, swiping his Blackberry from the nightstand for a read.

As he called up the Internet on his phone, he went to the *Journal* home page. The minute he saw the picture of the Keep on the front page with the FOR SALE? sign on it, he realized something was wrong, a fact confirmed by Wyatt's voice mail.

He had dressed, packed, and vacated the room in 15 minutes, leaving Winona in the bed. By way of apology, he arranged with the front desk to make sure she had the suite for the rest of the weekend.

Gus's estimate of how long it would take John Michael and the other executives to get back to Chicago proved to be accurate. At noon, a harried John Michael, lead Edson council Perry Reeves, Reed Burkes, the chief technology officer for the company, and chief financial officer Hector Walsh streamed into the lobby of the Keep. A worried Mary Kennedy and a chastened Wyatt Walker met them there. Walker looked like he'd slept in his suit and not had a bath for 24 hours because it was the truth.

With the others behind him, John Michael strode right to Wyatt and halted when they were able to touch chests. "What in the hell happened, Wyatt?" John Michael made a whisper seem like a shout in the cavernous lobby.

"I got goat-fucked, John Michael; that's the only way to put it," Wyatt said, causing Mary on his right to flinch. "One minute I'm walking to my car after lunch, the next minute, I'm getting arrested for possession of illegal explosives."

"Christ, am I going to have to pay Perry more to keep you out of prison?"

"No, sir. They already dropped the charges."

"Thank God for small favors." John Michael turned to Mary. "Has Lord Melchester called back?"

She shook her head. "I've left three different messages for him at different numbers. Still nothing."

He lowered his voice yet again. "What about Cathy? Has she called in?"

"Nothing sir. Left messages on her home and cell voice mail."

"And..."

"I've done the same thing for Sonny Turner. No response."

"OK," John Michael said, calming down just enough not to yell. "You are going to continue to call all three of those individuals at their numbers. *The minute* you can get one of them on the line, you patch them through to me, I don't care if I'm in the can. You keep calling them until I've spoken to all of them. That's your job for at least the next 24 hours, understood?"

"Understood."

John Michael turned back to Wyatt. "Let's talk over there." He pointed down the hall.

The two of them went away from the elevators and huddled together, voices low. "Are all of the papers out?"

"From what I heard, the last of them had left the plant by 10 p.m."

"Jesus. Any way to get those papers back?"

"At this point? They've already been out on the streets for the entire morning. Everyone's seen it now."

"Shit. What about the Web site?"

"That might be easier to do, but we don't have control of that right now. *They* do."

"What the hell are *they* doing?"

Wyatt gestured toward the upstairs. "Getting out the Sunday edition."

"We should have the cops here."

"What are they going to do? Arrest them for putting out a paper?"

"For keeping us away from our property, that's what!"

# The Holy Fool

"We can go up to the offices whenever we want, according to them."

John Michael waved him off. "Asses are getting fired around here, I can guarantee it. Speaking of firings, where's Massino and Pulaski?"

"Upstairs, in the executive conference room. They have a… delegation with them. They wanted to speak with you."

"I'll fucking bet they do." He adjusted his tie. "OK. I'll let them do their little song and dance. And then, everyone will see who's really in charge here."

\*\*\*

Flanked by his people, John Michael walked down the long hallway in the Penthouse toward the executive conference room.

Everyone was seated around the table, although they had left the head of the table vacant for John Michael's party. Seated at the other end were Carlo, Gus, Bill, Oscar, Ed, and Mark. The sight of Ed and Mark caused him to do a double-take. "Didn't realize it was Old-Timer's Day here," he said. "Mark, what lured you out of New York?"

"A strange situation, John Michael," Mark said, "a strange situation."

John Michael was about to reply, but he noticed two men at the other end of the table, next to where Perry Reeves sat. One of the men, a beefy blond man with hangdog eyes with arm muscles just contained by his shirt, he recognized right away.

"Gil?" John Michael asked in a whisper, walking toward him, "Gil? What are you doing out here?"

The CEO of UUF Bank stood to greet his old college classmate. "They asked if someone representing the bank might come," he said, his voice soft and – a first for Gil – unsure. "You've met Melissa Berg before, our senior VP for corporate accounts." He nodded to his partner, a thirtysomething brunette with a Roman-style nose whose sheared hair and business suit gave her a definitive androgynous vibe.

"But Gil," John Michael said as Gil stood up and stretched, "you could explain how the financing's going to work, how we're in great financial shape…"

"Can't stay, Johnny," Gil said. "There's a board meeting over at the bank I have to be at."

"What meeting?"

"We've been trying to quietly get rid of all of this debt we've got on the books, but that story your kid wrote blew that wide open. You didn't know about that." Gil said, noting John Michael's disbelief.

"Anyway, that really fucked us over… well, maybe it's not the whole reason. Shit's getting bad with the boys in New York and a lot of the deals we're in with them and others I don't even know about. A lot of firms are in trouble. There's talk of liquidating Lehman Brothers."

"What the hell?"

"They won't last 48 hours, I don't think. We might not either. And I think I'll be out of a job before the day's done."

"Jesus, Gil," John Michael said. "Well, getting $10 million in a single day's not the worst thing to happen to you," referring to the severance package that was a specific requirement of Gil's contract.

"I'd better enjoy it. I think this is the last time anyone's going to trust me with something like this ever again." He stared out at Lake Michigan through the windows. "I forgot how beautiful these views are. Looking at it every day, that can make you forget."

"Gil…"

Gil turned again to face John Michael. "Melissa can give you all the data and details, but here's what you really need to know – you're $300 million in the hole, and you've got two weeks to find a buyer for this place before Edson runs out of funds."

"You mean the *Journal*?"

"I mean *Edson Corp*. The *Journal's* already out of money. Well, that's it." He came around the table to shake John Michael's hand. "We need to drink a bar sometime, OK?"

"You mean, have a drink at a bar?"

"Naw, drink a *whole* bar, like the old days. I'm going to need a few days like that to get over this. See you." With that and a wave, Gil breezed out the door.

He turned to face Melissa. "Was he right?" he said.

"Short version? Yes," she said in a grating tone that brought *schoolmarm* immediately to mind.

"Heeey, sorry to cramp your style, John Michael, but can we talk?" Ed called out from the end of the table.

John Michael eyes shot knives at Ed as he stared at them. "Just because you don't work here anymore doesn't mean you're untouchable. I don't need to carry your column anymore."

"Go ahead – the Lord would be on the phone with my syndicate by Monday. Now that we've got the chest-beatin' out of the way, you think we can talk?"

John Michael began to gesture for his people to sit down at the table. "You want to talk? Talk. Explain why I don't fire everyone."

"You might be interested in why we decided to run that special edition last night," Carlo said.

"I'm guessing it had something to do with me wanting to sell this paper," John Michael said.

"Yeah, that's right," Bill said. "Basically, we don't want that to happen."

"What's the problem?" John Michael said. "You've survived a sale before. Besides, I'm not sure some of you wouldn't be happy to get rid of me."

"That's not the point," Gus said. "The point is, whoever's going to buy us would have to close the doors almost immediately. I'm thinking that almost any potential buyer would think that to be a deal-killer. I'm never the best with money, but $300 million in liabilities, that doesn't sound good to me."

"Even if those numbers are all correct, which I dispute," John Michael said, "That's not something that Melchester's going to fear. This is a man who's flirted with bankruptcy twice and come back wealthier than ever. He's not going…"

Mary entered the room. "What is it?" John Michael said.

"Lord Melchester on line two, sir."

John Michael turned to the newsmen, a finger in the air. "I'll need a moment…"

"Sure, go ahead," Gus said.

John Michael bolted out of the room and went to the reception area of his office, where Mary waited on with the receiver. He picked it up. "Lord Melchester? Is that you?"

"Edson, old man, beautiful day, isn't it?" Melchester said, a jolly lilt to his voice. "Had a chance to see your front page today. Bloody lively look to it."

John Michael took a deep breath before continuing. "Andrew, I want to reassure you that this is still a viable deal…"

"This little scheme of yours, *so clever* it was, I must say. It would have been amazing if you had pulled it off, but… it made a great story. Mr. Turner does have a talent of explaining the complex in simple terms, doesn't he?"

"You put him up to this, *Andrew*?" John Michael closed his eyes, shook his head, and continued in a lower voice, "I'm sorry, things have been stressful around here."

"Actually, he was perfectly willing to do it gratis. I did offer him a job after the fact – felt I owed him, anyway – but he declined."

"Look, the deal doesn't have to die."

"It's looking very good for me if I do nothing, which is what will happen," Melchester said, now matter-of-fact rather than jolly.

"Lord Melchester…"

"The best-case scenario is that in two weeks, you go bankrupt and I buy whatever belongs to you that looks appealing and hire any staff that might be a good fit for the *Star*. And I'll get all of that for nominal cost and none of that unsightly debt. The *worst*-case scenario is the status quo, of course, and I'm happy with our old-fashioned newspaper war."

"You able to keep things going over there on the other side of the river? Some of my friends keep asking me what I'm doing in a dying industry like newspapers."

"Why, Edson, newspapers won't die – not as long as I'm alive."

# The Holy Fool

"You're 70."

"That's 30 good years, old boy. By then, my grandchildren will have figured out how to run newspapers in the 21st century. Anyway, glad I managed to return your call. Cheers." With that, Melchester hung up.

After standing there for a few moments, holding a receiver with a dial tone, he finally handed it to Mary. "Keep trying Turner and Cathy's numbers." He walked back to the conference room.

Gus was leaning back in his chair when John Michael came in. "Didn't work out, John Michael?"

He said nothing in response but sat down at the table and looked around. "Where's Turner? He's got a lot to answer for today."

Gus nodded toward an envelope in front of John Michael. "That's his resignation letter there."

He picked it up for a moment, then dropped it. "Where is he now?"

"Gone," Gus said. "Don't know where. We had a little disagreement about him giving the *New York Times* and *The Guardian* those stories we decided not to run right away about Iraq, so he quit the paper."

"What!?"

"You didn't know?" Gus said. John Michael, stunned, hands in his pockets, didn't say anything, so Gus asked him, "Where's Cathy and Richard?"

"Cathy got off the plane, but I'm not sure where she is right now," he replied. "I fired Richard Connors before we landed in O'Hare. I can tolerate editors who don't do anything in their jobs, but those who don't know what's going on with their staff are useless."

"Good piece of advice, Johnny," Ed said.

Before John Michael could respond, Mary came into the room again. "Mr. Turner is on the line, Mr. Edson."

"OK." John Michael walked out of the room, pulling Wyatt with him. As they followed Mary to her desk, John Michael whispered to Wyatt, "Is that tracing system still active on my phone?"

"Yes, yes, it is."

"Can you get it going?" A nod. "OK, move, move!"

It took two minutes for Mary to stall Sonny and for Wyatt to get on John Michaels work laptop and get the trace set up. When Wyatt finally gave him the high sign, John Michael picked up the receiver. "Sonny, wonderful to hear from you today. How are things?"

"Ah, not bad," Sonny's voice, sounding bleary but clear. "A little tired. Anyway, I was just calling to make sure you'd gotten my letter."

"I certainly did. Your resignation has been accepted with *no* regrets."

"Damn, OK."

"One thing, Sonny. I'm wondering where you are now. It might be useful if the authorities ask about you, given that you used classified information for those stories."

"Well, there's a little deal called the First Amendment. You know that exists, right? Maybe it's not a surprise you don't."

"Are you in Toronto, Vancouver?" John Michael's voice purred. "I remember when Bush was re-elected, you wrote that column where you pondered moving to Canada. Did you really do it? Are you in the Great White North now?"

*\*\*\**

Sonny looked up at the windowed ceiling of the train station, the fog obscuring the sea of lights outside on the ground and the stars in the sky. "Yeah, I'm in Vancouver right now. You should come out here sometime. The view of the mountains is beautiful."

*\*\*\**

"You're actually in Vancouver, then?" John Michael asked back in Chicago.

"Maybe yes. Maybe no. Maybe go fuck yourself."

It took John Michael a second to process the words, then: "What?"

"Oh, wait, I guess you don't know your Scorsese quotes, then. Oh, well."

"You think you can get away with messing with me like this?"

"Happens all the time, brother. Life moves on, doesn't it? Later."

\*\*\*

As Sonny closed the phone, he walked down a flight of stairs to a restroom on a lower level of the train station. Finding a restroom, he went into the nearest stall and dropped the phone into a wastebasket. After a careful wash of his hands, he walked back up the stairs where signs read ST. PANCRAS INTERNATIONAL.

\*\*\*

After hanging up the phone, John Michael ran into his office. "Did you get him?"

Wyatt shook his head. "Somewhere in the greater London area."

John Michael seemed to shrink in size at the news. "That's it, then."

"It's not over, boss." Wyatt came around the desk to talk to him. "We can get some guys out there, dig around…"

"And WHAT, Wyatt?!? WHAT? Hunt him down… What the hell are you thinking?" John Michael rushed over to him, almost to challenge him, fists raised. However, Wyatt stood there, hands free and at his sides, not moving. John Michael realized what type of man Wyatt was, what he had done in his life, and he took a step back. "The information is out." John Michael looked up at Wyatt and laughed at something. "What?" Wyatt said.

"I just realized one of those stories, it was about your outfit, wasn't it? Foxwood Solutions? Weren't you out in Iraq when all of the things in the story happened?"

"Sir, I…"

"Psh," he said, waving dismissively, "I'm advising you to update your resume, of course, because I don't think any of our jobs are safe. But, maybe you should talk to Perry about getting a good lawyer." He walked away before Wyatt could say anything. "Make sure you lock up my office when you leave."

John Michael returned to the newsmen making some small talk as they waited. "Sonny was just confirming his resignation. Now, someone tell me about this idea you have."

Carlo nodded. "The idea is that you sell the paper to a cooperative, owned and run by the *Journal* staff."

"There's going to be some outside investors, but this entity, the Journal Staff Cooperative, or JSC, will be your workers," Bill said. "We name a fee, and we absorb the paper and all of its debt, and you get away scot free from any entanglements."

"Not that I'm agreeing to this at all, and not that I particularly care about the answer to this question, but what happens when UUF Bank comes along and wants their money and you don't have it?"

"It's probably unlikely that UUF will be doing the asking," Melissa said from the side. "More likely, it will be another financial institution that buys up either the company, its debt, or both. It might even be the federal government, at this point."

"Bush isn't going to go for a bailout," Walsh said.

"It's getting bad," Melissa said.

"Well, John Michael, that's a very good question, and it deserves a good answer," Gus said, getting up from his seat and pacing. "What's going to happen is that we're going to talk to whatever comes through that door asking for that debt. We're going to say that they have two options. They could decide to work with us to forgive a good portion of the debt and get the rest of it paid in a timely manner, maybe 10-20 years."

"That sounds like a nice fantasy," John Michael said to Gus. "What happens when they say they'd prefer it all?"

"Then we'll say shove it and walk out the door," Bill said. "The only way we can pay any of that off is if we're a working newspaper, and if they're willing to kill the golden goose, we're willing to provide the axe. We have the feeling they prefer a good chance of getting some of their money back rather than no chance of getting any of it back."

The room turned to look at Melissa. "Well, that's usually right."

John Michael stared across the room at the newspapermen. "You still might fail," he said.

"That's right," Ed said. "They might – we might. But in the end, this paper's not yours. It belongs to the people who worked for it and still work for it, and to the community at large. You were just *renting* the place, see?"

Before John Michael could think of another thing to say, Mary walked through the doorway a third time. "Is it Cathy?" he asked.

Mary shook her head. "Colton's waiting outside. He said he wanted to see you."

"One moment." With a single nod, he got up and went outside into the corridor. Colton was there, waiting by the elevators. "Hey, Dad."

John Michael stopped and glared at his son. "I have one question for you," he said, pointing at Colton.

"Sure." Colton remained calm.

John Michael inched forward, arm and finger extended at his son. "Tell me. You knew that they were writing all of that vile crap about me, right? And you let them. I just want to ask; whose side are you on?" He got louder, inching ever closer to his son. "Are you on my side, or on the side of those scumbags?" He briefly pointed toward the conference room before jerking his finger and fist under Colton's nose.

Colton, unfazed, now gazed at his father with a lazy contempt. "I'm on Mom's side, OK? I'm on *Mom's* side."

John Michael let his fist drop to his side. He somehow managed to stand up straight. "Of course you are," he whispered. "Of course you are." Then, his voice more modulated: "Why are you here?"

To John Michael's surprise, Colton braced himself against the walls and his hands shook for a moment. "Thought you'd be happy you got one over on the old man," John Michael said.

"That's what I thought, too. Guess you weren't the only one operating on false assumptions recently." He closed his eyes for a second and clasped his hands together to keep them from shaking before continuing. "Mom's downstairs. She needs to talk to you."

"Now?"

"Yeah, *now*."

He sighed as he looked back at the conference room. "Give me just a minute. Wait here; I won't be long."

He made a brisk pace back to the conference room, where he opened the door but did not go through all the way. He pointed at Gus. "OK. Do you have a written buy proposal?"

Gus got nonverbal confirmation by his fellow newspapermen, then turned to John Michael and said, "We do."

"Good. Show it to Perry and my people." He turned to Perry. "Take some time and look over it. I'll be expecting your opinion in an hour, understood?"

Perry stood up. "Yes, sir."

"Fine. I'll be back." He walked away with the door swinging closed before he could see the stunned looks of the men and women on both sides of the table.

Mark leaned over to Gus as the Edson people began pouring over the documents with highlighters and pens flashing across the pages. "Not that I'm telling you how to run the paper, but have you thought about running those stories Sonny had?"

"We're running them in tomorrow's edition, with more analysis and reaction from the administration and others," Gus said. "Sean Carlton, Colton, and that Casey Barnes kid are putting that info together."

"Surprised you went ahead with it."

Gus shrugged. "We got beat, and it's a story now, the leak. We have to cover it."

"Of course."

\*\*\*

John Michael walked back to his son in the hallway. When he got there, he reached out and made the smallest of adjustments to Colton's tie, then fussed with his own. "Does it look OK?"

"Yeah." Colton's voice was distant.

"What do you think? Do I have a chance with your mom? A reprieve?"

Colton stared at his father, then let a grin appear, the type you'd give to a friend or a brother before they would get bawled out by their mom or the principal. "You want me to be honest? I think she's kind of over it."

"Over what I did or over me?"

"Over you. And herself, too, if that makes sense."

John Michael nodded. "Maybe it does," he said. "Let's go." As they entered the elevator, the doors closed as John Michael Edson went down to hear his fate.

***

Joey sat in the window seat of a bullet-shaped silver train, stretching her legs so they extended in front of her. Business class in a 747 was just this side of comfortable; she was glad that this leg of the trip would be under roomier conditions. Although the fog was starting to lift overhead, a four-year old Rough Guide to France had her attention.

"Well, you found the best way to see Paris in a day?" she heard from behind her. She looked up to see Sonny saunter up and slide into the adjacent seat.

"Do you think we can make it three days, at least? There's some modern art museums I really wanted to check out."

"Not the Louvre?"

"I guess the Art Institute spoiled me on Impressionists," she said with a smile. "But I'm interested in seeing a couple of the historic sights, too. Maybe see Jim Morrison's grave at Pere Lachaise."

"I'm more of a Montparnasse guy. I'd like to see Sarte's grave, and Serge Gainsbourg's."

"Well, that's why we need more than just a couple of days, don't we? Besides, we see if we can stand being in the same place with each other for an extended period."

"We should be able to manage that. I'm wondering what's going to happen when we get out of tourism mode and have to settle somewhere around here."

"Any ideas about that?"

"A few. Here's this," he said, handing her an airline boarding pass.

"What's this?"

"Plane ticket back to Chicago if you change your mind. I figured it was only fair."

"I'm not going to need…"

"Just keep it for now."

"I'm humoring you, taking this, but OK," she said as she tucked the ticket into her bag. "You realized that we go under the Channel, no force on Earth is going to stop me from singing "Under the Sea."

"Except duct tape. I do have that."

She leaned over and kissed him on the nose. "Partners?"

"Partners. I like the sound of that."

She settled back into her seat. "Maybe we should see Notre Dame first. What do you think?"

"I'll let you take the lead on this one."

# Chapter 20

## Stories: 2008-2009

### UUF FINISHES LIQUIDATION; WILL NOT AFFECT JOURNAL SALE

CHICAGO (AP) – A spokesman with Goldman Sachs said that they will not challenge the debt reduction plan reached by USA Universal Financial (UUF) Bank and Journal Cooperative Corp. (JCC), the new owners of the *Chicago Journal*.

... Both sides signed the agreement Sept. 14, hours after JCC finalized the purchase of the *Journal* from Edson Media and just a day before UUF Bank would itself file for Chapter 7 bankruptcy.

... Mark Bauer, interim publisher of the *Journal*, said Goldman Sachs's decision will give the paper the opportunity to return to sound financial footing, pay back most of its creditors, and continue to serve the people of Chicago.

### ARGENTINA SAYS NO TO EXTRADITION

BUENOS AIRES, Argentina (REUTERS) – The Argentine Foreign Ministry has confirmed that it will deny the request of the U.S. Justice Department to extradite Marine Gunnery Sgt. Danielle Danvers.

Danvers, 30, an Iraq War veteran and winner of the Bronze Star and Purple Heart, is currently listed as absent without leave from her intelligence posting with the Pentagon. She is suspected of being the source of the leak of classified documents publicized in September by former *Chicago Journal* columnist Samuel "Sonny" Turner.

... In the U.S., Danvers' civilian attorneys say if the case goes to trial, they will be arguing that Danvers was under mental duress due to keeping her sexual orientation a secret from her superiors. Those mental problems grew, they say, after the woman Danvers considered her partner, Marine Sgt. Rachel Wilder, 27, was killed Aug. 7, 2007, by an IED while on active duty in Kandahar Province, Afghanistan.

## JOURNAL NAMES LEADERSHIP TEAM

CHICAGO (AP) – The *Chicago Journal* tapped former *Philadelphia Herald* editor Carlo Massino as Editor in Chief as part of a series of moves to solidify the paper's leadership under Journal Cooperative Corp. (JCC).

Massino, 48, a 25-year veteran of Philadelphia newspapers, first joined the *Journal* in January 2008 as managing editor. Since September of that year, he has served as interim Editor-in-Chief.

... Arthur "Gus" Pulaski, 52, a 35-year *Journal* veteran, will become managing editor after serving in an interim capacity since September...

... Ed Mauzr, a retired 40-year veteran of the *Journal*, has been tapped to serve as chairman of the *Journal*'s editorial board. Mauzr, 68, said the position is only part-time, adding, "I've earned the right to be as lazy as possible."

... Mark Bauer, 60, the great-great grandson of *Journal* founder Michael Bauer, said he will serve as interim publisher until Oct. 1, 2009. Once a permanent publisher has been selected, Bauer will join the JCC board.

## EDSONS REACH SETTLEMENT

CHICAGO (NY POST) – What if a media baron got divorced and no one noticed?

Former Edson Media head John Michael Edson managed this trick last week when he filed a divorce settlement in the case of John Michael Edson vs. Diana Edson, a case notable for its media silence.

Full details on the settlement were unavailable, but it is believed that Diana Edson, 49, will not get alimony. However, sources close to the case indicate she will receive, among other assets, a home on the north shore of Oahu, as well as a trust fund set up to cover maintenance, household expenses, and property taxes.

John Michael, 55, has kept incognito since his buyout, dividing time between his Chicago condo and Montana ranch while living with his current girlfriend, former Edson Media employee Jenni Hardin, 28, and their daughter Caity.

## TURNER REACHES THREE-BOOK DEAL WITH VOYAGER PUBLISHING

NEW YORK (AP) – Blogger and former *Chicago Journal* columnist Sonny Turner has reached a three-book deal for an undisclosed advance with Voyager Publishing.

The first of the books, *Dispatches: 1998-2008,* will be a collection of Turner's columns and writings, to be released Dec. 15. The writings span articles Turner, 32, wrote as a graduate student at Northwestern University, up to his last column with the *Journal*.

The other two books will be: *A Seat at the Revolution*, his memoir of the 2008 sale of the *Journal*, and *A Fool's Thoughts on Journalism*, described as an outline of Turner's journalism philosophy and ethics. They are scheduled for release in December 2009 and 2010, respectively.

## APOLOGIES FROM 'FOX AND FRIENDS'

NEW YORK (MSNBC) – The Fox News morning show "Fox and Friends" issued a rare apology today after mistakenly identifying blogger and former *Chicago Journal* columnist Sonny Turner as a suspect in the rape of two university students at a north London party last week.

In its initial discussion of the case Monday, it was disclosed that a man matching Turner's physical description had been spotted at the party, according to Scotland Yard sources. At one point, co-host Steve Doocy even said the Metropolitan Police were consulting with Interpol to track down Turner.

However, Facebook and Twitter posts placed Turner in Stockholm during the night of the attacks, speaking at a meeting of Amnesty International and meeting with potential donors for his upcoming nonprofit media project.

Two days later, the arrest of another man, 28-year-old reality TV star Eddie "Panda" Behr, forced Fox to air the apology the next day...

... Behr, who bears a strong resemblance to the writer, originally starred in the Chicago edition of *Real Life Drama* on Culture TV in 2006. Ironically, that series was filmed in the same Wicker Park neighborhood that Turner lived in at the time. Behr then starred in three different spin-off shows while dealing with various drug and assault charges, many of these stemming from incidents on those shows.

# Chapter 21

## Sept. 7 (Labor Day), 2009, Plainpalais District, Geneva, Switzerland

Sonny started his Labor Day stroll at seven that morning. He was ultra-casual that day – a black Iowa Hawkeyes hoodie, cargo shorts, and Birkenstock sandals, but with his satchel he'd carried from Chicago with him.

He also had a new friend. The beagle was a year-old pup, rescued from a French pound just across the border. It was Joey's dog, the one who would give her some companionship. He was a mellow soul, bright but quiet unless threatened, and had single-handedly overcome the man's reluctance to have pets in his home.

He had named the dog Pica, which was always a good conversation piece when meeting new people. He shook his head. He'd run away from newspapers, but the old terms, the old lore, continued to stay with him.

There was a nice café just six blocks north from their building along the Rhone River, up Georges-Favon Boulevard. He was still getting used to the city, the rhythms. It was no problem walking through the city, like Chicago, and the transit system was usable. It was also a bit more expensive to live in Geneva, but some clever planning and good support had made it tolerable. It was beautiful, especially walking near the river with the mountains in the background. He laughed to himself, remember that crack he'd made to Edson about the Vancouver mountains.

Once he got to Café Lachaise, he made sure to take his seat at one of the outdoor tables. Pica crawled underneath his seat and behind his feet.

One waiter he'd gotten to know well, a slight, well-mannered student at University of Geneva, was the first out to see him. "Monsieur Turner, how are you?" Jean-Paul said in French.

"Could you get me some eggs, scrambled, sausage, and some toast?" Sonny replied in Chicagoese-accented French.

"Of course. What to drink?"

"Coffee with cream would be great."

"Great. I'll get the order in right away."

"*Merci*, Jean-Paul," Sonny said as the kid walked away.

Within a couple of minutes, the kid had brought his coffee out to him, and he sat and let the lakeside breezes cool it down just a touch. He took some time checking out Reddit on his mobile browser as Pica let the breeze blow around his ears.

Out of the corner of his eye, he noticed his appointment showing up as he strode up the sidewalk. Henri Roussou was one of the brighter young attorneys in Geneva, having worked as an in-house council for the United Nations before going into business for himself. Immaculately dressed in a crème suit and custom-made shoes, Henri made Sonny think that he would be what Colton might look like in a few years.

"Monsieur Turner, how are you today?" Henri said in French.

"Good, good. Glad to see you."

"Yes, I am early." He switched to English. "I thought you might appreciate the break from French. Your French is getting very much better, I think."

"Thanks. You want a coffee?"

"No, no, I won't be that long." He sat down across the table from Sonny.

"OK, so, what do you have for me? Good news, bad news, a mix?" Pica began scratching his butt up against his shin.

"A mix, but more good than bad, I think."

"OK, give it."

"I have been conferring with my colleagues in Chicago, and they have been discussing matters with the Illinois Attorney General's Office. They all agree there will be no charges for any of the actions you undertook as part of the Sept. 12 incident, or leading up to it."

Sonny nodded. "Good to know."

"Even in the matter of the money... the accounts were in her name, and she willingly released it to you."

"So, you're talking about the state authorities. I'm not hearing anything about the federal authorities. What's going on with them?"

"Yes, well. I and my American associates have been in contact with certain federal agencies. The Defense Criminal Investigative Service and the Naval Criminal Investigative Service are assisting the FBI. It is their opinion that Danvers is your source, but they have not made an official finding of facts. They are also trying to trace what exactly had been leaked."

"They don't even know what's been leaked, that's what's so hilarious. What about charges?"

"That is a good question. With complicated federal investigations, we could be talking years before there are charges filed, and they still may decide against it. The same if they put it before a federal grand jury to investigate."

"And all the time, I'm playing a waiting game, wondering whether I'll ever feel safe going back to America without getting my ass sent to Gitmo."

Henri shrugged. "Perhaps the new administration will look more favorably on your case..."

"That's not going to make a difference, not really," Sonny said. "The new guy's different, but he's not *that* different. I still embarrassed America."

"The case is a concern, perhaps, but not a major one. Anyway, the good news is here." He placed his briefcase on the table, opened it up, and handed two envelopes to Sonny.

"What are these?"

"Your permanent residency papers," Henri replied. "Yours and that of Ms. Halvorsen. I will be sending these to the other American members of your staff, but I thought that you would want to receive these personally. How is she, by the way?"

"Doing quite well, actually."

"My wife and I saw her installation in Carouge a week ago; very stunning."

"I'll pass along your well-wishes." He reached into his satchel.

"What is this?"

He pulled out a white coffee mug with a picture of the fool Joey had drawn a year ago with THE FOOL written in block lettering below, and, below that lettering, www.thefoolnews.org in lighter letters. "For you. Typical of the swag we try to sell to keep the place going." He handed it to Henri.

"Ah, *merci*. It will go to my office." He put it in his briefcase and shook hands with Sonny. "I will call midweek to update you on matters, yes?"

"Sure thing."

"Happy Labor Day."

"Workers of the world, unite."

"Ahaha, yes. *Bon chance*."

\*\*\*

Joey woke up in bed.

She wasn't surprised to find herself alone – during the past several weeks, Sonny had been in the office early getting prepared for today.

The four-story building that housed her apartment dated from the 1880's, when it first served as a factory and warehouse. The design of the apartment was basic, right down to the red brick walls and the metal columns supporting the ceiling. After you left the bedroom and bathroom area and walked past the kitchen and dining space, the rest of the apartment was open space. Joey used salvaged cubicles and false walls to create some separate areas there, including a living room/parlor, a work space for herself, and a small home office for Sonny, even though he did most of his work upstairs.

Except for their memory foam mattress and the TV, all the items and appliances in the room had been salvaged from junkyards, garage and storage sales, or thrift stores. Most of her possessions she used to have were still in storage at her parent's place, and it surprised her how little she missed them. *How much do things just take up space? What's their point*? she thought. For her, it just gave her another chance to use her artistic talents to her advantage.

## The Holy Fool

Sonny rented out the top two floors of the building. The top floor contained the offices for The Fool; the other floor had apartments Sonny and several members of his staff lived in. Sonny and Joey were in one loft, and at least eight other staff members lived in the building with room for more if needed. *Almost like the dorms at the Art Institute*, Joey thought.

She went into her work space. All her old artwork not stored at her parent's place was in galleries in Chicago and New York, so she was busy creating new works to help decorate the apartment. Some of the work on the walls depicted landscape vistas in Geneva or street scenes in Carouge.

She saw that she had left her laptop on last night, checking out some emails from her agent in New York – and then Sonny had interrupted... *that* part of their relationship was still going strong, growing in inventiveness as time passed. Looking on the screen now, there was an email from one of her new friends, a former Boston resident turned UN employee.

Just as she prepared to type a response to the email, Sonny and Pica opened the door to the apartment. Sonny reached down and undid his leash, and the beagle walked toward the faint sound of tap-tap tapping in the distance.

Pica walked around one of the dividers between the main area and Joey's work area. Looking at the sated expression on the dog's face, Sonny said, "Wish I was in his paw tracks."

Joey looked behind her at him and smiled. "Hi, did your meeting work out?"

"I've got something for you."

"Oh, me too." She reached for what appeared to be an envelope on her work bench. "Do you want to take turns, go together, or..."

"It's great to see you." He came to her side and enveloped her in a hug and kiss. As he broke off the kiss, he tucked his envelope into her crossed arms and plucked out the thing she was going to give to him out of her hand.

"You too. So, what's this...? Oh, the residency card, cool! That means we can stay here as long as we want to, right?"

"Exactly. We're all set here for as long as it's needed. What did you give me..." He looked down to see the plane ticket he'd given her in London in his hands.

She shook her head. "I'm not going to need it. I was thinking, actually, that you could trade that in to help pay for my parents to come on over for the Fourth of July, since there's all these celebrations here."

"They'd want to do that?"

"I think so."

The two of them stood together, Joey staring at her card, Sonny staring at the plane ticket. Joey was the first one to look up at Sonny. "You get the feeling that somehow we just got married doing this?" she said.

"I thought we already got married a few months ago, when you agreed to go on the run with me like Luke and Laura. Maybe this was a recommitment ceremony or something like that."

"I love you." They embraced.

"Love you too."

"So, speaking of marriage and family, would you ever be interested in one?" Joey said.

"One what? Marriage or family?"

"It'd be nice to have a wedding, but honestly family was what I really wanted."

"What? You're serious?"

"Mom was on Skype the other day asking me if I was pregnant yet – she sounded disappointed that I actually wasn't. This is from a woman who never admitted to me until I turned 18 that she had sex with my dad before she got married. Attitudes change, I guess, or maybe she just wants grandkids that badly." She looked up at him. "What do you think?"

"About you as a mom? I think you'd be great at it. I always wondered what I'd have to offer to a kid."

"A lot." She hugged him again. "You're always talking with the staff's kids whenever they bring them to work. I can tell."

"So, when do you want to do this?"

# The Holy Fool

"How about we not put pressure on ourselves? Let's just say we're going to stop *not* trying to have a kid? How does that sound?"

"I can live with that."

\*\*\*

An hour later, Sonny and Joey got on the elevators to go upstairs. He ran a key card through a special slot on the elevator's control panel before pressing the button to the fourth floor. Joey looked stunning in a sea green and blue patterned dress that flowed around her and white sandals, along with the usual collection of bracelets. She looked at Sonny, who'd gotten dressed back into his half-and-half black and red hoodie with The Fool logo on the back and khaki cargo shorts. "Feeling underdressed for American television?" she said.

"Actually, no. Mark Zuckerberg can pull this off, I can too. Leadership has privileges."

"Oooh, you bad boy." Joey took his hand.

The two stepped out into the empty foyer area of the offices of *The Fool*. Nobody had considered getting administrative assistants, but Sonny realized they'd probably need one or two soon. There were three conference rooms to the left and a break-room/kitchen to the right as they took the narrow hall into *The Fool*'s newsroom.

The interior was simply red brick walls and steel supports in the middle of the room. A T-shaped desk ran the length of the room, lined with fiber optics and electrical plug-ins. A big spray-painted picture of The Fool's Head loomed above it. On the opposite wall, above the hallway, six large plasma screens loomed over the room, able to show online footage or televised material.

"You need to get more decoration in here," Joey whispered to Sonny.

"I told you this might not be the permanent HQ for us. I guess if you'd like to spray-paint some more stuff on the wall, that would be cool."

"Anything in mind?"

"Maybe some male and female nudes, give the staff something to look at."

"Typical."

Two things caught his attention. First, he saw a NBC camera crew starting to get set up in front of the desk and the mural. Second, he saw an old friend acting pissed about it.

"Goddamned amateur-hour video techs," said Woot, resplendent in shredded jeans and a black T-shirt declaring <u>Actually, I'm Kind of a Big Deal</u>. "Hey, Joey," he added, waving at her.

"And how's my CITO, then?"

"Well, they insisted on getting here early, even though they're getting in the way of my guys working," Woot said, waving at the camera crew.

"Woot, you got most of your guys working down at the other end of the table. What are you talking about?"

"Ah, OK, sorry. I'm just getting nervous about the launch. Worried trolls, government affiliated or not, might start screwing our stuff up."

"So, are your boys ready?"

"All hands are on deck." There were about a dozen staff in his tech crew, more than the news staff. They were huddled around their own work station in the back of the room, and ducking in and out of a separate, heavily air-conditioned room that stored their servers.

"Didn't know why you insisted on having your own servers here," Sonny said as he saw someone duck into the server room.

"It was cheap as hell to build those servers ourselves and use open-source programming on them. The more I think about it, the more I'm happy we went open-source on everything. I'm worried about the security measures some of these companies like Microsoft have going on."

"OK." He walked around the camera crew to get to his "battle station," a desktop in the middle of the T-table with three big screens and as much sheer processing power as he needed. "When do we formally go online?"

# The Holy Fool

"Formally, informally, or however," Woot said, checking the clock on his cell phone, "That is going to start happening, right... now."

The top center screen flashed to life. It was an elegant page, with plenty of white space and just the right amount of flashes of black and red in it. Right at the top center part of the page, TheFool.org was spelled out in bold letters with the Fool's Head just to the right.

"Isn't that something, though?" Sonny said.

"Sure is. The dream comes true, huh?"

"Good job, Woot."

"I've got some ideas on placement of featured stories, things like that."

"Yeah, that should be easy to tinker with. People starting to log on?"

"Klaus, can you get the stats up?" A few moments later, the lower center screen filled with graph charts and numbers, constantly fluctuating as more started to visit the site.

"Nice."

"Well, your lady had all of the good design tips. I'm gonna need your guys' help today with not only keeping on top of the web site, but moderating what I'm doing," Woot said. "There's *The Fool*'s Facebook page and Twitter feed that you'll be operating for a while, right?"

"Yeah. I'm going to be live for two hours on those feeds. I suppose I can even monitor this while the NBC interview is going on if they're shooting us from here." Sonny turned to the producer, a blond woman in her late 20's with steel-rimmed glasses who looked too harried to be intimidated. "Are you sure you want to shoot us in front of this?"

"Those visuals look the best," the producer replied. "Wait, what do you mean, 'us?'"

"I've got two guys I'll have up here with me, and then the one we can conference in via Internet... Woot told you about this, didn't he?"

"I didn't realize he was serious," she said.

"OK, whatever... Woot, you can get together with her, make it happen, right?"

"Yeah."

Sonny turned his attention back to the screens on the desk. "So, that's Facebook, Twitter, plus the comment thread on the site... I'm forgetting something, right?"

"The Reddit AMA," Woot said.

"The AMAs, right, the AMA."

"American Music Association?" the producer said, looking totally lost.

"Ask Me Anything," Woot explained to her. "It's a new section of Reddit they started earlier this year. They basically bring interesting people there, they prove who they are, and then they answer questions about themselves. It's pretty cool, actually."

"Maybe your morning guys should try one sometime," Sonny said. "They might escape alive. Woot, better make sure the Reddit guys get the proof."

"Not right now, brother. I've got to make sure our servers aren't going to crash the first hour out."

"Well, all righty, then," Sonny said, getting the computer camera on his desktop ready to go to grab a picture.

***

The Anchor was giving his lead-in for the interview. "...he's been called the most dangerous man in journalism, but some of his critics' question whether what he's doing now is more partisanship or political action than journalism. This morning, his new venture, *The Fool* news site, becomes active for the first time. Joining us now from *The Fool*'s offices in Geneva, Switzerland, is blogger, former *Chicago Journal* columnist, and now, Executive Editor and CEO of *The Fool*, Sonny Turner. Sonny, great to see you today."

Network viewers flashed to a split screen of The Anchor on one screen and Sonny on another, with *The Fool* mural behind him. "Mike, great to see you today."

The camera pulled out to show Sonny with Woot on his right side. On Sonny's left was a beetle-browed man, with black hair and eyes, built low and thick. He was a little under 30 and was wearing a hoodie identical to Sonny's.

"Also joining us today are Jeff Mackenzie, the chief information and technology officer for *The Fool*, and Dieter Weber, a former investigative reporter for *Der Spiegel*, who has just been named new managing editor of *The Fool*.

"Finally, joining us via satellite is *The Fool*'s Washington Bureau Chief, Casey Barnes." An inset screen popped up on the view of The Fool offices and Barnes was smiling back, from his bedroom in southeast DC. "And like Turner, formally of The *Chicago Journal*.

"Anyway, welcome. Sonny, I was curious as to why you insisted that this be a group interview?"

"Well, Mike, there's been a lot of attention on me, about what I write on my old blog, but I want your viewers to understand that this isn't just about me."

"I was a bit surprised to see a Swiss managing editor; I got the impression that *The Fool* is intended to be American-focused, if not based."

"About 50 percent of the staff are Americans," Weber replied in English that almost sounded like it came straight from the Midwest. He was another Northwestern University graduate that had met Sonny at school there. "The remainder come from around Europe – UK and Switzerland, mostly, but we have staffers from France, Germany, Holland, and Spain, among others. It's an international effort."

"Many of those American staffers are concentrated among our technical staff," Woot added. "There's talent from all over America keeping us online and functioning."

"That's also not counting the handful of correspondents in America and throughout Europe," Barnes added.

"For the first 10 years of my career, promoting me and my career was what I was all about," Sonny said. "Now, I'm trying to build something that's going to outlast me. I've always admired the teachers that I had at Northwestern, the guys I learned from at the *Journal*, and if I can be as good as them, I'll have accomplished something."

"OK," Mike said. "Some of my other co-hosts might have some questions."

"It seems strange to call a news organization *The Fool*," said Wendy, the blond, blue-eyed ex *Sports Illustrated* model that held down the other side of the screen for them. "Why that name?"

"It's like the old iconography in European myth, the fool," Sonny said. "The Fool was the member of the king's court that everyone laughed at, but he was the one who could tell the truth about what was going on at the court and everyone could accept it, because he was the fool. That's how we see ourselves; we see ourselves as the people who can speak truth to power."

"There's been concern that the top-secret files you've been releasing have the potential to harm American military lives or those of our allies," Mike said. "What do you say to that?"

"I recall in your promotion for this interview, that you called what is on our site right now as a 'massive data dump,'" Dieter answered for Sonny. "This only constitutes one percent of all of the government files that we have at our disposal. We will be reviewing these files very carefully before making them public. Of course, this means that many of these files may take months or even years to release."

"Sonny, you've said on your personal blog that you're on the fence regarding whether you will ever return to America. Why is that? What are you afraid of?" Wendy asked.

"To be honest, Wendy, I'm nervous about what the US government will do, despite the new president," Sonny said. "We see a push by the mainstream media to campaign against us and the people who are brave enough to give us information through the criminal courts. Even you - you said on Twitter that we should face 'some sort of charges' from what we did."

"But how do you call yourselves journalists?" Wendy said, her frustration starting to show. "You've just got a web site and some documents. How do you call that a news organization?"

"Which one is the news organization, the television network that runs cooking tips for housewives and shut ins, or the web site that gives information about what its government is doing?" Woot said. "We're journalists because we act like them, and we have a code of conduct and stick to it."

There was silence for a few moments before Mike jumped in again. "I was curious as to why you decided to go a nonprofit route for this news site."

"I've seen profit concerns hinder many different news organizations, including, no disrespect intended, the *Chicago Journal*," Sonny said. "With the ongoing changes in the shape of the news business and media in general, I believe a nonprofit format is the best way to present what's newsworthy, not just what we think is going to make us money or get us pageviews."

"And this is the impetus behind creating the Defoe-Mazur-Bauer Foundation?" Mike said.

"It's intended to provide primary financing for the news operation," Sonny said. "We have numerous donors that have contributed to the fund. That includes the revenues we receive from things like these," he added, pointing to the hoodie he was wearing and the coffee cup he raised in front of the camera. "All of it goes directly to supporting newsgathering resources."

"Not to you?" Wendy said.

"I'm living pretty sparsely," Sonny said. "Most of the money I live on comes from my books, the courses I teach in France and Switzerland, and a very modest salary as CEO, which is public. I'm not making a fortune at this. And that's as it should be."

"OK," Mike said. "Well, we wish you the best with your new endeavor, Sonny. Best of luck to you."

"We look forward to you featuring our reports on your network, Mike," Sonny replied.

***

"Everything looking OK?" Sonny said as he and Woot sat next to each other at the head of the newsroom table as the rest of the staff hummed along away from them.

"Everything five by five," Woot said. "No DDos problems, everything going smooth. Hey, can I ask you something?"

"Yeah, sure."

"Since our main source is sunning herself in Argentina or whatever, how are we supposed to get all of these new scoops without her?"

"I'm a journalist; we're all journalists. We will find new sources."

"Educate me, great warrior-poet, Lord Sonny," Woot said straight-faced.

Sonny glared at him, then smiled before continuing. "Let's play a little math game, here. Total up the intelligence services, the military, government officials, and the private contractors - don't forget those private contractors, my man – and we're talking maybe four million people."

"Wow, OK."

"Now, here's where the math comes in. How many of those people *despise* the current government, or maybe the government in general?"

"Hm, shit if I know. Probably 30 percent of them would vote against Obama when he runs in 2012, even if the GOP was running an actual turnip against him."

"Let's say 10 percent. So, that 10 percent is..."

"400,000 people, right?"

"Right. Now, how many of those people hate the government enough, or hate what it has done, enough to even consider snitching on them?"

"Would be small... maybe 10 percent of the those 400,000, so... 40,000."

"Yeah, 40,000 people thinking about betraying their co-workers, makes sense." Sonny nodded. "Now, out of those 40,000 people... what if I said that out of those people, only one-half of one percent had the guts to not only spill those secrets, but give them to us?"

"OK, let me think," Woot said, scratching his head. "One percent of 40,000 would be 400, so one-half..."

"...200 people." Sonny shook his head. "There's 200 potential sources out there *at the least*, I know it. And all we need to do is find them."

"And sweet-talk them."

"And sweet-talk them, true. It's nothing but journalism, except with more technology and ways of telling a story."

"What now?"

"Now? Now we act like we know what we're doing and hope that the finances work out."

"There's a lot more in that foundation that you're letting on. How much did Melchester donate?"

"Enough that I offered to add his name to the foundation," Sonny said. "He turned it down; said he didn't want people thinking he was against capitalism."

"Funny."

\*\*\*

Colton heard the song "Party in the USA," emanating from his iPhone next to the nightstand. He thought it was the radio waking him up, then realized Kyra had screwed with him because she was always getting new ringtones. He heard her in the shower, getting ready for her day at work.

Shaking his head, he picked up the phone. "Colton Edson."

"Colt 45, brother! How are things?" Sonny's voice boomed over the speaker.

"Uhhmm," Colton grunted, pulling himself up into a sitting position in the bed. "How did you get this number?"

"Your mama. Seriously, though, she really did give it to me."

"Fuck. What did you want?"

"Saw a lot of your writing the past few months. You've been doing a lot of great work."

"Yeah. Well, I guess nobody's saying I've still got a job because of nepotism now."

"You surprised?"

"To be honest, a little. What started as kind of a side internship turned into a job."

"Honestly, I think you've got a talent for business reporting. Not too many people can make that stuff interesting or understandable, but you do. So, you have any plans?"

"I'm not sure right now. Kyra got an internship with the ACLU last semester, and they want her to work for them. She wants to get married, which is crazy, because I thought I'd be supporting us. But, she doesn't care that I'm not working for my dad – she's just as happy being the main income as anything."

Sonny began to cackle. "Like you don't have that trust fund coming to you or help from your mom."

"Sound like you're swimming in millions from that 'foundation' my mom helped you set up, so you'd know about getting funded by my mom, wouldn't you?" Colton laughed.

"Ah, I don't see barely any of that money."

"Just so you get your cable and Internet, plus as much as you can drink."

"As long as I can get lunch at the hot cafes, I'm OK," Sonny laughed. "Christ, we're a couple of First World pricks, aren't we?"

"Speak for yourself."

"I've got a better idea – work for me."

There was a pause as Colton almost dropped the phone. "What?"

"Right now, I might hang out in Europe for a while, but I still think *The Fool* needs a presence in the U.S. I'd like you to help run one of the shops, be a correspondent/bureau chief."

"What? You serious?"

"Sure, why not? Casey's already got DC covered, but I still want to get someone out in Chicago, New York, and LA/Silicon Valley. Anyone of those sound interesting?"

"I... don't know. I'll want to talk to Kyra. You want me to work for you?"

"You're a talented reporter, Colton. Why wouldn't I?"

Colton was quiet for a moment. "OK. I'll talk with her and call you back. This number OK?"

"Sure. Look forward to hearing from you."

"OK. Bye."

"Bye," Sonny said as Colton killed the call.

Kyra came in, wrapped up in a towel from the shower. "Who was that?" she said.

"Sonny." Colton went on to explain what Sonny had offered.

Kyra got into bed next to him, acting like she was lost in thought. "So, what are you thinking?"

"I'm thinking that doing this might piss some people off, like the type of people Sonny likes to report on."

"You mean, like the type of people *you* pissed off with your reporting the last two months? I thought you got off on that."

"You're a riot."

"Hmmmm." She leaned her head over to touch his shoulder, twirling one end of her hair as the towel started to slip. "New York sounds interesting but staying in Chicago near my family might not be a bad idea. What do you think?"

\*\*\*

"You think he'll go for it?" Woot said as Sonny got off the phone.

"Yeah, he'll go for it." Woot and Sonny sat together on the roof of *The Fool*'s building, in chaise lounges getting some sun that afternoon. Joey was on the other side of Sonny in another lounge chair. As they relaxed, most of *The Fool*'s staff populated the roof as barbecue and tunes wafted through the air.

"You think Gus will go for it? You've been poaching a lot of his talent."

"It'll work out. I've already have a deal with him that we'll run some things by him, help him out on some assignments. It's a fair trade."

"A deal? I'm surprised either of them talked with you again."

"Time heals all wounds." Sonny saw his phone vibrate. He checked it out. "Shoot. Something downstairs. It's too beautiful a day to spend it indoors," He pointed at the clear skies and mountains in the distance.

"You'll be wondering what it was all afternoon," Joey said, peering at Sonny over an oversized pair of sunglasses. "Go ahead."

Sonny rolled over to get up. "I'll just be a few minutes…"

"Go on." Joey kissed him on the forehead. "Have fun. Love you."

"Love you too. Wait a minute, why are *you* up here?"

"My boss gave me the day off."

"I'll have to talk to him about that."

"You tend to talk to yourself a lot, I've noticed."

"Nutso," he said, blowing her a kiss. "You stay here," pointing to Woot. "If I need you, I'll call."

Sonny rode the elevator down to the newsroom, where one of the newest staffers, a young guy from Sweden named Eric, was waiting. "The person on our IRC channel, he kept on insisting to chat with you," he said, pointing to the station right next to Sonny's.

Sonny sat down at the computer and saw on the chat page:
&lt;drfunksjunkk&gt;Need proof of Sonny T here now. I need to talk.

Sonny looked over at Eric. "Have you got the encryption rolling?"

"Yes, all set."

"Come here and sit down next to me. You should see how to handle one of these things."

"OK."

Sonny began typing:
&lt;SonnyT76&gt;right here.

After a minute, he saw:
&lt;drfunksjunkk&gt;need proof
&lt;SonnyT76&gt;What proof?
&lt;drfunksjunkk&gt;timestamp with shoe on head. You know rules.
&lt;SonnyT76&gt;Seriously?
&lt;drfunksjunkk&gt;Rules or GTFO.
&lt;SonnyT76&gt; I'll send it, you'll see it.

"OK, they didn't teach this as Northwestern," Sonny said. He pulled off a shoe and scribbled the day's date and time on a piece of paper. Holding the shoe over his head and the paper next to his face, he had Eric take a photo of him with his own cell phone camera. Within three minutes:
&lt;SonnyT76&gt;1 attachment
&lt;drfunksjunkk&gt;Ma nigga.
&lt;SonnyT76&gt;OK, what would you like to talk about?
&lt;drfunksjunkk&gt;Have something that might interest you

<drfunksjunkk>Some files from the State Department about Iraq and Mideast. Heard you were interested in that stuff.
<SonnyT76>OK.
<drfunksjunkk>So, you want to see it? Would like to see some people get embarrassed.

Sonny had a big cackle at that one. "Can't believe I get to do this."
<SonnyT76>Let's talk.